A Rebellious Mind

KC Thompson

This book is a work of fiction. Names, characters, places and incidents either are the products of the author's imagination or are used fictitiously, and any resemblance to actual persons, living or dead, business establishments, events, or locales is entirely coincidental.

ISBN: 0-6155-2773-6
ISBN-13: 9780615527734
Library of Congress Control Number: 2011917189
KC Thompson, Cortland, New York

Dedication

I dedicate this book to my wife and children who give meaning to my life, and to my parents who gave me a love of history, reading, and freedom.

I

The thin officer in the purple uniform tapped his boot impatiently as he waited for the doctor to make his way down the long row of beds towards him. His face was strained, anxious about the results of the pilot test which would either propel his career to almost inconceivable heights, or end it completely.

"So, Doctor," he began as soon as the doctor was within earshot, "was the pilot study for the Procedure 23 a success. Have their traitorous memories been erased?"

The doctor returned the stern officer's gaze with a frown. He knew what the officer wanted to hear. He also knew that there were few certainties when an operation of this complexity was involved.

"Well, Citizen Security Regent Peloreid, our initial review looks promising. The subjects had their memories scanned before the operation and then again after. The monitor showed no response to the undesirable images after the operation. We believe that indicates that all the objectionable memories are now gone. Everything about their families and upbringing, and everything regarding the government, has been erased. From that standpoint, it seems to be a success."

"Excellent. So everything was successful."

"We can't be sure if their other memories were affected. Not at this time. That will have to be monitored on an ongoing basis for the next several weeks. We really won't be sure until they take their IQ and Aptitude tests," the doctor continued.

"So, there may still be a risk of undesirable activity?" questioned the officer.

"I don't believe so. I'm more concerned with loss of intelligence or technical skills. That would make their reorientation longer and more costly."

"I see. While inconvenient, that is probably to be expected." The officer paused, contemplating the situation. "How many died during the operation?"

"I'm happy to say none," replied the doctor. "However, I see we have several due for Procedure 66's. Is that still necessary?"

"The government has already spent too much time and money on them. The sooner they're eliminated, the more we will save."

"Doctor, the patient in bed nine is coming around," the nurse called across the room. The doctor turned his head towards her and nodded.

"If there is nothing else, Citizen Security Regent, may I return to my duties?" asked the doctor.

"Yes. Fine," the officer responded. "Keep me updated on the status."

As the officer wheeled and walked away, the doctor picked up a chart and walked down the long row of beds towards number nine. The hospital ward was filled with patients, most of whom were asleep. The doctor could see this patient coming out of the anesthesia and beginning to move his head. The man was rubbing his eyes and yawning as the doctor checked the vital signs as shown on the computer screen attached to the bed.

"Well, Mr. Johnson," the doctor said as the patient slowly focused his eyes on the doctor's face, "how are you feeling?"

"Where, where am I?" the patient asked, still not fully awake.

"You're in Hospital 371. You've had an accident. I'm afraid we needed to operate to relieve pressure on your brain. It may have affected your memory," the doctor explained quickly.

Johnson was confused as he looked around the ward where he could see about 50 beds lining the walls. "What kind of accident? I don't remember anything."

"Yes, that's what we thought would happen. Luckily, there was no other damage so physically, you're fine. We'll need to keep you here for another day for observation. Then you can be released."

"Released? Released to where?"

"Well, we can't just throw you on the street, now can we?" the doctor replied with a chuckle. "We have a reorientation therapy program that you'll participate in. The program lasts six weeks and, by the end of that time, you'll be ready to move on with your life."

"I don't understand. What happened? I don't remember anything. I…I want to go home," stammered Johnson, confusion growing.

"That's perfectly normal. You've had a serious operation which has affected your memory. You're domicile unit has already been reassigned but you'll get a new one after the reorientation. Your domicile unit, economic role, and your personal necessities will be assigned when you complete the reorientation. You'll be given everything you need. The government will see that you're well taken care of," replied the doctor, looking down at him calmly. Yes, he thought, you'll be much better cared for than the patients that will be terminated tonight. The government will definitely take care of them.

"You'd be surprised how many people go through this process every day," continued the doctor, signing the electronic chart. "You will not be alone, that's for sure."

"I don't understand any of this. What's happened to me? I can't seem to remember anything," the patient said, his voice rising as he attempted to push himself up on the bed.

"You're name is Charles Johnson," explained the doctor, quickly moving to the side of the bed and forcing the patient to lay back. "You're 42 years old and, right now you're in Hospital 371 in Capitol City. That's about all I can tell you now. The rest will be explained in a couple of days when you begin at the Reorientation Center. For now, just get some rest."

The doctor motioned for the nurse to come over. In a low voice, he instructed her, "Increase his sedative for the rest of the day. Make sure he's scheduled for a reorientation pickup on Thursday. Otherwise, it looks like the procedure was successful."

"It's amazing what they can do with Procedure 23 these days," the nurse replied. "What a miracle. A year ago, none of these patients would have made it."

"That's true, but it seems like we do more and more of these every day. How many of these patients had a 23 done to them?"

"Of the 68 patients on this ward, 59 had Procedure 23's done to them and nine are here for a Procedure 66."

"Wow, nine in for 66's today? That's a lot," the doctor remarked with surprise. "I thought with all these 23's we wouldn't have as many 66's anymore." He shook his head, "I don't even want to think about all the paperwork I'll have to fill out this week."

"Doctor, the patient in bed 42 is coming around," called a nurse from the other end of ward.

As the doctor walked away, the patient in bed nine was fading into a drug induced sleep. His mind kept hearing one term echoing over and over, "Procedure 23. Procedure 23. Procedure 23. "

At the other end of the ward, an orderly in scrubs, cap, and mask walked down the corridor to a small examination room. He entered, closed the door and stood to the side, peering through the small window in the door to see if anyone was outside. He pulled his mask down to reveal an old, weathered face and gleaming green eyes. Looking down at his watch, he extending his hand into the darkness towards the phone that he knew was hanging on the wall. An instant later, the phone rang.

"Ward 2," he said softly into the handset.

"Albert, it's Andrew. Is he there?" asked the voice on the other end.

"He's here."

"So he survived. That's wonderful," said Andrew Sinclair with a deep sigh of relief. "Do you know how the procedure went?"

"Unfortunately, I think it worked. The doctor said he was pleased when he spoke to Peloreid."

"Peloreid! He's there already?"

"He just left."

"Damn vulture doesn't wait long, does he? If they're happy with the outcome, that's not good news."

"No, it's not. I'm not sure how much of his brain was damaged by their goddamn Procedure 23. But, at least the boy's alive."

"That's something to be thankful for," agreed Andrew. "Lord knows, he's given enough of his family to our Emperor. Do you know where they're moving him?"

"All I heard was something about a Reorientation Center. Nobody seems to have any idea where or what it is but he'll be heading there in a couple of days," replied Albert.

"Reorientation? They must mean brainwashing. They must be planning on getting everyone ready to reenter the workforce. How many patients are there now?"

"A few dozen. And more to come tomorrow. By the time this is fully operational, there will be hundreds every week."

"What about those with the death sentence? Will they get the Procedure 23 instead?"

"No. I heard Peloreid say that they've already cost the government too much money. They'll be killed as soon as possible."

"What a wonderful world we live in. The great Barahu, freer of the masses. That's why it's important that we fight. Most people don't even realize what's happening to them. That's why it's up to us to keep the idea of liberty alive."

"Yes, but we're a lot further away now than we were before. It's going to be almost impossible to replace Charles," stated Albert glumly.

"Yes, it will. We have to hope that somehow we can reach out to him. If not, our plans may be set back by years. Well my friend, you'd better get out of there. I can't afford to have you captured too. At your age, it would mean certain death," advised Andrew.

"I'm well aware of my age, thank you," stated Albert in a bitter tone that can only be used between the best of friends. "I'll leave as soon as I can."

"Good. We'll need to get the group together by this weekend. I don't know what we can do, but we've got to start thinking of something. The Purple Shirts won't stop until we all have our memories erased. Be careful, my friend. I'll see you soon."

"I'm always careful. That's the only way I've lived so long. I'll be at the hole if you need me."

The old man hung up the phone and slowly opened the door. He slid the mask back up over his mouth and nose. Leaving the examination room, he grabbed a gurney and began to push it down the hallway past the purple shirted guards who paid no attention to him at all.

2

The brown bus pulled up to the hospital and opened its doors. Eighteen patients filed out and climbed on. Each was dressed in beige shirts and pants and carried a file folder with their personal and medical information enclosed. As they took random seats on the bus, they looked around nervously, both at their surroundings and each other. All were confused at exactly where they were, why they were there, and more importantly, where they were going. None of them had anything but vague memories of their previous life.

"Ladies and Gentlemen," began a pretty, smiling young woman, "please get comfortable. I'm Citizen Wainwright and I'm your Reorientation Coordinator. We've got about an hour trip in front of us to the Reorientation Center. We understand that you're confused about what's happened to you. You're all in the same boat since your memories have been affected by your operations but once we begin the Reorientation Program, things will begin to make sense again. You'll learn all about our society and your place in it. You'll be assigned your economic position, your personal domicile unit, and be provided with your personal necessities. So just settle back and relax. There are snacks and water in the seat pocket in front of you. "

The passengers leaned back and most just looked out the window. A few peeked at the food in front of them but none ate. Most were still groggy from the anesthesia. Some had only been out of surgery a few hours.

Charles Johnson leaned his head against the window and watched the miles go by. He, like the others, was confused about what was happening. He didn't know who he was or what his past was. He couldn't remember where he grew up, where he lived, who his friends were, or anything else. He had been told that he was in an accident, but he had no idea what type of accident. He just kept looking out the window, wondering what had happened to his life.

After a few minutes of staring at the landscapes flying by his window, Charles opened the folder. He scanned the medical information showing his height, weight, and age. He didn't understand much of the medical jargon, but that wasn't what he really wanted to know anyway. He wanted to know who he was. His folder contained no personal information about his life before the accident other than that he had been a research scientist. We'll, at least that was something. Perhaps they'd fill him in more during reorientation. A feeling of melancholy was seeping into his body. It was of complete emptiness. How could his whole life disappear from his mind? He closed his eyes tightly, trying to fight off the depression which was engulfing him.

A little over an hour later, the bus pulled up in front of a non-descript gray cement block building, with few windows and only a single door with an awning. The young woman stood up and instructed the passengers to follow her. She led them in as guards stood by the bus door to ensure that everyone got off and entered.

"OK, ladies and gentlemen," Wainwright began as the passengers grouped together in the lobby. "Let me welcome you to the Barahu Imperial Reorientation Center. This will be your home and school for the next six weeks. During that time, you'll be instructed on our country's history, the rules of our society, and where you fit in. By the time we're done, you'll be all set to reenter and restart your lives. It's almost lunch time so we'll give you your private room assignments, let you get settled in and freshen up, and then we'll meet for lunch. Your instruction will begin right after that. On the wall are your names and room numbers. Girl's rooms are down the hall to the left and boys' are down the hall to the right. Please stay in your own wing and in your own room. You aren't allowed to visit other rooms. Until you get back on your feet more, that could cause you to get disoriented and that could prolong your recovery. So, just stay in your own rooms and on your own wing. You'll have plenty of time to socialize with others during the breaks in your training. So go get your room numbers and drop off your folders. If anyone forgot their names, just look on the front of your folder. It's right on the front." The young lady said all of these things, as she had been trained to do, with a permanent smile on her face.

Charles waited his turn, looked up his name and saw the "7" after his name. He moved down the "boys" hallway until he came to Room 7. Opening the heavy metal door, he found himself surprised that there was such a substantial door for what looked like a typical college dorm room. Then, he wondered how it was that he knew what a typical college dorm room looked like. He shook his head, partly in disbelief and partly in another attempt to remove the cobwebs from his mind. The room had a small dresser and bed as well as a desk, chair, and lamp. He pushed open another door to reveal a bathroom with sink, toilet, and shower stall. All was painted a beige color which was nearly a perfect match to his outfit. As he turned, he saw a line of five beige shirts and pants neatly on hangers on a single bar hung on the wall. He pulled out a shirt and saw "Johnson C" on a patch above the left breast pocket. Above the right pocket was "845607". He turned and looked around the windowless room again. No, this wasn't a dorm room. It was more like a prison cell. Now, the heavy metal door made sense.

Charles slumped to sit on the edge of the bed. A prison cell. He was being imprisoned, but for what? For being in an accident? He searched his mind to try to remember the accident. Where had he been? What had he been doing? Nothing. There was no memory to answer his questions. Charles rubbed his temples, trying to ease the pain. While his memory wasn't working, his logic was. He pictured all those people getting on the bus. He thought of all the beds that were filled with patients in the hospital ward. And, he remembered hearing the nurse mention all the Procedure 23's that they had done. How could all of those people be in accidents which gave them amnesia? And why were they now put in these prison cells, nice prison cells, but cells none the less?

Something wasn't making sense to Charles. He shook his head. In his present state of confusion, he tried to reassure himself that things would begin to clear up as he was reoriented. He had to feel that way, he thought. It was all he had.

After utilizing the bathroom and splashing some cold water on his face, Charles walked back to the lobby where a few other "patients" were waiting.

"Well, Citizen Johnson, is everything in order in your room?" asked the guide from the bus.

"Yes, everything's fine, Citizen Wainwright," Charles replied with a smile. "I think anything's better than the hospital."

"Yes, those are such sad places," she responded with an immediate frown. However, the change only lasted for a split second before it reverted to a smile. "No need to worry about that now. And wait until you taste the food. The chefs here are great. I hope you're hungry."

Before he could respond, a 30ish woman walked up and Wainwright hurried over to ask her the identical question that she had posed to Charles. He turned to another man that was also waiting and said, "I hope she's right. About the food I mean. I'm pretty hungry."

The other man just nodded and looked down at his feet. Charles looked at him but didn't take offense. He didn't really feel much like talking either. More people were gathering now and Citizen Wainwright was taking a quick headcount.

"OK, everyone," she said a little more loudly but still smiling. "I hope everyone's hungry," she continued, rubbing her flat stomach for added effect. "Follow me to the cafeteria." She led the group down the center hallway and took a right through a door into a small cafeteria. "Everyone grab a tray. On the right are sandwiches. On the left are hot entrees. I think the special today is lasagna and take it from me, it's delicious," she said, again rubbing her stomach. "There are salads and soup in the center and a variety of drinks along the back wall. Grab whatever you want and as much as you want. Silverware and napkins are on the tables. You can sit wherever you want to. OK, help your self and enjoy," she finished. She turned and began walking towards the trays when she stopped, spun around and, bouncing up and down, began waving her hands to the group. "Oh my goodness," she yelled. "I can't believe I forgot the most important part...the desserts. They're on the table in the corner. And it doesn't matter what you choose, they are all yuuuumee," she squealed.

Charles browsed the offerings, chose some soup and a sandwich and found a table with two other patients. He nodded at the other two men as he sat down. No one spoke for several moments. Then, Charles broke the silence.

"Did you two have accidents too?" he asked quietly, looking at their faces for a reaction. The small, plump man on his left nodded while the other across from him said nothing, staring only at the lasagna that he was wolfing down hungrily. "I can't remember a thing from before. Can you?" he asked the plump man.

The man looked around nervously before leaning forward and whispering, "I don't think we're supposed to talk. I heard one of the guards warn someone in the lobby. But, no, I can't remember anything either. Just what they told me." He stopped abruptly as a purple shirted guard stared at him from across the room and began moving towards there table.

"The salt, there in the white container," he stammered, pointing to the salt container near Charles' elbow. The guard passed their table, eyed them cautiously, and then continued on as Charles handed over the salt. "Like I said, we're not supposed to talk," he finished in a whisper, never lifting his eyes from his plate. Both of the other men finished their meals and quickly left the table, leaving Charles alone with his thoughts.

Charles shook his head slowly. Why? Why can't we talk? Why aren't we told about out past? Wouldn't that help up to become reoriented sooner? Charles took a spoonful of soup. It was tasty, but he wasn't hungry anymore. He just wanted to lie down and sleep, hoping that this was all a bad dream which would be gone when he awoke.

After lunch, the new Reorientation Program participants were herded out of the cafeteria and into a large auditorium. People chose their seats, usually with the others that had been at their lunch tables. Charles instead took a seat halfway back and to the right side of the auditorium where he could observe most of the other students. He sat alone, not feeling in the mood to chit chat. He noticed a lot of people in the auditorium whom hadn't been at lunch. He could pick out several that had been on his bus but there had to be at least 200 people in the audience. There had been less than 40 in the cafeteria. Who are these people, Charles asked himself? His confusion was evolving into frustration. He was frustrated with himself for not begin able to remember and for getting into whatever accident he had been in. But frustration with the administration of this Reorientation Center was also taking root. Why wouldn't they tell him who he was? Why wouldn't they take him to his home, his friends and co-workers? Wouldn't they be wondering what had happened to him? Why wouldn't they help him to recreate his life? Wasn't there anyone that cared about him?

The low murmur in the audience faded as the lights dimmed and Citizen Wainwright made her way to the podium on the stage. A spotlight directed towards her smiling face provided the only light.

"The next few days will be the most enlightening of your life," began Wainwright. "I know you're all confused right now, but things will start to become much clearer for all of you over the next two weeks. Today, we'll begin to go through the history of our country. You must know why we work the way we do, and it's very important that you realize how our Supreme Being and Most Holy Leader, Emperor Barahu II, cares for us and takes care of all our needs", she continued, pointing to a large picture as she mentioned the Emperor's name.

Charles didn't remember anything about the country or the man in the picture. It was as if he were hearing it all for the first time. As he sat listening, his anxiety began to subside and, while he was alert, he was becoming at ease for the first time since he had awoken in the hospital several days earlier. Citizen Wainwright's words flowed over him like a light breeze. He remembered what she was saying but didn't seem to focus on anything in particular.

He found himself with a slight smile on his face as he looked around the room and saw most others in the same pose.

"After today, we'll go through what you'll be provided with as the beneficiaries of our Supreme Being. You'll also learn what is expected of you as members of the Union of Socialist Alliances. The USA is the greatest country ever conceived because everything is provided for you. All that you will need to do is follow the rules. And that is it," she said, emphasizing the last point with an even bigger smile than the one she normally wore.

"OK, so let's get started. In front of each of you there is a packet with everything you'll need for today. There's a book which has all the information that we'll cover in case you want to refer to it later. This is such joyous information that I've read the book at least eight times myself. I just loved reading about how the Supreme Being saved us all from the wickedness and greed that was common before his arrival. And even better than learning about it is teaching it. I encourage all of you to read more tonight.

Our country began in the year NA one, NA standing for New Age. That was when Barahu I was elected as this nations first Supreme Being and Most Holy Leader. To fully understand what a wonderful thing this was, it's necessary to describe the uncivilized society that existed before his emergence as our messiah and savior. I hope this part won't scare too many people. It was a terrible, wicked time that, thanks to our Supreme Being, the Supreme Council, and our Purple Shirts, will never reappear."

A hand was raised in the middle of the auditorium. Citizen Wainwright stopped, somewhat surprised that someone would interrupt her. She looked around nervously, as if she was unsure whether it was appropriate for her to acknowledge the person or just continue. Since she was alone at the front, there was no one else to help her make the decision so, after a moment, she pointed to the person and said," Yes, is there something you need?"

"I'm sorry. I couldn't make out what you said after Supreme Council. I missed that part."

Citizen Wainwright exhaled loudly and smiled again. "OK. We don't usually stop the lesson unless it's an emergency so please hold any questions to the end. But, I do want you to learn as much as possible, so I'll answer this one. I mentioned the Supreme Being and Most Holy Leader, Emperor Barahu I, the Supreme Council, and the Purple Shirts," she restated, counting the three names off on her fingers as she said them. "We'll talk about the Emperor quite a bit more so I'll move on to the others. The Supreme Council is a group of advisors to the Emperor. These are the brightest and most dedicated people in the country. They represent all areas of learning from Law, Science and Scientific Law, Medicine and Medical Law, and our Future Planning, which helps create new Laws. For our country to continue with its incredible record of achieving cultural balance and equality, we must ensure that the laws are updated frequently. There should be nothing that is not covered by some law or rule. These are the things that keep our country running smoothly. This is also what was missing in the Dark Age before our enlightened Emperor led us to the New Age. Now most of these Councilors have been on the Supreme Council for decades. Many even advised Barahu I some 30 years ago! No one really knows who they are or how many there are. This is to protect them so no one tries to give them special treatment. In the Dark Age, the rulers were lavished with riches. Oh, oh, I'm getting off track. We'll talk more about that soon.

The other group I mentioned is the Purple Shirts," Wainwright continued. "These people are very important to our society. They are extremely loyal to the Emperor and the USA. These people were the ones that helped crush the despicable rulers of the Dark Age and bring upon this Age of Enlightenment, the New Age. Now, they enforce our laws, encourage people to maintain order and discipline, and ensure that our Population Mandates are followed. They provide an incredible service to our country. The Purple Shirts have total authority over each of us so if one tells you to do something, anything, you must obey at once. To disobey would disrupt our entire society and cause much pain on others. That cannot be tolerated in an enlightened age. So, make sure you listen to and respect any Purple Shirt you meet. They're easy to spot because, well, they wear Purple Shirts! No one else is allowed to wear that color. Now, let's get back to the program."

From the back of the auditorium, in the shadows, a man smiled. Citizen Wainwright was doing well. Her smile seemed infectious as he noticed that everyone in the room smiled when she smiled and laughed when she made even a small joke. Her training had gone well and she seemed like the perfect choice to run the Reorientation Program. This would please his superiors. They had argued that a more authoritarian figure was needed, not the cute young woman with the perpetual smile. He had disagreed. He felt that the warmth and personality of the woman would make people more comfortable. Her voice and figure were more appealing and therefore, she would gain more trust and people would accept her words more easily. He was willing to bet that there would not be one harsh question or comment at the end of her presentation. Not only would that be a first, but it would also be with a large group of people that had just received their Procedure 23s. Normally, they would have been kept in hospitals for several weeks until their systems had built up enough "vitamins". That would ensure they would be accepting of the reorientation training. But, the Council had wanted them pushed into the program earlier to control costs.

Either that or to increase the odds of his failure. But, it didn't look like that would happen. Everyone was alert, listening to Wainwright. Some nodded in agreement with her words. Some followed along in the book. But everyone was engaged. Of course, his decision to seed the audience with dozens of his Purple Shirts, in plain clothes so they would blend in, should ensure that the audience was receptive. Like cattle, he thought. Get a few to move in a direction and rest of the herd will follow. No, he saw no problems with the outcome of this class. That would increase his standing with the Council. And that always led to good things.

"Again, I don't want to scare anyone but the information and the images you'll see on your monitors are disturbing," said Citizen Wainwright to the students. "This is only to show you how our society would be if we failed to follow the rules handed down by our Emperor and the Supreme Council.

Some 30 years ago, at the end of the Dark Age, our society was in chaos. Greed, gluttony, violence, famine, and poverty ravaged the land. There were things called businesses which were the worst organizations ever conceived. These were wicked, evil enterprises that enforced a type of slavery where one person could essentially own another. In a business, if you needed something, you had to give them what they called money. If you wanted food, you gave them money. If you needed medical care, you gave them money. If you wanted clothes, you gave them money. To have a domicile unit, you needed money. Everything revolved around this thing called money. In and of itself, it was worthless. But you could take this money somewhere else and give it to them for something you wanted. To get money, you had to agree to be a slave for someone else until you had enough money to hire your own slaves. You had to go where they told you, do what they told you, when they told you. If they didn't like what you did, they would throw you out in the streets and not give you any money. For many hours every day, you had to be someone else's slave. If they threw you out, you could go for weeks without money, unable to get food, clothing, a domicile, or medical care. Because some people didn't have money, they were starving, living on the streets. According to Barahu I, nearly everyone wanted more money. This was called greed. Greed was the main reason that this society was failing. Barahu also tells us in his writings that most people didn't have enough food or clothing. Most lived in boxes on the street. Almost no one had access to doctors or medicines. Most children were abused by their parents and were taught to hate other people. People died in the streets every day."

Behind the speaker, pictures were shown to add emphasis to the issues she mentioned. They showed death camps with the naked bodies of the deceased, homeless people in cardboard boxes, and starving children. Whenever she mentioned business or greed, there were pictures of men and women in expensive clothing, with elaborate jewelry, standing in front of huge mansions. The pictures were interspersed with simple slides with word like "Greed" written on them before the pictures of wealthy, and with "The People" before the pictures of the starving. The effect was complete. The students were visibly moved by seeing the tragic pictures and then appeared angry as they saw the next slide showing the greedy, wealthy and privileged.

"This was in what they then referred to as 2012 AD. AD means the Age of Darkness. This was the world that Barahu I was born into. He saw how people fought and died over money. He saw how businesses controlled people, making them beg for money. He saw how they were mistreated by businesses. If you couldn't work, businesses wouldn't even give you money to buy food. It was a very uncivilized time. Barahu knew that he was the only one that could lead the USA out of this despair. He knew that he was the Messiah, sent to become the Supreme Being. He had a far greater intelligence than any other person ever born on Earth. He, with a few others, knew that this was not a civilized way of life. To make people spend hours and hours, just hoping that they would be paid for their slavery! And then, to have to turn around and give that money to someone else just so they could have food…or clothing…or a place to sleep."

The man in the back smiled again. The young Citizen Wainwright was a gifted speaker. She paused at just the right time to drive home the point. She emphasized just the right word and even had a tear in her eye as she spoke of the suffering. She was a treasure! Their training system certainly was working. His mind moved to what his report would look like in front of the Council. The videos of this session would bring them to their feet. He would have his choice of spots in the hierarchy. Perhaps his name would even start to be mentioned for future vacancies on the Supreme Council. To be a member of that august body would be the highlight of his career. Keep talking, Citizen Wainwright, he thought. With each word, he was getting a little bit closer.

Charles looked around at the others. They all seemed to have a sense of disdain and fury. He could hear them quietly voicing the questions that were stemming from the lecture. "How could civilized people treat each other that way? To have to work for money, really for food and clothing! Those are necessities to stay alive. How could you survive if you had to rely on others to give you those things? And for some to have more while others didn't have enough!"

He stared carefully at individuals in the audience. The patients he recognized seemed to look around at the others anxiously, not seeming to comprehend the rage that was building. They, like him, seemed to be unmoved by the presentation. But others, mostly those that he hadn't seen at lunch, were becoming agitated. It was all they could do to not shout out their protests with rage. Charles could almost read their thoughts. While a few lived in huge homes, everyone else lived in squalor. It wasn't right! They were thankful that they didn't live in 2012 AD but rather in 31 NA. And they were thankful that Barahu had saved them.

"Barahu and the others planned very carefully for the take-over of the country. In those days, there was what was called elections. People had to select who would run the country. It's a very archaic idea but you had to keep going back to say who you liked. And, you could change your mind whenever you wanted. No wonder there was such confusion," Wainwright said, throwing her hands in the air and with a look of bewilderment on her face. A ripple of laughter swept across the crowd. "Most of these 'elections' were fraudulent. A few very wealthy people, those were the ones that had lots and lots of money, decided who would run the country based on how much the ruler would pay them. Whoever would pay them the most was allowed to run the country. That person, who they called the "President", would then take money from all the rest of the people in the country. No wonder everyone was poor and had no food. The President and the wealthy had it all. There were also advisors called a "Congress". They also took money from the poor and either kept it for themselves or gave it to the wealthy. So the wealthy who ran all the businesses and owned most of the slaves, and the President, and the Congress had most of the money and they all took care of each other. The people thought they controlled the country by the elections. They would argue with each other about who was President and in Congress because they didn't know that a small group of people were making all the decisions. And they even gave more money to the President and Congress so they would stay. They must have been crazy!" she added, again with emphasis and to laughter in the crowd.

"Barahu knew this wasn't right so he formed an incredible plan to take over the country. He convinced the wealthy that they would get a lot more money if he was elected. Not all of them believed it so he made sure that the elections were set to come out in his favor. It wasn't easy. He had to give money to some people, he had other friends go to the machines and make sure that people only voted for him. These people were the original Purple Shirts." As she exclaimed this, a large portion in the audience applauded, which brought and even bigger smile to her face. And to that of the man in the back.

"Barahu won the election and also had most of his friends in Congress. But he was afraid that the wealthy would soon catch on that the money would be going to the poor people and not to them. That would mean that they would throw him out or even kill him." She said this with such passion that there were audible gasps from the audience. "Barahu had to work fast. He knew that the key to controlling the country was to control the money. If he had the money, everyone would do what he wanted. He needed them to do this until he could reform the society to become what it is today. So, he went after the people and places that had the money. In those days, all the wealthy people had to keep their money somewhere so they usually put it in a bank, which is just like a warehouse. Barahu made laws that said that the banks were now owned by the government. That was a major move because that meant that the wealthy had to come to him for money. This was not easy. Wealthy people got nervous that the government would take all their money. Barahu was doing EXACTLY that, but he didn't want them to know yet. He knew that if they figured it out too soon, they would get rid of him. So, he kept telling them not to worry. This was only for a short time and, after that, they would get back even more money. I said before, Barahu was the most intelligent man ever so everyone believed him.

But, his greatest move came next. He knew that as long as the wealthy owned the businesses, the people would be slaves to the wealthy. He knew he had to take over the businesses, but how?"

Marvelous, simply marvelous, he thought. She's spinning this old tale like a mystery novel. People are literally on the edge of their seats, waiting for her next word. I wonder if she even knows how big of a lie, or rather, the series of lies, that she's telling? He doubted it. No textbooks, magazines, or newspapers existed from that period. She was too young to be around in the old education system so everything she learned was from the Barahu teachings. She was probably raised by the government, most likely part of their genetic engineering program. The blond hair, blue eyes, large breasts, and small waist looked to be the target outcome of the Genetics Engineering Department. That was the standard model that had been produced about 20 years ago. They certainly had done a nice job on her, he thought smiling. His scheduled visit to the Relaxation Center wasn't for another week and a half but, being a Purple Shirt did have some advantages. He might need to find a reason for an extra visit.

3

Citizen Wainwright continued her lecture. "Emperor Barahu I, as I have said several times, was the most intelligent, most caring, and most eloquent person ever to be born. He could mesmerize people with his voice and eventually, through his repeated assurances, people who once opposed him, would come to love him. He used this ability to outsmart those who were against him. They were murderous mobs who protested against him because they were slaves to the rich and forced to do it on punishment of death. In reality, no one that wasn't one of the wealthy could possible be against his programs. They just needed to be freed of the wealthy people who controlled them. So, Barahu knew that in order to bring protection to all of those millions of slaves, he needed to destroy the wealthy."

"As I said, he had already seized many of the largest banks. He waited until there was a crisis and then he went in to rescue them. The wealthy who thought they would lose all their money welcomed him then!" she said with added emotion. "These greedy, despicable people allowed him to take over their companies as long as he promised to let them keep some of their money. Soon, he controlled the banks. Then, the automobile companies who made products that were destroying our planet. He learned that the wealthy would give up their control if there was a crisis. The bigger the crisis, the more they would give up. So, in order to destroy the wealthy, he created a huge crisis and then waited for the wealthy to beg his help."

The audience was in rapt attention as she spoke. She was a gifted storyteller who could change her voice and emotions to perfectly fit the moment. Her face would be covered with concern as she spoke of the evil wealthy people but then become beaming as she explained Barahu's brilliance. Charles watched her with an odd fascination that he really didn't understand. He somehow couldn't absolutely believe every word. He was very relaxed and found her speech entertaining, but it did seem more like entertainment rather than a history lesson. Maybe part of it came from those around him. While he sat back with his legs crossed, others were literally on the edge of their seats with their mouths open in excitement and anticipation. Maybe it was just him, but he just couldn't get that engaged with the lecture. He wasn't sure why, but his attitude was troubling for him. What would happen if he didn't remember this? Would he be in trouble of some sort? A big part of his problem was that he didn't know what he should be doing or what the rules were. Well, he sighed, I guess that's the purpose of the reorientation, to help people become re-acclimated to society. He tried to focus on Citizen Wainwright and try to retain as much as he could. Maybe that would help him to remember some things about his former life.

"Barahu," continued Wainwright, "defied normal logic. He did the opposite of what people expected so they wouldn't know his true motives. So, he did what people said would destroy him, but in reality they made him stronger. At the time, many people had no food, clothing, homes, medicines or any of the items that we need to survive. The country was deeply in debt. People said that the government should stop helping people and should stop spending money. But, Barahu knew that this would only help wealthy people and not the poor people. So, Barahu started spending even more money. As I said, he promised to give money to the wealthy so he could control the banks and automobile companies. Once he had them, he could make them do what he wanted. In fact, you'll see that today, there are no banks or automobile companies. The only automobiles you find belong to the government," she said with a big smile. "Next, he forced power companies to spend so much money to clean our environment that they could no longer exist. To "HELP" them, "she said, using her fingers to form mock quotation marks when she said help, "he offered them money to "SAVE" their companies," again with the fingered quotation marks around save. This brought giggles from many in the audience. "Once these people accepted Barahu's money, he had control of the company. He did the same thing with doctors and hospitals. He made them treat everyone, from the wealthy to the poor but he limited how much they would receive. Soon, so many people were at the hospitals that they didn't have enough money to pay for things. So, Barahu "SAVED" them." More giggles from the audience.

"Soon, Barahu had SAVED the banks, automobile companies, hospitals, airlines, and insurance companies. His officials ran these businesses based on how Barahu instructed them. Soon, all of those businesses were part of Barahu's government. And now," Citizen Wainwright continued, pausing to denote that something truly astonishing was beginning, "Barahu could complete his plan. Now, he controlled many of the largest companies. The country owed trillions and trillions of dollars to other countries and Barahu's opponents announced a crisis for the country. They said the country would run out of money. Most people believed them. Barahu said that the only way to give things to the poor and to save the country was to take some money from the wealthy. Soon, most people agreed that the only way to save the country was to take the wealthy's money. Even some of the wealthy agreed because they thought Barahu would take other wealthy people's money, not theirs, or they thought that Barahu would only take a little money. So, Barahu had convinced the people to make him SAVE the country by taking all the money that the wealthy had! He got them to demand that he do exactly what he wanted to do all along! Is it any wonder that he was proclaimed as the smartest person ever?" she exclaimed to a roar of applause from the audience. Several people even leaped to their feet in excitement. Behind her, the screen which had been showing black and white scenes of poverty, sickness, and murder began showing full color videos of Barahu waving cheerfully to throngs of supporters. People were shown reaching to simply touch his hand. Teary eyed women were shown holding their babies out to be touched or kissed by Barahu.

As the audience calmed down, she continued her lecture. "First, Emperor Barahu, or President Barahu as he was then called, took the wealthy's money. Then, he took their homes, their automobiles, and their other belongings. Soon, there were no wealthy left in the country. The people that had been their slaves left them. Some went to become slaves in other places but many decided to have the government take care of them. There were other people who wanted to be wealthy. They were called the middle class because they weren't wealthy but neither were they poor. But, since these people wanted to be wealthy, they were really evil. Barahu knew that they were a danger to the country if he didn't destroy them as well so he also took their money and homes, and other belongings. Within five short years, Barahu was able to do what others had failed to do in over 200 years. Now, the all the people were cared for, not just the wealthy. The government gave all people food and clothes and domicile units. They had doctors take care of all the people. They had teachers instruct all the people. Is it any wonder that Barahu was deemed as the greatest person ever to exist?"

As she finished the crowd stood and cheered. Charles found himself following the others, on his feet and clapping his hands. As he looked around he saw others that were jumping up and down. Some were screaming out Barahu's name. He couldn't remember seeing the loudest and most animated people at lunch, but he supposed that there must be other groups that had all been combined for today's lecture. He just couldn't jump up and down and yell like those people did. It had been interesting, but his skepticism still nagged him. After a few moments, Wainwright motioned for the group to sit down.

"Yes, it's easy, and proper I might add, to show this kind of enthusiasm and thanks for Emperor Barahu. However, at the time many people were very upset with him. The wealthy didn't like giving up their money and the middle class could no longer steal their way to become one of the wealthy. Many hated Barahu. Luckily, he had his Purple Shirts ready. They went to meetings of the wealthy and made them go home. If someone threatened Barahu or his supporters, they were quickly silenced. While it took only five years for Barahu to destroy the wealthy and middle class, it would take longer for him to reorganize our entire society. The old laws said that even those that opposed you could speak and write what they wanted. This was a serious danger to the country. Barahu took over all the radio and television stations so these dangerous people could not be heard every day. Then, he seized the Internet so people couldn't contact others with their lies and deceit against Barahu. He made sure that papers and books with the lies could not be printed. And he changed what was taught in the schools to ensure that all children knew the truth. He did all these things to make sure that the wealthy could never take over the country again. This took several years. When he was done, he knew that the country no longer needed the "Congress". Remember, those were the people that the wealthy elected to keep them in power. He convinced his friends in Congress, of which he had the most, to promise not to meet every year like they had been. He told them that if they would promise not to meet, that they could be his most trusted advisors. Of course, who wouldn't want to be a trusted advisor to the great Barahu? They agreed. So, while our country still officially has a Congress, it hasn't met in almost 25 years. The last time they met, they made a law that said that Barahu was no longer President, but was our Emperor so we would always have him as our leader. It was in the year 7 NA that President Barahu became Emperor Barahu, now known as Emperor Barahu I."

Again, the audience rose to their feet and roared with approval. Charles felt like a yo-yo by getting up and down all the time. While he was still pretty relaxed, the lecture had tired him and he really wanted to go take a nap. He was hoping it would end soon.

"This has been a very brief history of our country and how it was saved by Barahu I. Over the next few days, you will learn more about how he saved this country and how much we owe to this remarkable person. After breakfast tomorrow, we'll start learn about how this country cares for its people by providing domicile units, food, clothing and other necessities. While you'll hear a little about how things used to be, more of it will be about how our society works now. Three days from now, each of you will take your economic benefit test. This tells us what you will be doing to provide a benefit to the country. Some of you will be clerks, laborers, teachers, and maybe even a scientist. By next week, you'll be getting any economic benefit training you need. Then the government can see where you will be sent to provide the greatest benefit to the country. This next week will be some of the most exciting days of your life, so get ready! I thank you for your attention this afternoon. Please take your materials from the table. You have 30 minutes before dinner so please return to your units and review the learning materials. Then meet in the cafeteria for dinner. Thank you."

The crowd rose and gave Citizen Wainwright a loud round of applause. She smiled and waved to everyone, obviously happy with the response. As the people filed out of the auditorium, the man from the back of the room waited patiently. When the crowd was mostly gone, he moved forward into the light for the first time. Wainwright saw him and her smile vanished for just a moment before returning to her face. It was obvious that she had not known that he was in the back. With a forced smile, she moved quickly towards him with her hand outstretched to shake his.

"Security Regent Peloreid, I didn't know you would be here," she said, squeezing his hand warmly and smiling until her cheeks began to hurt. "I'm honored to have such an esteemed member of the Purple Shirts in attendance."

Peloreid smiled smugly at her. While he knew her flattery was more a response to his authority rather than a sincere appreciation of his attendance, he couldn't help but smile back and the pretty young lady. Although sexual relations outside of the Relaxation Center were strictly prohibited, he knew some other Purple Shirts that had done so in the past. Of course, that had compromised their careers so he had no intention of following in their footsteps but he did feel a physical attraction to her. As his eyes scanned her figure, his mind moved to what it would be like to have her at the Center. He quickly shook that image from his mind as he returned to his business here.

"Now, Citizen Wainwright, how could I not attend your initial session under the new format? As you know, I've been a big proponent of this method of indoctrination for those who have undergone a Procedure 23. I think this is much better than traditional classrooms."

"Oh, I couldn't agree with you more," she exclaimed, as she dropped his hand and linked her arm in his. As she did so, she rubbed her breast against his arm. She wasn't sure why, but this seemed to please the older man. It did nothing for her and she couldn't imagine why he would like it, but, you needed to keep the Purple Shirts happy. This was a wonderful assignment for her. The domicile unit she had here was the nicest of any she had seen and the food was a delight. She has been assigned as a government clerk for several years and hadn't really enjoyed her smaller unit and the cafeteria at that office. This was much nicer. They really provided the best to their Procedure 23 patients in order to bring them back into society. She felt happy to be even a small part of that process. While she didn't know what a Procedure 23 was, her training had told her that these people would have no memory of their former lives and would be very confused. The more she could reassure them that their government would provide everything necessary for a satisfying life, the quicker they would accept their positions. Her work not only helped these patients but also helped the society as a whole. The nicer living arrangements and better food were just fringe benefits. And, if she had to rub a breast against an old Purple Shirt to ensure she could remain in this position, it wasn't that much to ask of her. "Let me show you the new auditorium. They've actually built sensors into the seats to track student's heart rates and breathing rates. That way, I can tell if they are really enjoying the presentation or not. The system even adjusts the air temperature and lighting if people aren't as responsive as they should be."

Peloreid let her lead him to the front of the auditorium. She showed him her monitors, the different digital displays, and various controls and adjustments she had. It was obvious to him that she was the perfect person to run this program. She was intelligent, but no so much that she might question some of the material. She was attractive and young, which would reduce any perceived threat to older audience members. They were particularly dangerous to this program. The older the student, the more likely that they might actually remember events that occurred when Emperor Barahu dissolved the former republic and established his government. That had been about 30 years ago, so there weren't many people left that would have been born then. The population control program had been hugely successful. The average age of the population was 25 and it had been relatively steady for several years now. By controlling the birth rate and enforcing the euthanasia policy, Barahu had eliminated most of the people that would have remembered the former regime. Within two years, there would be no one left over 65 years old. That would mean that there were very few people who would have been adults when the events happened. Then, and pretty much only then, would the Grand Society of the Union of Socialist Alliances be secure. He dreamed of that day since it would be the fulfillment of his lifelong mission which was the support of Barahu and the longevity of the Purple Shirts. However, he was also going to be 57 soon. He knew that, some day in the not so distant future, his medical officer would give him a pill that was not a vitamin. He didn't know exactly when that would be but he knew it would come. It could occur anytime after your 65th birthday. Even Purple Shirts were not exempt from the Population Control Directive. Not many people knew about it. They just took the pill just like they did every time they visited their medical officer. That way, no one was afraid of the pill or wondering what it was. I guess being a Purple Shirt does have some drawbacks, he thought. Most people don't know what really goes on in this society. He was sure he didn't know all the secrets, but he knew many. They were all designed to exert the maximum amount of control on the citizens without bringing them to the point of revolt. Control. That was the primary goal of the Barahu administration. It had worked better than ever before in the history of civilization. People had willingly given up their freedom. Once Barahu got it, they weren't getting it back. Now, almost two entire generations had been raised by the Barahu government. Two older generations had almost entirely been disposed of. Soon, the only collective memory that would exist was that of Barahu. Too bad his pill would probably come before then.

"Security Regent Peloreid?" Citizen Wainwright called from across the room. "Citizen Peloreid, is everything alright?"

"Yes, yes my dear," he responded, jolted back to the present. "Just admiring this wonderful technology. I must bring the Council Chairman here for one of your lectures. I think it would impress him immensely."

"But of course. Anytime you would like. I'll make sure you have the schedule of our classes."

"Thank you but no need. I have your schedule," replied Peloreid. His wry smile indicated a degree of control which he enjoyed, and which he wanted the young woman to recognize. He could see her face go blank momentarily and then return to her forced smile. Message received.

4

The next few days moved rather slowly for Charles. He felt like he was in a dream most of the time. He always felt a little light headed and never seemed to be able to focus on a subject for very long. While the food at the center was fine, he rarely felt very hungry. He just seemed to be in a daze. He watched others in the sessions and saw them in rapt attention, often standing and cheering. He went through the motions but never with much enthusiasm. He could feel people, those people who worked at the center, watching him. He knew they were judging his reaction but he just couldn't elicit much emotion, on any subject. He felt lost. He had no friends, no one to really talk to. He just wanted out of the place. At night, he would pace like a caged animal in his room. Over and over he would ask himself, I'm a prisoner, but for what? One night, tired of looking at his four walls, he had tried to open the door in order to walk around the building. The door was locked. Within moments, a voice came over a loudspeaker asking him if he needed something. He responded that he only wanted to walk around. "Not allowed", came the response followed by a loud click as the speaker was switched off. So, he paced in his cell. Why won't they tell me who I am?

He knew that there was something in his mind which he just couldn't get to. It seemed so near, but impossible to grasp. It was causing his frustration to continue to grow within him, becoming an anger at himself and his situation. He didn't know what to do, how to overcome it. So he kept searching his mind. And pacing.

The lectures that he received seemed unending and redundant. He heard over and over how Barahu I had saved the country, transformed it really from an uncivilized wilderness of greed, gluttony, and violence to the orderly society of the present. He heard again and again how the seizing of people's property, the censorship of opposition, and elimination of the elected government was all for the good of the people. To Charles, it appeared that Barahu had systematically taken over every part of society, piece by piece. "It's the economy, stupid," kept repeating in his mind but for the life of him he couldn't figure out where he had heard it. Once Barahu controlled the majority of the economy, people would either do what he said or be thrown out in the streets. Faced with that option, people did what he said. Charles was somewhat surprised that Citizen Wainwright didn't even hide the fact that Barahu had planned it that way. She celebrated that fact. She admitted that most people were unhappy and even demonstrated against Barahu. She stated proudly that, without the Purple Shirts being willing to violently put down the opposition on Barahu's behalf, he might never have succeeded. In the end, the people just gave up the opposition because they were afraid of the violence that would befall them if they continued. She was not apologetic, she was proud. The end justified the means. And it was very clear that, in today's USA, the beginning and the end was Barahu.

Every necessity of every citizen was granted by Barahu, so everyone depended on his government in order to survive. There was no lack of food, clothing, shelter, health care, or education. People received the food they needed, appropriate clothing, and a domicile unit to satisfy their basic desires. If they were sick, they could go to a clinic, although this seemed somewhat frowned upon. "The best medicine is rest at home," was the advice from Wainwright. "Only the very sick should ever go to a clinic since that is a sign of weakness and we are a society of the strong." Charles didn't quite understand how that worked but he figured he would find out in time.

It was the educational system that was the most interesting piece. Citizen Wainwright explained it on the third day of her lectures.

"In today's world, we must maintain order. It would do no one any good if everyone wanted to be a doctor since there are very few sick people. They would have nothing to do and would therefore not be helping society. Rather, they would be a curse to society. So, the Imperial Department of Education mandates that a certain number of people are trained in certain fields. They are selected based on aptitude. Usually, when children are 13 years old, they take an IQ and Aptitude Test. This test tells the government where the child will best fit in society. Based on their scores, they are divided into different groups and given specific training in that area only. In this way, they become experts in their field and it is much less demanding than trying to educate them in a variety of fields. In the Dark Ages, these children had to figure out what they were good at on their own! Can you imagine?" she asked. "These poor children had to struggle to learn all these subjects that they'd never use again. Then, they needed to get more specialized training and hope to find a place to work. It was really inefficient. Now, we know what you will be best at, give you only that training, and guarantee that you will provide a benefit to society. That way, we always have the right number of scientists, cooks, government clerks, and relaxation workers. It's a perfect system. No waste at all."

When it was time to ask questions, there were several. Most were fairly simple such as what was on the test, if everyone took it, and a few others. Charles hesitated, but finally raised his hand.

"Yes, Charles?" said Wainwright.

"What happens if you don't want to do what the test says you should?" he questioned. He wasn't sure what to expect. He saw a few others turn and look at him with surprised expressions on their faces.

Citizen Wainwright smiled even more, something that Charles had noticed occurred whenever things didn't go exactly as she planned. "Why, don't be silly," she began. "Who would want to do anything other that what they were best at? That just never happens," she finished as she moved onto another question. That was a very simple answer. It just didn't happen. Something in the back of Charles' mind just couldn't believe that it was so simple.

"What's the top vocation?" asked one student.

"Well, that's a great question," she replied. Behind me on the board you will see a sample of some of the professions and the score ranges. Each of you will be taking the exams in the next two weeks. I know all of you have training in certain fields, but we must be sure that the procedure, uh, I mean your operations didn't impact your scores. But please don't worry. The people that fall outside their prior professional range will be quickly trained in a new profession."

On the screen behind her, a list of several jobs and score ranges appeared.

Scientist	130—150
Instructor	120—140
Administrator	110—130
Political Administrator	100—120
Administrative Clerk	100—120
Food Service	90—110
Relaxation Specialist	70—90

"As you can see, the brightest of our people are our scientists that help to ensure that our society maintains its high level of advancement. Others include administrators, like you would find in our factories, administrative clerks like you would find in the product exchanges, and food service personnel like those that make and serve you the yummy meals you eat," explained Wainwright.

"Citizen Wainwright, what's a relaxation specialist?" asked on of the patients in the middle of the group. Wainwright blushed at first, looking down at the floor and then regained her composure before answering.

"We usually review that during the Health and Wellness portion of our program but I can give you a brief answer now. During the Dark Ages, men and women had very uncivilized relationships. Men would use women for sex, often forcing themselves upon them and sometimes even killing them. Women were forced to have children, a process that dehumanized them to baby producing machines. Men did this in order to keep them subservient, since most women would need to stop producing economic value for society when they had children. These women were sometimes forced to teach these children for years, another way in which the male control oriented society forced women into second class status. Often, women would even die in giving birth under very primitive circumstances. These living units of a man, women, and any number of children were a huge waste of resources for society. Most of the time, they would not properly care for each other and these "families" as they were called would usually end in violence and even death. Emperor Barahu understood that this cohabitation unit was the major problem with society so he began a process of abolishing them.

First, Barahu began a process of sterilizing people as they reached their teenage years. This was done through a mandatory inoculation that everyone received. We all realize that, without children, our society would perish but Barahu had already developed the Imperial Child Development Agency. They created children using specially selected citizens whose economic benefit role was to produce children. That's all they did. The children were raised and educated by the government in order that each received the proper training and instruction into their responsibilities for aiding society. In this way, people weren't forced to reside and interact with others and forced to raise children which they would usually abuse. People are now much better off and more adequately prepared for their roles in society than ever before.

There was one aspect of life that this didn't solve and that was the animalistic desire for sex. While children were now adequately cared for, women were still abused by the men. Barahu then mandated that men could no longer use any woman they wanted for sex. He set up Relaxation Centers, where men, and women if they choose, could go once every month in order to release their physical sexual urges. They are provided with a subject for 30 minutes. These are called Relaxation Specialists and are those at the lowest end of the testing range. However, please don't think this is an unimportant or useless position. These specialists have helped to end violence in our society. In fact, our Genetics Engineering Department has developed several models that have been proven to be the most effective in speeding up the sexual release process and have led to increased productivity in that segment of the economy. What used to take one hour now usually takes less than 30 minutes, which is a 50% increase in productivity. This is an example of another of Barahu's incredible success stories which have improved our society," she finished, beaming at the crowd.

"Excuse me, Citizen Wainwright," said a young patient that was sitting in the very front row. "I'm trying to take notes but I wasn't sure what you said about Genetics Engineering. Can you repeat that please?"

"Of course, of course. After our government took responsibility for population control, we had to ensure that we had the best, most advanced population available. Hundreds of genetics researchers worked to develop traits that could be of the most benefit to society. Some aspects, like appearances, were fairly easy to manage. However, others, like intelligence, were harder. As you look at the table, you see a wide range of scores. Our researchers are becoming better and better at being able to produce people that fit into a particular scoring range. That will help us to manage the population so we always have the right number of scientists, political administrators, and relaxation specialist to fill our requirements. The essence of the Barahu society is to properly manage every aspect of life to the fullest benefit of society. Population control is the most important way of doing this. It's been in existence for years now, so some of you are the output of this incredible system. Unfortunately, many of you are still the product of the ancient style of child rearing. But that's fine too. You should feel grateful to live in a society that continues to improve itself. And one of the benefits of the operations that you've received is that you can no longer remember those terrible times," finished Wainwright, flashing her big smile, particularly towards the older patients scattered throughout the crowd.

Charles didn't quite know what to think of the information he'd received that day. Something just seemed wrong about a government producing the people that would then support the society. Rationally, it seemed like the perfect system. But where was the humanity. At present, he felt no sexual desires. While some part of his brain understood sex and somehow he could even remember having sex at times, he didn't seem to be attracted to anyone in the group. He imagined it was due to the operation. But something gnawed at him. He didn't remember a family. Certainly, he couldn't remember being beaten or abused as Wainwright said happened with most children. But he felt like there was something missing in the equation. Somehow, the things that were said to be wrong with the ancient society didn't seem so wrong. Charles was getting more and more worried that he wasn't fitting in this society. He wasn't sure why he felt that way but he was concerned that, in a society that was so controlled, you either fit in or you had some big problems. The number of purple shirt wearing security guards that were a constant presence throughout the center reinforced the notion that you were meant to stay in line and follow the rules. He just couldn't figure out why the rules seemed so wrong to him when everyone else accepted them readily.

Charles took his nightly vitamin pill and fell into a restless sleep. That night, he had a dream about two older people, one man and one woman and a little boy, which he knew was him. They were in a crazy world where they lived on a boat that could fly. They walked across the water to the shoreline and began having a picnic. Then, men with clubs and guns burst from the bushes and they had to run towards their boat. As they got to the boat, the man and woman jumped in but he fell. They screamed and stretched out to him as the boat began sailing away. He tried to reach them but they were just too far away. They were screaming to him and he was yelling for help. But the boat just kept getting further away, little by little and then it lifted off from the water and slowly flew away, being replaced by a bright light. Charles screamed and flailed his arms as the water began to cover his face.

He awoke in a fright, a cold sweat running down his face. He looked at the clock on the stand and saw that it was 4:14 AM. Still about two hours before he needed to get up and get ready for the next lecture. His mind was still filled with the nightmare. Those two people that he wanted to save him. The reaching. The screaming. The boat flying away and the feeling that he was going to drown. He couldn't remember seeing those people before but then he couldn't remember seeing hardly anyone before. Why was he having this dream? Who were those people? He could remember the picnic. He had felt so secure, so happy. The emotion was almost overwhelming. The warmth and security that was so realistic in his dream. He could still feel the arms wrapped around him as the woman hugged him It was everything that he didn't feel now, in his locked room and in this Reorientation Center. It was the missing part of him.

The part that was human.

The part that realized that something was wrong with this "reorientation". Was that the family that Citizen Wainwright had said was so evil? Were those his parents, the ones that would have beaten him?

It was becoming more apparent to Charles that the government sought to control every aspect of your life. It was also becoming apparent that they had yet to discover how to control your dreams. And perhaps his dreams would lead him back to his former life.

5

"Charles Johnson?" a voice called in the hallway. Charles stood up and made a slight wave to the middle aged woman holding his file.

"I'm Charles Johnson," he said, moving towards her.

"Hello, Citizen Johnson. I'm Citizen Chapman, your economic position counselor. Please step into the office and we'll review your test results."

Charles made is way into the office which housed a small metal desk, with one chair for the counselor and one metal chair for him. A desk lamp, computer monitor, and keyboard were the only other articles in sight. Citizen Chapman motioned for him to sit and he did so. He was a little anxious on how he had done on his exam. He thought he did well. Answers seemed to jump into his head although he didn't know how. He couldn't remember attending any classes in math or science but yet he understood each of the questions and knew their answers. He just didn't know why his mind could remember facts but not how or where he had learned them. It was the most difficult thing that he was trying to comprehend.

There was also another reason why he was anxious. These results would indicate what his job would be and where he would work and live. Everything in the society revolved around your economic position. It reflected your value to the society and how much they needed you. The lower your score, the less valuable you were to them, whoever "them" was. He still was unsure if things were really as organized and structured as he had been told in the Reorientation Center. According to Citizen Wainwright, everything worked on an absolute schedule, from the time you showered and dressed in the morning, (if you had a non-physically exhaustive job, otherwise you showered at night), to when and what you ate and the vitamins you took, to when you needed to sleep. Domicile units, where people resided, were controlled so that the interactive education and entertainment monitors started and stopped automatically, indicating when it was time to watch. Lights came on or went out automatically, based on whether you were supposed to be awake or asleep. Food was obtained in a cafeteria area in each domicile residence unit building and adjusted specifically for the person consuming it. There were no chairs or tables so you just got your meal and went back to your unit to eat. Your choices were hot or cold. Even the streetcars stopped automatically outside your building to take you to your Economic Position Location, where you did your work. Miss the streetcar and a Purple Shirt would call your unit. If you were sick, they would come to escort you to a health clinic. If not, you would be escorted to their offices for a "performance evaluation". Citizen Wainwright indicated that it was never a good thing to have your performance evaluated. It usually only occurred once and the poor performance was never repeated by the offender. Life revolved around going from your domicile unit to your economic position and back. One day every week, you had free time. That's when you could walk to a park to relax, go to the relaxation center if it was your time, or remain in your unit to watch a variety of videos on the history of Barahu and the advancements being made in his society or a governmentally approved and produced show. Otherwise, your only choice was hot or cold meals.

"Choice makes for inefficiencies in society," stated Wainwright forcibly in one of her lectures. "And inefficiency means a waste of resources. That's why everything is programmed from the lights to the streetcars. To conserve energy and reduce inefficiency in our society."

Charles wasn't sure that he agreed, but he had to admit that the schedules would force efficiency. It just seemed to him that there had to be more to life than efficiency for the sake of society. Charles looked expectantly at Citizen Chapman while she scanned his file and reviewed the information from the computer monitor.

"Very impressive, Citizen Johnson, especially after the operation you had," stated Chapman after a few moments. "You continue to rank near the top of the ratings, just as you did originally. That's a wonderful testament to our medical capabilities."

Charles listened to her words, at first with relief and then with some consternation. He felt like his success on the test was due to his intelligence, not the medical capabilities of Barahu's Grand Society. While he was grateful for the medical treatments he had received, it was still his brain that answered the questions. However, he had an idea that those sentiments wouldn't be shared by Chapman.

"Yes, the doctors and nurses were wonderful," he responded. "Does it say what my economic role will be?"

Chapman looked at him with a trace of disdain. "The term is economic position, NOT role. And yes, that is MY responsibility to explain to you. Now, if you'll let me execute the responsibilities of MY economic POSITION, you'll find out what YOUR economic position will be," she said smugly. "You were a research chemist for the government's nutritional additives section. Those are the wonderful people who provide us with the vitamins that are added to our food to keep us healthy. Every time you eat, your body is filled with the vitamins these people create. Do you understand?"

"Yes, ma'am," was the sheepish response.

"Good. Your overall scores as well as your economic position specific results would put you in a similar role. You'll be working with other scientists to enhance the health effects of the nutritional supplements that the entire population eats daily. In this capacity, I feel you will provide the greatest economic benefit to the government and overall society. This will also eliminate the need for costly retraining since it appears that you have retained most, if not all, of your former training and education. It's a very good thing that the government hasn't wasted all of that valuable learning. Now it's up to you to repay their efforts by being a productive and conforming presence in the nutritional additives section of the Health and Welfare Directory. Is that all understood?"

"Yes, ma'am. When do I start?"

"If you'll ALLOW me to continue, I will give you all the specifics. I certainly hope that you show more self restraint when you begin your assignment than you has here. Your interruptions are causing me to run behind schedule."

Charles nodded and looked at the floor. His first taste of the government bureaucracy outside of the Reorientation Center was not particularly to his liking. This condescending attitude didn't sit well. She was already late when she called him in, and she wouldn't need to take as much time as she had if she would just stop reprimanding him and get on with it. But, he figured that this was probably the last time he would ever have to deal with Citizen Chapman so he might as well keep his mouth shut and get it over with.

"You'll be placed at Unit 1125. That's a laboratory that you'll get to by taking Electric Transport Vehicle, or ETV, number 17. It will pick you up outside of your domicile residence unit building beginning at 8 Barahu Mean Time on August 24th. Now, in case you can't remember that, it's all contained in this packet, along with other required information for you to review. Don't sign anything until you get to Unit 1125. The clerk there will verify your identity and take you through their security process. This is an extremely high security area so you will need to conform with their policies completely. Failure to do so will result in a visit from the Purple Shirts and I'm sure you DON'T want that, now do you?"

Chapman looked at Charles who shook his head slowly.

"No, of course you don't. Now, if you have no further questions, I have many others to meet with today."

Charles got up and thanked her. He extended his hand to shake hers but she simply looked at his outstretched hand with contempt.

"You can't possibly believe that I'd risk a trip to the health facilities because I picked up germs that you might be carrying?" she asked him, incredulously.

He simply replied, "No, ma'am. Sorry, ma'am."

She pushed past him and moved out the door, mumbling something about the problems with Procedure 23 patients and wondering what in the world they were teaching them at the Reorientation Center.

Charles followed her out and made his way to the stairs without saying another word and without looking at Citizen Chapman.

"You're welcome," he heard sarcastically shouted after him as he reached the door that led to the stairway. Charles didn't look back. He just kept on moving. He just wanted to get out of the building. As he exited, he saw Wainwright and some of the other patients waiting near the entrance. He walked over to the group but stood a little apart. He looked at the bright blue sky with the sun warming his face. Except for some mumbles he could overhear from the group, the street was mostly silent. The only other sound he could hear was from the ETVs moving by on the street. The electronic streetcars were the only vehicles allowed in Barahu's society. Those and official government vehicles, that is. While most of those were also electronic, they were all painted black or purple, with darkened windows. Some were small, with probably no more than a few people inside while others were larger than the ETV's that Charles had used to get from the hospital to the reorientation center or to the government building where he now stood.

Charles looked at Citizen Wainwright who was standing alone, just a few feet away, enjoying the warm summer day. It was a sudden impulse that made him approach her.

"Excuse me, Citizen Wainwright," he began, without really thinking this through. "I've really enjoyed your lectures so far," he lied, "but I'd like to know when we will be learning about ourselves?"

"Learning about yourselves? Whatever do you mean?" she replied, with an astonished look on her face. Rarely had a patient, or rather student, approached her and never to ask a question like this.

"My life. When do I find out what my life was before my accident?"

"Your life!" she exclaimed, not comfortable with where this conversation was headed. "Why would we teach you about your life? It really isn't important now."

"Not important? It is to me. It's my life. I want to know where I'm from. Where I lived. Who my friends were. What kind of accident I was in. I want to know who I am," Charles demanded, his voice rising.

Others in the group had turned to watch the pair. Wainwright looked around nervously. She knew she could call a Purple

Shirt but she didn't want to. This may be a test for her to pass. Peloreid could be nearby watching her right now. No, she would handle this on her own.

"Mr. Johnson, your life before doesn't matter. Your responsibility is to the government. What happened before will not help you with that. You had better spend less time worrying about things in your past and spend more time understanding how to serve this society in the future. Otherwise, I'm afraid the Purple Shirts will need to deal with you."

Charles understood the threatening tone of her voice. He knew he shouldn't have asked her. But some part of him just didn't care. His life had been lost, or had it been taken, from him? Only through his dreams was he able to catch even a glimpse of it. And now, after Wainwright's words, he knew that the government didn't want him to have it back.

"Sorry, ma'am," he mumbled and then moved away from Citizen Wainwright and the other students.

"Are you ready, Citizen Johnson?" Wainwright harshly yelled to him a few minutes later.

Wainwright's voice jolted him back to the present moment. He quickly looked around and saw his group entering the ETV which would take them back to the center. "Yes, Citizen Wainwright. Sorry. I was just enjoying the warm sunshine."

"It is a beautiful day, isn't it? If it weren't for Emperor Barahu, we wouldn't be seeing a nice blue sky. They were called the 'Dark Ages' because there was so much pollution in the air that you could barely see the sunlight. Barahu's reforms saved the entire planet," stated Wainwright, seeming to have reassumed her previously happy mood.

"I'm amazed he could do it all by himself. Didn't the rest of the world have to do it too?" asked Charles.

Wainwright looked at him with a mixture of surprise and perplexity. She hadn't expected a question in return of her statement of fact. And, to be honest, she had never stopped to think about what the rest of the world had done. She couldn't even remember learning about the response of the rest of the world to any of the teachings and principles of Barahu. For a moment, she was puzzled as to how to answer Charles. Then, the most obvious answer struck her and she ridiculed herself for even wavering for a moment.

"Well, of course, the rest of the world was grateful for Barahu to show them the way out of their problems. He was the most loved and revered leader the world has ever known. They followed his example without question."

She didn't know if the response was factually true, but what other answer could there be? How could anyone, anywhere in the world question the decision of the Divine One? Was he not the Messiah meant to save the world from themselves? Had he not led the USA into the utopia in which they now existed? While she never heard reports from other countries, she could think of no other plausible answer to the question. If there was no other answer, the one you had would have to be the correct one. Simple logic dictated that. And so, with a smile that reflected her inner happiness with her own, carefully thought out answer, she led Charles to the waiting ETV.

Charles looked down at the pretty, young woman leading him. She seemed precious, like a little child. She so wanted to believe all the good things about Barahu. It was obvious that she would never question anything told to her about the Divine One. She would not question the good and not accept the bad. That was the definition of faith, he guessed. He just seemed unable to have the same blind faith in this man, this government. Something told him that this was not right, but he still couldn't understand where that feeling was coming from. Maybe it was the questioning nature that was also leading him toward science. That, at least, was fact based. The laws of chemistry and physics held true. The results of the experiments were whatever they would be, not what someone wanted them to be. All was based on facts and real logic, not the patronizing babble that passed for education at the Reorientation Center. Sitting in his seat on the ETV, silently rolling down the streets, he wondered what would happen to him if he said those thoughts aloud. There seemed to be no debate anywhere in society. You went where you were told to, ate what they gave you, and slept when the lights went out. There was a sort of comfort to that, to the rules that you learned and were told to adhere. Not thinking did have its advantages. No decisions to make. No mistakes. As long as you liked what they provided, everything was great. The only problem that kept nagging him was that there seemed to be no choice. There was no way to choose something else to eat, or someplace else to work, or something else to wear. His meals had started with many choices but that gradually faded to one meal choice for everyone. It hadn't been explained. It's just the way it was. His wardrobe had been cleaned daily, but it hadn't changed. Everyone wore the same colors every day. His job, no that's ECONOMIC POSITION, was assigned to him as it was to everyone. A test told you how best to serve the government. All decisions, all choice remained with the government bureaucrats. As Wainwright had said, "that's the only way to retain order and ensure that everyone is cared for in an equitable way."

Charles, for some unknown reason, was having a problem with that. As he looked around the ETV, he wondered if he was the only one having these thoughts. Most people seemed happy and content. But, as usual, most people were sitting by themselves, not saying a word. A few chatted quietly with one other person but most were like him. Solitary. Alone. That feeling wouldn't leave him anytime soon.

Several days later, his reorientation was officially complete. All patients had finished the six week program and learned all about the storied history of the Barahu system of governmental control of society. The group stood and cheered after a pre-recorded message from Emperor Barahu II was played. They were even more vocal as Wainwright announced that their program was complete and deemed a total success. She beamed as the audience applauded her efforts. She was doubly pleased when she saw Peloreid clapping in the back of the auditorium. It had been his program and she had personally been selected to execute it. It was rumored that he was in contention for a spot on the Supreme Council one day. It would have to occur soon or he would be deemed too old to serve. This was to be his prized program, one that would save the government millions of dollars in population engineering and training costs. For her, a friend on the Supreme Council could only improve her standing in society. And so, if he was happy, she was thrilled.

And, Peloreid was happy. It was all coming together. His plan for saving money was working perfectly. Procedure 23 had been a gamble. If he won, he would almost certainly be seated on the Supreme Council. If he lost, well he just hoped it would end quickly and painlessly. He also knew that wasn't always the case. Procedure 23. What an innocent name for such a powerful solution to the government's problems. Few knew about it, although the word was spreading. He knew it wasn't going to be kept secret for long but now that this first group was successful, he didn't really care. Let people know. That would make them hold their tongues.

The problem was one that plagued strong, centrally controlled governments for ages. At some point, people revolt. No one could explain why. The pigs were given all they could want. But, they weren't satisfied. They wanted theoretical ideals. Liberty. What was liberty except a license to steal from others because you were born wealthier, smarter, or just worked harder? Why should some have more just because luck had been kind to them? Freedom. Why should people have choices which might not benefit others but only themselves? The rights of man. What kind of idiotic notion was this? Freedom of speech and assembly. A right to revolt from the kindness and generosity of the government. Peloreid couldn't understand why people would be willing to fight and even die for these concepts. They were outdated notions going back to a time when people wore powdered wigs. Back to a time when people built grand temples to some god figure. How could people really believe in a power and essence of creation? Government was the grand creator of society, not some unseeing being. He remembered being dragged to church as a youth. He hated it. What kind of grand being would create people that could be as cruel as the other children were to him? There was no god, of that he was quite sure. He smiled at the memory of when Barahu I had outlawed religion. What a glorious day that had been! He remembered joining other Purple Shirts in burning churches, temples, and mosques all around Capitol City. They were overjoyed with the official condemnation of any grand being other than Barahu. Of course, the empty headed populous had screamed bloody murder. He snorted. There had been a lot of bloody murder that day too. Actually, it wasn't murder. He had freed their spirits to return to their creator. They should have thanked him. They were so stupid that he almost felt sorry for them. It had taken years to weaken the population's grasp on religion. Now there was only one religion, Barahu. And he, Peloreid, a somewhat frail, slow child from a stinking religion was on the verge of joining the inner circle of the new religion. He was at the threshold. And all because of Procedure 23.

All of these "geniuses" with their grand ideals like liberty, freedom, and rights. They were now at his mercy because of Procedure 23. It had taken months to develop but was primarily based on research already available. They had been working on a way to control people thoughts, mostly through inserting small chips in the brain to generate electrical charges when necessary to promote or prohibit certain thoughts and behavior. They needed a way to stop the small revolts that were becoming more frequent. Personally, he liked to just line up the offenders and shoot them with the electro-bullets, small pellets that held an electrical charge for a short time. Being hit with a small charge would stun the target. A strong charge would kill it. No blood, no flying body parts, no wounded running off only to fight again on another day.. It was neat, clean and quick. Its efficiency should have been welcomed.

The problem was twofold: dead bodies and the lost productivity. While the millions killed during the revolution had typically been dumped in mass graves, hauling thousands of dead bodies out of the urban areas was time consuming and costly. While loyal citizens didn't give a damn how many rebels were killed, they didn't seem to like seeing the bodies. To Peloreid, it was a sign of the security they were providing but others seemed squeamish. So, what do you do with the bodies? That was a problem but, in his mind, not the one that would gain him a promotion.

The more significant problem was the economic impact of these traitors. The Barahu Population Control Program had been a greater success than he had ever felt possible. By limiting the number of births through forced sterilization and abortions, and by "managing" the elderly, they could control the total number of people. But the number wasn't the important part, it was the type of person. They needed a certain number of chemists, doctors, and ditch diggers. Too many of one and not enough of the other caused enormous problems for the government. They were spending huge sums of money by producing too many people that needed to be terminated once they proved to be of the wrong type. Usually, you couldn't judge their overall intelligence until they were about five years old so you ended up feeding, clothing, and training these people for years until you could determine if they would be of any benefit to society. When the population control program first started, they let all these unneeded children grow up at an enormous cost to the government. Barahu had tried educating them to do something else but that didn't work. They finally began terminating them by age five if they weren't needed, but that was still five years of costs for nothing. Then, the Genetics Engineering Division had developed a method for managing intelligence. Their success rate had gradually grown so that they could provide almost the exact number of required IQ types. Their failure rate was only five percent, which saved billions of dollars in food, clothing, and training expenses. Now, only a few thousand children had to be exterminated every year. It had been in the tens of thousands before the breakthrough.

The system worked extremely well. Genetics Engineering produced the right number of people to fill each job type. For the lower level jobs, like Relaxation Specialist, they could be trained to provide economic benefit by age 15. For higher level positions, it could be as long as 25 years before they began to generate a payback for society. The system worked well since Relaxation Specialists were usually "retired" by age 25 while higher level positions like chemists were in their 60's before "retirement". After all, who would want an old Relaxation Specialist?

Unfortunately, the system was so efficient that it didn't allow room for any failure. When a group of scientists were tied to a local revolt, their deaths caused a shortage in the laboratories. All of their projects came to a screeching halt. It was years before the labs were totally back on line. And therein lay the problem. For some reason, it was the higher level professions that seemed caught up in the liberty/freedom/blah blah blah movement. When the protesters and rebels were killed, it was the high level professions that lost their workforce. That was the real problem of the revolts, the economic impact of the lost professionals.

And so, the government sought to be able to control these thoughts through inserting the chips. The first experiments were gruesome failures. The test subjects either died on the operating tables or became blathering idiots.

Then, one magical day when Peloreid was reviewing the security at a chemical laboratory, he overheard a chemist saying how they were now able to identify certain micro-proteins in the brain that controlled different types of memories. Peloreid had no idea of what a micro-protein was. In questioning him on the new discovery, he also asked, if there were different micro-proteins for different thoughts, whether or not certain chemicals might be able to alter those micro-proteins and thereby eliminate the thoughts. While the scientist wasn't sure, he thought it possible. The next day, Peloreid made his proposal to his Security Regent. His long service as an original Purple Shirt, his eagerness to suppress any revolt, by whatever means was necessary, and the imagined rewards of the projects success had convinced the Regent to approve the project. It had taken several years, but finally the chemists had developed a process to eliminate the targeted memory of the subject. They would retain their knowledge of language, the learned skills of their profession, and would retain anything new taught them, but they could have certain memories, such as those of their childhood or their traitorous ideals, removed. In essence, the useful knowledge would remain intact while the destructive, unnecessary ones would be erased. Not destroyed, but erased.

As with the other experiments, it had taken time. Thousands of subjects had their brain functions totally destroyed by the wrong mixture or potency of the chemicals. Peloreid's Security Regent had been retired and Peloreid had ascended to his position, largely due to the progress made on this project. And then, on the 23rd version which combined a small chip with a 20 hour period of chemotherapy, they had success. The chip helped to monitor the protein levels in the brain and adjusted the amount of chemicals provided. The result was a procedure which eliminated the undesirable memories without destroying others. The patients would lose their insane notions of liberty, freedom, and rights but maintain their knowledge of their professions. They could then be retrained, or reoriented, in order to emerge from the treatments as a productive member of society.

Procedure 23 would take about two months to complete. The cost was a small fraction of the cost of raising a new chemist or physicist or of maintaining an inefficient quantity of those professions to make up for any lost to revolt. It was going to be a huge success. And today was the final day of the pilot study. It was the graduation of the first 50 subjects, or rather patients, of the procedure. These people would reenter society and provide immediate benefit at a very small cost to the government.

Peloreid looked across the auditorium with genuine pleasure. There was the group, standing and applauding as one. There was Citizen Wainwright, his hand picked instructor, smiling at him. Her red sweater was a stark contrast to the khaki clothing of the patients. It hugged her body and revealed all of her curves. A flush of excitement came over Peloreid. Tonight, he would grant himself a small treat. He wasn't due for another visit to the Relaxation Center yet but they never turned down a Security Regent of the Purple Shirts. Somewhere in that center, there was a young woman who would remind him of Wainwright. She would be the surrogate tonight. The thought made him smile with delight at her. She saw his smile and returned it.

6

"Next," said the male receptionist at the Relaxation Center. A middle aged, somewhat pudgy and balding man stepped forward.

"Number?" the receptionist asked.

"078579," the client replied.

"Very good. Right on time. I wish everyone could be like that," sighed the weary receptionist as he finished scanning the computer monitor. "Your specialist will be here in a moment."

Peloreid opened the door to the office and looked at the crowd of men waiting. The Center was very careful to keep the male and female clients separated. Each had different entrances and exits, as well as separate relaxation rooms. Sexual relations were strictly prohibited outside of the Relaxation Center. Before the rule was enacted, casual relations resulted in jealousies and acts of violence, as well as the very real threat of disease. Barahu once thought of prohibiting it all together, but decided that it was much better to tightly regulate it. Since this type of activity often led to increased passions, the government mandated that the sexes be separated in order to ensure that no "extra curricular" activity occurred. And so, Peloreid was greeted by a room full of eager men, all awaiting their turn.

He knew that he should really wait a few more weeks before his next visit. It had been less than two since his last one. But, the thrill of today's victory had his blood up, and there was only one way that would allow him to satisfy his desires. He also knew that this low level receptionist would never think to refuse a request from a Security Regent. In case this particular person didn't recognize him by name or number, Peloreid wore his uniform underneath his overcoat. That should be enough to persuade even the most officious clerk.

"Your specialist is here," the receptionist stated unexcitedly to the pudgy man.

"Um, I think there's been some sort of mistake," the client replied, looking warily from the specialist to the clerk.

"No, no mistake. You're next in line and this is the next specialist," came the blunt reply from the man who just wanted to be done with work. In 45 minutes his shift would be over and he could go home. Dealing with problems was the last thing that he wanted to do that night.

"But, but, he's a man," blurted out the somewhat confused client.

"Can't get one by you, now can we? Yes, he's a male. You're a male. I'm a male. You're next and this is your specialist. Now please go. You're holding up the line."

"But I don't want a male. I want a female," protested the increasingly nervous client, feeling more uncomfortable in the situation than usual, which was a great deal to begin with.

"Obviously, you aren't aware of the new regulations. The government did a study which showed that seven percent of men prefer relations with another man. Therefore, they decreed that one out of every twelve specialists be male instead of having all females. That way, there's no discrimination due to sexual preference," huffed the clerk.

"That's fine for those that prefer another male, but I don't," stammered the pudgy man, growing red in the face.

"You don't have a choice. It's the government's regulation. If you don't like it, why don't you contact the Supreme Council!"

exclaimed the clerk, frustrated by the delay. He didn't make the rules. He could care less whether this particular man had sex with a woman, another man, or a horse. He just wanted him to go somewhere so he could count off the final few minutes of his ten hour shift and go home.

He looked up to see a tall, thin, older man in a long dark overcoat make his way up to the desk. Just what he needed, another trouble maker. His routine day was getting worse by the minute.

"Is there a problem that I might assist with?" asked Peloreid, allowing his coat to open to show the dark purple tunic of a Purple Shirt Security Regent. He took great pleasure in seeing the flushed expression on the clerks face as well as the beads of sweat begin to flow from the pudgy client.

"Welcome, Citizen Regent. What an unexpected pleasure! I had no idea that we were expecting a dignitary this evening," replied the clerk, struggling to retain some dignity. "This client does not seem to appreciate the governmental regulations regarding this Relaxation Center. I believe you were going to protest to the Supreme Council, weren't you," said the clerk with a menacing smile to the now sweaty client.

"No, I mean, I wasn't arguing about the regulations. I, I, I just, uh, wasn't aware of this particular regulation," replied the client, painfully aware that his complaint, while not serious, would be noted on his file. And now, what were the odds of a Security Regent being there the same night as him? This was far from a relaxing night.

Peloreid looked down at the balding, sweaty little man that was standing between him and the physical release that he so deserved. He looked through the entryway to the relaxation rooms and saw a man in his 20's wearing only a light pair of loose fitting cotton pants. The male specialist was tanned, tall and muscular, as though he had been carved from a block of amber granite. Now, he understood the client's dilemma. He wasn't a homosexual, but he either had to go with this man to have sex or loose his opportunity for at least another month. The computers would think that his failure to complete his monthly relaxation appointment meant a decreased desire. That could mean that he wouldn't be able to return for anywhere between two and six months. And so, the man was desperate to have sex but, was he desperate enough to go with the man. Peloreid had just decided to extend the man's discomfort when he saw the next specialist come into view. She was young, probably around 17 or 18, with long blonde hair and beautiful full blue eyes. Her loose fitting pants and blouse couldn't hide her sumptuous curves. Oh, that genetics engineering department! This pretty young girl had to be one of their finest creations. And, being so young, she was probably barely used. She reminded him of a younger version of Citizen Wainwright. Perhaps this girl's waist was a trifle smaller and her breasts a little more full, but the face was almost identical.

The muttered explanations of the little client brought his attention back to the current situation. Only, Peloreid no longer had a desire to lengthen this little man's discomfort. He was now thinking about his own desires.

"Perhaps, we should escort this citizen to the local Purple Shirt Directorate. I'm sure they would be happy to let you dictate your complaint," interrupted Peloreid, in the most contemptible tone of his possession.

The client turned white. He could feel the sweat running down his cheeks and neck. The Purple Shirt Directorate? He had heard stories of people that had been taken to the Directorate. He had never heard of anyone returning from the Directorate.

"Um, you know, I think I was mistaken. Yes, yes, it is my turn. I think I should just go ahead now."

The clerk smiled. The little play that had occurred in the past few minutes was unlike anything he had participated in before. The sheer power of the Security Regent was very impressive. His position had no such ability to instill fear in others. He had very little authority, but decided to be as authoritarian possible before the Regent.

"That's more like it. Off you go then. Your specialist is waiting," he said in a deep voice that he hoped would impress the Regent.

The male specialist walked forward and took the client by the hand. The client looked sheepishly down at his feet, then up to the Regent before again lowering his head and following the specialist down the hallway. Peloreid smiled as he heard the specialist look down at his newfound friend and say, "don't worry, most people are nervous their first time. I'll take such good care of you that you'll feel silly for ever worrying about it. You wouldn't believe how many first timers I've had lately..."

The conversation faded down the hallway so Peloreid turned to the clerk and smiled. The clerk returned the smile in kind, feeling as if he had shared a little triumph with the very impressive Security Regent.

"Now, if I may," began Peloreid, "I was hoping that I might be accommodated next."

"Of course, sir. I am Citizen Rangelo and am at your service, sir. May I have your number please?"

"PS-R12597."

"Ah, Security Regent Peloreid. Yes, I see that you are not yet due but give me just a moment and I'll get you straight in. One more second. This system seems a little slow tonight. Ah, yes, there it is," Rangelo said looking up at the Regent as if he had just supplied a vital service to the government.

Peloreid looked at the clerk with an appreciative smile. He had many years of experience in dealing with low level administrators and knew very well when he was receiving a first class boot licking. He also knew that these lower level people could be useful at times so it was usually wise to at least acknowledge their efforts, as limited as they might be.

"Oh, that's very good of you, Citizen Rangelo, was it?"

"Oh yes sir," beamed Rangelo. He motioned the young, blond specialist to come forward. "I hope this specialist will be satisfactory. If not, I will do my best to find you an acceptable substitute."

"No, no, this one will serve nicely I think," smiled Peloreid as she entwined her arm in his. "Thank you for your accommodation. I shall not forget it."

The clerk beamed with excitement. Gratitude from a full Security Regent. And one that even remembered his name. Perhaps soon he would be able to advance to a better shift and be able to avoid the lesser people that always seemed to show up at this time of night.

The young specialist led the older gentleman down the hallway to a small, dimly lit room which contained a small bed and table. She closed the door behind them and stood, smiling lovingly towards Peloreid who was already sitting on the bed, removing his boots. He looked at her with an appetite prepared to be satiated. She leaned her back against the door and slowly undid the blouse tied loosely around her neck. The blouse fell to the floor, exposing her perfectly smooth skin. Slowly, seductively, she loosened the tie on her pants and allowed them to slowly fall to the floor, revealing her perfect, fully nude body to Peloreid. She smiled at him, a smile which he returned, as she moved over to help him remove his tunic.

It had lasted only minutes, but she would feel the affects for weeks. He stood above her now, redressing in the light as he looked down at her contorted body. He could hear her soft whimpering, which helped to extend his excitement of the evening. The bruises were starting to form on her neck and back and blood trickled down from her nose and mouth, turning the white sheets a crimson red. She lay there on her stomach, naked except for the sheet which covered her lower legs. Her left hand was holding her right forearm, which had a slight curve to it due to the broken bone just below the skin. Peloreid straightened his shirt and buttoned his slacks. With a smile on his face, he bent down and whispered in the girls ear, "thank you, my dear, for a most enjoyable evening. I can't remember when I last felt so relaxed." And with that, he turned and left the weeping teenager alone in the room.

The next day was a beautiful summer day, sunny and warm with only a trace of humidity in the air. This was the day Citizen Peloreid had been anticipating for months. He was to address the full Supreme Council with the results of the Procedure 23 Pilot Study. It would be the greatest achievement of his career, one that would save untold millions of dollars over the years. The pilot had been an incredible success with no test subjects being lost, either from death during the procedure or significantly disrupted brain functioning. Their reorientation had gone according to schedule and, with the reductions of meal choices that he had directed, it had even come in under budget. In three days, the study participants would be reentering the workforce in their previous professions. While there would be some required training to get them caught up and involved with current projects, this was minimal compared to the cost of training a brand new employee. This would also reduce the need of additional bodies from the Population Control Division and eliminate the costs that would have been spent to dispose of the participants bodies if they had undergone a Procedure 66 instead.

Peloreid took a deep breath as he exited his personal transportation craft in the basement parking garage and entered the elevator to take him to the chambers of the Supreme Council. He had only been there once before, as an assistant to the former Security Regent. It had amazed him and opened his eyes to a world that few even knew existed. The entire population knew that a Supreme Council advised Emperor Barahu, and now Barahu II. But the members themselves were supposed to be unknown to the public, although Peloreid realized that many of their identities had become known over the years. The people were told that the Councilors were everyday people, chosen from a broad spectrum of society. Most thought that the members lived and worked just as the general public did, with no special privileges or powers. At least that was the propaganda that had been forced into the public mindset for the past three decades. Peloreid had believed it himself. And why wouldn't he? The building that housed the Supreme Council was the most bland and benign in the entirety of Capitol City. Cement walls with no windows and only two doorways for entry or exit. At least, that was the building that people saw from the outside. Even most of the workers in the building saw it the same way.

But, what people couldn't see, was the top two floors that could be accessed only from these elevators. Most employees didn't even know they existed. The staff that worked on these two floors was selected from the most loyal of all the citizens in the country. While it was a great honor, they were forbidden from revealing anything about the contents or work done on these floors, or who the members were. The penalty for divulging any information was more terrifying that anyone was willing to risk. Peloreid didn't know if they had ever actually inflicted the penalty, but he was sure that he would not be one of its recipients.

The elevator stopped but the doors didn't open. A voice came over the intercom asking for his name and ID number. After responding, a panel opened on the side of the elevator and an eye scanner extended itself out towards Peloreid. This was normal security for most high level government sites. Peloreid stared into the scanner for a second or two before he heard the familiar tone of acceptance. The scanner retreated into the wall and, a moment later, the elevator doors opened.

It was as if Peloreid had stepped five years back in time. The lobby of the Supreme Council Chamber was one of the most magnificent sites he could remember. Instead of the dull gray concrete of most government offices, the lobby was covered in Italian marble. Light seemed to flood the space with windows surrounding the entire lobby and a vaulted, domed ceiling which allowing it to pour in from above. Peloreid rightly guessed that these were not real windows, but panels which reflected the climate outside, unless of course one of the members wished it to be otherwise in which case the "windows" would reflect any climate requested. But Peloreid understood, this was not about authenticity, it was about opulence and control. Where else would the weather be as you requested, not as nature regulated? Where else could it be sunny at 2 AM or totally dark at 2 PM? The Supreme Council was all about control. That was the fact the Peloreid had learned those five years ago. That was a day that had changed his life. From then on, he had devoted himself fully to gaining access to the world that he had only glimpsed that day. He wanted to become part of the powerful elite, instead of residing forever in the world of the everyday citizen. Now, he was closer to realizing that dream than ever before.

"Welcome, Citizen Security Regent Peloreid," said the receptionist from behind her computer monitor. "The Council is nearly ready for your presentation. I'll let you know when you can go in." While her words were decent, there was no sincerity. She said them out of duty and routine but didn't even try to fake warmth. Her job put her in daily contact with some of the most important people in the country. There was no need to be warm. It wouldn't do anything for her, so why bother.

Peloreid wasn't concerned with the cool receptionist. He couldn't care less about her and just assumed that she felt the same way about him. They were civil servants, not nursery maids. Although, with the nursery maids being civil servants too, he wouldn't have expected warmth from them either. Peloreid paced back and forth across the lobby, repeating his presentation to himself over and over. This was his best chance ever to impress the Council. To fail now would be worse than he was willing to contemplate. Never again would he have such an opportunity.

After what seemed like an eternity, he heard the receptionist call to him.

"You may go in now," she stated plainly, pointing to an opened door in the rear of the lobby. A purple shirted security guard held it open for him as he walked into the Council chamber.

It took a moment for Peloreid's eyes to adjust to the dim light. While the lobby was flooded in bright sunlight, the chamber was nearly totally dark. A bright desk lamp illuminated each Councilor's location behind a high desk. The remainder of the room was dark, with the exception of a single podium which was lit by a spotlight from the ceiling. There was no stool, indicating that the presenter was expected to stand.

"Welcome, Citizen Security Regent," said a gravelly voice from behind the middle light. "We are most interested in the progress of Procedure 23."

"Thank you, Chairman Baucman," answered Peloreid, with a touch of anxiety in his voice. "Please project the presentation." Behind him, the title page of his presentation was projected on a screen.

"As you all are aware, our country has had a crisis due to rising costs in two main areas. The first is the disposal costs of retired bodies. As these statistics show, the reduced life allowance to 65 years old has caused an increase of 23% to the bodies to be disposed. In addition, there were the bodies of the undesirables. This chart shows that 38% were adults critical of government policies, 27% were children below the age of five that had birth defects such as being overweight, without perfect vision or hearing, or with diseases such as asthma, 24% were from the genetic engineering department due to overages of certain intelligence ranges. The remaining 21% are for a variety of other reasons for extermination, but most were due to medical reasons that were cost prohibitive to treat. The combination of these issues drove disposal costs of the bodies up by 87% over the past 5 years alone.

Our choices were limited. We could either build twice as many crematory ovens at a huge expense and devote even more land to dispose of the ashes or we could come up with a different method of disposal which would take years and cost additional funds."

He expected they all knew of this problem very well. This very committee had decided that people over 65 years old, as well as those that were sick or born with the wrong attributes, were too costly for the society to support. They provided too little and took too much. Their decision had replaced the normal life cycle with one that ended at age 65, or even younger. That meant that 20 years worth of people had to be eliminated in only a few months. While that would save money, where did they think all the bodies would go? Obviously, no one had thought about it ahead of time. They started burning them and dumping the ashes but, after strong windstorms caused the entire city to be covered in a layer of ash, the Supreme Council had instructed the Imperial Disposal Agency to do something. While Procedure 23 didn't solve that problem entirely, it would help with the governmental critics, which was the second largest group after the older people.

Peloreid continued, "The second major increase in cost was due to the replacements for those adults that were disposed of due to their criticism of our policies. For some reason still unknown, a high proportion of those critics come from some of the highest intelligence rankings. Replacement of these people in their economic positions takes years and at huge costs. We needed a solution for both of these situations.

Through a variety of tests and trials in our laboratories, we were able to develop a process which would dramatically reduce the costs incurred because of the government critics. Through this process, we insert a small chip in the patient's neck as well as deliver chemicals directly to the brain. With the proper coordination of these, we have developed a process to erase certain memories in the patient's brain. They retain knowledge of language and any mathematical, technical, or scientific skills, but most of their personal memories are eliminated. They can't remember their youth or upbringing which is the main driver in developing their political views. In essence, we were able to keep the good and dispose of the bad. This Procedure 23, as it is known, will eliminate all costs for disposal and reduce replacement costs by 78%."

Peloreid paused at this point, letting the impact of the cost savings sink in. While he hadn't expected applause, a savings of this magnitude was unheard of. He knew that most divisional chiefs presented increased budget requests with trepidation and fear. Those that needed even 5% more were criticized and demoted. One had asked for 15% and was retired early, some said on the spot. To save money, and to this extent, should at least merit a compliment, if not a promotion. And yet, the Councilors were silent.

"If we no longer need to exterminate these political critics, then why are the savings only 78%?" asked a voice that Peloreid couldn't identify. "Shouldn't there be total savings from it?"

"Citizen Councilor," began Peloreid, "while we have full savings from the body disposal services and the training areas, we also have costs for the procedures and the necessary reorientation. I have deducted these expenses from the savings received. That is the 78% to which I referred."

Peloreid was confused. This was not at all the response that he had anticipated.

"You may continue," advised Chairman Baucman.

"Of course, sir. The savings I mentioned are after the costs of the procedures, retesting, and reorientation. Through our trial process, we were able to ensure that we did not erase their memory totally."

"How long did it take you to ensure this?" interrupted a woman's nasally voice.

"The total program development time was over four years. We had to do numerous studies until successful, 23 to be exact. Hence the name Procedure 23," answered Peloreid. He was becoming more concerned by the minute. "This type of research is painstaking in its detail. Hundreds of tests were performed to ensure the memory retention."

"And how many test subjects were used?" asked the same Councilor.

"Approximately 350," he responded. "We tested at least five per test in the beginning, and increased to a final test of about 30 subjects."

"And how many of these test subjects needed to be terminated at the end of the testing?"

"All of them Madame Councilor. Our first tests were complete failures. The subject's brains were completely destroyed. They died painful deaths, I'm afraid, but they provided us with valuable information. With each new set of tests performed each month, we learned more and refined the process. Of the 30 subjects in the final study, only one had substantive brain damage. The others tested in their normal intelligence range."

"And so why were these last few eliminated? It seems like a waste of money to eliminate and dispose of them once the procedure was successful," sneered the nasally woman.

"Yes, so it would seem," agreed Peloreid. "However, at that point, we did not have the reorientation program structured. Until we could validate the intelligence testing results, we weren't sure how to set up the reorientation. Our cost analysis told us that feeding and housing the test subjects until the reorientation program was ready would actually be more expensive than disposing of them. By doing so, we saved our government over $50,000."

"I see. While I don't see the logic, I'm glad you at least did a cost study of it," came the high pitched, monotone response of the woman. "So why do we need to pay to have these people reoriented? Reoriented to what?"

"While the subjects have most, if not all, or their prior technical knowledge and skills, they have no idea of who they are, where they are, or how our society works. To send them back to their economic positions would cause enormous turmoil, for them and their entire departments. So, we have developed a six week Reorientation Program. This instructs them on the rules of our society and their place in it. Allow me to show you."

On the screen that had been showing the figures and charts from Peloreid's presentation, there was shown videos from the Reorientation Pilot Program. Numerous scenes were shown of Citizen Wainwright instructing the students in a variety of subjects. Several included her rousing praises to Barahu and the society that he had constructed. The subjects were shown standing and cheering the smiling Wainwright.

This is what should put me over the top, thought Peloreid. How could they not be impressed by this? Here were political opponents to the government who now, after Procedure 23 and its Reorientation Program, were applauding the very society which they had criticized only a few weeks earlier. Procedure 23 would save millions of dollars over the next few years alone. It would eliminate the need for all of those crematories to dispose of the bodies.

"In conclusion, as I have shown, this program will save an enormous amount of money from disposal and retraining. The results from the Reorientation Program show that we have produced productive, law abiding citizens. I hope you agree that Procedure 23 is worthy of approval by this esteemed body and should be made standard procedure for all sectors of the country. I thank you for your time and attention," finished Peloreid.

Silence.

For what seemed like an hour.

Just Silence.

And then,

"Thank you, Citizen Security Regent Peloreid. Are there any questions from the Councilors before I dismiss him?" asked the Chairman, looking around to the others. "Very well then. Please excuse us, Citizen. You may wait in the lobby."

Peloreid clicked his heels together in a salute and made his way out through the opened door. His mouth was dry and his hands were shaking. What a fool he had been, he thought. He had raised his hopes that perhaps one day he, yes simple Citizen Peloreid, servant to the state, could sit with those people on an equal basis. For years, he had let nothing get in his way. Some of those very subjects in the initial study of Procedure 23 had been his co-workers that he, himself, had turned on in order to move them out of the way. He had watched the agony of their deaths with only one thought, to get to the Supreme Council. And now, in what should have been his finest achievement, he had been met with… silence. Were they blind to what he had done? He didn't think anyone could be. Did they dislike him for some reason? Why should they? His divisions had always placed in the top 10% every year.

He took a seat in the bright, sunny lobby. Less than an hour ago, he had enjoyed the sunshine. Now he detested it. He wished they would darken the lobby as they had the chamber. He leaned his head back and closed his eyes to block out the light. Silence. He had wanted anything but silence.

7

Charles slowly adjusted to life after the Reorientation Center. His daily routine was organized down to the minute. The lights in his domicile unit illuminated automatically to wake him up and darkened when it was time for him to go to bed. His meals were delivered to a room off the building's lobby where breakfast and dinner were warmed before eating. Each tenant ate by themselves in their units as any interaction was discouraged. An intercom would announce departure times for different workplaces and those workers would assemble in the lobby before boarding the transport.

While his work was interesting, he struggled to fully understand the goals he was given. He worked in a chemical laboratory doing research on behavior enhancement. While developing chemicals to aid people in extending their lives or overcoming mental disabilities would be of major benefit to society, his work seemed to be more aimed at reducing mental abilities rather than increasing them. He spent hours in lectures where researchers review the results of previous experiments. All of their efforts revolved around getting subjects to limit their behaviors in certain circumstances. Charles felt that it was essentially chemical mind control. He made the mistake of making an offhand remark to that affect in one meeting. Afterward, he was criticized and questioned by the supervising manager for over an hour. He made a mental note to never question their objectives again, at least in public.

Charles also noticed that, within two days of asking his question, he was required to take additional nutritional supplements, these in the evening. He had to admit, they seemed to help him relax and sleep at night. He had trouble sleeping many nights. Usually, he could get to sleep easily enough, even before the additional pills. But the nightmares that began at the Reorientation Center had followed him to his new residence. Several times every week, he would be awakened after another horrible dream, panting and wet with sweat. Occasionally, they would be good dreams of him surrounded by friends. They would be laughing and eating, all enjoying themselves. But those were rare with the nightmares much more common. When the lights came on after a restless night, Charles would drag himself out of bed and shower. After breakfast, he would take his vitamins and then catch the transport. Within a few minutes, he would begin feeling better and carry on with his day.

It was a lonely, boring existence with one day fading into another. On his one day off, he would sometimes wander the streets, looking at the different buildings. Most were like his residence unit and workplace, dull, faceless concrete buildings with a few windows. Sometimes he would walk to a neighborhood with older buildings. These somehow lifted his spirits with their unusual architecture. He enjoyed looking at the archways and windows, the masonry work and detailed metal railings. They were unique from the dull buildings which seemed to surround him.

Sometimes, he would wander to the park and lay on the green grass, looking up at the sky. There was a definite chill in the air these days, but that didn't bother him. In fact, the crisp, fresh air seemed to clear his head. Things didn't seem so bad at those times. He even contemplated joining in one of the group activities that were allowed. While each person was given one day off every week, not everyone had the same day. That enabled the government to run their operations continuously, which improved efficiency. On the off day, citizens could participate in a number of activities designed to enhance fitness and reduce health costs. There was running, swimming, aerobics, and other exercises that could be done with others. These, along with attending film festivals about major government achievements, the life of Barahu, or other governmentally approved films were the only allowable group activities. Charles hadn't joined in any of these activities yet. He hadn't overcome his anxiety over his missing life, all those years that he couldn't remember. The feeling that the government was responsible for his situation, just as it was responsible for everything else in society, continued to grow and fester within him. That resentment was always present in him now. He couldn't help but feel that the government had done this to him, not for him.

It was the evening after one of his visits to the park that Charles had one of the worst nightmares yet. He had been a small boy, playing with a middle aged man and woman when he fell off a balcony railing. He could see them rushing to try to catch him with outstretched arms. He screamed as he was falling, reaching for their hands but continuing to sink further and further away from them. He awoke with a start. He sat up on his bed, his heart racing, and the images of their distraught faces fresh in his mind.

Those faces, they were much clearer this time than the others. He could see the woman's brown eyes as she screamed and ran towards him. The man's dark brown hair, with patches of gray, was vivid in his memory. These were the people in his other dreams, both the good ones and the bad. They were familiar but unknown to him. He could only imagine that they were people he had known before, but from where. He could barely conceive of the idea that they were his parents since the reorientation only instructed about the government raised children. He knew that he was from the outdated child rearing model. But the notion of what a parent actually was remained a mystery to him. He was lost and dumbfounded. He tried to go back to sleep but couldn't. Those faces were haunting him.

When sleep finally came, it was nearly daylight, or at least the artificial daylight that arrived at the same time every morning. Today, it didn't awaken him. He slept on until the loudspeaker announced, "Transport to Sector A departing in 10 minutes. All riders should assemble in the lobby now."

Charles awoke with a start at the announcement. Ten minutes. He couldn't be late or else he'd get a visit from a Purple Shirt. He shaved as quickly as possible, cutting himself twice in the process. After brushing his teeth and running a wet comb through his hair, he pulled on his uniform and raced for the door. He saw his vitamin pill lying on the counter with his ID badge and grabbed them both on his way out the door. He jumped on the transport just before the doors closed. People looked at him oddly for a moment, and then returned to staring out the window or sitting with their eyes closed.

Charles made his way to his usual seat, fifth on the left. He tacked on his ID badge and looked at the pill in his hand. It was rather large. He had never tried taking it without water. He thought it would probably make him gag. While he knew it would help to calm him down, he also didn't want to choke on it. This day was starting out rough enough as it was. He closed his eyes and leaned back. His head was pounding and he couldn't get the picture of those two people out of his mind. His commute was about 10 minutes long and he figured he could just sit quietly until his stop.

"Don't take the pill."

Charles heard a voice whisper that behind him. He started to turn around to see who had spoken to him since speaking was expressly prohibited on transports.

"Don't turn around or someone will notice. Just sit there quietly," the voice continued. Charles did as he was instructed.

"I'll bet you're having nightmares about people you don't know. They can stop if you quit taking the pills. It may take a few days, but you'll start remembering your life again."

Charles didn't know what to think. How could that person know he was having nightmares? Didn't everyone take the pills? So, why should he stop? They were the only things that made him feel better. His mind was buzzing as the words repeated in his head. Remember your life, remember your life. That's what he wanted more than anything else.

"If you stop taking the pills, your memory will return. The pills are how they are controlling you, just like the experiments you are conducting. If you understand me, nod your head slightly."

Charles thought, what if this is a Purple Shirt sitting behind me? What if they are just waiting to haul me off? But why? Other than that one comment at work, he'd caused no problems. If they wanted to haul him off, they could do it whenever they wanted. They didn't need a reason. That much he knew from the reorientation. The government had complete control. He had been in a real prison cell during reorientation. Now, he felt like he was in a prison with no bars. His entire world was one big cell, keeping him in line, always being observed. But, wasn't he helping them through the chemical research studies he was conducting? Of course, he was. The realization struck him suddenly, as the unknown man's words sank into his brain. That's what the pills were. That's why they gave him more pills when he questioned them. It was to control him. He felt like an idiot. Why hadn't he seen it sooner? Were the pills that effective? Maybe they were. Charles wondered, what should he do? Just sit there? Nod?

Very slowly, Charles nodded his head.

"Good. We understand each other. If you stop taking the pills, your memory will start returning within the next couple of weeks. Perhaps not all, but you'll begin to remember parts of your life before the accident. I'll contact you again in two weeks. But, you must not do anything unusual. Don't say anything to anyone. Trust no one."

With that, the transport pulled up to Charles' laboratory. He stood up and moved to the aisle to wait his turn to exit. As he did so, he glanced at the seat behind him. It was empty. He looked at the others in line. It must be one of them, wasn't it? How could he be sure? He never looked at the person behind him before. For that matter, he never paid any attention to anyone else on the transport. He wondered how he could go back and forth with the same people on the same transport day after day for weeks and never noticed anyone else. For that matter, other than the people he worked with closely, he couldn't describe anyone else. Other than Citizen Wainwright of course, but that was because he had focused on her for six weeks straight. Otherwise, no one.

Charles was uneasy. What had he just agreed to do? It was definitely inviting trouble from the Purple Shirts. But, he had to know more that he did. He had to find out who those people in his dreams were. He had to make the nightmares stop. More than anything else in the world, he wanted to know who he really was. His logical, scientific brain had gone through the past few weeks over and over again. It didn't make sense. All those people in accidents. All that reorientation. Being told that his former life didn't matter because it wouldn't help the government. But, what about him! His anger and agitation continued to simmer. Maybe this was the way to take back some semblance of control.

As soon as he had been checked through security, he made his way to the restroom. He quickly flushed his pill. He didn't want any evidence on him. That day, his normal routine went by slowly. The lack of sleep was catching up with him and his brain seemed slow and fuzzy. He sat through the mandatory meetings, saying nothing, and when his workday was done, he quickly made his way out to the transport.

He waited anxiously for the transport and his heart was racing as he walked up its steps. He moved towards his normal seat and looked at the seat behind his. It was empty. He looked around at the rest of people on the transport. They looked perfectly normal. No one paid any attention to him as he sat down. He began to question his memory of the morning's events. Did they really happen? Was the voice inside his head? Was it a continuation of the nightmare he had the night before? Was it a side effect of not taking his pill that morning? His mind spun through the different possibilities.

He had decided nothing by the time the transport dropped him at the domicile unit building. Charles picked up his meal in the lobby and walked slowly up to his unit. His lights came on when he opened the door. He walked to the table and sat down, opening his dinner. Meatloaf. Again. It seemed like they had meatloaf about three times a week. He wasn't even sure there was any real meat in the loaf. It just looked like a big blob in the container. Dog food he thought. That's what it reminded him of. Dog food!

Charles caught himself. He had just remembered feeding a small beagle. He had been young, just like in his dreams. The sudden memory of the dog, running, jumping, licking his face, began to overwhelm him and he began to cry. The tears ran down his face, falling on the table. He had never felt like this, at least that he could remember. His heart was aching as he thought of the dog. How much else had he forgotten because of his accident? Since he had awoken from the surgery he had been trying to understand these feelings. Now, it seemed like things were coming back to him. Maybe the voice was right. Maybe the pills had been repressing those memories. But why? Why would the government want him to forget his past life? What had he done?

He was tired. His mind was filled with questions but the fatigue was overcoming his ability to think. The waves of tears wracked his body, making him shake. That dog. That silly faced, black, white, and brown dog. It was the only part of his prior life that he could remember, although honestly he didn't know if the memory were real or more like a subconscious dream. Before going to bed, he brushed his teeth and drank a big glass of water. He looked at the bottle of pills sitting on his bathroom counter. He knew he was supposed to take one. They had helped him sleep but he didn't think that would be a problem tonight. He took out a pill and looked at it. He couldn't identify what it was. Then he took it into the kitchen and cut it open. A reddish liquid oozed out. He smelled it and dabbed his pinky in the liquid, touching it to his tongue. It had a bitter taste but otherwise he didn't recognize it. He washed the remainder of the pill down the drain. Not today. It was painful remembering the little dog, but it was also comforting to remember part of his life. He had decided. No more pills. He would remember if he could. He knew it was against the rules of the government, but he didn't care. Come what may, he was going to run his own life.

For the next ten days, Charles didn't take his pills. Everyday, he got on the transport waiting to be contacted again but never heard the voice. He was beginning to think that he had imagined it all, that it was a continuation of a dream. But, he had to admit that the voice had been right. His memory was slowly returning.

While he still had some nightmares, they had been fewer. He was beginning to remember his life and, in fact, memories of his earlier years were returning faster than his later years. Charles was also remembering more at work, like the effects of the chemicals his team was creating. He now understood that his job was to create mind control drugs that the government could use to make the populace more subservient. He realized that the "vitamins" he had been taking were more for mind control than health and he began to question many of the things he had learned in the Reorientation Center.

It was the Friday of the second week he had been "pill free" when the next contact came. This time, it was on the transport back from his laboratory. He was sitting, staring out the window when he heard the voice again.

"Don't turn around, Citizen Johnson. Have you stopped taking the pills?"

Charles slowly nodded his head.

"Is your memory returning?"

Again, Charles nodded.

"And do you want to know the truth?"

Charles sat motionless for a moment. Nodding his head would mean taking a step that he couldn't back away from. He always had some questions regarding the propaganda that he heard from Citizen Wainwright. Now, there was a chance for the truth. Charles' heart was pounding. He had heard the rumors about the Purple Shirts, how they would come for you and you'd never return. He was sure that, by nodding his head, he was running the risk that the Purple Shirts would come for him someday. Or, had they already? Was his accident really the result of a visit from the

Purple Shirts? Charles could feel the anger welling inside of him. They had taken his whole life from him., he thought. But, he wanted to know for sure. Charles slowly nodded again.

"Very well, Charles Johnson. Tomorrow morning, go to the park where you like to lay on the grass. By the path, there is a bench. Be sitting on the bench at eleven o'clock. Wait for us. If it is safe, you will be met. If no one is there by noon, you must leave. Say nothing to anyone."

Charles slowly nodded.

When his stop came, he didn't look back. He very quickly got off the transport and walked into his building. He began walking quickly up the stairs.

"Citizen Johnson!" a voice yelled. Charles froze. It had been a trap. For some reason the government had set up a test for him and he had failed. They were here to arrest him, Charles thought. They were probably doing this to all the reorientation patients, to see if they were really loyal to Barahu. He had failed, and now he would pay the consequences. Charles exhaled loudly and turned around, his shoulders dropping.

"Citizen Johnson, your dinner. It's Friday and yours is the last meal I have. Will you take it so I can leave?" asked the attendant. Charles stiffened a little, his heart still pounding and he had to remind himself to breath again.

"Yes, of course. Citizen," he added quickly, for how much affect he wasn't sure. The attendant looked at him oddly and then handed him his meal box. "Thank you for waiting for me."

"I can't leave until I hand them all out or until 8 PM," muttered the attendant, as if any idiot should know that. He turned, shut of the light in his room, and walked quickly out of the building.

Charles slumped against the railing on the stairway. He made his way up to his unit with his hands shaking and knees a little wobbly. He threw his meal on the table and fell into his living room chair. How could he go through with this? A simple meal attendant had almost given him a nervous breakdown. What would happen if it had been a Purple Shirt? He probably would have had a heart attack. Maybe he couldn't do this. Perhaps he would be better off taking the pills and going with the flow. Why make trouble for himself? Everyone else seemed to be doing OK. Why not him?

And, where did the voice come from, or rather not where but from whom? How did they know about him, his name, the transport he took, where he worked? They even knew the park he liked to go to on the weekends. It was obvious that they had been following him, observing him for some time now. Why? What did they know about him? The questions swirled through his suddenly tired mind.

Then, it hit him. He just couldn't do this. Yes, he wanted to know about his life, but he didn't want any trouble. It seemed like the whole world was watching him. He knew there were video cameras at work and on many outside buildings. He wouldn't be at all surprised if they were in his domicile unit as well. Someone in a purple shirt was probably watching him right now. He couldn't live with the anxiety. He didn't want to spend the rest of his life looking over his shoulder, jumping at every sound. He couldn't deal with that. He had decided. He wouldn't show up tomorrow. That was it. He was tired and went to bed

That night, the faces reappeared in his dreams. He could see them clearly, taking him by the hand and walking through the grass. The man was chasing him playfully while the woman opened a picnic basket on a red, checkered blanket. They were calling to him. One part of his mind was telling him that this wasn't right but another part didn't care. He was having fun and being loved. That's what this feeling must be, love.

He sat up in bed, wiping the sleep from his eyes. Love. Nowhere in Wainwright's description of Barahu's world was love mentioned. She had talked about everything Barahu had done for the people, how he had destroyed the wicked rich people. She had talked about how the government had taken over entire industries and run them so they could better manage the economy. She told how the government had taken over raising children so they would be safe and instructed properly. That was it. Children. In Barahu's society, his government produced the children in laboratories. The government trained them to take their place in his society. But what about before then? Wainwright had only said that they lived with people who usually abused them. Could it be that the people in his dreams were his parents? Were these the people who bore him and raised him? If the dreams were an accurate reflection of reality, then they did not seem terrifying. In fact, they seemed exactly the opposite. They seemed loving. Love was the emotion missing from Barahu's world. There was security, no doubt. There was food and clothing, and shelter. He had an occupation that kept him, well, occupied. You wanted for nothing. Except love. Very few in this society seemed to speak to each other. It was frowned upon, and in some cases even prohibited. There was no love, or even friendship. It was a soulless society.

Charles' consternation about what to do returned.

"And do you want to know the truth?"

The words repeated over and over in his head.

"And do you want to know the truth?"

He did.

8

Charles didn't sleep much for the remainder of that night. Without the "vitamins", he found it increasingly difficult to sleep through the night. Especially this night. In the morning, he would go to the park and sit on a bench, waiting for some unknown person to approach him. Some unknown person with "the truth". Charles still didn't know why he would even risk something like this. His life, if unfulfilling was at least safe. He was fed, clothed, and housed by the government. He worked for no pay but then there wasn't anything to spend money on anyway. The government ran all industries so they provided whatever was needed. It was rigorously controlled, but safe and secure. Why would he risk that?

Inside, he knew why and that was what kept him awake that night. He knew there was more to his life. He had caught glimpses of memories over the past two weeks, some in his dreams and some when he was awake. A face, a smell, the memory of a little dog. They seemed to come at him randomly, like pieces to a jigsaw puzzle without benefit of knowing the full picture.

And so, he dressed early in the morning and went downstairs to receive his breakfast from the attendant in the lobby. He couldn't eat but did drink a cup of black water which they tried to pass off as coffee. The caffeine revived him somewhat, but the black bags underneath his eyes betrayed the fact that he hadn't slept.

At ten o'clock he left his domicile unit and made his way in a roundabout path to the park that he liked to frequent. He walked around the outskirts of the wide open lawn, staying in the shadows of the now leafless trees. It was a chilly morning, although not bad for early November. Charles zipped his jacket and was appreciative that it wasn't windy.

It was 10:55 when he moved to the bench. He sat, alone, leaning back and scanning the park. He tried to look relaxed, but he half expected some purple shirted officers to approach him at any time. But no one did. Charles sat and looked. For ten minutes. Fifteen minutes. Twenty minutes. He began to think that it was all a mistake, that no one would be coming to meet him.

He saw an old man walking down the path towards him but paid little attention. The man seemed ancient, especially in this new era when everything was new and young. Old people were rarely seen. They had all been "retired" according to Citizen Wainwright. This old man looked about 80. He couldn't be part of a conspiracy, could he? And then it dawned on Charles. He was about to be part of a conspiracy of some sort, wasn't he? What else could it be? The secrecy, the hidden knowledge. It had to be a conspiracy for something.

The old man continued to approach slowly and then sat down on the bench with a thud, more falling onto it than lowering himself down.

"Do you mind if I share your bench, young man?"

Charles didn't know what to say. He didn't want this person sitting there if he was supposed to get a visitor. And what conspiracy group would have an old man as a contact?

"Well, I am waiting for someone but I'm not even sure they will show up," Charles responded.

"Oh, I'm sure they will. Snow will start coming soon so I'm sure no one will miss meeting you on a nice day like this."

"Maybe," Charles mumbled.

"There's something about this time of year that I've always loved. The crispness in the air, the smell of the fallen leaves. When I was a lad, this would have been football season, but alas, the government doesn't allow thousands of people to gather at will any longer. I do miss football. Wonderful game, plenty of action. Teams of eleven men all working in unison. One person out of place and the whole team could fail. Wonderful game."

The man sat silently for a couple of moments. Charles wished that he would leave. He continued searching the park with his eyes, hoping if his contact was watching him that they would realize that he didn't want the old man to be there.

"You look old enough to remember sports, football, baseball. Did you play as a youngster?"

"I'm afraid I don't remember much of my childhood. I had an accident and lost most of my memory."

"Oh, you must know that it was no accident," the older man replied. "You had a Procedure 23."

"I had a what? What did you call it?"

"A Procedure 23. I can tell by your jacket. The olive green color is only given to those that have had a Procedure 23. It helps the purple shirts identify you."

A chill went down Charles' spine. How did he know what had happened to him. A Procedure 23. He had heard that before at the hospital but he thought it was just a medical term.

"I'm afraid I don't know what a Procedure 23 is," stated Charles softly.

"The government erased your memory, Mr. Johnson."

Charles stared at the ground. This was it. This was his contact. The old man knew the secrets that Charles did not.

"Why?"

"You were a danger to them. Yes, you were a very dangerous man indeed. You wanted to think for yourself. That," paused the grey haired, green eyed man, looking at Charles, "is not allowed by Barahu the Great," he finished with disgust.

"Then why didn't they just kill me?" snorted Charles.

"Because they need you. You're a scientist, the highest level of professional achievement and training. Basically, it costs too much to replace you," he replied, pausing a moment. "This is a wonderful spot, but not secure. Purple Shirts will split us up and record our names if they see us talking. That would not be good for either of us. You had a Procedure 23 and I'm 73 years old. So, we should be going. I'm going to go two blocks north and then one block east. You go one block east and then two blocks north. There's an overpass where the trains used to run. A transport goes by there now. Meet me there in ten minutes. Oh, one thing first. We need to remove the chip in your neck?"

"The what?" asked Charles, stunned.

"The locator chip that they placed in your neck. It's a tracking device. Turn around please."

Charles wasn't sure why but he turned his back to the other man. He felt a sharp pain in the back of his neck and pressure from the old man's hands.

'There we are. Hold still while I put this bandage on it. Here, chew this gum."

From behind him, his contact handed him a stick of chewing gum. Charles stuck it in his mouth and began chewing, although why he wasn't sure. He could feel the bandage being applied to the cut on the back of his neck.

"Alrighty then. We're set."

Charles turned around and was shown a small, bloody computer chip on the tip of the man's index finger. Charles had never known that was in his body.

"Gum," the man said.

"What?"

"Give me your gum," he instructed.

Charles spit his gum into the outstretched hand, wondering why he had just been given it. The old man took the gum and placed the chip into it. He then reached behind the bench and stuck the wet gob on the back.

"There," he said with a smile, "as far as the government knows, you spent the afternoon in the park, as you're apt to do on such a nice day. Now, off we go." Without another word, the older man rose and walked north at a brisk pace.

Charles waited for a few moments, somewhat from the shock of the whole experience. A locator chip in his neck? A contact that should have been "retired"? He wasn't sure what would happen next. Adrenaline flowed through his body. While this life wasn't safe and secure, it was definitely more exciting. Charles got up and set off east.

As he made his way through the park to the street, he saw the old man's back, heading north. He crossed and made his way east. His heart was pounding, as was his head and neck. Was this a trap? Could be, but if that was the case, why remove the chip? If the old man was part of a government plan, why would he remove tracking devices that Charles hadn't even known about? Charles frowned, his head down and staring at the sidewalk directly in front of his feet. Tracking devices implanted in his neck? Why? He didn't feel like a threat to anyone, particularly the government. He did have some misgivings and doubts about all the reorientation he had received, but it wasn't like he was out to overthrow Barahu because of them. He had to admit, he was having more doubts since he stopped taking his vitamins. The dreams were more frequent and vivid than they had been. He could see the faces of a young man and woman, playing with him, pushing him on a swing. But he didn't know for certain who they were. Was he on his way to find out?

After a block, Charles turned to the left and headed north. The street was mostly empty. The buildings looked gray and deserted. Windows were broken. Weeds grew between the cracks in the sidewalk. Garbage lay strewn across the ground and the wind scattered papers and dirt as it blew up between the buildings. It was a dreary, empty part of the city.

Charles thought about the brief conversation that he had just had with the old man. The government had erased his memories? Was that even possible? Of course, that would explain a lot. Like why they didn't want to tell him about his past. He could feel his jaws tighten. His anger grew. They had taken his life. They had swept away every part of what made him an individual, at least the ones that they found useless. What gave them the right to decide what memories he should have or not? What had he done that was so dangerous that he deserved to have that kind of punishment? And now, the government of the Supreme Being and Most Holy Leader used him to help enslave the rest of the population. The anger was turning to hatred within Charles' heart.

Charles could see the old man appear in front of him, turning to the left and proceeding towards a train overpass. It didn't seem like it had seen a train in a very long time. The street sloped down at a steep angle to go under the tracks and Charles could see it appear again, rising on the other side of the tracks. The man walked down into the darkness of the overpass. Charles slowed his walk slightly, waiting to see the man emerge from the other side, but he hadn't. Charles' eyes darted around him. Was there a Purple Shirt waiting in the shadows? Was the man already in their grip? Or was the man one of them, baiting Charles to enter the trap? Charles stopped. He peered into the darkness, but could see nothing. He waited, moving towards the side of the nearest building, looking up and down the street for signs of, of what? He didn't know. Of purple shirted officers? There was nothing around him. He stood there, looking around and wondering what to do next.

Then, the man emerged, not on the other side of the overpass but on the side he had entered. He motioned quickly for Charles to follow him. Charles stared at him. The man had a look of urgency on his face. He quickly moved his hand three times, appealing for Charles to follow him. Charles hesitated for another moment or two, and then moved forward towards the man, towards the darkness.

As Charles neared, the old man took a couple of steps into the shadows. When Charles slowed, hoping his eyes would adjust to the near total blackness, his arm was grabbed suddenly. The old man had a surprisingly strong grip and pulled him roughly further under the overpass.

"Good Lord," he muttered quietly to Charles, "if you move any slower it will be spring before we get there."

Charles held his free hand out, feeling for any wall or obstruction that could be in front of him. The two men stumbled together for several steps before the old man stopped and Charles bumped into him. His eyes adjusting, Charles could make out the outline of a doorway in the middle of the cement wall supporting the tracks above. He heard the old man fumbling with some metal keys. He dropped Charles' arms as he felt in the darkness for the doorknob and lock. A moment later, Charles heard a metallic click as the lock opened. The old man turned the knob and swung a doorway open. Bright light flooded out, momentarily blinding Charles. The old man pushed him roughly in the back, forcing him through the doorway. Charles raised his hands, shielding his eyes from the intensity of the light as he heard the door swing shut behind them.

He was there. He was in. He knew there was no going back now.

9

"Well, it's about time," said an unknown voice situated to the left of the intense light.

"Turn that damn thing down," yelled the old man. "You know I hate having that in my eyes.

The light dimmed. Charles looked around. The man was removing his jacket and hanging it on a hook near the door. Charles could see a cluttered little room. It smelled of oil and grease and contained a small bed, an old easy chair, a kitchenette with hotplate, sink and refrigerator, and a folding table with a few chairs around it. A tall, thin, balding man, not nearly as old as Charles' guide, beamed at him from behind the table. He rose and walked quickly towards Charles, smiling at him. He grasped Charles and hugged him firmly.

"I'm so glad you're here, my boy," he whispered in Charles' ear, his voice thick with emotion. "I've missed you so."

Charles pulled back and looked at the man, who held Charles' head in his hands, staring into his eyes. He was beaming, and Charles could see tears forming in his eyes.

"I'm sorry," said Charles, pulling away, "but I don't who you are. Do we, do we know each other?"

The man turned away slightly, moving back towards the table from whence he'd come. He sniffled and wiped his eyes before returning his gaze on Charles.

"We do. At least, I know you very well. I've known you for years. Of course, after what you've been through, I know you don't remember me. Hopefully you will, in time."

The man looked down at his hands and saw the blood stains.

"God, Albert. Did you have to slice his head off?" he said with a raised voice.

"Now, don't you start on me! You know damn well that I had to cut his neck to get the chip out. Better to do it quickly, even if it's a little deep. I didn't see you out there risking your ass to bring him in."

"We've been through that. I made contact on the tram. It might have caused notice if I had been seen with him on the bench too. Besides, if he had remembered me, it might have given us away."

"As if a 70 year old man walking around on the streets wouldn't give us away!" replied Albert, who had been Charles' guide to this place.

"You? It was you on the transport?" asked Charles, looking at the tall stranger.

"Yes, my boy. It was me. We have much to discuss today. Hopefully, it will clear up many things which are disturbing you. Like your nightmares. And your Procedure 23."

"But I don't understa. ." began Charles.

"Oh for Christ sakes," hollered Albert. "Why don't you start with introductions? You've known him for 30 years but as far as he knows, he's just met you."

"Yes, you're right, Albert," he replied. "Charles, I am Andrew Sinclair. I've known you since you were born. I was your father's best friend and I'm happy to say that they gave me the honor of being your godfather as well. I know nearly everything that has ever happened to you, at least the important things. I'm here to help you understand, and remember."

"Ahem", sounded Albert, clearing his throat.

"Yes, yes. And this is Albert Brown. He's part of the Liberty Tree. And he's one of the most brilliant men in the country.

Unfortunately, he's well aware of his intelligence which makes him damn near unbearable sometimes."

While the words had a harsh tone to them, the look on Andrew's face bespoke a definite liking and friendship towards the older man. Charles turned his head to look at Albert.

Albert sprang to attention, clicking his heels slightly and, giving a short bow, said, "Your servant, sir."

"OK, Albert. Try to remember that we're not in the 1700's," chuckled Andrew.

Charles looked at the two men. He didn't really know what to think. He was wondering if he were just with two crazy old friends, one of whom had been a friend of. . his parents? Was it possible that this balding man might be the key to his dreams, to finding out who he really was?

"You, you know about my life, my parents?" Charles asked. While he desperately wanted to know about all of that, he still had some doubts about who these men were and what kind of conspiracy he was being pulled into.

"Come, sit down Charles and we can discuss all of that," offered Andrew, pulling a chair out by the table. "Albert, I think some tea would be in order, don't you?"

"Yes, yes. A cup of tea sounds lovely. Feel free to get one for your self as well," he replied, moving towards the easy chair. He looked at Andrew and saw the frown come across his face. He smiled and continued, "Oh, of course. It's in order if I'm making it." He moved toward the hotplate, picked up a tea kettle and began pouring water in it. "Thinks I'm his Alice, doesn't he," he muttered, under his breath but loud enough for all to hear. "I'm not his wife, he should know that by now," he finished, setting the kettle on the hotplate and returning to sit in the easy chair.

Andrew looked down at Charles for a moment before sitting across from him at the table. He took a deep breath and sighed.

"I'm afraid I don't quite know how to begin. There are so many things I have to tell you. I know this must be a little overwhelming for you and I want you to be as comfortable as possible with me, us," he quickly added with a glance to Albert, "but you also have to understand the danger that we're placing you in."

Charles stared at Andrew. The danger they're placing him in? So, there was a conspiracy of some sort. These men were doing something against the will of the government and now he was involved. But, he hadn't really done anything wrong. He just wanted to know about himself, about his past. How could that be a crime? Charles felt like he could still step back from the edge. He could still walk away. But, he wanted, needed really, to know about himself. He needed to know what his life had been, and why the government had decided to remove his memory.

Andrew returned Charles' gaze. His concern for the younger man was evident. He wanted to help him, but would the information that he held really help? Or, would Charles reject him. Would he just want to live his life without knowing about his past, but with the safety of his current situation? While there was little choice and even less freedom in Barahu's society, there was security. You didn't need to worry about where to work. Or where to sleep. Or what to eat. All decisions were made for you, and for the good of the state. It was simple. Go where they told you, eat what they fed you, and do what you're told. Don't think. Just follow. For Andrew, that wasn't enough. He wanted to be in control of his own life, his own decisions, his own thoughts. Wasn't that what separated man from the beasts, the ability to reason and make their own decisions? While Barahu's world promised security, it took your humanness. It removed your ability to make mistakes but the price of that was your individuality. In Andrew's mind, survival was not enough. He desired the ability to make his own decisions, good or bad, right or wrong.

But would Charles? It's hard to understand what it's like to really be free if you've never known freedom, or in this case if you can't remember it. But Andrew believed it was in every person. It was a part of being human, just like your ability to think, or see. The yearning to breathe free was the essential humanness. Not blindly following an emperor, king, president, or anyone else. He could remember reading about slaves risking their lives for a chance at freedom. He could remember life before Barahu. That seemed like several lifetimes ago. Most people didn't remember. By exterminating, or "retiring" in Barahu-speak, anyone over 65 years old, the government was systematically erasing the memory of real freedom. By controlling education and travel, they ensured that people wouldn't learn about it. The people of Charles' age were the last hope to revive the freedoms that the country had enjoyed before Barahu. He had to believe that Charles would agree. He had always had an independent spirit, from the time he was a small child. His parents had raised him to make his own decisions, to think freely. It was in his blood. And Andrew just had to remind him of it.

"Maybe you should tell me about this memory erasing that Albert mentioned. And why I'm in danger," Charles replied after several moments.

Andrew smiled at him. "Yes, of course," he said. "The government has a new medical procedure they named Procedure 23. It's a very complicated process of using micro-chips inserted in the brain along with chemical agents to erase certain memories. The purpose is to erase memories that may be anti-government but to retain those that are useful. It's imprecise at best. The first trials left most patients brain dead. Or fully dead. The chemicals they used destroyed too much of the brain. They had to keep ratcheting it back until they could maintain at least most of the intelligence. They put probes into the brain and then try to stimulate certain thoughts, like of your childhood, parents, friends, or the government. As the probes indicate those types of thoughts, the chip signals the computer to shoot the chemicals into the particular part of the brain where the thoughts occurred. Again, it's highly imprecise but successful enough that the government began rolling out the program to dozens of patients."

"You said they removed thoughts about childhood, parents, and…the government? Why would they do that?" interrupted Charles.

"They want to remove the memories that might lead you to undesirable actions. Memories of a childhood with loving parents might make you wonder why people are now sterilized and all children are raised by the government. They want people to forget that anyone used to care for them except Barahu and his minions."

"But why forget thoughts about the government itself?"

"The process is not yet good enough to distinguish good thoughts from bad. They would rather you didn't remember anything that something bad. So, they try to erase anything to do with it and then teach you what they want you to know. I'm sure your reorientation training was full of wonderful words about Barahu and the state which he created."

"Yes, it was mostly about Barahu and how much he helped the people. And, what was expected out of us to aid the government," agreed Charles. "It did seem like he fixed a lot of problems. People are fed, housed, protected now. It didn't seem like they were before."

"Barahu has a powerful propaganda machine. The reality of life was a lot different. Most people opposed the moves. They didn't want the government controlling every part of their lives. They wanted freedom and choice. They wanted to make their own decisions. Barahu tried to convince them that he knew better. He promised to give them everything they wanted if he was given control."

"So how did he achieve power if the people opposed him?" asked Charles, a little skeptical of Andrew's assertions.

Andrew paused and smile at Charles. "You always did jump to the heart of the matter," he stated. "Just like your father. And you always loved to argue. He used to say that you were a born litigator. You'd argue about what color the sky was." Andrew paused again and looked down, lost in recollections about his dear friend.

"Before we go there, let's get back to your first questions. Why the government stole your memory and why you may be in danger. What's the first thing you do remember?"

"Well, the first thing I clearly remember is waking up in a hospital. They said I'd been in an accident and my memory was lost. I don't have any clear memories before that. But I know how to do things. I understand the chemicals that I work with, their uses, how to mix them. I just don't know how I know those things."

"As I said, only certain memories were destroyed. In reality, you can probably remember a lot of things from before you woke up in that hospital. The vitamins that they gave you had nothing to do with your health. They were drugs used to reinforce the Procedure 23. They help to deaden your thoughts. They don't so much control them as to reduce your brain activity. They keep people in a constant stupor. You can think, but it's like you're in slow motion. Barahu has drugged the population in order to control it. However, once you stop taking the drugs, your memories may return."

"I stopped taking them after you spoke to me on the transport. But I still can't remember much of anything before the hospital."

"That's because they don't just drug your vitamins. Those are additional for people that are special threats. Everyone that had a Procedure 23 is given additional medications. But most people, I'd say, don't get them."

"Then how do they control everyone like you say?" asked Charles, the skepticism strong in his voice.

"Easy. Where do you get your food?" responded Andrew, with a slight smile on his face.

"My food? From the cafeteria at work or in the lobby of my domicile unit."

"And who prepares the food?" questioned Albert, interjecting from behind Charles as he brought over two steaming cups of tea.

"I don't know. I never thought about it," he replied honestly.

"The government has very tight controls over all food production and processing," stated Albert. "They add the drugs to the food. Everyone has to eat. When they do, they ingest the drugs and, there you go, the population is so brain dead that they can't even think about opposing Barahu," he finished with obvious disgust in his voice.

"You're telling me that the government is knowingly drugging the food supply?" Charles exclaimed incredulously.

"They are," replied Andrew, very matter of factly.

"So, why aren't you two under their mind control?"

"Simple. We don't eat their food, at least anything processed. The raw vegetables are usually fine since they normally add the drugs only to the food that is cooked."

"Now wait a second, you said that the government controls all food production and processing. So how can you NOT eat their food?" he questioned.

"The answer to that is also the answer to the other part of your question. The danger. We've included you in part of that already by contacting you and bringing you here. These actions would mean the death penalty for both Albert and me. Before we continue, you need to decide how much more you want to know. Because to continue would mean that you too would face the death penalty, a Procedure 66 they call it."

Andrew paused after saying these words, staring down his straight nose at Charles. His eyes were serious, although not threatening. Charles looked back at him and then at Albert who was also staring at him intently.

"You're saying if I turned you in, they'd kill you?" he asked.

"Most certainly. After trying to extract everything we know about the resistance of course. We would be drugged and probably tortured. And then we'd be injected with a chemical that would kill us in a most painful way," Andrew replied, still staring at Charles, measuring his response.

"So why are you taking this risk on me? How do you know that I won't run out this door and turn you in?"

"While you don't know or remember me, I know you. I loved your parents, both of them. They were my best friends. We did nearly everything together. Your mother and my wife were inseparable. Your mother introduced me to my Alice. She wasn't sure about going out with your father at first. She would only go if she could bring a friend and, of course, he brought me. She was the love of my life. She made my life worthwhile." Andrew paused here. His voice had become choked. Tears welled in his eyes.

"They killed them, your parents that is," he said softly as the tears ran down his face. "They just let my Alice waste away because they didn't want to pay for the medical treatment she needed. Said her life expectancy wasn't long enough to justify the expense. So, they just let her die."

Charles was moved by Andrew's show of emotion. He watched as the man turned and rummaged through a small box that sat on one of the other chairs. Andrew pulled out a photograph that showed four young adults, all smiling broadly. Charles recognized Andrew, about 25 years old with a full head of light brown hair. A pretty woman was kissing him on his cheek as the other couple in the picture laughed. Charles looked at the faces. It was them, the couple that he had seen in his dream. They were a little younger in the photo, but it was definitely them. The dark hair. The smiles. It was them. He looked up at Andrew.

Andrew seemed to be reading his mind. "You recognize them?" he asked hopefully.

Charles nodded slightly, "I've had dreams about them. But I didn't know who they were."

"They were two of the most wonderful people the good Lord ever put on this earth," Andrew replied. "They're your parents. Harry and Eva Johnson."

He stopped and stood up suddenly. "So, Charles Johnson, do we live or die? Do you want to learn about yourself, your parents, your life? Do you want to take back control over it, even though you could lose it? Or, do you want to walk out this door and go back to the safe, drugged up existence that most people have? You need to decide before we go any further. Too many lives are at stake for to go forward without your commitment."

10

"Citizen Security Regent Peloreid to see Chairman Baucman," stated Peloreid clearly to the receptionist at the Supreme Council. The woman looked at her computer screen to verify the appointment and the security checks that had been done as he had entered the premises.

Without looking at Peloreid, she responded, "Chairman Baucman would like you to join him in his private office. Do you know where that is?"

Peloreid cleared his throat quietly and murmured, "No."

"Very well." She motioned to a security guard with a purple shirt and gold braiding around his shoulders. "Escort Citizen Security Regent Peloreid to the Chairman's private office," she ordered.

The guard nodded curtly and motioned for Peloreid to follow him. Peloreid gave a slight nod to the receptionist as well but her head was still down and she failed to notice. The two men walked through a paneled doorway and into a marbled hallway with several wooden doors on each side. Peloreid looked at the brass nameplates on each door. They glittered in the faux sunlight with the name of the Council Member that occupied each office. Tonklin. Baxter. Rahmer. His head spun back and forth, trying to catch every name on every door. Of course he knew the names of the seven members of the Supreme Council but he had never been this close to their individual thrones before. The seven Supreme Councilors! To even be amongst their offices gave him a mild thrill. After what he considered a failed presentation, he felt further away from power than ever before. He had even gone to witness some 66 procedures to cheer himself up. Nothing like seeing some deviants exterminated at his command to return a sense of power to oneself. But even that feeling had been temporary. But now, here he was. After the Supreme Being and Most Holy Leader, Emperor Barahu II, these people were the most powerful in the country. No one could counter their orders. In a world that gave the appearance of complete equality, even with the outward appearance of this building, these people were above all others. Peloreid's heart beat faster as they neared the end of the hallway. The largest brass plaque simply read "Chairman Baucman". The guard opened the door, held it for Peloreid, and closed it behind him.

Peloreid found himself in an office that could only be called opulent. Crystal chandeliers lit the large space that held two desks, fine leather furnishings, artwork, vases, and sculptures the likes of which Peloreid had never beheld. An extremely attractive, dark haired female sat behind one of the desks. She quickly rose when Peloreid entered and gave him a very big smile.

"Welcome, Citizen Security Regent Peloreid," she said, moving toward him quickly. "Please allow me to take your coat and hat. Chairman Baucman will be dining in his office today and he would like you to join him," she continued, taking his garments and hanging them in a closet next to the door. "I'm afraid he's running a few minutes behind today. I hope you don't mind waiting for him."

"Of course not," exclaimed Peloreid quickly. He imagined that few people would have shown displeasure at having a private lunch with the Chairman of the Supreme Council, even if it meant waiting for hours. His heart had leapt at the assistant's words. He was on the threshold of great power. This could only be good for his career. Oh, to be in one of these offices. He looked around at his surroundings and at the pretty girl. Her auburn haired companion at the other desk had not risen when he entered but had given him a warm smile as he gazed at her. While Peloreid was partial to blonds, he could certainly see the attraction of the brunette and redhead in this office. He wondered if Chairman Baucman had any "special" duties for these women. His thoughts were interrupted by the brunette assistant.

"Please make yourself comfortable," she said, with her hand extended towards an overstuffed sofa and armchairs. "Can I get you any refreshment?"

"No, no thank you," he answered. His hands were shaking with excitement and he was concerned that he might spill something on the oriental carpet or, even worse, on his uniform. "I'll just browse the Chairman's art collection." He smiled at the young woman.

"Do you like art, Citizen Peloreid?" she asked, hoping that she could be of some special service to the visitor. She really didn't care at all if he liked art or not. However, it was unusual for the Chairman to have a private lunch with anyone so she thought that it might be wise to stay close to this particular visitor.

"To be honest, I have very little appreciation for art, and even less knowledge. But, I'm interested in what Chairman Baucman likes," he replied, a slight grin on his face as he looked down his crooked nose at the assistant.

She returned his smile, "Of course. Please let me know if I can be of any assistance." She returned to her desk, knowing that his eyes were on her, examining the lines of her body through her tight sweater and skirt. The pig, she thought. Just like the rest of this "august" body of civil servants. He didn't care about anything that wouldn't further his career. At least he'd been honest about it. Few people were honest in this building. Of course, he probably felt that she was too low level to worry about. She was amazed at how those in very high levels of authority would say anything in front of their servants. They would say things in front of her that they would never say to their peers. It was like she was invisible. They were sure that she wouldn't hurt them, or more likely, that she couldn't hurt them. She had learned secrets that others in the country would kill for. She had a better understanding of the true source of the government's power that almost anyone else because she knew the Chairman's secrets. She wasn't sure exactly what Peloreid's role would be going forward. But he was definitely someone to keep an eye on.

Peloreid scanned the paintings on the office's cherry paneled walls. They were good, he guessed. There were a variety of different scenes. Old battles. Landscapes. Seascapes. People in old styles of dress. He didn't recognize any of them. While they were nice to look at, they really didn't do much for him. He turned and looked at some of the sculptures on small tables situated between the paintings. Again, nice but he really didn't care. They seemed like just clutter to him. If he had an office like this, he reasoned, he'd also have these niceties around. If nothing else, it gave the appearance of culture, wealth, and power. And, at politics of this level, it was appearance and perception that counted. The people here worked and lived in opulence, with every desire fulfilled several times over. That was the reality. But the appearance from the street was that these people worked in the same cramped, austere office spaces that everyone else did. The appearance of equality led to that perception. The perception was the reality of politics. Let the people think that you work for their best interests. In reality, you worked in your own best interests. Tell them that you all suffer together. The reality won't make them feel any better so why worry them? They need to keep their perceptions intact. If they really knew, they might want to share in some of the indulgences which the Supreme Council held for themselves. And that would take away the whole point of being on the Supreme Council, now wouldn't it? No, it is better this way. The people work to serve the government. It's obvious that they can't take care of themselves, so they might as well serve the government. Particularly if he were about to take a much larger role with this government.

"Citizen Security Regent Peloreid, please follow me," said the auburn haired woman.

Peloreid was a little startled by the interruption of his thoughts. He turned quickly and straightened his uniform tunic. Following the assistant, he walked through the opened doorway into another, larger office. The immense oak desk was covered with papers. Windows covered most of two walls and bookcases the other two. A large rectangular conference table was set with two place settings. A uniformed orderly stood at attention beside the larger of the chairs. Peloreid looked around, waiting for someone to indicate what he should do. The orderly just stared at him. The red headed assistant had left, closing the door behind her. Peloreid stood in place, a little confused and embarrassed.

This only lasted for a moment however. A door on the right wall opened and the corpulent form of Chairman Baucman slid sideways through the doorway, wiping his hands on a hand towel which he threw on the bathroom floor before kicking the door closed.

"Welcome, Citizen Peloreid," muttered Baucman, no hint of affection in his voice. He plopped his hefty frame into the large chair and, with the assistance of the orderly, moved as close to the table as his stomach would allow. "Sit, please," he said, motioning Peloreid towards the chair in front of the other place setting. Peloreid immediately did as directed, keeping his eyes on Baucman, hoping for some indication of the Chairman's frame of mind.

"So, are you wondering why you've been invited to dine with the Chairman of the Supreme Council?" asked Baucman, obviously enjoying the stress he was causing his guest. He motioned to the orderly to begin serving. Steaming bowls of lobster bisque were placed in front of the two men. Baucman immediately scooped a large spoonful into his mouth, with drops rolling down his cheeks and dripping onto his shirt.

"I assumed you wanted a further update on Procedure 23, Citizen Chairman," replied Peloreid, eying the bisque hungrily but worrying that he would need to answer a question while eating.

"Not really. I'm sure that's going according to plan," stated Baucman, with the smallest hint of a question in the last sentence.

"Yes, of course it is," exclaimed Peloreid, a little more enthusiastic than he had meant it. Small beads of sweat were forming on his forehead. Whether these were from the heat of the sun beaming through the windows, the steam from the soup, or the immense anxiety which was now like a weight on his chest, he was unsure. "We are reviewing all cases in the first grouping now. Initial results are very encouraging."

Baucman, swallowing the last of his bisque as if he were a starving man, interrupted "Yes, yes. As I said, I'm sure it's fine. Now, tell me what you know about Madame Tonklin."

Peloreid paused. This was totally unexpected and he hadn't prepared anything at all on this subject. He looked down at his still steaming bowl. The orderly had removed Baucman's empty bowl and was reaching for Peloreid's. He had yet to taste it and his mouth was watering with the smell of the brown liquid. He took his eyes off the bowl as the orderly removed it and focused his gaze on the Chairman seated at his right.

"I must admit, Citizen Chairman, that I haven't updated her profile in some time now. From memory," he began. One of the things that Peloreid had been blessed with was an incredibly accurate memory. Very little escaped his notice and anything he noticed was instantly stored. While he didn't consider it photographic, it had never let him down. "Citizen Councilor Tonklin has been a member of the Supreme Council for 22 years, two less than yourself," he continued, nodding to the Chairman who was now biting into a piece of chicken marsala. "She was a Security Regent for eight years before that, in the Western Sector. She was instrumental in limiting the revolt casualties. Some have deemed that partly due to Emperor Barahu's large base of support in the West and partly due to her aggressive use of immediate termination of anyone opposing the absolute authority of Emperor Barahu and the dissolution of the governing bodies of the old America. She was able to deliver the West to Barahu with fewer than ten million casualties which was less than any other sector."

Peloreid paused for a moment to study Baucman's face. He wasn't sure if he had listened or not. The man was eating the chicken and potatoes at a rapid rate. Peloreid's own plate had yet to be touched while the delicious smells were making his stomach growl in protest. Baucman, finally noticing the pause, looked up at Peloreid and, with his left hand which held half of a dinner roll, motioned for him to continue.

"Councilor Tonklin was largely responsible for the food service industry takeover. Utilizing the Purple Shirt Security Guards, she quickly gained possession of nearly 70% of the country's food production and preparation capacities. She also was a driving force in the behavioral control enhancement methods used in the food preparation processes that are so important to the government's continued peaceful dominion over the population. At her direction, the nation's chemical laboratories develop several ground breaking methods to distribute better and stronger medications which assist in placating the populace. It was this work that many feel was largely responsible for her invitation by Emperor Barahu I to join his Supreme Council," he concluded, just as the orderly removed the plates from in front of both Baucman and Peloreid. While Baucman's had been wiped clean by the last piece of the roll, Peloreid's had not been touched.

"Do you know how old she is?" questioned Baucman.

"She will turn 65 in about six month," replied Peloreid.

"And you are well aware of what happens to people after their 65th birthday?"

"They are…retired"

"Yes. Retired. Few people know of this, although of course I would expect someone in your elevated position to be aware of it. Most people are unaware of the retirement process because they may not willingly allow the state to take their life. Citizen Tonklin is one of those people. I happen to know that she has developed a plan to evade her retirement."

"Oh, I…"

"I don't expect you to know this. What I need are three things. First, I need to know more about her plan. I have only the barest details and I can't very well ask her about it. Over the past two years, she had strengthened her security detail. They are much more loyal to her than to me, or Barahu for that matter."

Peloreid's raised his brows at this. He knew that Councilors had their own security attachment but it had never occurred to him that they would be more loyal to the Councilor than the state.

"I need to know her plan," continued Baucman. "Next, I need a plan to prevent her evasion. And finally, I need someone to take her place on the Council. Someone who is well aware of where their loyalties should lie. In my mind, whoever can deliver the first two would be the natural candidate for the last." He stared intently at Peloreid between spoonfuls of the chocolate mousse that had been served. Peloreid returned his stare, his spoon suspended in his hand, his heart beating furiously.

"Do you have anyone to recommend for this assignment?" asked Baucman with a mischievous smile on his face.

"You know that I am here to do your bidding, Citizen Chairman," replied Peloreid. He wanted there to be no misunderstanding. He would do whatever Baucman wanted. He would do anything, kill anyone, to get a seat on the Supreme Council.

"I was hoping as much," said Baucman, dropping his spoon into the empty dessert cup.

"May I ask what boundaries I have?" questioned Peloreid.

"Obviously, there is a great deal of discretion and secrecy involved. If it's discovered that I'm investigating another Council member, it could be...uncomfortable, even embarrassing. You cannot question Tonklin directly. However, I believe that security in this sector is your responsibility. I'm certain you can utilize some of your contacts within her security detachment to gain information, either willingly or unwillingly. We are under some time constraints because I do not believe that she will wait until her birthday to act. She is not the type to go quietly, unless she hopes to slip away to avoid capture."

"Would that be so bad? If she slipped away quietly?"

"Disastrous. The law states that a Councilor cannot be replaced unless Barahu approves. I know his response. He will not act until he sees her dead body. A vacant seat means that the Council will be split on many issues. She has been a thorn in my side for years. She may at times agree with me, but only after exacting a price. I will replace her with someone of MY choosing. In that way, I will have a majority of Councilors. I will need to negotiate with no one. That is why you must not fail."

"But why can't we just follow her and take her before she can do anything? It would be very simple to just detain her for a period of time."

"I thought of that initially. However, she has a, shall we say, special relationship with Barahu. He is very fond of her, one of his many faults."

Peloreid stiffened at Baucman's criticism of Emperor Barahu II. He had never heard anyone speak negatively about the Emperor. I would mean a severe beating, or worse, for most people. But the Chairman was not "most people".

Baucman continued, "Barahu would not be pleased if I detained her. Also, I know that she has spoken to him about her own replacement, with someone not entirely pleasing to me. And of course, that would not help you either." He eyed Peloreid. He knew he had been right about the Security Regent. He was ambitious. He loved the finer things in life, to possess even if he could not appreciate. He had read the reports of Peloreid's beating of the young relaxation specialist and knew that it was a demonstration of his control and power that really excited him, not the sex. He had watched the monitor as Peloreid had viewed the art and sculpture in his outer office. Peloreid wouldn't know a Picasso from a pig's ass, but he knew that they were valuable so he would want them. Baucman had seen it in his eyes, his demeanor, his attention to anything that gave the appearance of prestige and power. And now, Peloreid would be his possession, his tool to use. The price was a seat on the Council. But this would also benefit him since Peloreid would never dare to challenge him. He could not lose.

"Now, if I can go to Barahu with proof of a plan that Tonklin has to break one of the laws that his father had enacted, her credibility would be gone. He would not trust her or any recommendation she had given. That's why I need the proof."

"Does it have to be real?" asked Peloreid.

Baucman smiled. "Real? No. But the appearance of authenticity is very important. Tonklin will deny any charges so we need to have enough evidence, real or invented, to convince someone who will not want to believe it."

"I understand," said Peloreid quietly. "I appreciate your trust and confidence. I will not disappoint you."

"Then you are everything that I believed you to be, my friend," finished Baucman, rising from his chair with the assistance of the orderly. He stretched his hand towards Peloreid. Shaking the Regents hand, he walked him towards the door. "Call my office when you have any update. This should be your highest priority, I believe."

"Of course, Citizen Chairman. It shall have my undivided attention."

Baucman nodded to Peloreid and closed the door behind him. Peloreid was elated. This was his opportunity, his chance to become a member of the Supreme Council. It would probably mean disposing of some of Tonklin's security guards but that was nothing. His orders had caused the loss of tens of thousands of lives. Actually, he thought, sliding into the coat being held by the brunette assistant, it was more like hundreds of thousands. He had cleansed a large portion of the undesirable elements in this sector. At one time, people had chanted about freedom. He had seen that they were freed from their earthly bodies. Freedom. Liberty. Stupid theories that assumed people would take care of themselves. Only people who took responsibility for their own lives could be truly free. But people were stupid and lazy. They didn't want to work. They wanted the government to meet their every need. And so now it does. Some complained that they were losing their freedom and liberty. But you can't expect the government to support you and then be able to criticize the manner in which it's done. They needed to decide between freedom and the risk of failure or security and the loss of choice. When they couldn't, Barahu had decided for them. "Let no crisis go to waste" was a motto of the movement. And if you had to create a crisis in order to lure the stupid public into supporting the usurpation of their power, so be it. Those that didn't agree to let the government make decisions for them had to be dealt with. Peloreid pulse quickened as the remembered the heady days of the takeover. They had created wars, invisible enemies, joblessness, hunger and fear. And when the people were screaming for the government to help them, Barahu had agreed, for a price. He would fix everything, but his way. Agree and be fed. Or fight him and die. He took more and more power from elected officials, private business, and individuals. And their fear caused more and more people to grant him more and more power. Looking back, Peloreid almost felt that it had been almost too easy. "A drowning man will grasp even the edge of a sword." When you're afraid, you'll try anything. But once things are set in motion, sometimes you can't go back. By the time people had learned that, Barahu was well established. Millions fought him and millions died. Most of that occurred before Peloreid was made a Security Regent. He was only a Purple Shirt Area Security Manager at that time. He had executed, what was the number? Probably not more than a million people. Maybe not all from executions. There had been battles too. But the stupid freedom fighters were no match for the government's tanks and planes. They were mowed down. Bulldozers had pushed them into mass graves. His area had been small. Others had to kill many more. He thought about 100 million in all. Now that was a cleansing. Those that remained were either in agreement with Barahu or too scared to oppose him. And, after Tonklin's food service had introduced the sedation drugs, the population had settled into their new arrangement.

Tonklin. Yes, Tonklin. The early winter wind struck him in the face as he emerged from the Supreme Council building. As the driver held his door, Peloreid slid into the back seat of the car. What to do about Tonklin? He had felt assured in the Chairman's office but he seemed less so now. If her security detail was so loyal to her, how would he get them to provide him information without tipping his hand? He didn't want her aware of his presence or she would either change her plan or accelerate it. Neither of those options was good for him. But, she only had a few months to live so she couldn't wait too long. Once she passed her 65th birthday, she couldn't refuse. It would cost her life but it would also probably cost Peloreid his Council position. He needed information and soon.

"Take me to the Central Security Office," he instructed his driver through the intercom.

II

Charles stared back at Andrew. On one hand, he had a burning desire to learn about his life and his family. But what danger were they really in? He still didn't understand what this Liberty Tree was or why they had to sneak to an oil-stained maintenance closet to meet. He looked Andrew in the eye.

"You keep saying that we're in danger. Why? From whom? Why would anyone want to stop us from talking?" he asked, the skepticism heavy in his voice. "I just want to learn about my life."

Albert rose from his easy chair and moved rapidly to the table. He pulled out a chair and dropped into it. "You must understand, this society, this government of Barahu allows no dissention. We are not meant to communicate with each other. They fear us. They fear people with their own ideas. They fear a free populace. People that want their God given freedom and liberties would destroy this government. They want to keep their power. They did it at first by promising people that they would be given their every desire and that someone else would pay for it. When it was obvious that wasn't working, they scared the public. And then they resorted to killing anyone that opposed them."

Albert's eyes had not left Charles' since he had begun speaking. While his voice was steady, his emotion was evident.

"Barahu's government killed your parents because they wanted to return the country to the republic that existed before Barahu. They were victims of the clinical trials that led to your Procedure 23. But those didn't go so well. The drugs that they injected ended up destroying their brains, not erasing their memories. Dozens, maybe hundreds, died like that before they reached what was used on you. Now, does that indicate what sort of danger we're in? Does that tell you why we sneak around? Why we hide? I'm alive because I am careful. I live in this pigsty because I chose to live rather than die. I don't believe the government should be able to control every part of my life. For that, I'm an enemy of the state. For that, I'm hunted. And, if captured, I'll be killed. So, young man, I'm very concerned about the danger that we've put ourselves in by contacting you. And you need to decide if you'll share that danger with us or not."

Charles looked back and forth between Andrew and Albert. He knew they spoke the truth. He could see it, even feel it from them. This was about much more than just a curiosity in his background and understanding who the people were that invaded his dreams.

"Why me," he asked quietly, looking down at the cup of tea in his hands. "I understand that you were close to my parents... and me, I guess. But why put yourselves in danger for that?"

"I see they didn't destroy your intelligence with their Procedure 23," said Andrew calmly. "There is more than just that connection. We need you."

"What do you mean, you need me? It seems like you'd be better off without me. Safer."

"Not just Albert and me. I mean our organization. The Liberty Tree."

"What's the Liberty Tree?"

"Ah, and there's the question. To know the answer to that means that you're in. You're one of us. You're committed. There's no going back. It means having a price on your head. It's a death sentence if caught. So, again, do you want to know the truth?"

The same question. It kept coming back to the same question. His answer had been yes before. But, he hadn't known that it carried a death sentence. Now, although he wasn't sure why, he understood that this answer could cost him his life. Did he really want to know? They needed him. What the hell could he do for them? He couldn't even remember his life from more than four months ago.

His eyes fell on the picture of his parents again. The Johnsons and the Sinclairs, together, arm in arm. Alice Sinclair kissing Andrew. Harry and Eva Johnson smiling happily. Three of the four were now dead according to Albert. Killed by the government because, because why? Because they wanted to live in freedom? To make their own decisions? What the hell did that mean? He stared at his parents. He could see the resemblance to his father. The same nose and eyes. His hair seemed to have come from his mother. And then his eye focused on her smile. That look of pure, unadulterated joy. As he stared, Andrew slipped another picture over the one that he was memorizing. It showed a boy of about 10 with a birthday cake in front of him. His parents were standing behind him, again smiling broadly, as was he. Again, his focus was on his mother's smile. It was that same smile that had haunted his dreams. And then, he remembered the nightmares where he was pulled from them. He thought about the terror he felt as he was pulled further and further from their grasp. Had it been real? Had the screams that had awoken him really the sound of his mother's voice? Had the government really taken that smile away from him? Had they caused the scream that echoed in his sleep?

"I want to know the truth. I just want to know who I am," he said, with finality.

"Very well," responded Andrew, quietly. "What do you want to know first?"

"This picture is of me and my parents, isn't it?"

"Yes, it is," confirmed Andrew. "You were their only child. They doted on you. You were their whole world. They loved you very much."

Charles shifted around more pictures of his parents, of him as a child, of the Johnsons and Sinclairs. A lump formed in his throat and his eyes began to water.

"I wish I could remember them," he said finally. "They took my whole life from me. Barahu took my life."

He paused, staring at the pictures, trying to memorize every line, every color. He knew these people. He knew them from his dreams. He wanted them to be real.

"I hate them. They had no right to do that. This was my life and they had no right. How can I hurt them? What can I do?" he asked, searching the faces of both Andrew and Albert.

"Your parents always did say that you had a rebellious mind. Albert, why don't you describe where we are now. I'll fill in the blanks as we go."

"So, not the full history lesson?" questioned Albert, with a weak smile towards Andrew. "Where we are today. OK. We, Andrew and I, and now you, are members of a secret organization, the Liberty Tree. Our goal is the same as your parents, to restore the old American republic. We want to give the people back their freedom of speech, of religion, of individual choice. To do that, we need to awaken the populace from their stupor. We need to foment a revolution."

"I don't understand. What's the old American republic?" asked Charles, a confused look on his face.

"You've heard of the USA?" asked Albert, his eyes twinkling.

"Yes, the Union of Socialist Alliances."

"That's Barahu-speak. It originally stood for the United States of America. That was the country before Barahu and his cronies stole it. In those days, the people voted for who they wanted to run the country. You see there were Congress and a President. ."

"Albert, please, the Readers Digest edition. We don't have time for all the details."

"Yes, yes, OK," he replied to Andrew's plea. "The people had a choice in who led the country, the laws that they lived by, and the direction they had. They could speak their minds without fear of retribution. They could write their ideas and share them with others. They could meet to voice their support for the government or with their anger and disagreement with it. They could live where they wanted, work in whatever field they chose. Some failed. Some were hungry, sick. Some had few possessions and little money. But most worked hard. They married and raised children, like your parents. They loved and laughed and yes, sometimes cried. But all of it was primarily due to their God given abilities and to their own choices. Of course, when those worked out well, they were happy and content. When it didn't work out so well, they were unhappy. They let power hungry politicians convince them that it wasn't their fault. It had to be someone else's fault. The successful people, it was their fault. They were to blame. They didn't deserve the things they got. The bastards convinced people to let them punish the most successful people in the country. The idiots agreed and so, the politicians went after these people. It wasn't the first time in history that wealthy people were attacked but, in a country that had always prided itself on allowing and even enabling people to succeed, it was a shock. So, surprise, surprise, with no successful people, there was no one to create new businesses and new jobs or new opportunities for people. Once the government did this, the only place people had to turn was to the politicians. Instead of the people controlling the politicians, they became their servants, relying on them for their most basic necessities, even food and clothing. As long as the people needed the government for their very survival, the politicians' power was secure."

Albert paused a moment and took a sip of tea, seeming to ponder how to continue. "By destroying wealth, redistributing it to others, they destroyed the ability of their enemies to challenge them. The only ones with any real power remaining were the politicians themselves. The people that had been rewarded were those that did as Barahu's government wanted. Those that had worked hard but wanted some self-determination had been punished and saw that it was more beneficial to just let the government take care of them. And so, the country began to fail. And that's exactly what Barahu wanted. He wanted a global depression so that he could use it to take over those elements of society that he hadn't yet. So, he took over banks, since that was where most people held their wealth. He regulated them, made it impossible for them to succeed and, when they did indeed fail, he stepped in and seized them. He said that it was a rescue which he really didn't WANT to do but HAD to do." Albert emphasized the words. His face was turning red and Charles knew that his blood was beginning to boil.

"The car companies were next. It wasn't that he really wanted to take them over. He really just wanted to see if anyone would stop his RESCUE of the industry. No one did. Next, he wanted something bigger. His greed for more power was growing, as was the greed of his supporters. He went after the medical industry. Barahu actually met some resistance there. The industry was actually doing fairly well on its own so they didn't need to be RESCUED. He tried calling it REFORM but that didn't fly. So, since he couldn't rescue or reform, he regulated. He set up so many rules that the companies couldn't survive. He cut the amounts that people had to pay which put hospitals, doctors, laboratories and pharmaceutical companies into bankruptcy. Now, they needed to be RESCUED. It's similar to what they did to the banks. They made it impossible for them to succeed and survive, and then criticized them for failing. So now, Barahu's government controlled the banks, the hospitals, drug companies, and doctors. Once you've got their health and wealth, it's a very small step to the rest."

When Albert paused, Andrew continued for him. "Barahu instituted educational REFORMS. Basically, he mandated what schools taught so that children became indoctrinated from an early age. One of his most important takeovers was the communications industry. The government had always controlled radio and television airwaves but now Barahu wouldn't allow certain types of radio broadcasts that were critical of his administration. He eliminated them off so people couldn't hear them thereby removing any opposition. The Internet takeover was the most hurtful though. He said that he needed control of the computer networks in case of an emergency."

"They had a saying, 'Let no crisis go to waste.' For them, that meant that if things were really bad, it was an opportunity to use that fear to grab more power," interjected Albert.

"That's right. They were unscrupulous in their use of scare tactics in order to get the public to go along with their plans. They warned that terrorists were using the Internet to attack government and private computers. They tried to convince the public that only the government could possibly protect something as big as the nation's computer network."

"And did the people believe them?" asked Charles.

"Not hardly!" answered Albert. "That's when things really began getting out of hand." He chuckled. "It was known as the Porno Revolution. Barahu grabbed the Internet and decided to cut off access to certain sites. It was mostly to anti-government sites but, you see, the government isn't really good at running things. So when they tried to limit access to some sites, they overdid it." He began laughing uncontrollably.

"Millions of hard working American men and women were cut off from their pornography sites. You want to talk about a rebellion! People were walking into their elected officials offices with shotguns demanding that they turn the Internet back on. It took a week for Barahu to figure out that it had more to do with porn than anti-government forces." Andrew too was laughing heartily.

"That dumb son-of-a-bitch," roared Albert. "He was so far removed from the people that he thought everything was about him. The Chosen One people were calling him. Well, actually I think it was something that he himself was pushing, but he definitely thought that his words were gold and he had sunshine flowing out of his ass." Albert was laughing so hard that he began coughing uncontrollably, finally getting up to get a glass of water.

"Barahu used that crisis to implement gun control regulations and imprison those that were caught owning weapons. He was successful in controlling almost every form of communication. People would gather to protest, but he'd send in the Purple Shirts to break up the meetings."

"And people's legs," shouted Albert from the kitchen area.

"Isn't the Purple Shirts the army or police?" asked Charles.

"It is now. It used to be just an organization of workers that supported Barahu. But he kept giving them money for their support. He used them more and more for his personal purposes. They became his own personal security force, loyal to no one but him. The army reported to generals that were supposed to uphold the laws, not one person. Same with the police forces. Barahu wanted someone loyal to him alone. Eventually, the Purple Shirts replaced the army and police into one security force."

"So, there was an army. Why didn't they stop him?"

Albert had returned. He was no longer smiling. His face was drawn and gloomy. "That is one of the most disgusting events of Barahu's takeover. It's a sin what he did to our glorious armed forces." He paused looking at Charles, composing himself before continuing.

"Our country had been attacked by militants. We fought them overseas, which moved the battles away from our soil. Barahu pretended to defend the country. But, he had infiltrated the services. He learned who would be loyal to him and who would fight him. Over two years, he moved those that would oppose him to positions overseas. While they battled our enemies, he restructured the military leadership. We have some evidence that he actually leaked information to our enemies. Instead of imprisoning the enemy soldiers, he put them on trial. In our own courts! He gave the people that were trying to destroy us the very legal protections which they sought to destroy! During that process, much of our intelligence and strategy became known. The enemy learned what we wanted to do and how we would do it. And then," continued Albert, "he left our people to die!"

Charles looked at him, struggling to fully comprehend what he was saying.

"Barahu had those supposed 'disloyal' forces sent overseas and he left them there. No supplies. No reinforcements. No support. He left them out there by themselves and let the enemy destroy them. He blamed it on disloyal officers, on terrorist attacks, on anything he could. But basically, he left them on foreign soil alone, with no supplies. Eventually, they ran out of food, water, ammunition. And then, they were overwhelmed by an enemy that knew they could not fight back. Thousands, tens of thousands of brave men and women were sacrificed. Those 'loyal' forces sat here at home and waited for the revolution that would surely come."

"And it did at last," said Andrew, taking over for the emotionally drained Albert. He looked at Charles as he moved around the table to put a hand on Albert's shoulder as the man began to weep. "Albert's two children were part of those forces left to die in the deserts and mountains of those foreign lands."

No one spoke for a few minutes. Charles looked at his hands, his feet, his cup, anything but Albert and Andrew. Both had lost so much. Friends, children, wives, all to fuel Barahu's greed. This was a much different version of events that those explained by Citizen Wainwright. Charles could not envision the victory parades for Barahu that she had mentioned. Neither could he see the bloodshed and famine which she claimed had led to his ascension. All he saw was greed for power. He saw a hunger to control this country, these people. He saw an all consuming desire for the government to control the people so that the people could never again control the government.

Finally, Andrew carried on. "There was a revolution. But it was short lived. Unarmed protesters are no match for government guns and tanks. Even millions of protesters are no match. They were gunned down, trampled, or arrested. No one knows how many were just lined up and shot. Bodies lay in the streets, rotting. They were trucked to fields and dumped. The carnage was incredible. We're talking tens of millions of people over just a few years. The few battles died out in a couple of months. Then the government began rounding up suspects. Anyone that was registered with a different political party. Anyone that had spoken out against Barahu. They were gathered up and, just disappeared. Sometimes, people were just standing in a group waiting to cross a street. A truck pulled up and they were all herded in. Didn't matter if they were pro-government or anti-government. They were standing on the wrong corner at the wrong time. And then they were gone."

"It was a very dangerous time, as you can imagine," stated Albert, wiping his eyes. "And that's when the Liberty Tree was formed."

"How is it that it wasn't discovered?" asked Charles.

"It has been, many times," Albert answered. "But the strength of the Liberty Tree is that it's all branches. No one knows more that a handful off others. I know six, not including you. You, now, know two. For most people, they don't know more than a few. The government can grab a couple of people, but that only gives them a couple of names. And that's if they don't screw up and kill the people before they get the names, which happens much of the time."

"And so, the Tree has survived and even grown, right under the noses of the government that is so sure of it's own security," interjected Andrew. "While I don't know many names, I do know that we have people extremely highly placed in all parts of the government. People are beginning to awaken. And that's were you come in."

"Me?" said Charles incredulously.

"You. You are a senior chemist at the lab that develops the sedation chemical that go into the food supply. The government research has shown that the current chemicals are losing their effectiveness and they need something new in order to maintain their control over the population."

"And you want me to stop the development? Not possible. There are a team of scientists working on various parts of that project."

"No, we don't want you to stop it. It needs to continue. They'll know if it stops. We need an antidote. Something that will counter the effects of whatever the drug ends up being. Once we have that, we can get the antidote into the food or water supply. When people wake up, the revolution will begin," stated Andrew, a slight tinge of excitement and desperation in his voice.

"Why do you think that you were given a Procedure 23?" asked Albert.

Amazingly enough, Charles had never asked himself that question. He had been too busy listening to the history lesson being given by the two men. Why had he been given a Procedure 23? What had they wanted him to forget?

"I don't know," he mumbled in reply. "I guess because of my parents," he half answered and half asked.

"No, your parents died months ago when they began developing their Procedure 23. No one knew what happened to them with any certainty until about a year ago when one of our operatives discovered the list of test subjects for the experiments. That's when you joined the Tree."

"So, if they knew I was in the Liberty Tree, why didn't they just kill me?" asked Charles.

"You're too valuable. And, you had provided good service to the government in the past. You're one of the top chemists in the entire lab, and that means the entire country," Andrew said, giving Charles a proud, fatherly smile. "They need you. And, they weren't sure you were in the Liberty Tree. They suspected it, but they weren't sure. Your team leader, Ben Jorgenson, was taken and he implicated you. He was at a higher level while you had just joined and were at the lowest level. You were questioned but you didn't know much more than gossip that you could have picked up from

Ben. He was killed. They decided to be safe with you and give you a Procedure 23 instead of a 66."

"What do you mean that I had provided service in the past? I don't understand," asked Charles.

Andrew stared at him uncomfortably, cleared his throat, and responded. "You didn't always agree with your parents views. You were young and you believed much of Barahu's propaganda. You were part of the team that helped create the additives that are in use now."

"So I betrayed my parents?" asked Charles, afraid of the response he might get.

"No, you never betrayed them. You disagreed. You argued. But you never betrayed them and they never stopped loving you."

"You mentioned a 66. What's that?" asked Charles.

"A Procedure 66 is how they exterminate the undesirables," answered Albert.

"They inject you with a chemical that causes massive internal hemorrhages. Your cells essentially explode. It's the most painful way of dying that they could develop," added Andrew. "That's what Jorgenson got. But you are the brightest chemist they've got. Now, they're using you to develop the replacement. We need you to develop the antidote at the same time."

"That's it, huh? Be able to undo by myself what a team of people are doing together. It could take me years by myself."

"I hope not. I believe that, if we have the formula within six months, we may be able to topple this government."

"Why, what's so special about six months?" asked Charles.

Albert and Andrew stared at each other, trying to read the other's mind. After several seconds, Albert shrugged and nodded. Andrew turned to face Charles again.

"We think they are preparing to replace Barahu II."

"Replace the Emperor? Doesn't that solve the problem then?" responded Charles.

"Not in this government. The original Barahu was the leader, along with his henchmen. As he got older, they worried about a way to transfer power without a struggle ensuing. They cloned Barahu to create Barahu II. But, Barahu was sick. They couldn't wait for Barahu II to grow naturally so they injected him with all sorts of growth hormones, some even before birth. They wanted to speed up the rate of growth so they could insert him as Emperor whenever Barahu I died. It was a massive failure and has been an even bigger cover-up for years. Barahu II is almost 28 years old, is much larger than a normal person with a misshaped head and body and the maturity level of a 12 year old. He has real authority but is manipulated by the Supreme Council. They get him to sign whatever they want by giving him a new toy or something. Over the past few years, control of the Council has been split between two factions that have largely offset each other. However, we've received word that one of the parties may be making a power grab soon. They may be trying to take over the Council and impose their will on Barahu II."

"And this is going to happen in six months?"

"Maybe sooner."

"Probably sooner," added Albert.

"There's more. A second clone of the original Barahu was developed a few years after Barahu II. This version wasn't given growth hormones but was allowed to develop naturally. He has grown and was taught about life according to his, well, it's not quite his father but I'm not sure what else to call him, so he was taught everything according to his father, Barahu I. Ohnoma is scheduled to assume power when he turns 25. That's in just over six months."

"So, how will that cause a revolution," asked Charles.

"Whenever there is a transition of power, there is instability in the government. This will be at least a three way struggle for power. You have a split on the Supreme Council, both trying to retain or even grab more power. You also have Ohnoma, who will certainly try to assert his own authority to replace his father and, I guess you'd call him his brother," instructed Albert.

"And, don't forget about Barahu II. He's been told his whole life that he's all powerful in this country. How will they push him out of the way? So, the greatest point of instability that this government will probably ever see will be in three to six months. We need the new chemical to be introduced along with the antidote by then," said Andrew.

"Or," added Albert, "we need an antidote to the current drug and the new drug to be delayed."

Charles paused, thinking about everything he had been told. "The second option might be easier in that timeframe. We certainly have a lot of data on the existing chemical components and, as you said, the effects are already diminishing. It would also probably be easier to slow down the current experiments than to complete a whole set of parallel experiments on my own. That could work." Charles looked up at the two men who had both risen.

"Charles," said Andrew, "don't forget to pick up your tracking chip on your way home." He smiled at Charles and pulled him into a hug.

Albert held out a small medallion for Charles. "Turn it over," he said. "There's a place on the back for you to insert the chip. Much easier than sewing it back into your neck."

"Thanks," said Charles. "So, how do we meet again."

"When you have news for us, stand outside five minutes early for the transport. You'll be contacted soon after," instructed Albert.

"You mean, someone's going to watch for me every day."

"Charles, you are our most important resource right now. Without your brains, we will have no chance to overturn this corrupt government. You'll be watched almost constantly, just as you have been for the past few months."

Charles looked at Andrew's face, almost thinking that it was a joke. He could see that it wasn't. Charles nodded at the two men and walked through the door into the blackness.

12

Citizen Security Regent Peloreid leaned back in his chair. The charts that he was reviewing showed the security organization for his area, which included the Supreme Council. He needed to get close to Councilor Tonklin, but how? He reviewed the officers posted to her security detail. The most senior members had been with her for over 10 years. Many had risen through the ranks with her, as she had done the same. They had literally been through the war together, and he could not see any of them betraying her confidence. There were some new additions, but they were probably not trusted enough to have the in depth knowledge that he needed. It seemed like a dead end.

"I would like a listing of all security officers by rank for my areas," he commanded into the speakerphone.

"Of course, Citizen Security Regent Peloreid," came the immediate response. "It will take me only a few moments. I will bring it in as soon as it is ready."

Within three minutes, a middle aged woman walked through the door, carrying several pages of the report. She was attractive, with only a few wrinkles around her eyes and gray hairs amongst her blond. She smiled slightly at Peloreid as she handed him the report. He didn't glance up from his computer screen as he reached to take the papers. Without saying a word, she turned and walked quickly from the room.

Peloreid had watched her walk away before turning to the report. Could he use her to infiltrate Tonklin's group? She might not draw their concern. Perhaps she could seduce her way into...

No. He shook his head. While she was loyal to him, none of Tonklin's security officers would divulge their secrets just for sex. They probably had their own special access to relaxation specialists just as he did. Purple Shirts open many doors closed to others.

Peloreid scanned the page. His name appeared on top, of course. The highest member of Tonklin's team was 12th on the list. He ran his finger down the list, looking for a name that might be familiar, that might lead to a plan. He could just grab one. He could certainly get the truth out of them. He had several methods of procuring information from even the most confidential source. The problem was two fold. First, he had to get access to a source of information soon. Time was not on his side. Secondly, he had to do it in a way which would not cause suspicion to arise in Tonklin. She didn't get to her level without having a keen sense of danger. Suspicion bordering on paranoia was second nature to people in the Barahu government, especially at the highest levels. So, how to get someone knowledgeable, in secret, and fast? He needed to give Chairman Baucman an update within a few days and he had nothing.

He rose from his chair and went to the window. He stared at the sidewalk, the people walking in and out of the security building. While there was no snow on the ground, he could see the breath escaping people as they moved about. He didn't recognize most, but that didn't surprise him. Thousands of people worked in this building, the vast majority of which were at much too low of a level for him to be concerned with. They were clerks, technicians, and others that dealt with the huge volume of data that the government collected on its citizens. Nothing was unimportant. Tracking devices were in most people now, at least anyone under 30 years old. Computers tracked where people went, when they moved, and who they associated with. If more than 6 people were together in any unusual location, Purple Shirts would be notified and would investigate. The computers knew where you lived, worked, and even what transport you rode. If you got on the wrong one, a computer would warn the security department. It would do the same if you went to someone else's domicile unit. The government controlled by separating individuals so that their primary contact was always with someone of government authority. Citizens didn't interact with each other, they interacted with the government, or more accurately an appropriate government representative. Everyone was a government employee so, to maintain control, you just had to ensure that people in authority were true to the government and not whatever department or industry they may happen to work in. As long as loyalty was to the government and not other individuals, the government could carry on in perpetuity. Therefore, individual interactions were strictly limited and were monitored closely.

Peloreid saw the smiling face of Joyce Clifford, the Area Security Manager, as she walked up the steps of the building. Clifford was the only person that Peloreid knew that was always smiling. He didn't know why. He'd never been able to figure it out. The woman always seemed to be in a good mood. Peloreid had recruited her out of the training academy. While she was never a great beauty, her long, lithe body at the time had attracted Peloreid to her immediately. He frowned, remembering the one time when he had made an advance towards her. She rebuffed him, in the friendliest way possible. It had been a humiliation that he hadn't forgotten but of which neither had ever spoken. He shook his head. That was many years ago. Then, he'd not been in a position to punish her. Thereafter, she had proven herself to be so intelligent, crafty, and supportive that he'd never thought about punishing her even though he had certainly continued to think about doing other things to her.

Peloreid returned to his desk and scanned the listing. Clifford had progressed to 37th on the listing of over 3000 security officers in his district. He personally knew all of the top 100 and she was the only one he would classify as "cheery". He reviewed the names above her. Not much there. People in all different departments under his command. No name that seemed to help create a plan in his mind. He looked at her name again and noticed the name directly below hers. Oliver Matthews. Oliver Matthews of Councilor Tonklin's private security detail. 38th on the list. Not among the highest, but certainly someone that had been around Tonklin for a while. He turned to his terminal and chose the appropriate screen before typing in Matthew's name.

Could he? Could he possibly substitute Clifford for Matthews? What would he need to do? Certainly grab Matthews and then provide Clifford as a replacement. Would that work? Probably not. As soon as he detained Matthews, Tonklin would be on alert. So, how do you get Clifford in if Matthews isn't out? But wait, the issue might not be getting Clifford in, but rather how to get Matthews somewhere so the information could be gathered from him?

Peloreid grabbed Tonklin's org chart again. Matthews held the second highest ranking on her security detail. Certainly, if there was a plan, he would be involved. So, how to get Matthews on his side, Peloreid thought? How had he done it with others? It was usually fear or greed. Fear wouldn't work. Matthews would feel protected by Tonklin. Greed? What could Peloreid offer that Tonklin couldn't? There had to be something. The problem was that it had to be something natural, something that wouldn't cause concern. Peloreid paced before his window again. What could he offer that wouldn't raise suspicions? It flashed to him in an instant. The one thing that he could offer that no one else could was a promotion. Officially, Matthews was part of his sector's staff, even if he reported to Tonklin. But, what kind of promotion? What wouldn't raise suspicions? How did people get promoted? A new position? No, there hadn't been a new position added in six years. That would certainly raise eyebrows. He looked at the rankings again. Matthews. Above him, Clifford. Above her, well above her were other Area Security Managers with more experience and seniority than her. There were eight Area Managers before you got to Sector Chief. He couldn't promote Matthews that far. The only person he was really close to on the ranking was Clifford. He had actually been in the Purple Shirts longer than Clifford. But, Clifford had progressed through the ranks a little faster. Peloreid smiled. That was because she had tied her tail to his kite. He had seen to it that she was promoted because she had been useful to him, even if she had refused him as a sexual partner.

He thought of Clifford for a few moments. She had certainly helped him along the way. Some of his greatest achievements had originally been her ideas. Oh, he made sure that she was rewarded, after him of course. He reflected on their parallel careers, hers always slightly behind his. But, over the past three or four years, he hadn't relied on her as much. Things had been quiet in the region and his major initiative, Procedure 23, hadn't required her attention. Could she be useful to him once again?

The plan started formalizing in Peloreid's mind. If Clifford was no longer in her position, there would be the inevitable climb up the rankings for everyone below her. Next on the list would be Matthews. He would certainly be expected to assume her position as Area Security Manager. There was no refusing of a position. To do so would be a direct refusal of the government, which was never allowed. Matthews would have to work for him.

But, then what? Peloreid could certainly detain him and extract the information. However, even though Matthews would report to him, where would his loyalties lie? And, even more importantly, where would his protection come from? He was sure that Tonklin would be keeping an eye on him, out of suspicion if nothing else. Peloreid was close. He could feel it, almost taste the plan. He always has a sense of excitement when he felt a plan coming together. It was a wave of stimulation and invincibility. He was setting something in motion that would propel him forward in his career, even while it was at the expense of others. They were placed at his disposal to serve him and the government. To Peloreid, those were one and the same.

"Tell the Developmental Lab that I'm on my way. I want a complete status update prepared when I arrive," Peloreid barked into the phone. He disconnected without waiting for a reply. A broad smile crossed his face. The plan was nearly there. He looked around his drab, bare office. There were none of the fine furnishings of the Supreme Council. His desk and cabinets were metal, painted a dull gray color. His chair was of metal as well, not the overstuffed fine leather of Chairman Baucman's. There were no paintings or sculptures to be enjoyed, only an old photograph of Barahu I. Standard issue, Peloreid thought. But soon, he would no longer be looking at the putrid trappings of his lowly office. While the best in the building, he had seen what was enjoyed by those with real power. He wanted it, and he was convinced that it would be his. Soon.

A few minutes later, Peloreid was charging into a conference room. Several men and women immediately rose from their seats as he entered. They stood at attention as he strode to the end of the table. After he sat, the others resumed their seats.

"Status update, Citizen Sinclair," ordered Peloreid, nodding to the tall, thin, balding man on his left.

"Of course, Citizen Security Regent," came the soft voiced reply. Andrew Sinclair looked at the Security Regent with a smile. "We have all departments assembled. Rogers, please begin first."

In turn, each department head made a short report of their various projects. The Development Lab was primarily responsible for new means of public surveillance. They developed the tracking chips, the software for determining which people should be interacting with which others, and the monitors to scan the various devices. While not responsible to analyze the data, they were intimately involved with the software used by the analysts. Their job was to constantly develop new methods for checking every movement of the population in order to uncover anti-government groups and rebellious plots. They were very good at their work and Andrew Sinclair was the best.

Andrew had been in charge of this particular department for several years now. Originally, he had been posted in the Western sector, the same one that had caused the rise of Councilor Evelyn Tonklin. He had been so successful at uncovering plots that he was moved to the Capitol sector, deemed the most important in the nation. The Supreme Council felt sure that, with Sinclair in charge, they would be well aware of any plot weeks before it was ready to strike. And, to support this confidence, not one anti-government attack had occurred in this Sector since he had been assigned. The Chairman himself had awarded Sinclair the Golden Crescent, the highest award possible for non-Purple Shirts.

Peloreid listened carefully to the reports. Without surveillance, the state was at risk and, even more important, his career was at risk. The Supreme Council felt safe with them on watch. That was why he was afforded special privileges. That was why he had been given this assignment. That was why he would be the next member of the Supreme Council.

The reports were completed. Peloreid had asked the obligatory questions of each. He would pick out a minor detail and ask for further information. This made them think that he had a grasp of the scientific concepts which they were discussing. In reality, he had no idea of the physics, chemistry, and biological compounds and methodologies of which they spoke. But, he didn't need to understand. They only needed to believe that he understood. That would keep them honest, and on their toes.

As the meeting ended, Peloreid rose as did the laboratory staff. He turned to Sinclair, "Citizen Sinclair, I need to speak to you in your office."

"Of course. Anything you please," came the warm, if wary, reply.

Sinclair followed Peloreid next door to his private office. While furnished in a similar fashion to Peloreid's, the laboratory was in the basement of the building. There were no windows or nice views, only hard, cold concrete surfaces which were covered with mechanical diagrams and computer data reports.

"What can I do for the Security Regent?" asked Andrew Sinclair as the two men sat across from Sinclair's desk.

"When will your thread be ready for actual use?" asked Peloreid flatly.

"As we said, we're nearly ready for the prototype stage," replied Sinclair, a question in his voice.

"I know what was said in the meeting. I also know that you are usually two to three months further along than you admit to me," said Peloreid. "What I want is the real date."

Sinclair flushed. It was true that he padded his time estimates to Peloreid. That always allowed him to complete his tasks on time, if not early. He had assumed that Peloreid recognized this fact, but this was the first time that he had been accused of the practice.

"Well, we have the cloth woven to include the fiber optic thread. It's really the download device that is causing the issue right now."

"And why is that. I would think downloading would be the easy part."

"To develop a capable device is quite easy. In fact, it's done. The problem is that it's big. It's doubtful that we can use it unnoticed."

"Explain."

"As you know, the fiber optic thread we've developed is itself a long, thin micro processor. It's able to trap and record sound and video like a recording device and uses its entire length as storage. That part is fine. The issue is removing the stored data from the tread. Depending on the amount stored, it can take several minutes. And the retrieval download device is very large in order to probe and extract the entire length of the tread. Additionally, the thread is interwoven with normal threads so the retrieval device has to penetrate those to retrieve the data stored below. It's all requires a large, powerful monitoring processor and a number of minutes to complete. We haven't developed a smaller, faster device yet. Otherwise, we feel that it would be too noticeable. Even putting the monitor in something like an elevator wouldn't work because the normal ride isn't long enough. That's our struggle."

"But, the technology works?"

"It has tested out perfectly. Now it's about the miniaturization of the retrieval device."

"How close does the garment need to be to the device?"

"Within about six feet. Probably closer with a smaller device."

"And the thread really records all sound and video?"

"Too much. That was part of the problem. Much of the data is useless. The ruffling of the fabric. The wind. Only about three percent of the sound is useful. The video also has caused problems because there's too much data. The thread is like a 360 degree camera. Obviously, more than half the thread is either inward facing or covered by other threads. That part of the video is useless. We have developed software filters to use on the data, but that has taken a great deal of time. Also, all the sound and video requires a huge amount of storage capacity before we can get to filter the data. Hence the long download times."

"Are you sure this thread is not detectable by security scanners?" questioned Peloreid.

Sinclair looked up at him quickly. Just who was he planning to monitor, he wondered? "The device is only slightly thicker than a single thread. While its presence would be detected if it were in a mass, the long, thin nature of the device makes it essentially undetectable. Most sensors look for concentrated electronic current so, to sensors, it is invisible."

Peloreid nodded in understanding. "I would like to see a prototype garment by next week," he demanded.

Sinclair nodded. "Anything in particular?" he queried with a slight smile on his face. By now, he knew when Peloreid was up to something.

"Area Security Manager."

Sinclair stopped smiling. Peloreid was serious about tracking someone at a fairly senior level. "Do you require a particular size?"

"Ah, good question. I'll have the answer to you by the end of the day."

"Yes, sir, Citizen Peloreid." Sinclair stood as Peloreid stood and left the room. Why does Peloreid want to know what an Area Security Manager is up to? They're all his people, loyal to him more than anyone else. Does he think one might be a security risk? Sinclair ran through the list of area managers in his head. He couldn't see a weak link. None of them were even on the radar of the Liberty Tree. They were devoted to the government. So, why does Peloreid want one of them monitored? Sinclair knew that Peloreid never did anything without a motive. He was up to something, and, if it involved one of his area security managers, it was something big.

Sinclair was correct. Peloreid was up to something. Something big. Peloreid allowed a smile to creep across his face during the elevator ride back to his office. The plan had materialized. Most of it was in place before the Development Lab update. But that information had finalized it. Peloreid knew how to gain access to Tonklin's inner security circle, although it would cost him one of his most trusted assistants. Now, he knew how to gather the information on their plot. While it was not impossible for the plan to go wrong, it had a better likelihood of success than many he had attempted. Of course, the consequences of failure had been much smaller for those. Hushing up a poor operation or project could usually be done if it wasn't highly visible. But this one would be for the Chairman of the Supreme Council and include a high ranking member of the government. This operation was definitely a high visibility one so it had to be right. The consequences were too dismal to consider. And so, before Peloreid picked up the phone to schedule a meeting with the Chairman, he ran through the plan again in his mind. He would have liked to have seen the garment before committing, but that would cost more time. Could he wait that long to begin initiation? He didn't think so.

Citizen Security Regent Peloreid's hand was shaking as he pushed the intercom button on the telephone. "Get me an appointment with Chairman Baucman," he instructed his assistant. Then, he turned in his chair to face the window, looking out at the sky which approached dusk. He knew that a momentous event had been put in motion. He had yet to realize how right he was.

Five stories below him, Andrew Sinclair began typing into his computer system. As with every project initiated by his department, he needed to set up the security protocol to be used.

"FOG LTI" he typed.

"Fiber Optic Garment—Live Trial I"

"Security Clearance Required—Level 5—My Eyes Only"

He paused after typing the last line. Would this cause a stir? Would people begin questioning why only he could see the data results from the fiber optic garment? In his gut, he knew Peloreid's demands were caused by something big. This could be the event that the Tree had long waited for. It would be a little earlier than they had anticipated. But he knew that this project would be a part of the true revolution, the Second American Revolution towards which they had worked for so long. He needed to know what the data showed first, before anyone else. But, if high level government forces like a Security Regent and an Area Security Manager were involved, he wasn't sure if his presence on the project would raise eyebrows. He was never involved in live operations, only development and testing. How could he set up the security without drawing attention to himself?

Sinclair picked up the phone and dialed an extension he rarely used. He asked for the person and was put on hold momentarily.

"Peloreid here," came the voice on the other end.

"Sir, it's Sinclair. I'm setting up the security protocol for the test we discussed. I sensed that it was highly confidential so I wonder if we should restrict access to the test results."

"Absolutely," declared Peloreid. "This is most sensitive."

"If you like, Sir, I can put my name as the analyst so the results would be for my eyes only. That would ensure that no one else in the development area or lab could access the data. It's a little more work on my end, but it would enhance the security."

"So, do it," replied Peloreid, sounding indignant that his time should be wasted with such administrative decisions.

"Of course, Sir. I just need your approval since this is outside the normal protocols. If you give me just a moment, I'll record your voice authorization into the database. One moment."

Peloreid sighed. He hadn't considered of others gaining access to the information from Tonklin. Of course, now that he thought about it, he would need someone to do a first pass, filtering the data and sending it to him. While Sinclair wouldn't have been his first choice, he was in charge of development and had the highest security clearance available. And, at least that would mean only one set of eyes to eliminate if it came to that.

"OK, sorry Sir. Here we go. This is voice authorization from Security Regent Peloreid for Security Development Lab Director Sinclair to set security protocol as my eyes only for project FOG—LTI. That's Fiber Optic Garment, Live Test One. Is that correct Security Regent Peloreid?"

"This is Security Regent Peloreid. Security protocol set at Director Sinclair's eyes only for FOG—LTI."

"Thank you, Security Regent. That was all I needed. Sorry to bother you but I wouldn't want everyone to know about our little test here."

"No. That was good thinking." He hung up the phone. That was good thinking. Sinclair was sharper that he had given him credit for. He was obviously intelligent, but now he had shown a level of loyalty and discretion that Peloreid had never noticed before. Those were traits that a new Supreme Councilor would need in their Security Regent. He'd have to keep that in mind.

Sinclair smiled as he completed the security documentation. Now, he would be the first one to see everything from Peloreid's little surveillance project. Whoever he was spying on would be known to Sinclair before anyone else. From all the signals that he had heard from his Liberty Tree contacts, cracks were beginning to form in the government's façade of unity. As was natural, human cravings for power were overwhelming their original idealism, if in fact idealism ever drove their actions. But now, Sinclair felt that a different revolution was approaching. The time was drawing ever nearer for something that he had worked towards for many years.

13

Charles' life had taken on new meaning after the clandestine meeting with Andrew and Albert. The pictures of his parents were etched into his mind. The contact with Andrew had given him a link to his past that was more than he could have hoped for and he had every intention of learning everything he could. If they weren't his own memories, Andrew's were the next best thing.

By eating only the unprocessed vegetables that he received daily, Charles had avoided the sedatives included in the other processed foods he was served. He had stopped taking his "vitamins" several weeks before and, the combination of these two efforts enabled his memories to partially return. It didn't happen all at once but through short glimpses of his past. A sight, a sound, a word overheard in a stranger's conversation, any of these could trigger a sudden insight into his past. They would be memories which would only last for a few seconds, but it was a reattachment to his parents, his childhood, to the reality of who he was as a person.

As these fleeting moments occurred, his hatred of Barahu and his government grew. It bred in Charles' heart and he could feel it growing a little more each day. How dare Barahu or his Supreme Council, or anyone else for that matter, decide which memories he could keep and which he needed to forfeit for the good of the state. Was there anything more personal than your memories? Did he have no right to really own anything? Was every fiber of his body, his mind, and his spirit owned by the government? The arrogance was appalling to him. He couldn't believe that one elitist group of people decided that they knew what was best for everyone regardless of what the individual might feel. Charles' identity had been stolen from him, a victim of the drugs used to erase his mind. He desperately wanted to get it back. To him, it was becoming more important than life itself. He watched the people moving around him, sedated so that they wouldn't recognize their own circumstances, controlled so they wouldn't have either the energy or the willingness to question, much less overturn, the government that imprisoned them with invisible chains. As everyone had to work to support not their own necessities and pleasures but those of the state, they had become enslaved to the decisions of the government. Charles saw that it was a house of cards, a pyramid scheme that doomed each successive generation to more enslavement by Barahu.

It was a simple premise really. The government gave you everything you needed. Then, once you had total reliance on the government for your food, clothing, medical care and shelter, you wouldn't dare disrupt the government. And so, to receive the necessities of life, you did what you were told. You willingly enslaved yourself to their demands. Eventually, the population would know of nothing else. They would never threaten the very institution that saw to all of their needs. The circle would be complete, from a government working for the people to people working for the government. And it would all start innocently enough by the government officials declaring that a "redistribution of wealth" would solve all the problems. That simple statement, willingly accepted by the populace that thought they would receive something for free, would begin the enslavement of a people. Even then, Barahu didn't trust that everyone would fall in line, even after exterminating most of his opposition, so he tainted their food with chemicals to stunt their thoughts. Or, he gave them a Procedure 23 to eliminate their memories harmful to him while maintaining those helpful to him. Or, he would just kill them. Procedure 66 was a much more innocent term than murder.

The anger welled in Charles. Barahu had taken his memories, his parents, his freedom. But, as the chemical imposed haze continued to lift, he saw his way to fight back. He would help the Liberty Tree. He would find a way to slow down development of the new sedative and to counteract the effects of the old one. That had started immediately after his initial meeting with Andrew and Albert and, within days, he had a plan developed in his mind. Now, he needed to see if he could put it in motion.

"Alright, that concludes our briefing for today. Are there any questions?" asked Chemical Development Lab Director Horner at the end of their weekly status update session. Charles raised his hand. "Yes, Citizen Johnson?"

"I'm afraid I'm having some issues recalling the neurological interference capabilities of our Omega 4 and Alpha 12 formulations. I believe these are the foundation of the current formulation, are they not?"

Horner nodded at Charles, a slight frown on his face. "Yes, you should know. You were the primary development scientist on both of those chemicals."

"Yes, but that was before my accident. I'm afraid that I can't recall the details of those interactions. It's making it difficult for me to comprehend the changes that would occur from using the Omega 7 formulation or by adding the Theta 1 component. I was hoping someone could work with me to refresh my memory."

"Hmm," muttered Horner, grasping his chin in one hand and pacing across the front of the conference room. He looked at his feet, pondering Charles' request. "That does pose a difficulty. You were the expert. Omega 4 and Alpha 12 were introduced before most of the others were part of the team. Everyone else has either been reassigned or has retired, I'm afraid. Would you be able to remember if you reviewed the original test data?" he asked hopefully.

"I would hope so, but it would probably take me a little longer that way."

"Yes, I'm sure it would but I don't see any other way. What would this do to the timeline for our initial test trials? They're due to begin by the end of the year. That's less than two months away."

"I think I'd need at least two weeks to review all the data. Assuming that I have a limited number of follow up questions, say another week or so. That would mean at least a month before I felt confident in moving forward."

"A month delay in continuing the formulation? Hmm, that's not good," replied Horner, continuing to pace without looking up at anyone on the team. "Robertson, what does that do to the testing schedule?"

A short, mustached scientist responded, "That would not be a major issue. We've found about half of the required test subjects from people about to be retired. An extra month would provide more than enough time to validate the remainder of the test subjects. We'll just have to guarantee that none of the subjects already accepted are retired before the testing begins. No, for me this is not a hindrance but a help," he finished with a look of relief on his face.

"And Murray, what about the delivery system development?"

"Well, we've developed the inert ingredients based on our current formulation," replied a tall, thin, rather dull looking woman from the back of the room. "I don't see any issue unless the Omega 7 or Theta I causes an unforeseen interaction with one of the inerts. Not impossible but, I think, most unlikely. No delay at all from our end."

"Do we feel that the testing can be shortened to make up for the delay caused by Development and Test Supply?" asked Horner. While Charles continued to look at the other scientists in the room, Robertson's face turned pale and he looked nervously around the room at the others. It was apparent to Charles that Robertson would not have acquired enough suitable test subjects if the testing wasn't delayed. He had hoped that this fact would go overlooked due to the delay Charles had introduced, but Horner was too smart for that. Robertson would share in the notoriety of the delay. While Charles wasn't sure what the penalty was, based on Robertson's response, it probably wasn't good. Charles felt that his excuse, that the government had inadvertently erased some memories that he might need, would be justification enough for him. Obviously, Robertson didn't have that luxury.

"I'm not sure how we can," replied Charles. "I believe we've already removed one round of testing due to delays caused by my accident. I'm not sure that we would have a very good statistical basis if we remove more testing." Charles surveyed the room and saw nodding heads and murmurs of agreement from the others. "I'm afraid I'm the main culprit behind the delay. I wish that accident had never happened."

Charles saw Horner raise his head suddenly with his last words. He knew, Charles thought. He knew that what happened had been no accident. Charles wondered if Horner felt he was a threat to Barahu's government. Did he even care? Based on the look on Horner's face, Charles didn't think so. Like the other bureaucrats he had seen here, they were only worried about their own jobs and performance. As long as they had a scapegoat, they could care less about anyone else. Charles had banked on this.

"Very well, I agree. I guess it can't be helped."

"Perhaps, Director Horner, I may be able to develop a recommendation for lengthening the useful life of the current formulation," offered Charles.

"Explain," responded Horner.

"Perhaps, I can develop a small increase in the current ingredients or a simple additive that allows our current formulation to be used a little longer. That could make up for the delay."

"Do you think that's possible?"

"I believe it might be. Of course, we can't just increase the dosage without causing irreversible neurological damage, but we may be able to adjust the ratio slightly, or add a very small dosage of another ingredient. That could buy us at least a couple of months longer. If it's a chemical component currently in use, we wouldn't need the testing required for new development."

"Uh-hm," Horner nodded. "Yes, we'd only need to increase it for a short period of time. As long as there were no long term negative reactions, we could get away with it. Good. I like it. When can you have it to me?"

Charles pondered the question for a moment. He already knew the answer, but he didn't want to seem too forthcoming. "Let me review the data and I'll give you an update by next week's meeting. I feel pretty confident that we can do it," he concluded, with a nod of his head and a smile.

Horner returned both the nod and smile. "Very well. Meeting adjourned," he said, heading for the door. Horner knew that the delay would not be taken well by Security Regent Peloreid. Delays of less than this had caused some Development Lab Directors to disappear overnight. That was one of the things that had bothered Horner about this position from the moment it had been offered. He had rather liked his predecessor so, when he was told that his predecessor had retired due to a failed experiment for what would become Procedure 23, he was reluctant to replace him. But, of course, you couldn't decline a promotion. At least this delay could be explained. He didn't know why Johnson had needed a Procedure 23. To be honest, he didn't care. He was happy to have him back on the team now. Charles Johnson was the brightest chemist he had ever known. Horner had been hard pressed to replicate his knowledge while he was recovering. Now he was back and the team was functioning fairly well again. After a procedure like Johnson had endured, some memory lapses were to be expected. At least, that's what he would tell Peloreid in a few moments. And, if they could introduce an extension to the current formula, they would be no worse off. For a bad report, this was about as good as he could do.

Horner stepped into his office and dialed a number on his phone. "This is Chemical Lab Director Horner. I need to speak with Security Regent Peloreid," he said to Peloreid's assistant.

"Reason for your call?" Peloreid's assistant asked.

"Important update on the Food Additive III project," he replied.

"One moment."

The line went dead. Horner' forehead was sweating and his heart began to beat more rapidly. It was never good to present bad news and he never knew what it would take to be prematurely retired. He hoped his excuse would be acceptable to the most powerful person Horner knew.

Peloreid hung up the phone. A delay on the Food Additive III project. Usually, such a problem would cause him to be infuriated. Someone would pay dearly for their error. But today, he was more concerned with other matters. It sounded like Horner had things under control. Something about side effects of Procedure 23 for Johnson...he didn't remember any Johnson on the list but, no matter. The end result would be the same. The current sedative would be extended somehow and the new one would be introduced after the required testing. Blah, blah, blah. How Peloreid detested these scientist and their babble! They always seemed to sound smarter than him, even without trying. Of course, intelligence wasn't the primary requirement to reach the highest levels of power, now was it? Cunning, loyalty, and sacrifice were what mattered in those circles. He was definitely cunning. He was loyal to those that could help him the most. While that person had changed from time to time, his loyalty had always been to that person. And sacrifice. He was about to sacrifice someone that had been immensely loyal to him. But that was how the system worked. Sometimes you had to sacrifice people close to you in order to achieve your objective. If you weren't willing to do that, you were no better off than the ignorant scientist in the lab, going about their business with no appreciation of the what Peloreid was about to do. Indeed, he would forfeit anyone to get what he wanted. So, a two month delay on a food additive meant nothing to him today. He was too concerned with the sacrifice he would be making tonight.

The plan had come together. Sinclair had delivered the garment and shown him the audio and video recordings from the fiber optic thread. Peloreid was thrilled to see the clear video images. The downside was the size of the retrieval monitor, but he had already thought of a plan for that. Now, he just had to get his test subject to wear the garment. Once that was done, he felt confident that he would have access to Councilor Tonklin's plan. He was hoping to get approval from Chairman Baucman, but had been disappointed at their meeting.

"Security Regent Peloreid, please understand that I am very happy that you have developed a plan for our, ah, shall we say situation? However, you must understand that I cannot be aware of your plan or its details. How could I feign ignorance if it is uncovered if, in fact, I know all about it? No, it would never do for me to have knowledge of, or certainly to give approval to, a plan which may actually be illegal. No, no, my dear Peloreid. We have a firm understanding. You of the objective that was discussed and me of the reward if successful. That is all we need to discuss."

It had been short, but not sweet. Peloreid was on his own. If he failed, he knew the consequences. But, if he were successful, he would be a member of the Supreme Council, the most elite level of government. And so, Peloreid had the authority to do as he saw fit and the responsibility to get it done. It would require a large sacrifice, but the reward was worth it.

So now it was time. He could tell by the darkening sky but he looked at his watch for confirmation. He went to his desk and unlocked a drawer. Opening it, he shuffled around a few objects before he came to the envelope he wanted. It had been some time since he had needed this. Over two years in fact. His mind went back to the years that it had taken for him to climb this far. It had required strong action, harsh, perhaps excessively harsh at times, but necessary to get this far.

At first, it was ideology. Barahu had captivated the world. His mere presence was enough to silence all but the most bitter of rivals. He was tall, strong, and intelligent. He gave a vision of life where all people shared in the bounty. Wealth redistribution. Tax the rich. Barahu had been a disciple of Marx, Mao, and Lenin, but he had taken it to heights never before seen in Western societies. Europeans had dabbled in full socialism. Russia had the façade of socialism but it was really despotism. Other European countries provided government largess, but none had dared take over all industry. Some countries had, but most had been small. Castro and

Chavez had been contemporaries that had survived repeated attempts to usurp their authority. But Barahu had outdone them all.

Peloreid had seen the opportunity. He was poor, with no job, no education. Why should others get big houses and fancy cars? Why should they be able to buy whatever they desired? Hard work? He could work hard too if he so chose. Education? Sure, some had gone to college and worked to improve themselves. But school had never come that easily to him. Did they understand how hard he would have to study to get through college? Ridiculous! So, when officials were willing to give him money, why shouldn't he take it? He was as deserving as the next person. And, if some fat cat was paying for it, so much the better. He hadn't had the advantages that others did. But that made him no less deserving. He could remember the warnings of those wealthy entrepreneurs and business people. "We're dooming our children and grandchildren." What did he care? He didn't have any kids. "There is no free lunch! Someone has to pay for all of these things." Sure there's a free lunch and, of course, someone else would be paying for it. If that someone else is some greedy millionaire who didn't deserve what they'd gotten, so much the better. All he had to do was vote for the socialists and his lifestyle would be maintained forever, on someone else's dime.

But, eventually, others stopped seeing it that way. They started voting against the promises of Barahu. That was the flaw in the system, that others could decide who made the rules. It wasn't right, it wasn't fair. Now, after years of the government supporting him, they would take that away? No, it couldn't happen that way.

Luckily, Barahu saw the warning signs. He formalized the Purple Shirts into is private police force. They would stop the anti-Barahu demonstrations. Watch them run like scared little chickens when some people with baseball bats show up and crack a couple of heads! He had joined willingly after seeing some of the Purple Shirts in action. We wanted to be part of something big, something that would ensure that his way of life was maintained. So, some blood needed to be spilled. That was work he was willing to do.

Peloreid thought back to those days with a rush of excitement. How close it had been! Many Purple Shirts had been arrested. Luckily, the judges were mostly on their side. They wanted Barahu to succeed. Most of the media portrayed Barahu opponents to be greedy, wealthy opportunists that were heartless. When other media outlets disagreed, Barahu took over the Internet, television, and radio waves. He thought of everything. Except, the opposition continued to mount. Un-democratic. Un-American. Un-Constitutional. The attacks kept coming. Peloreid gave a little shudder as he remembered the last election. Barahu had lost! Had the world gone mad? How could the people of his country choose someone other than the Chosen One? How could they not understand the wisdom of the Supreme Being? That they would choose someone else to replace him was unconscionable.

Barahu only had months to react. Most thought he was finished, but not Peloreid. He had never given up hope. And so, while many left the ranks of the Purple Shirts, he stayed, and flourished. With each departure, he moved up. When there was a particularly nasty or gruesome job to do, he volunteered. He would prove his worth and loyalty in a thousand different ways. And he had.

Peloreid had a key role in the main act. He had planted the explosives in the largest gathering of Barahu opponents in this sector. He had carefully ensured that all evacuation routes were covered, that the fleeing bodies would run into more mayhem, more murderous bombs. Yes, he had been only one of dozens of such events across the country. But, his had been the biggest. And the most lethal. When the smoke had cleared, thousands of Barahu opponents, including the woman elected to replace him, were dead. Of course, they had to kill some of their own supporters. Otherwise, it would have been too obvious. Barahu was a genius at the spin. Terrorists had done it to disrupt the country. Martial law was required. National, state, and local governments would relinquish all control to his government until security was restored. Since the most senior members of his opposition were killed, few opposed him. The populace was in shock. They needed to trust him, he told them. And they did.

It was over 30 years later. Martial law was still in force, but was a way of life now. Within a couple of months of its imposition, the citizenry had begun to revolt. But, it was locals with shotguns against a well trained army. Barahu had ensured that the military was loyal to him above all others. The Purple Shirts had played a crucial role as well, weeding out the insurgents. Extracting lists of people involved with the opposition. They had killed millions. Tens of millions. They needed to. By doing so, they stabilized the population to a level that could be supported. Now, there were jobs for everyone. By eliminating the sick and elderly, Barahu had saved the country trillions of dollars in support payments. There was security, both economically and politically. Life was good. And, the loyal, dedicated Peloreid had been rewarded.

From time to time, there was still an occasional obstacle to overcome. Which is why he kept these items in this locked desk drawer. You never knew when you had to remove an obstacle. Or, in this case, sacrifice a supporter. But, it happened. Just as Barahu had to sacrifice millions to achieve his vision, so too did Peloreid need to sacrifice to achieve his.

He closed and relocked the desk drawer. Straightening up, he carefully placed the envelope into his side tunic pocket. Sliding into his winter overcoat, he glanced around his office. Dull, drab, metallic gray. Only Barahu's framed picture looked down at him from the wall. Perhaps people would refer to him as dull, drab, and gray as well. But not for long. His image was due for an upgrade.

Peloreid got into the backseat of his waiting car. As the driver pulled away, he reached for one of the crystal tumblers next to the scotch whiskey decanter. Alcohol was one of the privileges of his position, and one of the few treats that he could offer subordinates. He looked at the wrinkled envelope with its faded writing on the outside. It had been years since he needed to use this. He had doubted that he would ever need it again. But, his intuition had made him hold onto it, and tonight he was glad he had. It would be much cleaner than the other methods. No bloodshed. A delayed reaction so he wouldn't have to witness it. Distasteful tasks had never bothered him before, but this one was different. Yes, he'd disposed of many subordinates in the past, but they had always done something to warrant it. Joyce Clifford only had her name in the wrong position on a list. She had been nothing other than a loyal and devoted servant. But now, she was an impediment to his progress. A roadblock. Well, maybe more of a speed bump. Still, it was the first time that Peloreid actually felt some remorse for what he was about to do. He thought of Joyce's smile, how she always seemed to be in a good mood. He would miss that. Such a sacrifice that he was making.

He steadied his hand on the side of the glass and poured some of the white powder into it. He then carefully tipped the envelope up and shook the remaining powder back down into its bottom. He refolded the envelope and slid it back into his coat pocket. As the car approached the curb, he could see Area Security Manager Joyce Clifford waiting at the curb. He quickly poured some of the brown scotch whiskey into each glass, watching to ensure that the powder dissolved fully in her glass. The car came to a halt and the driver jumped out to open the door for Clifford.

"Good evening, Security Regent Peloreid," she exclaimed with a wide smile as she slipped into the seat next to Peloreid. The driver closed the door and then Joyce leaned over to Peloreid and kissed him once on each cheek. "I hope this evening finds you well."

"Very well, Citizen Clifford," he replied, formally but with a smile on his face. "Due to the chill in the air, I brought something to warm us both up," he continued, motioning to the waiting glasses.

"Oh, very nice," she said, reaching excitedly for her glass as Peloreid did the same. "To be honest, I've been dying for a nip for weeks now."

Peloreid's heart skipped a beat. "Dying for a nip?" How ironic that she should use that term. And, he could have sworn that she was smelling the glass and staring at it before drinking. Did she know? How could she? Smiling at him, she raised the glass to her lips and took in a big mouthful. He watched her swirling it around in her mouth before swallowing. A smile spread across her face, and he finally relaxed and took a sip himself.

He watched her intently. He knew that the effects wouldn't begin for a couple of hours. It was the delay, combined with the almost undetectable nature of the poison that made it such an effective weapon.

"So, I'm sure there was more than good scotch that you wanted me for at such short notice," she said, staring at Peloreid with her big, brown eyes.

"Yes, Joyce, there is. I need to know everything you know about Oliver Matthews," he replied, an official sound to his voice.

She looked at him, a slight look of surprise on her face. He rarely used her first name, although it was not totally unheard of.

But to ask about Oliver Matthews? That was very odd. As Security Regent, he had a much better dossier on all security agents and government officials that did she. Why would he ask such a strange question?

"Well, let me see," she began in response to his unusual question. "I think, I think. . " The car was getting blurry all of the sudden. The lights in the ceiling and sides were spinning. She was getting an odd feeling in her throat and chest.

Peloreid stared at Clifford, a sense of dread spreading throughout him. Her eyes were beginning to roll and she was stretching out her hand, seeking for something to grab onto. Peloreid hadn't expected this. The powder wasn't supposed to begin its work for hours. What was happening? What was going wrong?

Clifford began tugging at her coat, moving her hands to her throat as if to remove the clothing that was slowly strangling her. Her throat was closing. She began gasping for breath. Her stomach and lungs were beginning to burn, as if acid had invaded her body. She looked towards Peloreid, her old friend and mentor. She was screaming for him to help her, but no sound was coming from her mouth. The only sound was a gurgling from deep in her stomach. Her eyes were watering, tears streaming down her face. She reached out for Peloreid, wanting his help, desperately needing him to help her breathe.

Peloreid stared. Clifford's face had turned red, and now was bluish. Her hands were at her throat. She began thrashing, twisting in pain as the poison attached her stomach, intestines and lungs. She began coughing. At first, it was phlegm and then it turned crimson, as her lungs exploded and the blood began spewing through her mouth.

She kicked her feet, her body convulsing automatically as the poison made its way throughout. Her vision dimmed, and then she was in darkness, her last image that of Peloreid's contorted face. Why didn't he help her? What had he done to her? Those thoughts were driven from her mind as she frantically tried to save herself, without knowing what was happening. She felt the blood rushing from her throat, through her lips and felt its warmth falling across her hands, face and chest.

As the blackness continued to close around her, Joyce Clifford made one last painful convulsion and then lay perfectly still.

Peloreid stared at the body before him. It was covered in blood, as was his coat and much of the car. He had not wanted this. He hadn't wanted it to be painful, or to be in his presence. She was just supposed to go to sleep, gently slipping into a sleep from which she would never awaken. It wasn't supposed to be like this. He was supposed to have been removed from it. He had to do something, but what? He couldn't just pull up to her domicile unit like nothing had happened. What could he do? The reports would be everywhere when her body was discovered. And, if it was discovered that he had poisoned his own deputy, the trial would be swift. His execution would be almost immediate. And, he was sure, that it would be at least as painful as Clifford's death.

His brain immediately turned from the horror of the death scene he had just witnessed to something even more powerful for Peloreid, self-preservation. He pounded on the security screen between him and the driver. The wheels of his mind were spinning as he thought of a way to conceal his crime.

The screen lowered and he could see the face of the driver reflected in the rear view mirror. "Quickly," Peloreid screamed to the driver, "get us to the nearest medical unit. Something terrible has happened!"

The driver stared at Peloreid. While he couldn't see Clifford's lifeless body, he could see the blood on Peloreid's face and coat and the terror in his face.

"NOW!" screamed Peloreid and the car immediately accelerated. Peloreid raised the security screen. He took Clifford's glass from the holder and poured the remainder into his own glass. Then, he took the envelope from his pocket and poured the rest of the powder into the decanter. He shook it slightly, trying to hold it steady as the limo careened around a corner. He took a napkin and wiped down the bottle. Then he stopped. No, he couldn't do that. They would expect to find his fingerprints, and only his on the bottle. He took it and removed the stopper, pouring a little more of the liquid into his own glass. Then, he restored it to its holder.

He looked down at the grotesque body lying next to him. Joyce Clifford's face had always worn a smile, but now the last memory he would carry of her would be this. Her face was contorted, covered with blood. Her neck was covered in deep scratches from her own fingers caused as she had clawed at the invisible tourniquet that had choked the life from her. Her eyes, still opened, reflected the pure horror that was her last moment.

The car came to a screeching halt at a medical unit emergency entrance. An orderly, warned that a senior government official was on his way, hurried over and opened the door. The limp body fell against the ground as the orderly made a crude attempt to catch her. The sight of her caused him to pause, startled at the blood covering her face and chest. He had never seen a sight such as this.

"Hurry, you fool," cried the uniformed man in back seat of the limousine. His face was a mixture of anger and fright. "She needs a doctor."

The orderly picked up the woman and placed her into the waiting wheelchair. He turned and hurriedly pushed her towards the emergency room. Looking down, he saw her vacant eyes. He noticed her uniform, covered with her own blood. No, he thought, this woman doesn't need a doctor. She's well past that now.

14

Charles was awake and showered before the government had turned on his lights in the morning. He rushed down to the lobby to get his breakfast, which he flushed as soon as he'd returned to his unit. He was taking no chances with ingesting any added sedatives from his processed food. He checked his watch and, at seven minutes before eight o'clock, he put on his coat and walked down to the entryway. At five to eight, he walked out and waited for the transport. He looked around but saw nothing out of the ordinary. No one unusual was standing along the street. He didn't see Andrew or Albert anywhere around. All he saw was the blue sky with a few traces of clouds, the light layer of snow lying where the breeze had deposited it, and a few pieces of paper blowing along, unobstructed by any automobiles on the empty street. He was alone, cold, with a feeling of abandonment.

It was almost as if his rendezvous had never happened. It seemed like another one of his dreams which, while it was realistic as he slept, faded into obscurity when he awoke. But even as these thoughts passed through his mind, he could see the photos of his parents with the Sinclairs and with him. That was his face in the picture. Those were the faces of his parents, the same ones that dominated his sleep. And, the flashes of memory, of his youth and adolescence, his college years, of discussions with his parents around a dinner table, these flashes kept coming, like a constant drip from a faucet. They were random, sometimes in bunches, and could leave him as quickly as they came. Then, he'd be left with a feeling of emptiness, of something that had been in his grasp and then lost. No, not lost, he thought. Taken from him. It was that feeling that overwhelmed him now.

There were times that he hated his life, when he wished that the procedure would have been a 66 instead of a 23. To have lived for, what, 42 years, in reality he didn't know, and remember only the barest of moments was torturous. He began to sense that he was being driven by his anger towards the government which first took his parents, and then took his memories of his life. He also could see that his anger was becoming his obsession. He wanted to hurt the big, all knowing, all seeing government which restricted his movements, eliminated his ability to make even the most basic choices in his life, and would 'retire' those people who objected to their arrogance.

He hated them. He could name only Barahu, and it was his face that became the target for Charles' anger. The videos and pictures that he'd seen during the reorientation had shown a tall, thin man who was constantly posing for cameras. The man appeared to always be 'on', an actor always playing a part. He spoke about providing for the poor, taking care of the elderly, doctoring the ill. But Charles saw his eyes, he sensed that there was no conviction behind the words. They were the words that the populace wanted to hear. And he would tell them anything they wanted, as long as, with each word, they ceded more and more authority to him. Let me run your life, and you'll like it. That's what he meant. I'm smarter than you, so let me make all the decisions for you. Self-determination? Personal choices? You don't want that. What if you're wrong? Then you have to take responsibility for the lousy condition of your life. No, you'd be much better off with me making all the decisions. Then, you have no responsibility for anything. I, Barahu, the Supreme Being, the most intelligent and charismatic person ever to be placed upon this measly planet, I should have the responsibility. And, of course, the authority. If only Barahu had been that honest. But he never had been. And, once enough people had given up, the others had no choice.

The day moved slowly for Charles. He spent most of it reviewing the data from the original sedative formulation. There had been thousands of test subjects and hundreds of thousands of data points. While there had been reams of analysis, Charles' mind was not really engaged with the information. This was as much about convincing Horner that he couldn't remember as it was in jogging his memory. Charles was more concerned about finding a formulation which would offset the effects of the current sedative. So, he was searching for failed experiments, not successful ones, and that was taking much longer. He had an idea, one that he thought would work, but he needed some confirmation that he was correct. He hoped that it had been used in one of the original trials and ruled out. He had a dim memory of it, but wasn't sure.

As he made his way through the various reports, his mind began to see glimpses of what he needed. As with much of his recent recall, it was fuzzy and unclear, but it was there. He could almost make out the report in his mind. His heart began to pound. He was close, so close he could taste it. He could see himself reviewing a report from years ago. He could remember the frustration that he felt at the time because the formulation wasn't working the way he wanted. Now, he felt frustration because he couldn't remember what it was that caused the prior formulation to fail. He pulled file after file onto his computer screen, scanning the summary page. All of these showed the varying degrees of successful test results. It had to be earlier, before these. He went further back, six, then seven, then eight years back. He saw his name on the reports. If only he could remember writing them. But the memory wasn't there, at least not yet.

After several hours, he stopped. His eyes burned from looking at the screen. His head pounded from the force of will that Charles had exerted, compelling himself to remember what he could not. He looked at the clock. Two in the afternoon. His stomach rumbled. The lack of any breakfast and the stress of his search were causing a hunger that he tried to fight. How could he even think about eating, ingesting the very drugs that he was now seeking to block? Maybe just some water, he thought, rising from his desk and walking down the hallway towards the cafeteria.

"I thought you had died in there," said a woman's voice from behind Charles. He turned to see Charlotte Murray coming up behind him.

"Yeah, trying to remember everything I did five years ago," he replied with a slight smile. "It's like learning all over again."

"That must be tough," she said warmly, smiling at him. "Let me know if I can help at all. I wasn't part of the team back then but I can help pull data if you need me to."

"Thanks, I'll let you know. Right now, it's just getting to the right information to reorient myself." The term reorient stuck in his mind. That was the whole purpose of the reorientation center wasn't it. Not to help you remember but to change your orientation so you were pro-government, not anti. Now, he was seeking to reorient the formulation, from one that stunted your cognitive powers to one that allowed you to think freely.

"Oh, since I didn't see you at lunch, I grabbed yours for you," she stated, handing him a plastic container. "Can't have you starving on the job."

He took the container from her and smiled. "Thanks, I was just headed to get something. Saves me a trip."

"No problem. Like I said, let me know if I can help out," she finished, turning and heading back down the hall towards her office.

Now that was strange, thought Charles. While she'd never been cold towards him, he had never considered Charlotte to be the helpful type. She was reserved, as were most in the office, and somewhat standoffish. Charles continued down the hall, got a cup of water from the cooler, drank it and then refilled the cup before returning to his office. He sat down at his desk and opened the container. Inside was a salad of greens, cucumbers, and carrots as well as a packet of salad dressing. He tossed the dressing in the garbage, not taking any chances in that being drugged, and picked up a baby carrot that he bit into with a crunch.

His mouth stopped in mid-chew as he looked at the top of the container. On the inside cover was written "Sunday—9 AM—St. John's Cathedral." His heart skipped a beat. This had to be a message from the Liberty Tree, didn't it? What else could it be? But, who sent it? Was it Charlotte? Was she a member? Or had someone asked her to give it to him? He looked at the outside of the container. "C. Johnson" was written on the top in marker, the same writing as on the inside cover. There could be no mistake that the message was written for him. Sunday at 9 AM was obvious enough. But St. John's Cathedral? Where was that? What was that? While Charles had some vague notion of churches, his memory, largely based on the reorientation instruction, told him that they were some outdated gathering places that were seldom used anymore. Well, the seldom used part would make sense. But where was it? How would he find it without being too obvious? Since today was Thursday, he would have a couple of days to find it.

Great, he thought. Another mystery to figure out. Just what he needed. He threw the other half of the carrot into his mouth and munched, his heart a little lighter than it had been. We'll, at least he wasn't alone. The Tree had obviously been watching him. And, they must have people in the building. He wished he knew who they were. But, he understood how limiting each person's knowledge of the organization provided an important safety device. If someone was caught, they could provide two or three names, but it would take weeks and months to track down everyone. And by then, he was certain that key people would have gone into hiding. Still, it would be nice to know who his friends were. He took a bit of the salad and wished that he could trust the dressing. At least it was better than nothing and should stave off starvation for a while. Charles returned to his computer screen, more determined than ever to solve the formulation problem.

Several hours later, the bell rang notifying people that it was time to go. Charles shut down his computer. He looked at the box top again. He needed to dispose of it somehow. Having his name on the outside and the meeting time and place on the inside didn't make him feel too safe. He looked around for something to use to cover the writing. He had pens and pencils but those wouldn't cover up the marker. Should he cut it up? That would look odd, he thought. Who cuts up their food container? So, how do you make it so someone doesn't want to look at it, he wondered? Then he thought about the dressing. He pulled it out of the garbage, tore open the package and spread the thick, creamy white substance on the inside of the cover. He added some on the inside of the bottom tray as well and then stuck the bottom on the inside of the top, covering up the writing. The dressing held the two separate pieces of the container together. There, he thought. If anyone looks at it, it just appears to be the garbage left from his lunch. If someone is watching him, they'll find out where he was going anyways. At least the casual observer will probably be dissuaded from looking through his trash can. He rose, grabbed his coat, and switched out the light. The janitorial crew should remove the evidence when they cleaned his office that evening. Now, all he needed to worry about was what he would tell Andrew and Albert when he saw them Sunday.

Charles made his way to the lobby of the office building and bundled himself up against the bitterly cold wind that had enveloped the city. He stepped outside and walked to his normal spot at the curb, waiting with others that were going on his ETV. People going in other directions waited at their spots, just as they did every day. Most of the faces were familiar, even though Charles didn't know their names. No one spoke and most just stared straight ahead, looked down the street for the transport, or looked at their feet. Since everyone worked a six day week but had differing days off, the crowd changed slightly every day, but it was essentially the same. It was the routine, that mind numbing constancy which sometimes drove Charles mad. Of course, he was cleansing his body from the massive amounts of sedatives that the government forced on the unsuspecting population. And so, even if the routine wasn't numbing, most people's minds were anyways due to their daily intake of government mind control.

Charles, who had been looking at his feet, huddled with some others against the wind, heard a general murmur of excitement, something that had never occurred before at the stop. The crowd parted, pushing Charles back against his neighbors, everyone turning to see what was happening. A small bus had pulled up, and a number of purple shirted officers, actually purple jacketed officers due to the cold, had moved into the crowd. They had clubs out, as well as pistols and stun-guns. The crowd continued to back away from them, partly from their own fear and partly from the pushes of the Purple Shirts.

Charles felt his pulse rate quicken. Had he walked into their trap? Was Charlotte an informer for the deadly Purple Shirts? But, his logic kicked in. What had he done wrong, at least today? His lunch really proved nothing. He could always say that he hadn't even seen the note, or rather, that he saw it but didn't understand what it meant. Yes, that was better. He thought someone had just written down a reminder for themselves and didn't realize that it was on his container lid. Until he actually showed up on Sunday, he would be innocent. At least if he didn't include the initial meeting with Andrew and Albert. He watched, trying to slow his breathing, as an officer moved through the crowd, examining identification badges and matching the names to a list he had on a digital clipboard.

"Citizen Greene," the officer called out, standing in front of a large, brutish looking man of about 25 years old, "you are under arrest for conspiracy to commit murder."

The crowd moved away from the man who was now wearing a puzzled look on his face.

"Me? Commit murder? I don't know what you're talking about," he exclaimed in a mixture of confusion and fear.

"You are the Greene that lives in Unit 17, Block C, on 112th Street?" asked the officer, already knowing the answer.

"Yes."

"And, you live next to Citizen Weiner?"

"Yes."

"And you joined Citizen Weiner in attending the film presentations last week?"

"Yes, but we didn't…"

"Silence. Citizen Weiner has admitted to murder. He is now listing his accomplices and your name was provided. You will come with us," finished the officer, with a smug sense of contempt on his face.

"But, but, I didn't murder anyone. I don't know what you're talking about. He, he must be wrong. I didn't do anything at all. I don't know what you're talking about," Greene repeated, pleading with the officer and the crowd.

The senior officer stepped aside and nodded to a subordinate, who moved in with shackles for Greene. Greene automatically pulled back, moving closer to the crowd of people, even as they continued to move further back from him.

"Take him," shouted the senior officer.

Immediately, a large Purple Shirt moved in with a stun-gun. He struck Greene in the abdomen. The young man went rigid, his muscles involuntarily tightening. Uncontrollably, he fell forward on the officer that had just stunned him. The officer pushed him back and struck him again with the stun-gun in the neck. Greene's eyes bulged in their sockets as the second wave of electric current paralyzed his nervous system. This time, he fell to the side, smashing into the pavement with a thud and a crack.

Charles could see the man's face bleeding onto the concrete. Several fragments of his teeth were lying near his mouth as blood rushed out of him. His nose was also bleeding profusely, obviously broken from the fall. His body convulsed as the crowd watched, a group fear clutching them. The senior Purple Shirt looked around at them, smiling from the fear that he saw on their faces. Another officer went over to Greene and rolled him over by kicking him in the ribs with his boot. The body had stopped moving. Even the eyes were listless.

"I think he might be dead, Sir," said the officer quietly. He leaned down and placed his fingers on the man's neck, checking for a pulse. "Nothing. He's gone."

"You fool," cried the senior Purple Shirt, looking at the officer holding the stun gun. "Why did you hit him again?"

"He attacked me. You saw it. He came right after me."

"Idiot. He couldn't attack you. He was paralyzed. He just fell." The senior officer looked around at the crowd. He was losing his arrogance as the potential consequences of the error hit him. He cleared his throat before loudly stating, "All witness what happens to murderers and enemies of Barahu. Beware. Next time, we could come for you."

He turned looking down at the dead body. Then, he looked up at the officer holding the stun gun. With a sly smile, he asked, "So, what is it you didn't want him to tell us?"

"Sir? Excuse me?" spit out the officer, fear creeping into his eyes.

"There must be some reason you killed him. Why don't you take his place in the back of the van?" he said, motioning to two other officers to escort him.

The others took his stun-gun and belt, before shackling his arms and feet. They each grabbed an arm and half-walked, half-dragged the shaking officer to the van. The officers then moved back and took Greene's ankles, dragging the body along the concrete sidewalk to the street, before heaving him into the back of the paneled security van. They slammed the back doors shut and then moved back to the sidewalk, awaiting orders. The senior officer looked up from his digital clipboard after making a few marks on its surface. He looked once more at the crowd and then turned abruptly towards the van. One of the junior officers opened a door for him, and after closing it, jumped into the front passenger seat. The van moved off , disappearing from view as rapidly as it had emerged.

The crowd looked around at the sidewalk. There was a maroon circle of blood, which had been swept towards the curb by Greene's body. The crowd moved around it, staying several feet away. Three transports pulled up next to the curb in unison, having been kept waiting by the Purple Shirt's security van. The crowd piled on the appropriate ETV, which quickly departed.

Charles stared out the window at the stained sidewalk. A janitor was already there with a hose, spraying the blood and pieces of teeth down into the sewer drain. Within moments, no trace of Greene remained. How quickly Barahu and his Purple Shirts can erase your existence, thought Charles. Would that be him in a few days, he wondered?

Meanwhile, a trembling purple shirted officer was pulled from the security van and ushered into a confession chamber. The small room had a chair which was bolted to the floor. The shackles from his arms and legs were attached to the chair and he was left there, alone in the dark, empty room, to ponder his now perilous future.

Security Regent Peloreid looked at the officer as the door was being closed. He shook his head before turning to the senior officer that had been on the scene. "Report," he commanded.

"Well, sir," began the red faced, panicked officer.

"Your name and rank?" growled Peloreid between gritted teeth. He had been in a foul mood since the spectacle with Joyce Clifford. Things had spiraled out of control for several hours before he began to rein in the disorder. His luck, prestigious position, reputation, and quick thinking had most likely saved his career and quite possibly his life. By pouring the remainder of the poison in the whiskey bottle and some of that into his own glass, he had been able to convince the Internal Affairs Officer that someone had tried to poison him and that Area Security Manager Clifford had unwittingly saved his life by taking a drink first.

Of course, while this deflected suspicion from Peloreid, at least for the moment, the next question was who had access to his car that would have tried to murder him. The obvious answer was his driver, Citizen Weiner. He had been a good servant to Peloreid. Punctual, polite, and discrete. What more could you ask for in a servant? But, another sacrifice that he had made that night. He knew that Weiner was weak minded. He had lasted only three hours in the confession chamber before admitting to planning the murder of Peloreid. He gave no reason, but named a few accomplices. Peloreid, and for that matter probably those from Internal Affairs, could tell that Weiner was just providing any name he could think of. Peloreid stood by and watched the confession being extracted although he didn't particularly care for this examination.

Usually, he somewhat enjoyed watching the suspect forced to reveal the true nature of their crime and the others associated. He felt that it was their natural punishment, inflicted with maximum pain. It was the only way to protect the government, and thereby himself. Of the more than one hundred that he had witnessed over the past few years, intuitively he knew that the vast majority of people were innocent of any crime. But, the government had to inflict the pain. It was the only way to maintain the fear factor in the population. Who would be afraid of going into questioning and being given coffee and donuts? No, it was the threat of absolute pain, the kind that made you long for death, that would keep the population in line. And, if a few hundred innocent people had to undergo this, and some even die, then so be it. That's what would keep the Barahu government in power.

But the interrogation of the past few days was a little different. In his career, Peloreid had pulled hundreds of innocents in for questioning. But, this was the first time that someone was undergoing it to cover up something that he had done. He really didn't consider Clifford's murder as a crime. It was an inconvenient reality that sacrifices had to be made for the overall good, and by that he meant his overall good. The political animal that he had become was always about self-promotion above all else. He knew this. He understood it. And he saw nothing wrong with it. That was life. Someone would do it to him just as quickly so, if he beat them to the punch, so much the better. But he was taking no pleasure in Weiner's interrogation. Luckily, it didn't last long. Some went on for days. Weiner's had been a few hours. He gave some names of acquaintances, which Peloreid had ordered to be brought in for questioning. That should ease the concerns of Internal Affairs and allow him to pursue the investigation as he saw fit.

It had gone just as he had expected. Having been around political stooges for so long had its advantages, after all. He knew how they thought. He could put on the appropriate front, use the right voice, feigning disgust or anger. His theatrics had always been convincing, and they had worked again in this instance. But, a dead 'accomplice' and an officer under arrest were not things that he had planned. While neither was a large concern, although the officer could cause embarrassment, he didn't want to give Internal Affairs any reason to be poking their noses into his business. Not now, when he was so close to the goal. And so, his glare was real as he stared down his nose at the Purple Shirt Officer stammering in front of him.

"I'm sorry, Security Regent Peloreid. I am Senior Officer Franklen. I was in charge of the detail to apprehend suspect Citizen Greene."

"Continue."

"Yes, sir. We apprehended Greene as he was departing from his economic position location. He didn't come willingly at first, so Officer Barney stunned him. As the suspect fell, he was stunned again. I believe this killed him."

"Why was he stunned a second time?" requested Peloreid.

"Sir, Office Barney mistakenly believed that Greene was attacking him because Greene had fallen towards him. In pushing him away, Officer Barney stunned him again, killing him."

"I see. Incompetence. Total incompetence."

"I agree, sir. That's why I had him arrested as well. I wasn't sure if it was only incompetence or if Officer Barney was attempting to cover up some relationship that he might have with Greene."

Peloreid started at the officer. He didn't know whether to laugh or cry. The imbecile. Didn't he realize that he was talking about his incompetence, not Officer Barney's?

"Open the door," Peloreid instructed a guard. "Follow me," he said to Barney.

The two men moved into the room. The guard flipped the light switch to reveal a weeping security officer, his head on his chest, his whole body heaving with his sobs.

"Leave us," Peloreid ordered the guard. After the door closed, he turned to Barney. "Stop that damn crying," he bellowed. "Are you a Purple Shirt Security Officer or a baby?"

Officer Barney looked up at him. His tears had wetted his cheeks and run down to darken his purple jacket. Peloreid glared down at him.

"Do you know who I am?" he asked. The man nodded. "Answer me, damn it!" he shouted.

"Yes, Security Regent Peloreid," mumbled the officer.

"Good. Do you know why you're being held?"

"Because I killed the prisoner, Greene. But sir, it was an accident. I didn't mean to. I, I panicked. It just happened. And then Senior Officer Franklen ordered me held in case I might have done it on purpose. But sir..."

"Enough," barked Peloreid. He now turned his gaze upon Officer Franklen. "You told me in the hallway that Barney mistakenly believed that he was being attacked. How do you know this?'

"I have seen several people stunned, sir. I know that they have no bodily control immediately after being stunned."

"That's true. Did you know that?" he asked, turning back to Barney.

"No, sir. I, I never used the stunner before. I didn't know what it would do. I just thought that it sort of, just sort of froze the person."

"It makes their muscles freeze in a way," lectured Peloreid. "However, it does not diminish the laws of gravity. Why were you using a weapon that you hadn't been trained on?"

"Senior Officer Franklen told me to get it when we arrived, sir."

"So, Franklen, you had an untrained officer use a weapon. It that how you were taught?" glowered Peloreid. He was beginning to enjoy this playacting. But then, he had always enjoyed playing the bad cop.

"No, no, sir," stuttered Franklen. "I didn't realize that Officer Barney didn't have the appropriate training. I . . I"

"Is it not your job to know who has been trained on which weapons?" said Peloreid, continuing his interrogation.

"Yes. Yes, sir it is. I just, I just thought that . . "

"Enough," shouted Peloreid. He looked at Barney, who looked up at him, his face pleading for mercy. His eyes traveled over to Franklen. "It appears to me that we have one person here that is ignorant about weapons and one that is ignorant about leadership. Does that summarize the situation?"

Both men nodded.

"Answer me!"

"Yes, sir," said the officers in unison.

Peloreid could see the sweat break out on Franklen's forehead. His face had become ashen and it looked like he was very near to fainting. Good, Peloreid thought. Now, to reel in these fish. I'll make sure they will be forever in my debt. That's how loyalties are formed. He turned to face the two men.

"This was an unfortunate incident. Unfortunate in that the suspect did not do as instructed. His death sounds entirely accidental. I see no benefit in pursuing this matter further." He could see the relief break across the faces of each man. "Senior Officer Franklen, please review your team's training and see that each is fully up to date on all weapons and vehicles. I want to see your report on this matter by tomorrow morning. I see no need to include the section regarding Officer Barney. He was following orders and accidentally caused the death of a man that was attempting to avoid arrest. The details are not important."

Officer Franklen nodded and then, remembering Peloreid's earlier instructions said, "it shall be done, Security Regent Peloreid. And, thank you sir."

"And, Officer Barney, you are a highly skilled member of Emperor Barahu's Purple Shirt Security Forces. You're training is expected to be exemplary. See to it that you never again are untrained in any aspect of your duties."

"Yes, sir. I will, sir. Thank you, sir. I shall never forget your kindness sir," he stammered, the choked words coming out of his mouth as quickly as he could form them.

"And neither will I, sir. Anything you ever require, sir, you have only to ask," added Franklen.

"Good. Now, Barney is a member of your team. Why do you keep him shackled to a chair?" finished Peloreid.

Franklen's eyes widened and shot to the other officer. He thrust his hands into his pocket for the keys and immediately knelt on the floor to unlock Barney.

Peloreid went to the door and knocked, waiting for the guard to open it for him. As it swung open, he saw a nervous looking man standing by the wall on the other side of the hallway.

"These men are free to go,:" instructed Peloreid to the guard.

"Yes, sir," replied the guard, moving into the room to help Franklen unharness Barney.

"Excuse me, Security Regent Peloreid," interrupted the waiting man. "My name is Officer Matthews of Councilor Tonklin's Security Detail. I was instructed to report to you."

Peloreid smiled and nodded at the man. "Yes, Matthews. Please follow me to my office where we can talk," responded Peloreid, striding down the hallway towards a bank of elevators. Act II had just begun.

❖ ❖ ❖

15

"So, Officer Matthews, are you aware why I summoned you?" asked Peloreid, after they arrived at his office.

"No, sir," answered the pasty faced, middle aged man.

Peloreid observed the man, trying to gauge his value to Tonklin. His hair was graying prematurely and had thinned on the top of his head. He was developing a pudge around his middle. His eyes were droopy, his nose was round and lifted up slightly, giving him a piggish sort of face.

"Perhaps you've heard that Area Security Manager Clifford was assassinated three days ago?" queried Peloreid.

"Yes, sir, I had. A tragic loss."

"You are in line for the Area Security Manager position. You're seniority is ranking for the spot," explained Peloreid.

"Oh, really, sir. I didn't realize," said Matthews, shuffling nervously in his chair and pulling at his tunic collar. "I did hear that you two were very close. It must be very difficult for you to replace her so soon," he added.

"Yes. But, much as that is, the responsibilities of the state do not stop for funerals. We have a vacancy in a critical post and you are to be promoted into it. Assuming, of course, that you accept the position."

Matthews squirmed some more. Peloreid was taking an instant dislike to this pig-like man. He obviously lied about not knowing that he was next in line for Clifford's position. Every civil servant knew where they stood in seniority at all times. So, he was either a liar or a dullard. There were more than enough of both in Barahu's government.

"Of course, I would be honored to accept, of course I would, now wouldn't I?" answered Matthews, pulling at the cap that he held in his hands and looking down at it. He sounded like he was trying to convince himself that this was the right answer to make.

Peloreid smiled, although a deep disgust was building in his stomach. He was also beginning to worry if his plan was at risk. Would anyone trust this oaf with sensitive information? He thought of Clifford, her efficiency, her intelligence, her long, thin body. He had thrown that away for this clod. If this man cost him his entrance to the Supreme Council, he would undergo a death a thousand times worse than Clifford. His mind shot back to that night in the car, Clifford's scratching at her own throat, the convulsions, the blood. He could see the look in her eyes. That confused look. She knew that he had betrayed her, of that he was sure. And now, smiling, he looked at her replacement. The balding, graying, pig faced man that he needed to complete his plan.

"Good," said Peloreid, standing up at once. "I'm glad that's settled. And, as a reflection of your new authority, you must forfeit this drab tunic for one with a little more color," he said, striding to a garment bag hanging on the closet door. He unzipped it and pulled out a dark purple tunic with gold braids on the left hand shoulder.

Matthews rose too and moved closer to the closet, looking wide eyed at the garment in Peloreid's hand. Then, he gazed down at his own faded uniform and noticed some stains that must have been the residue from a meal eaten long ago. Looking back up at Peloreid, he saw the name "Matthews" on a nametag above the left chest pocket. A little slowly, it dawned on him what Peloreid was holding.

"For me?" he asked in amazement. He had rarely been given anything by a supervisor before and certainly nothing as nice as this.

"Of course. You are now a member of my personal staff. I expect you to look presentable. I know that it can take several weeks to get a full wardrobe updated so I took the liberty of procuring this one for you. I believe the size is right. Why don't you try it on?"

Matthews again stared down at his uniform. He wasn't quite sure what to do. On one hand, the new purple tunic was appropriate for his new rank. That he knew. However, he had been warned about trusting Peloreid. That had come from Tonklin herself when he informed her that he had been summonsed to Peloreid's office. He was unsure what to do, but he was very concerned with seeming disrespectful or ungrateful for Peloreid's gift. He began unbuttoning his tunic, his thick fingers moving from button to button as if in slow motion.

Peloreid paused. In any other circumstance, he would have thrown the idiot out of his office. But, this was not an ordinary circumstance. He needed Matthews much more than Matthews needed him right now. That wouldn't last for long, but it was the case for now. And so, he waited for the dumpy man to remove his dirty old tunic and helped him put on his new one. He still couldn't believe that someone like this could rise to such authority in government. Of course, he had always known that it wasn't based on proficiency, but on politics, or in this case, simply by staying in line for 20 years.

"There," Peloreid said as he smoothed the tunic and Matthews finished buttoning it. "A perfect fit."

In fact, the fit was rather good. Peloreid didn't know who Sinclair used as a tailor, but he must find out when he wanted a new garment. Peloreid smiled down at Matthews, who returned his smile in kind, even standing a little straighter in his new uniform.

"Welcome, Area Security Manager Matthews. Report back tomorrow morning to my assistant and she will show you to your new office and introduce you to the staff," instructed the security regent.

"Uh, sir. According to my schedule, tomorrow is my day off," replied the shorter man.

Peloreid looked at him, amazed. You just get a ranking position on my staff and you're concerned about your day off. Incredible!

"Of course. The next day then," he said, continuing his smile.

"Yes. Good. Thank you, sir," muttered Matthews, unsure about what to do next.

"That's all, Matthews. We don't have a car assigned to you yet but that should be done when you return. I hope that's not a problem."

"No. No. I think not. Good night, sir. And thank you, sir."

"Yes, good night, Matthews."

Peloreid had returned to his desk and was staring at his computer monitor, apparently looking at emails. He didn't look up at Matthews as he said the last words. Matthews stared at his feet for a moment, again, spinning his hat through his fingers. Then, without saying another word, he turned and walked, head down, out the door.

Peloreid stared at the door after it had closed. The huge sacrifice that he had made of Clifford was tormenting him. He had already forgotten about the sacrifice about to be made by Weiner, who was to be executed the following morning. Then, he turned and picked up the phone.

"Sinclair here, Security Regent Peloreid," came the voice at the other end of the phone.

"Yes, Sinclair. The test subject is wearing the garment and has just left the building. Please begin tracking."

"Yes, sir. The monitor was installed in the man's domicile unit closet today. I supervised myself. It is unnoticeable. We should be able to retrieve the information nightly."

"Good. And you know the information goes to no one but me?" confirmed Peloreid.

"Of course, sir. For your eyes only. I'll report as soon as we receive significant data transmissions."

"Good." The phone clicked dead.

Andrew Sinclair hung up his receiver. Yes, he thought, Peloreid would receive the information, after he had reviewed it himself of course. Sinclair still wasn't sure what Peloreid was up to. He was shocked to learn of the death of Joyce Clifford. He knew that she had been extremely loyal to Peloreid for years now. He didn't buy the story that someone had intended to poison Peloreid and got Clifford by mistake. The only group that he knew of that would try something like that was the Liberty Tree, and he would have known if that type of plan was in the works. There were plans, certainly, but nothing as obvious as killing a Security Regent. But who else would have tried it? A different Security Regent, hoping for Peloreid's job? Probably not, since most likely they would promote from within the sector, as had been done with Clifford's replacement. The only other people powerful enough would be on the Supreme Council. But, it was well known that Peloreid was a favorite of Chairman Baucman's, so it wouldn't be anyone in that camp. The other side was controlled by Councilor Tonklin, who had her own issues from what Sinclair could tell. So who? And why had Peloreid had an Area Security Managers tunic ordered for Clifford's replacement? And why before Clifford was even gone? Had he planned on promoting her?

The wheels were spinning in Sinclair's mind now. The puzzle pieces were falling into place. Peloreid had ordered the tunic for Clifford's replacement before Clifford was dead. That means that it is quite likely that Peloreid knew that Clifford would be killed. And since she was poisoned in his car, even more likely that Peloreid had killed Clifford himself. But why? All indications were that they were very close. A sexual issue? Had she refused him? Perhaps? But would he kill her over that? It didn't seem likely when Sinclair happened to know that Peloreid was a frequent visitor to Relaxation Centers. However, he did like to beat the relaxation specialists, in some cases severely. That showed a violent streak. But poisoning isn't an act of passion, it's an act of planning.

No, he was missing something. He was pretty much convinced that Peloreid had killed Clifford. But he wasn't sure why. He was sure that Peloreid wanted to know of every move of the new Area Security Manager Matthews. So much so that he had the new fiber optic thread made into Matthews' new uniform. Was that it? Was it really about Matthews and not Clifford? No. No way. No one would kill a long term, loyal, trusted subordinate in order to track a moron like Matthews. What would he find out anyway? What he liked for breakfast? It didn't make sense. But why put the thread in Matthews 'uniform if he wanted to track something? Did he suspect someone on his staff of something? But then, why not enlist Clifford in the cause? Unless he suspected her? But then why not put the thread in her uniform? Or interrogate her before killing her? And what was Matthews anyway? He had no claim to fame. He had no major accomplishment in over 20 years of service. Sinclair had validated that by reviewing Matthews' file, another perk of his current security level. Matthews had done nothing, either positive or negative. He had never missed a day of work, had never received an award, and had graded as average on every personnel review ever done. He was nothing more than a member of Councilor Tonklin's security detail.

Tonklin! Was that it? Was Peloreid trying to get close to Tonklin? Now, that had a smell to it. But, kill Clifford to spy on Tonklin? No, Matthews was now on Peloreid's team, not Tonklin's. It seemed like another dead end. But it was just too coincidental.

Tonklin! Tonklin? He knew there was something in the wind about her. He had heard her name mentioned by several Liberty Tree members. But that was more about her upcoming 'retirement' than anything else. It was about who would replace her on the Supreme Council. Sinclair knew that Baucman was pushing for his lap dog, Peloreid. But, with that being said, would Peloreid do something as stupid as trying to spy on the person he was named to replace? If it was uncovered, the publicity would doom him since, if there was one thing that the Barahu government disliked, it was a scandal. They didn't want anything that might make the natives restless.

It made no sense. He was close, very close. He could feel it. And the timing, just before a potential chasm in the government that he had heard was coming. Was that it? Was the Tonklin replacement the chasm? Were the two sides going to battle it out for control of the Supreme Council? But, how would there even be a battle? Baucman had control now. Replacing an adversary, even with another adversary, didn't change the balance of power. Unless someone on his team were willing to change sides. But, who would that be? And how would Matthews help Peloreid determine that?

Sinclair shook his head to clear the cobwebs. It had been a long day. Time to go home, such as it was. He would try to get with Albert tomorrow to see what news he had heard and to learn some more about the Supreme Council members. He'd also ask some of the other Liberty Tree members about Tonklin and her security detail. He couldn't see the fire yet, but he could smell the smoke. And, he couldn't forget, Albert was supposed to meet with Charles in a couple of days for an update! What would Charles be able to tell us, he wondered. Yes, things were definitely beginning to spin. But in which direction? It all came down to Charles, but he didn't know how Charles was progressing.

"Hello, son," welcomed Harry Johnson as a 23 year old Charles Johnson walked into the living room of their small, neatly furnished apartment. "You look worried."

"I've got a lot to be worried about," Charles replied frankly.

"Yes, I think you probably do. I think you push yourself too hard."

"That's only because you don't believe in what I do."

"I believe that you're trying to make the world a better place through chemistry. But, it's the people you're working for that concern me. You know that."

"Yeah, sure, Dad. I know you hate Barahu. I know you think they're ruining the country. I wish you'd listen to what he really says. He wants to help people. Make their lives better. He's promising them hope. And a change to the hundreds of years of hardship that most people have to endure," pleaded Charles. "Why won't you just listen to the man?"

"Charles, you are a brilliant chemist. But you're looking for an outcome that will never occur, at least from this man. He's changing our very foundations of government. He set up martial law years ago and never lifted it. He dismissed our elected officials and replaced them with his own people. He's taken away our ability to manage our own lives."

"How can you say that? You still do the same job. I've gotten nothing except opportunities to perform important experiments. I've been nominated for another promotion if this project goes well. How can you say we can't manage our own lives? Mine has gone just fine by working with Barahu, not against him like you and your gang."

"Son, you're not working with Barahu, you're doing his bidding. You're working on some mind control drugs, are you not?"

"No, Dad, I'm not. It's a sedative to be used to help reduce people's stress. These are difficult times. Barahu's had to take over more segments of the food production because the damn businesses aren't producing enough food. They're waiting for prices to go up even higher so they can make more money. In the meantime, people are starving."

"Charles, that's Barahu's propaganda. It's his policies that are driving it. Believe it or not, the people running those companies want to produce more, not less. Barahu has so many regulations that they can't. He's putting them out of business and all this nonsense about rescuing the industry is just so he can control it."

"Good, I wish he would. I wish he'd control everything. Then maybe we wouldn't be having this goddamn civil war."

"This isn't a war. This is a massacre. Barahu's troops are shooting anyone that might voice a different opinion. These people are barely armed at all."

"So you say. I guess you get your information from your little group of revolutionary buddies. You better watch it, Dad. If you're right, they'll be coming for you next."

"You may be right. They may come for me sometime," agreed Harry, sorry that all their conversations seemed to go down this same path. "So, you're still struggling with your project?"

"Yes," admitted Charles. "I keep saying that we need to use the Omega 5 variant but they insist on using the old Sigma 6 because it's cheaper. It just isn't strong enough. But, they won't listen. One guy there, Jorgenson, is coming around but I'm not sure if we can convince Gibbert. He's such a moron. Talks real nice but doesn't know a goddamn thing."

"You'll convince him. You're smarter than they are and at the end of the day, they'll come around. I wish they wouldn't. I've got a bad feeling about their true use for your work. I don't think it will be as beneficial as you hope."

"Jesus Christ, Dad. Will you lay off. Someday YOU'LL be the one to come around. You'll finally have to admit that Barahu has built a great country. Either that or I'll read about you getting arrested," chuckled Charles.

His father didn't laugh. He only looked at Charles with a grimace. "Will you be coming to church with your mother and I on Sunday?" asked Harry.

"Maybe. You know church is frowned upon now."

"I know, but it is Easter. Your mother would like it."

"Where are you going?"

"St. Johns of course. You know we like to walk in the park afterwards. You still remember where it is, don't you?"

"I know I haven't been to church in a while but, yes, I still remember where it is," answered Charles a little bitterly.

"Son, we can't let politics tear us apart. Please come to Easter Mass with us."

Charles woke up with a jolt. It had been so real. My God, he thought, was that real? Was that a dream, or was it really a conversation that they had, returning to him in his sleep. Sigma 6, was that really the answer to his problem? Sigma 6 acted on a different part of the brain than the Omega drugs. We that the answer he needed?

Charles was up now, pacing around his unlit domicile unit. That was it. The Omegas worked on the emotional parts of the brain. They brought total control, even destruction, of those areas but only a slight sedating effect on the more rational areas. And now, after all these years, the body was becoming accustomed to this external control and was adjusting its own chemistry to make the sedation less effective. Wasn't the human body incredible, thought Charles. Even after years of mistreatment, it adjusts and tries to counter all of the control mechanisms placed upon it. He felt that he understood more than most others ever would. The government had sought to control him more than most others, but he had learned and adjusted, and was countering their attempts. He was fighting back, just as the bodies of the populace were fighting the governmental control, even without the individuals realizing it.

The Sigma compounds worked on the rational parts. That's why they weren't successful to begin with. You wanted the rational parts working. You just didn't want people to care about what they were doing which is why they had to introduce the Omegas. But now, how could he change it back? How could he get them to agree to use a formulation that didn't work to begin with? That would take some time to figure out.

The dream had been like a gift. He had gotten the delay, but now he knew the answer. It was like a gift from his father. His father. He had seen his father's face in the dream, even smelled the coffee that he was drinking. And, he had heard the disappointment in his voice. Charles had been working against everything his father believed in. How arrogant he had been about Barahu. And how wrong. His father had been right. Right about Barahu's desires, about the use for Charles' work, right about everything. Charles' warning about his father's arrest echoed in his mind. Had Charles betrayed his family? If not to Barahu, certainly his father must have felt betrayed by him. Had he gone to St. John's that Easter? He couldn't remember. Charles had been wrong. He knew that admission wouldn't, couldn't, bring his father and mother back. They had died for this cause. Charles vowed that he would finish their work. Tears ran down his cheeks as he replayed his dream over and over in his mind.

16

Friday and Saturday had come and gone for Charles. He still hadn't discovered how he would get the reformulation approved. The other problem was simpler, but didn't seem any easier to solve. How the hell was he supposed to figure out where to meet Andrew and Albert? Since religion was outlawed in Barahu's USA, there wasn't really anyone he could ask about the cathedral. He tried looking on bus maps, but saw nothing mentioning any church. Not surprising, he thought, based on Barahu's stance on religion. But, how was he supposed to find out where to go?

His father had said St. John's Cathedral was by the park, but which park. There were hundreds in Capitol City. The only park that Charles knew of was the one he had been going to where he met Albert. Was that the park that his father meant? Was there a subconscious connection with that park that drew Charles to it? Was that the park that he saw in his dream when he was eating with his parents as a young boy? That might be it, he considered. He didn't remember seeing a big church there, but neither had he been looking for one.

On Sunday, Charles dressed warmly and left his domicile unit early. His only hope was in the park. He walked there swiftly, partly from anxiety and partly to keep warm. He followed his normal route, looking around at all the buildings, searching for one that might be a church. While all the trees were bare of leaves, he could see very little past the first row of buildings that bordered the park. At each street, he looked at the street sign and then looked down the street to see if anything resembled a church. He wasn't really sure what it would look like. He just hoped that he'd recognize it when he saw it. And then, near the northeast corner of the park he saw a street sign, weather beaten but legible, which read "St John's Place". Peering down the street, he could see a large granite building with a steeple on top.

That was it. It had to be it. And, it was right near the park, just like Dad had said. Charles had a lump in his throat and choked back a tear as he began walking down St. John's Place.

St. John's Cathedral filled an entire city block and its high steeple rose so high that Charles couldn't see its cross due to the snow. It had red, wooden doors which didn't appear to be opened. Charles could see piles of snow in front of each, such that none of them could be moved without first shoveling. He wondered if he had the right place. The note had said St. John's Cathedral and this was it. Even the brass sign, somewhat dingy and coated with snow, confirmed that.

Charles was directly in front and looked up and down the street, wondering which way he should go. Along the left side of the church was a wide avenue and, along the right side, was a small alley, a one lane street which appeared dark and empty. Charles decided that was a more likely candidate to be used by the Liberty Tree, so he turned to his right, moved to the end of the block, and with a look around to make sure no one was watching him, at least no one that he could see, he moved quickly into the shadows of the alley.

While the wind blew snow in every crevice of the narrow street, Charles could make out one set of footprints in the snow. They moved in the same direction as he was headed and seemed to bob from left to right, as if the person had a bad leg. The footprints seemed to be parallel, as if one leg had stepped forward and then the other moved to the same spot instead of stepping ahead of the other leg. Charles didn't know why, but the footprints struck him as odd, and an internal alarm bell began to ring.

About halfway down the dead-end alley, he saw a door that opened into the church. The footprints in the snow had turned into the doorway and disappeared from sight behind the closed door. Charles looked at the snow beyond the doorway, further down the alley. He could see no footprints. He hesitated, knowing that the only entry to the church seemed to be through this door. His heart was beating more rapidly than it had been as he glanced both ways down the alley but saw nothing other than an old dumpster a little further down. He walked further, not really knowing why, but looking around, up at the high stone walls on one side and the brick walls on the other. There were no windows, no other doorways into the church. The brick building on the other side of the alley looked abandoned. While there were a couple of doorways, the doors were old, with broken windows or were nailed shut.

Charles neared the end of the alley A dead end. He turned around, still peering up into the falling snow, the sun invisible behind the clouds, just a mass of grey above him. He moved back towards the doorway, almost feeling like a cat that's been cornered, with no escape. He shook his head, trying to drive the fears from his mind. He wasn't caged, he was here to meet someone. To provide an update, whatever that might be since he still hadn't worked out a full solution, and, for at least a few moments, to have some companionship. As he moved down the alley, he thought he saw someone at the end by the street, looking down at him. He instinctively ducked behind the dumpster, crouching down. His cheeks were cold, and he could see his breath rising into the air as he exhaled. He wondered if the person down the street had seen him, was now wondering why he had hidden. In hindsight, his move was pretty dumb. If they saw him, they would know he was down here. Hiding would be even more suspicious than just walking back. If anything, his dart behind the dumpster would have made his situation worse, more suspicious, not less.

Charles decided. He stood up and shook his leg, acting as if he'd been tying his shoe. He looked down the alley and saw... nothing. No one was there. No one was watching him. Had he imagined it? The alley was fairly long and dark. The grayness of the day didn't help his visibility. Was his mind playing tricks on him? Again, the feeling of being caged began to grow. He needed to be somewhere, anywhere other than where he was. He needed to have another escape route than down a dead end alley. He moved quickly, determinedly, down the alley to the doorway. Without hesitation, he grabbed the handle, pushed and flung himself inside.

He hadn't known what to expect, hadn't even really thought about it. As he closed the door behind him, he found himself in a small hallway. On the right, facing him, there was a doorway. The hallway ran along the left side of this door until it reached another one, about 20 feet away. That door was ajar, but not enough for Charles to see what was on the other side. However, he could see some light coming through the crack between the door and its frame. It didn't provide much light, but it was the only light there was. It seemed obvious to Charles that whoever had come from the alley had probably gone through that door as well. He wished he could make out the floor to see if there were any wet footprints leading that way, but there wasn't enough light.

Slowly, Charles moved to the end of the hallway. He peeked through the crack in the door. He saw benches, pews he could remember they were called. They stretched nearly to the back of the church, row upon row of dark brown wood. No one seemed to be in there. There was no light except that which filtered through the stained glass windows, some of which Charles could see in the background. It was decision time. Go forward, or back. Charles reached for the door with his hand.

Just as his fingers were about to touch it, the door was pushed open. Charles jumped back in fright. There, standing directly in front of him, was a man in white robes, a white rope belt tied around his waist, and a hood covering his head and face. Charles' heart was pounding. He stood, shrinking against the wall, his mouth open but no words escaping, not even a breath. He wasn't sure whether he should attack the stranger or run for the door. He turned his head, looking back, waiting for someone else to come up behind him, wondering if he should run while he still could.

"Calm down, my boy. You look like you've seen a ghost."

It was the soft, calm voice of Albert. Charles looked back at the man, not sure he could trust his own ears. Not sure, like in the alley, if his mind was playing tricks on him. The man pulled back the hood, and there was the grey haired, kindly faced Albert.

"What the devil took you so long? I thought something had happened," he said, motioning Charles in towards the pews.

"I didn't have very good directions," he replied, his voice finally returning as his heart began beating somewhat normally again. "You scared me half to death."

"Me? Scared you? Now how did I do that?"

"Well, first off, how was I supposed to know where St. John's Cathedral was? And then, I didn't know how to get in. And then you greet me in that getup."

"You didn't know where St. John's was? I never considered that. You'd gone here for over 20 years, until it was closed."

"What? I? Gone here? What are you talking about?"

"This church. Your parents were members as were you. You were baptized here. Went here for years. In fact, this is where I first met your parents. You don't remember at all?"

Charles shook his head. He looked down at his hands, rubbing them to warm them up. Another part of his life, removed for the good of Emperor Barahu.

"Oh, I'm sorry my boy. I guess I figured with more of your memory coming back that you'd remember this place."

"That's OK. Not your fault," replied Charles quietly, with a trace of bitterness in his voice. He looked around, examining the huge stone pillars supporting the vaulted ceilings, the large stained glass windows showing a bearded man in different settings. Some showed him with lambs and children. Others surrounded by soldiers and dragging what looked like a big log. Another showed him nailed to two pieces of wood, his faced bloodied, with some women around his feet and a soldier stabbing him in the chest with a spear. Charles looked again at the different scenes, from ones of love and tenderness to a horrible torture.

"What kind of place is this?" he asked Albert.

"This is a place of contemplation, of reverence and reflection. This is where we admit that there is some life force greater than man in the universe. Where we acknowledge our imperfections, and seek to understand how we can better serve our neighbors. It is something that is sorely missing in this world. Although, heaven knows, mankind has not always lived according to the preachings. Certainly aren't now."

"I don't understand."

"The man you see in those windows is Jesus Christ. According to the Holy Bible, he was sent by God to help save his people. He taught of love, of service to others. For that, he was crucified, that's the scene with him on the cross," Albert continued, pointing to the final, bloody image. "It is said that he died for our sins. Basically, if you asked God for forgiveness for the wickedness that you've done, that Jesus will take on your punishment. That he would suffer so we could live. And, if we treat others well, follow the word of the Lord, at least try to do our best and ask forgiveness when we don't, then this mortal life is only one part of our journey. Our spirit, the soul inside us, will live on, and some believe, reunite with our loved ones, their spirits, after our bodies die.

But, to truly believe, you must acknowledge that man is not the ruler of the universe. That there is a life force that founded the universe, that creates new life, human, animal, or plant. A force that can form life from non-life. Create matter from nothingness. Something greater than Barahu. That's why these places aren't used anymore. Barahu would never allow anything greater than him."

"I don't know if my brain is ready to tackle these concepts right now," admitted Charles, shaking his head and continuing to look around the large cathedral.

"Not surprising. Man has been wrestling with the concept of God and his place in the universe for thousands of years. Probably will for thousands more."

"So, I used to come here?"

"Yes, every Sunday. Since you were born. Until Barahu that is?"

"I don't remember them telling me anything about this at the Reorientation Center."

"No, don't imagine they did. Wouldn't want people to begin asking about some of the bigger questions in life. Doesn't help them. That was one of the last things that Barahu destroyed. That and families."

"What happened? How'd he do it?"

"Slowly, bit by bit. In order for all people to worship the Supreme Being Barahu, they must not worship any other. The greatest threat to Barahu was twofold, families and religion. Families are the basic human group, the most fundamental relationships there are. It begins with the parents that give birth to you and extend to brothers, sisters, aunts, uncles, and then to your children. It's been that group for thousands, tens of thousands of years. But Barahu wanted government to fill every role in society. In order to have total control, he needed to be the glue that binds everything together. And so, he set out to replace each fiber of life with his government. We already talked about taking over businesses so he controlled that piece of life, and the medical system so he control the interactions with doctors that could help improve and prolong your life.

But that wasn't fundamental enough. He, and those like minded people that preceded him and his worshiping followers, knew that they had to destroy the family unit. So, they penalized married couple, through taxes, fees, and other costs of being married. They made it easier to divorce, so that people could destroy their own marriages whenever the going got tough. They advanced alternative lifestyles so that marriage became the old, outdated, uncool model of life. Television shows, movies, books, magazines, they had all of these vehicles to promote non-marriage. Then, they invaded schools, forcing them to teach about and promote the non-marriage lifestyles. Since children are more experimental and more easily persuaded, more and more adopted these alternative lifestyles. But, for Barahu, it was still moving too slowly.

He began a program which, when the truth is finally known by the world, will doom him to the lowest levels of humanity. He began a program of sterilizing people, those in particular that he felt did not fit his ideal. Basically, anyone who didn't agree with him. Scientists already knew how to fertilize eggs and implant them in healthy women. They were developing human cloning.

Through genetic engineering, Barahu mandated that all human babies were to be developed by the state. He began baby making factories at the same time that he began sterilizing people. Eventually, everyone was sterilized except those that were used as human baby making machines. Men produced sperm and women eggs. It was like farming. They were just used and then slaughtered when they didn't produce as much as they had, or when a better crop came along. The scientists modified the eggs and sperm genetically to produce the type of children, the future citizens, that they required. They split them into different intelligence types, trained them different ways, and set them up in different jobs, all based on what was needed for the state run enterprises. They were able to increase or decrease the supply of workers as needed.

Of course, there's a decent lead time with producing humans so they weren't always right. That's why they developed the Procedure 23, because they were exterminating more of certain categories than they could replace. They wouldn't allow anyone to think for themselves, but neither could they have entire industries fail because they didn't have enough workers so, erase the bad memories and problem solved. Once their baby production gets back to the right quantities, they won't need to do Procedure 23s anymore. They can just dispose of the trouble makers."

"But, what about the family units? There must have been thousands, millions of families. Those couldn't have all been destroyed," asked Charles.

"Well, yes and no. No, all those people weren't killed, although Barahu killed millions in his cleansing. But what they did was to separate the families. Husbands were taken to one part of the country to work. Wives were taken to a different one. Children were pulled away to go to state run schools. Then, as the mind control drugs doped everyone up, those relationships faded. The emotional bonds broke. That's what keeps a family together after all, the emotional bonds. The love, the support, the life long relationship of spending years together, through good times and bad. Existing families were broken up. Sterilizations, legal restrictions, forced separations, these all ensured that new families wouldn't begin. Once children are taken from parents, the family will eventually dissolve. And, the children will only know the state as their parents, so the attachment will be with a state, with Barahu. Then, they disrupt all of the personal relationships a person has and replaces it with the state. The government becomes your parent, your employer, and even replaces your spouse since the only place you can legally have sex are the Relaxation Centers."

"So," asked Charles after a moment of thought, "where does religion fit in?"

"Prior to the ascension of Emperor Barahu, this was a very religious country. The founding fathers looked to a Supreme Being, in the form of God, not a mortal man, as their guiding light. As with the family structure, the socialist predecessors of Barahu were trying to destroy religion. Most religious people on television or in the movies were extremist lunatics, out to kill in the name of God. They kept reinforcing this image of religious people, particularly Christians, as odd, or dangerous, or nerdy. In reality, most were normal, sincere, hard working people that believed in a force greater than mortal man. They believed that something greater created all of heaven and earth. Barahu had to substitute government for religion. It began before him but he extended it. Religion wasn't allowed at schools, public buildings or events, or even to be seen in public. You could no longer hold a wedding in a public park. They removed the word 'God' from any public building or paper, even our money. Churches were taxes harshly, causing most to shut down. But still, some religion continued.

And then, Barahu had enough. Look at the man in those windows," instructed Albert. Charles looked, again, at the colored glass and the various scenes containing the same bearded man as the central figure.

"Now," continued Albert, "look at the man on the cross above the altar."

Charles followed the outstretched arm of Albert, over the long rows of pews and to a raised platform. Behind it was a huge wooden cross. On the cross, arms extended as if to enwrap the people, was a different figure than that on the windows.

"Barahu!" exclaimed Charles.

"Barahu," Albert agreed, nodding. "Barahu replaced Jesus in churches wherever possible. It was now he on the cross, not Christ. We celebrated his birthday at Christmas."

Charles head gave a start. The term 'Christmas' caused a stir in his brain. He was flooded with happy memories of evergreen trees, food, parties, and of course presents.

"Christmas. I remember Christmas," said Charles, half under his breath.

"Yes, most every child remembers Christmas. Usually the presents mostly. But it was a time of love and friendship, of outreach and charity. It was a celebration of the birth of Christ. It became Christmas after Christ Mass, the church service celebrating his birth. He represented hope for millions of people, some of whom had nothing else to rely on. But, Barahu's government doesn't like competition so they took Christ of the cross and put Barahu's image there instead. They wanted to do the stained glass windows but the glass is too old and it probably would have shattered if they tried to change it.

Think of the imagery. Millions of people across the country going to church, kneeling down and worshiping Emperor Barahu.

The Chosen One. The Supreme Being. Truly religious people resented it and stopped going. After a few years, there were no more churches. That's exactly what Barahu wanted. Another form of human interaction and support where he substituted the government for people. Just like they planned, the government was involved with every decision in people's lives and took control of every aspect of their life. We were no longer families, we were individuals, separated and powerless, totally reliant on Barahu and his government for our every need. He had total control."

At his, Albert paused. He was looking at the church, its stained glass windows, it's altar of marble. Charles sat, quietly. The stillness was meditative, quieting his soul, calming his troubled mind. He felt as if he could sit there forever, at peace with the world. He could see the emotional draw of these institutions, where people could find hope and peace, friendship and companionship, support and compassion. It was everything that this all encompassing government was not. He looked at the cross, at Barahu with his arms outstretched. To Charles, it seemed like he was grabbing the whole world, engulfing it in his grasp, seeking not to comfort, but to control. This was what government could become if not contained. Charles wondered how many days he sat there, probably between his two loving parents. How could he have been so taken in with Barahu? How could he have forsaken the love of his parents for the government of Barahu?

Finally, after what seemed like hours, Charles broke the silence. "So, my work, the chemical formulas that I developed, they helped cause this, didn't they?"

Albert looked at him, stunned by the admission. "In a way, yes. I'm not a scientist, but I know those drugs help control the mind, help make people, well, distance themselves from each other. But, my boy, you were only one of the many tools that the government used to secure their power. If you hadn't, someone else would have. It was Barahu and those elected politicians that surrendered their souls, that sold out their constituents who trusted them. They were the ones that caused this. It was their thirst for power that did it. You were just a tool that they used. One of many."

"But I did it. I remember explaining how the original formula didn't work. It was controlling the brain's cerebrum, the logical, reasoning part. Instead, we need to focus on the amygdala, the emotional center. Originally, we tried controlling everything but the drugs powerful enough to control the cerebrum destroyed the amygdala. We developed a formula that would gradually build up in the amygdala, and maintain its control. I should say that I developed it."

Charles stopped speaking. He had risen and was pacing around the church, raising his voice until it was echoing off the high ceilings, bouncing back at him.

When Albert spoke, it was quietly and calmly. "And now? Now what will you do?"

Charles looked at him. It was really that simple wasn't it? He had done something. Now he needed to undo it.

"And now, I'll fix it. That's what I wanted to tell you. I've been able to delay the new formulation by at least two months, probably longer. Now, I just need to figure out how to get the formula changed back the original one that was less potent. I thought about it and I can't stop it cold turkey. People would be bouncing off the walls. There would be chaos. They wouldn't be able to understand where all those strong feelings were coming from. The government would see it and crack down. No, I think it needs to be more subtle, over time."

"How much time?"

"The biggest delay will be in getting the formula approved. I'm not sure how I'll be able to do that or how long it will take. After that, it will be another month for the full effects to kick in."

Albert sat quietly, considering what Charles had told him.

After a few moments, Charles asked softly, "Albert, did I betray my parents?"

"What do you mean, my boy?"

"I had a dream about my father. I think it might have really happened. I was having an argument with my father about Barahu and my work."

"You two had many arguments. You both believed deeply in your positions. You were young, idealistic. Your father was very wise. He could see things that others missed. He knew what Barahu wanted to do. You knew what he said he would do. Barahu was a great speaker. But, he was also a great liar. Your father saw that. At the time you didn't. But, no, you never betrayed them. And they never stopped loving you because of your views. In one of our last conversations, they asked that I look after you. We all thought Andrew would be arrested for sure. I have no idea how he's gotten by all these years. So, they asked me to be your guardian. They knew Barahu was closing in on them."

"I feel like I betrayed them," Charles said bluntly.

"After they were captured, and then when they were, were gone, you changed your feelings. You became part of the Liberty Tree. You were trying to avenge them. That's why you got the Procedure 23. Now, the government thinks you're back on board. That's why you're so useful for us. They trust you, at least as much as they trust anyone."

Charles sighed. "Thank you, Albert. I'm glad you're watching after me. I think I need all the help I can get."

"Don't worry, Charles. You're parents are watching after you too. And they're now with much stronger forces than us," Albert replied, pointing towards the stained glass windows.

Both mean sat in silence for a few moments.

"My son," said the robed figure of Albert, "I think you should sit here for a few minutes. I often find that some quiet contemplation does wonders for my mind. And spirits. It's best if we leave separately anyway."

"Albert, why is this building still here? Why to they allow it to remain?"

"Simple. Money. It would cost too much to tear it down. They probably figure it will fall down at some point, being vacant for all these years. Or, they just forgot about it."

"It looks pretty good to me."

"Well, there are still some of us that believe. We keep the faith, and keep the church maintained as best we can. I'll go now," he finished, lifting the big brass cross necklace over his head and beginning to remove his robe.

Charles' face went flush. He felt around his own neck and pulled out the medallion with the chip. "Albert!" he said, holding up the medallion.

"Good Lord, why didn't you take that off? You've got to get out of here. You've been stationary for way too long, particularly here. Go, go now!"

While Albert wasn't yelling, the fear and anxiety were evident in his voice. Charles rushed out to the outside door and gently pushed it open, just far enough for him to see. No one was visible down the alley. He moved out, closing the door and walking rapidly down toward the street. As he approached the main street, he slowed, holding his body close to the church wall. The snow was still coming down. Visibility was still poor. He could see no one on the street, no cars, no transports. He walked quickly out onto the sidewalk and crossed the street to the park. His heart was pounding. Had he just blown everything? Had he just condemned Albert? Another mistake, maybe not as far reaching as helping to develop a formula that would in essence enslave an entire population, but one that could hurt someone that had become a dear friend to him, one of his only friends. He imagined the kindly, green eyes of Albert, staring down at him as he sat in the pew. He had let his parents down. He would not let Albert down. He would finish his job this time.

17

"My, that Area Security Manager uniform does become you," said a smiling, welcoming Councilor Evelyn Tonklin as Oliver Matthews entered her office. "Congratulations on your appointment. You have certainly earned it," she continued as Matthews made his way to a seat at the conference table after shaking her hand and returning her warm hug.

"Thank you, Madame Councilor. I'm afraid it couldn't have come at a worse time for our, uh, the plan," he replied.

"Yes, that is somewhat inconvenient, now isn't it? But, it cannot be helped I'm afraid. To reject the appointment would raise many eyebrows and we don't need to give Chairman Baucman any more reason to mistrust us."

A broad shouldered, muscular man in his 20s was sitting at the end of the table, to the right of Councilor Tonklin. At Baucman's name, he looked up from his papers. "I find the whole thing rather odd, myself. A spot opens up at precisely this moment, all due to the poisoning of the previous Area Security Manager, all happening in Security Regent Peloreid's car. I don't trust that Baucman didn't orchestrate this whole thing to pull the team apart. And I don't trust Peloreid either. He's always been Baucman's lapdog."

"I had considered the same thing myself," replied the Councilor. "I would not put it past Baucman at all. However, I don't think it's likely. Area Security Manager Clifford was Peloreid's favorite. Clifford was Peloreid's right hand. He would never agree to her assassination. And, I don't believe Baucman would risk that

Peloreid and Clifford would both get poisoned. He wouldn't dare go behind Peloreid's back to kill Clifford and Peloreid would never do it himself. He needed Clifford too much. She always was the brainpower on his team. Without her, he wouldn't know what to do with himself."

"I hope you're right," he replied. "We should review the plans to ensure that our timing is exact. If there are any complications due to Oliver's new role, we need to have a backup plan. Otherwise, we are certain to be stopped."

With the last words, he looked over to Matthews, who blushed and looked down. Matthews, while blameless in this, nonetheless felt responsibility for putting the plan at risk. His was not a large role, but was critical. Now, on one hand he had more power to be used as needed, but on the other he would be required to do the bidding of someone the entire team despised. He was in a no win situation and he knew it.

"Very well, Vannie," said an older, gray haired gentleman sitting directly to the left of the Councilor. "Why don't you lead us over the plan once again?" He looked down the table to the muscular man, Vannie. Jefferson Tonklin had being in the background. While legally, he and Evelyn had been divorced once marriage was made illegal, they had never parted company. He had been at her side from the start, and many felt like he made more decisions than she did. Many wondered why he wasn't a Security Councilor instead of his wife, or ex-wife to be precise. But, his condescending attitude and arrogance had made him many enemies within the movement from the earliest stages. He hated Barahu and saw him as nothing but a farce, a punk with a good voice and expensive clothes. He thought Barahu was an idiot, but one that gave the appearance of great intelligence. He saw him as someone with no depth and could never fathom how he had gathered the power he did. Jefferson Tonklin thought that it was the ruthless team that Barahu had assembled, a team that used him to gain their own power bases, that had elevated him to Emperor. Barahu was the pretty face. They did the dirty work and gathered the power. Enough power that eventually they would establish the Supreme Council to advise Barahu. In reality, at the point when Barahu was dying, they had assumed complete control. The plan of cloning Barahu for future generations was never meant to imply that control would be restored to the clones. No, that was something the Council would keep for themselves. The Emperor would be powerless, nothing more than a figurehead. Jefferson Tonklin had pushed them in this direction through his wife. She was smart and ruthless, perhaps more ruthless than her husband, but didn't have his political awareness and insights. They made a wonderful team. He developed the plans and she executed them flawlessly. And, they deeply loved each other, even if that was no longer allowed by government. And so, Jefferson Tonklin sat by his wife's side, and waited to hear the plan yet again, the plan that would prolong their lives together, even if it defied the government. Both Tonklin's were due to turn 65 within the next few months. Neither was ready for "retirement."

"I'd be happy to, MISTER Tonklin," replied Vannie, more than a trace of irritation in his voice. Vannie Johannes had not risen to the level of Councilor Tonklin's Chief of Security by being inattentive to details. His job was to guarantee the protection of the Councilor, a job he relished. Unfortunately, in his opinion, that also meant dealing with her ex-husband. He did not even understand why she kept him around. He always seemed to be on hand, inserting himself in the discussions. He never did any work and rarely provided useful information. He was just there, getting underfoot, and often barking orders. Vannie didn't work for him and, in fact, had developed a hatred of the man over time.

But he could harbor no such dislike for the Councilor. He would gladly lay down his life for her. She had selected him for her security team years ago, when he was just out of the academy. She had helped him along the way, guiding him and promoting him up through the ranks. She had nurtured him as none of the government workers in the nurseries and schools ever had. He didn't know what it was like to have a mother, since children were created in government laboratories, but he felt a deep connection to the Councilor which he had with no one else. She was his only concern. He would not see her "retired", no matter how much he would like to see Mr. Tonklin "retired", and he would go over the plan a thousand times if it led to success.

"We won't know the start date until Madame Councilor has provided it, after obtaining the support of Emperor Barahu. Once we have his support, the plan will go as follows. Step One, I will escort Madame Councilor to Hospital 103. At the same time, two officers will escort Mr. Tonklin to the hospital. This step should be the easiest since we have full access to the vehicles and drivers so I see little risk here.

Step two, a helicopter will arrive at the airport and transport the team to Barahu's private airport. There will be three planes waiting there. Oliver, that's your responsibility. Are you sure that the helicopter and airplanes will be available when needed?"

"Yes. I moved two people into the helicopter pilot position last month. Both are on call when needed."

"Whom do they serve now?" asked Councilor Tonklin.

"They were newer members to the security detail that came on board last year. A few months ago, they were being reassigned to security at food processing plants but I offered them pilot training instead. They both jumped at it. They're certified now and owe me. I contacted them last week to notify them that I was planning a high security operation. They don't know what it is but they're both on board. The helicopter is set.

The bigger issue is the airplanes. One is no issue since Councilor Tonklin has the government plane for her personal use. One will have to come with Barahu's approval. That's the only way we'll be able to get it. The third, the one we'd actually use, is in for servicing right now. It will be shown as a service and inspection flight of 30 minutes. It will be the second one to leave, right after Councilor Tonklin's. The third plane should leave shortly thereafter as well," concluded Matthews.

"Very good," commented Johannes. "So the helicopter and two planes are provided. After taking off, the Councilor's official plane will go down halfway to the West Sector. If authorities are trailing us, it will take them at least several hours to determine how many people were aboard. With the third plane being Emperor Barahu's, they may think we used that and, if so, they'll follow it to the South Sector where they'll find it empty. The service plane will fly north and then west to the mountains. We'll land and drive through to the West Sector. We should be in the stronghold within 12 hours of our departure from the hospital. Once we're at the stronghold, Baucman will never be able to drive us out, especially if Emperor Barahu addresses the Security Council as we hope"

"That is the major question, isn't it," inserted Jefferson Tonklin. "Will Emperor Barahu agree with you, Evelyn? If he does, this entire plan is unnecessary or, at the very worst, temporary. If he doesn't, I'm not sure that our stronghold is enough."

"Mr. Tonklin, we have over 500 Purple Shirts, all well trained and extremely loyal to Councilor Tonklin at the stronghold. We have food and water to last for months. I have built this force and this plan for months. They will not be able to take us from that place," assured Johannes.

"Maybe not alive, Director", interjected Jefferson, "but they can destroy us if they want. And, even if they didn't, we would be captives. The key is Barahu. If he defies the Supreme Council to maintain the throne, he will need our help. That is the key question. Will he defy the Council?"

"I wish I knew," replied Evelyn Tonklin. "He has refused to discuss the subject of his removal, even as Ohnoma approaches his 25th birthday. He refuses to believe that Ohnoma is anything more than a safety net in case something happens to him. I haven't pushed the matter yet. He's very opposed to overruling Barahu I. I think he looks at the pictures and statues of Barahu I and then looks at his own misshapened appearance and feels he's unworthy of overruling any decree that Barahu I set down. He's been hidden in that palace so the people don't realize that he's not a carbon copy of Barahu I. He doesn't know what's going on."

"But dear," said Jefferson, "you must convince him. He must see what Baucman means to do. Baucman will use any means to stay in power. He will not allow you to live. He wants to control Barahu II just like he wants to control everything else in society. And, he's pretty close. We must alter the Supreme Council if we have any hope of survival. We must remove Baucman, and the only person that can authorize that is Barahu."

"I know, Jefferson, I know. I'll speak to him again," she said, softly with emotion and concern in her voice. She took his hand in hers. They had been together, well forever it seemed. She had always relied on him for direction. He was her compass. She did what he said and it had worked. Initially, it was to gain power from the ignorant electorate, then to solidify and keep what they had acquired. Her control of the West Coast was instrumental to

Barahu's rise. She was a natural to assume a position on the Supreme Council.

When Barahu was diagnosed with cancer, it was that Council who developed the idea of clones to replace him indefinitely. One clone would be conceived every 25 years. When the existing clone turned 50, he would retire and the younger one, then 25, would assume the throne and a new clone would be conceived. The only problem was with Barahu II. Barahu I didn't have 25 years to live and he didn't trust ANYONE to serve as regent after he was gone. He did love the idea of a clone, the thought that an exact copy of him would live on forever, taught to accept his theories as truths and continuing his government, his legacy intact in perpetuity. Barahu had videos made of his lectures and speeches, of him alone with the camera, speaking thoughts of wisdom that he wanted his successors to know and follow. He had hundreds of thousands of pages of laws, regulations, and codes written so that his thoughts on every subject would be the law of the land.

And then, Barahu I died after numerous operations and chemotherapy. Barahu II was barely 12 years old. He was twice the size of a normal 12 year old, due to the human growth hormones and steroids he had been given since birth, actually even before his birth. His appearance had become warped as his body reacted to the chemicals. In fact, he had become so misshapen that he was hidden from Barahu I during the last months of his life. After Barahu's death, the boy was crowned as the Supreme Being and Most Holy Leader of the Union of Socialist Alliances, Emperor Barahu II. But, in reality it was the Supreme Council that made all decisions. They relied almost exclusively on the writings of Barahu I, at least at first. The boy Emperor was not ready to reign, not in body or mind. He was a young boy that didn't realize his own strength, an oddity that was kept hidden from view. The Council ruled. And, they were determined not to relinquish power. They would destroy anyone that threatened their status. While the population had been reduced to half by the civil war and cleansing that had followed Barahu's takeover of the government, there were still over one hundred fifty million people to govern. To control them would take extraordinary effort. The masterstroke had been the sedatives added to the food supply. That, combined with the other moves to destroy families, religion, and personal interaction, paved the way for the complete control of the populace which the Supreme Council enjoyed. That, and a strong, determined, dedicated force of Purple Shirt Security Officers.

But a problem was developing now which threatened the Supreme Council, and the government as a whole. Ohnoma was approaching his 25th birthday. Largely isolated from Barahu II during his upbringing, he had been indoctrinated with the laws and regulations of Barahu I since birth. He knew that it was his right to assume the crown once he turned 25 years old. However, Barahu II, although he had reigned for over 15 years, was only 28 years old himself. He was not due to step down until his 50th birthday. He, too, had been indoctrinated since birth. He, too, knew the law. The man that was only supposed to be a stopgap until Ohnoma could grow and age naturally, did not expect to relinquish his crown for another 22 years. His clone, Ohnoma, was expecting to assume the crown, to become Emperor Barahu III, within six months.

The Supreme Council was in the middle, partly seeking to avoid a collapse of government, and partly seeking to maintain their own grasp on power. It was this debate which was tearing the Council apart. The debate was not really about whether to back Barahu II or Ohnoma, but rather how they could maintain their positions and their authority. It was readily apparent that

Ohnoma would be a much stronger leader than Barahu II, and as such he would assume some of the power they had sequestered for themselves. Others felt that keeping Ohnoma waiting, in the background was unwise, because either he would resent them once he did assume power or he would make a power grab. Either event would weaken the Council.

It was this debate that had Chairman Baucman and Councilor Tonklin at each others throats and building their own coalitions of supporters. And, while Tonklin was closer with Barahu II, she was due to retire within months. With her gone, Baucman would consolidate his power.

This was a struggle that few knew about, perhaps only a few dozen people in the entire country. It was a struggle in the Council chambers, not on the streets of the cities or in newspapers. Even the two Emperors didn't realize the dispute was shaping up as each felt that their viewpoint was the correct one and gave little thought to the other. It was the Council and their close confidants that knew of the upcoming struggle. And of the Council, it was really Tonklin and Baucman, the two most senior members, the ones that had been the closest with Barahu I. They would decide the fate of the country. Unless Tonklin "retired", in which case Baucman would win by default. But, she, Evelyn Tonklin, had Jefferson. And Jefferson Tonklin had no intent to go quietly off into retirement.

As Andrew Sinclair watched the video that had been retrieved from Oliver Matthews' uniform jacket the night after the meeting, he was stunned. He had sensed something was developing at the Supreme Council. In his position, both in government and the Liberty Tree organization, he heard things. He had always had the ability to put puzzles together, taking the different pieces of information and making a picture that was recognizable. That was an asset in his position. But, he hadn't recognized that this was coming. The government, he knew, was managed by the Supreme Council. He rarely thought of Barahu II or Ohnoma. His enemy had always been Barahu I who, while dead, had left behind the Council which maintained the government that he had created. Andrew had felt a crack forming in the Council, and now he knew why. He also knew many of the details of Councilor Tonklin's plan of escaping the fate of "retirement" that she had helped to force on millions of others.

"Retirement", what a novel word for government mandated murder. People were retired at 65, or shortly after, because that was when their useful life was deemed complete, at least in the eyes of Barahu I. After 65, people produced less for the state, and used more resources. Once people stopped working, they only took resources from the nation by receiving pensions and using a large amount of medical care. The drain on the national treasury to pay these bills was enormous, and had threatened to bankrupt Barahu's government. So, Barahu's analysts decided that it was more cost effective to eliminate the claimants than to pay the bills. And so began "retirement." At first, it was for those over 80 years old. But it worked so well that the age was lowered to 75, and then 70. And, while the government coffers were no longer bare, the program was producing so much money that the age was finally lowered to 65. At every person's medical checkup after turning age 65, they were given an injection or a pill. They were dead within a minute. No more medical care. No more pension. This was Barahu's form of retirement, and balanced budgets.

It seemed to Andrew that, now that the Supreme Council was nearing "retirement" age, they weren't willing to undergo the same treatment as ordinary citizens. Typical, he thought. The rules are great, as long as they're for others. But now, the conflict over the Emperors was something altogether different. Two sides of the government, warring with each other. That would be a chasm that he might be able to exploit, but, only if the Tree were ready to act.

Two things were of concern. First, how do they get in contact with either Barahu and which one do they approach for help? It's not like you could just walk into the Imperial Palace and ask to see the Emperor, or his, well what was he? Not a brother. A brother clone? Emperor in waiting? Maybe just Ohnoma, Andrew thought. His mind was wandering and he needed to concentrate. The time was nearing. How to approach Barahu? He had no idea. But, that was only one problem.

The second was when Charles' reformulation would be ready? Without the population awakening, seeing the inequalities of the government, and rising to overthrow the oligarchy that controlled them, his plans were worthless. The people must rise up. They would, he was sure, if they were able to think clearly, to function as normal, emotional people not the automatons that they had been turned into.

Andrew had to think. He needed to send this information to the Liberty Tree leadership and he needed to summon them quickly. It hadn't been done in years. Every meeting was with individuals, not groups. Groups of people could be noticed much easier by the government computers or the Purple Shirts. As he contemplated, his office phone buzzed, returning his mind to the present.

"Sinclair here," he announced into the speakerphone.

"Sinclair, Security Regent Peloreid here."

"Yes, Citizen Peloreid. What can I do for you?"

"I am waiting for the results of the video from Matthews' uniform. Do you have anything yet?"

"I was working on just that project as you called," replied Sinclair, honestly. "The video download worked perfectly. The monitor in his closet picked up everything last night. I'm running it through the filter now."

"And how long will it be before I see results?" demanded an anxious Peloreid.

"Hard to say. We've only done this in testing before. The more muffled or fragmented the audio and video, the longer it will take for the computer to analyze it. I think it will probably take the day. I think I can have the information to you first thing in the morning."

"An entire day. You expect me to wait an entire day?"

"It might be done sooner if I split the file and have someone else help filter the other half," replied Sinclair, unapologetically, anticipating Peloreid's response.

"No, no one else needs to be involved. Tomorrow morning will be fine. First thing."

The phone clicked as the line went dead. Tomorrow morning. Certainly not enough time to get the leadership group together. But now, he had to decide what he was going to show Peloreid. He wouldn't show him everything, that was for sure. But how much, which parts? The meeting with Councilor Tonklin had occurred late in the day, just before Matthews' went home. Perhaps, he could cut that section out and duplicate parts when the tunic was just hanging in his closet. Yes, that might work. The audio/video part was easy enough. It was the time tracking that would be the issue.

Sinclair's mind was racing now. This was when he was at his best, when he could see the different puzzle pieces and just had to put them in place. His adrenaline was up. His heart was pounding. Everything he had been waiting for over the past 20 years was beginning to come into sight. Now, to get over the finish line. His enemies were at hand. Thoughts flew through his mind, bits and pieces of his life up to this point. His parents. His dog as a child. His wife, Alice. He had thrown his entire life into avenging her. And now he was close.

The enemy. A puzzling thought crept into his mind. Who was the enemy really? He always thought of Barahu when he thought of an enemy of the people, of freedom. But, Barahu was dead. Barahu II? Perhaps. The Supreme Council? Definitely. And now, the Supreme Council was coming apart at the seams. Was that it? The enemy of my enemy is my friend. Baucman was in power. Tonklin was afraid. Tonklin. Tonklin? Tonklin!

That was it. Plans sped in and out of his thoughts. Yes, Tonklin was vulnerable. She needed help to save herself. She had a plan but one viewing of this video would have her executed before nightfall. He had leverage. It was dangerous, but then his life had been dangerous for years. All that he valued had been lost. No, not lost, taken from him. His freedom, his choice, his liberties, his love, all gone due to the egomaniacal Barahu and his lust for power. Now, he could strike a blow. Now, he could drive a stake in the heart of the Supreme Council. Now was his time. Now was his moment. He only needed one thing. Charles.

As Charles looked down at the notes on his desk he thought, I'm almost ready. He had the formulation in mind. But, he needed to test it. And that would require one of two things. Test subjects or use of the computer. The first was nearly impossible. While the government had no qualms about providing hundreds of test subjects if needed, the use of test subjects required additional supervision and oversight. Those were two things that Charles didn't want.

So, it was the computer system. But this wasn't just any computer system. It was one developed to replicate all human body activities from breathing to cardiovascular activity to nervous system responses. It attempted to determine the effect of chemical, environmental, or physical changes on a body. You could load in different menus and it would tell you what would occur in the blood vessels based on the amount of cholesterol consumed. It held over two hundred different body types and compositions, many to the genetic level, as well as thousands of different variables that could be changed. It was powerful. And well guarded since computers of this power could be used for many different uses, not all of which were acceptable to the government.

But, that was Charles' only hope. Now, he just needed to convince the Laboratory Review Board that he needed it. He was supposed to be working on the next formulation, not a revision of the old one, and certainly not one that would reverse the work that the team had done. He was being pressured for some results and, as yet, he hadn't given any. But his time was running out. He had to give them something. And, he needed to access the computer for his own ends.

As he made his way home that evening, he still wasn't sure what to do. He had been stalling, as he promised Andrew and Albert that he would, but that couldn't last. He was sitting on the transport looking out the window when a paper slid under his seat. He didn't turn around. Looking around to make sure that no one was watching him, he bent down and picked up the note. He slid it into his shoe, pretending to tie it in case he was being watched. His heart beat rapidly as he returned to looking out the window, watching the flakes of snow blow around the transport. He tried to slow down his breathing, to relax. As they reached his stop, he rose and walked to the front of the transport and out the door, not looking back. He was afraid of who might be sitting behind him. He had already put Albert in extreme danger with his mindless act at the church. He wouldn't put another in danger by even making eye contact.

Charles grabbed his dinner and walked up the stairs to his unit. His heart pounded as he threw his coat on a chair and immediately sat down, removing the note.

"Need solution soon. Execute to begin by end of month."

That was clear, brief, and direct. But the end of the month, Charles thought. That's only three weeks away. Yes, he had a solution in mind, but it hadn't been tested. He needed the computer system. But, he couldn't give them the real formulation that he wanted to test. But, to be ready in three weeks, he'd need to begin testing this week. That assumed a few days of rework and then another round of testing. Typically, these tests took months. He had three weeks!

Charles was pacing around his apartment, thinking through the possibilities. He didn't have months, but he did have a formula. His plan was to use the old, unsuccessful formula and then to slowly blend in an inert agent as he reduced some of the active. While the overall composition would have all the correct ingredients, it was the amounts and timing that would result in his desired outcome. His only hope was that the others weren't overly familiar with the interactions and wouldn't realize their effectiveness or, in this case, their lack of effectiveness.

It was a risk. He wasn't working with idiots, but they also didn't have his background and knowledge. It was the computer system that would be the problem. He needed to have the computer validate the results in order to get the formulation approved. But the computer would know and would report the true results.

How do you trick a computer? You don't. And that was where Charles was stuck.

Think. Think! There had to be a way. You must be able to fool the system into giving you the results you wanted to show. But that was it. The solution was so obvious. Too obvious. He could run a parallel test with another formulation which he was sure would generate the government's desired outcome. And, he would run his real test. Then, he could give one to the panel and, how would he do that? Would he give the real results to Andrew and Albert for them to pass on to the production facility? They had told him not to worry about that part. But, how would they get the chemicals to make his formulation? Charles reminded himself to solve his own problem and allow others to solve theirs. Andrew told him not to worry about the execution of the formula change. He had to trust him, trust him with his life.

Charles was sure the switch would also be discovered in no time. People would notice. Someone would investigate. And Charles would be identified as the culprit. If the plan didn't work, if the uprising didn't occur, Charles wasn't sure what his future would be. Taken away by the Purple Shirts, he imagined. He wondered if everyone, every patriot in a cause had to, at some point, make this decision. To succeed means freedom. To fail means death. He could hear the words, "Give me liberty or give me death" ringing in the depths of his memory, although he couldn't remember the source. Liberty or death. They seemed the only choices he had.

❖ ❖ ❖

18

"So, this is it?" questioned Security Regent Peloreid to Andrew Sinclair.

"Yes, sir. You can see that the audio and video quality is really quite good in the right circumstances. The filtering was more intensive than I had expected, but overall I'm happy with the outcome. Don't you agree?"

"Yes, yes. The quality is fine. I was expecting more...more substance," Peloreid admitted.

"Substance, sir. This is almost everything from the moment he woke up until he went to bed."

"Almost? What do you mean almost?"

"I mean, we only have data from when he was wearing his uniform. Time spent showering, at night after he hung it up, things like that, we'll have no record of."

"I see. Yes, of course not. So, he may have had activities without his uniform on. Yes, I see," replied the Regent, deep in thought.

"So, I believe this test has proven the capabilities of the fiber. Can I assume this test is now complete?"

"Complete? No, not complete. I want you to continue and report to me on anything, anything unusual."

"Unusual, sir? Can you explain what you mean by unusual?"

Peloreid stared at Sinclair. He didn't want to tell him, but, he needed Sinclair's assistance. And, Sinclair had been the ranking member of the Security Development Laboratory for several years. While not overtly supportive of Barahu, he had a spotless record.

Peloreid was an inch away from a seat on the Supreme Council. Without Joyce Clifford to help him, he needed someone. Sinclair was probably as good as anyone, he thought.

"Sinclair, what I'm about to tell you is highly classified. In fact, right now only two members of government know about this. You'll be the third."

"Of course, Security Regent Peloreid. I'll guard any secret with my life."

"Yes, I know you will. We have gained knowledge that Councilor Tonklin may be planning an overthrow of the Supreme Council. We believe that she may have caused the murder of Area Security Manager Clifford, either accidentally, targeting me instead, or as a way to insert Oliver Matthews onto my staff. The reason to eliminate me is obvious."

At this Sinclair nodded, an action which Peloreid noticed and approved of. He was powerful and his elimination could only assist Tonklin in her quest, he thought. Or, at least that's what he wanted Sinclair to believe. Sinclair's response confirmed that he was the man Peloreid needed. He was in his pocket and would do whatever Peloreid required. It was obvious from the body language, his shoulders leaning forward, his eyes never leaving Peloreid's. Sinclair wanted to be in Peloreid's inner circle, to serve him. And, serve him he would. Ah, power. There was nothing like it. That was what government was all about. The use of power. The ability to use people, to make them do your bidding. It was an aphrodisiac like no other.

Peloreid smiled at Sinclair and continued, "But, she had to know that Matthews was next in seniority to Clifford. So, either I'm gone and that helps her or Clifford's gone and Matthews is now inside my team. Matthews spent years on her security detail. I'm sure his loyalty is to Tonklin, and not to me as it should be.

For that reason, I need to know his movements. I need to know if he has any contact with Councilor Tonklin or her staff. That is the 'unusual' activity which I want you to watch for. And, that's why I want this to be for your eyes only. No one else must see this data. Is that understood?"

"Of course, Security Regent. I will run this project under maximum security. I can't believe a senior member of the Supreme Council would do such a thing. Despicable! I will report any contact only to you, Security Regent."

"Very good, Sinclair. I knew I could count on you. And, there will of course be rewards if we uncover this plot. I will not forget your service."

"You are most kind, Security Regent."

"You may go, Sinclair. Report any activity like we discussed to me, anytime, day or night."

"Yes, sir. I will, sir. Thank you, Security Regent Peloreid," stated Sinclair, rising from his chair and moving out the door.

Sinclair leaned against the elevator wall as he made his way back to the office. So, Peloreid knew something was up with Tonklin. He wasn't sure about the poisoning of Clifford, but that made more sense that the chauffer doing it. But, if they knew she had planned the murder of a senior Purple Shirt, why hadn't they arrested her for that? Why wait since that would be enough to warrant a death penalty? Something wasn't adding up there. But, if Peloreid had suspicions about Tonklin then she was at greater risk than she knew. And, based on the video and Peloreid's comment, Chairman Baucman was probably the other person in the know. But, how close were they to discovering her plan? They couldn't be that close or they'd just pull Matthews in for interrogation. No, they must know something was up, but not what or when.

Sinclair moved down the corridor and to his office, closing the door behind him. He needed to formalize the plan with the Liberty Tree leadership. He had leverage that he could use on Tonklin. He really had no leverage on Peloreid or Baucman, so it had to be Tonklin. She was the nervous one, the one at risk. She had the most to lose.

What do I even ask her for, Andrew wondered. He couldn't just go in and demand an overthrow of the government. It sounded, from the video, like she had a favored position with Emperor Barahu II. She would be using that position to request waivers of the 65 year retirement rule. But, Sinclair needed more that that. He needed something to break the government, to cause an uprising. He needed the two factions of the Security Council to battle it out. That would give the people a reason to revolt. That was the spark. The kindling was the newfound awareness of their situation which would dawn on them when they were no longer medicated. Again, back to Charles.

Andrew knew that Charles had received the note. He thought Charles must be close, based on the last meeting with Albert. But how close was he? Andrew needed to know. The timing of the plan was essential. He had to approach Tonklin soon, probably within the next few days. If her plan was due to take effect within two or three months, the formulation had to be in production within the next four weeks. While risky, particularly after the last meeting, Andrew had to set up another meeting with Charles. He had to ensure that the plan was moving along on time. If not, the Emperors would battle it out behind closed doors, the Supreme Council would change members, and the population would continue to be enslaved to a government that cared more for their own power and position than for the people that they ruled. This was government at its worst. This was what America had become under Barahu. It was time for the Second American Revolution.

Andrew picked up his phone and dialed a number from memory.

"Food services. Citizen Brown speaking."

"Citizen Brown, this is Citizen Sinclair. I need to order a special lunch today."

"You realize, it is very late to order something special. I can't guarantee delivery, even for the Development Laboratory Director."

"It's fine if it's a few minutes late. As long as it goes out today."

"Very well. What would you like?

"Turkey sandwiches. Four of them. One for Citizen Charles Johnson at the Chemical Development Lab, one for Citizen Ryan at the Capitol Sector Security Office, one for Citizen Pance at Supreme Council Security, and the last for Citizen O'Connell at Food Services."

"Very well. And when will this order expire?"

"I need this filled by tonight with the exception of Johnson. That can wait until Sunday afternoon."

"Understood. I'll see if we can rush it through."

Sinclair hung up the phone. Tonight, it had to be tonight. He couldn't wait longer to meet with the leadership team. It had to be tonight and they had to make a decision. Tonklin was the one to approach and to press. But the same question remained. How to push her?

"Ah, Councilor Tonklin," smile Emperor Barahu II as Evelyn Tonklin walked into his office. The sunlight from the large windows behind his oversized desk momentarily blinded her. As she moved forward, she could make out the enormous form of the Emperor sitting on a sofa, one leg on the cushions and the other on the floor. He was reading a book, something that struck Tonklin as very unusual. She rarely saw anyone read a book anymore. If people read at all, which most people didn't, it was from a small computer, not a leather-bound book. The only authorized literature was about Barahu I, either biographies or his writings and teachings, or books that had been approved by him. There wasn't a big demand from the populace. Most was done during their educational indoctrination when the government instructed the youth of the nation.

"It is wonderful to see our Supreme Being and Most Holy Leader today," replied Tonklin, beaming at the Emperor. "I hope I'm not disturbing your reading."

"Oh, not at all. Always a pleasure to see you. It seems that I get so few visitors. I don't know why more of my subjects don't come to me. I've never turned any away that wish to see me." Barahu motioned Tonklin to sit at the other end of the couch from him.

"They are busy serving you. They show their love and devotion by working for you. They are so dedicated, it leaves them little time for other things," she replied, taking her seat.

"Yes, I supposed that's true. I do wish there were more people around, other than these servants that always seem to be under foot. But, enough of my problems. What do we discuss today? Or, are you here to play another game with me?"

"I'm sorry, Excellency, I did not come for a game. I have a rather serious matter to discuss. I'm not sure how to begin," she said, a degree of sentimentality in her voice. She appeared nervous as she held her hands tightly to her lap and looked down at her feet.

"Councilor Tonklin, you have been a most loyal servant to me, and my father before me. There is nothing that you cannot say to me," stated the man, his oversized, bald, head nodding towards her consolingly.

"You know, I'll be leaving you soon," stated Tonklin, softly but clearly, looking up into the brown eyes of Barahu.

"And, why would you do that?" asked the Emperor, leaning in slightly towards her, lifting his large frame to face her more directly.

"I'm going to be...retired soon."

"Retired? You? I'm not sure I like that," he said, a strange, confused look on his face. "I will not be happy if you get retired."

"I know. I have enjoyed serving you. I wish I could continue."

"The law says that everyone must retire at age 65," Barahu sighed. He stared at his hands and there was emotion in his voice. He was obviously having a difficult time in accepting the news that his most trusted Councilor would soon be leaving him.

"I wish there was another way, that the law could be changed, amended slightly," she said, leading Barahu to ask the obvious question.

"Changed? Amended? Is that possible?" the Emperor asked, lifting his eyes to hers with hopefulness.

"You are the Emperor. Of course you could alter the law as you deem correct."

"But, my father set the law. Were you not with him? Are you saying he made a mistake?" asked Barahu, somewhat indignantly.

"I was with him, of course I was. And I never knew your father to make a mistake. He was, after all, the Supreme Being. But, when that law was written, it was a different time. The country was on the verge of bankruptcy. Older people were receiving billions of dollars in retirement payments for doing nothing. In addition, they required more doctors and nurses, more medicines and hospitals. The country could no longer afford to pay for the medical care. But, if you stopped paying, they would become sick and hungry. Then, they would protest and try to disrupt your father's government. That would harm all people. The only ethical way of dealing with the issue was to put the older people to sleep. Give them a painless injection. I thought it was a wonderful idea. The older population was reduced. With less people, we needed fewer doctors and hospitals. We spent less money and the country was no longer in debt."

"But now," continued Tonklin, grasping Barahu's hands and looking at him, nearly pleading with him, "now the situation is different. Your laboratories control the population and the number of people in each particular economic position. We have money to pay for things so that is not an issue. Now, we have fewer skilled people to take over key positions, such as a Councilor. You are very smart. You can obviously see how things have changed since your father made that law."

"It is very different, isn't it? But still, I have never before changed a law. I'm not even sure how to do it. And, what happens to all those people that aren't retired. Will they not eventually grow older and need medical care. Oh, I don't know. I'm very confused," he moaned. He put his hands up to his forehead and began rocking back and forth, in obvious distress.

Tonklin moved closer, putting a motherly arm around his shoulders, as difficult as that was because of his size.

"Don't worry, Emperor. I'm here to help you. You don't need to decide now. You can think about it and we can discuss it further," she said, softly, almost whispering in his ear.

"Yes. Yes. I'll think about it. I'll see what some others may think," he muttered, stopping his rocking but still sitting, elbows on his knees and his head in his hands.

"Oh, I don't think you should discuss this with anyone," Tonklin said softly.

"But why? This would affect many others."

"Yes, but some others may want me to retire."

"Who? Who would want you to go," he cried, angrily getting up from the couch and moving around the large office.

"I don't know for sure. I have heard talk that Chairman Baucman may want you to appoint one of his favorites in my place," she said, looking at him slyly, as if she had just spilled a big secret.

"Chairman Baucman? I don't really like him. He only comes to me if he needs something. Never to talk. Never to play a game. Of course," he continued, in a resigned tone, "I suppose it would be his job to name a replacement."

"Yes, but the replacement should show loyalty to you, not simply to Chairman Baucman," the Councilor replied, herself rising from the couch and moving towards the Emperor. "I will admit something to you that no one else knows. I have questioned Chairman Baucman's loyalty to you. He seems to run things that advance his desires, not necessarily in line with your wishes. That his why he rarely comes here."

At those words, Barahu turned quickly to face Tonklin. He rose to his full height, which was over seven feet tall. His enormous shoulders blocked the light that had so dazzled Tonklin when she arrived. He had a mad, menacing look on his face.

"He does not follow my wishes? How is that? Am I not the Emperor? Does he not know that I control the nation, not him?" he roared.

"Please, please calm down, Excellency," begged Tonklin, not just a little fearful of the outburst. She had seen the sudden mood swings before, but never the anger that was coming forth now. It was usually from happiness to sadness, from laughter to tears. The anger was a new dimension that she had not seen before, but which she was cataloguing in case she might have need of it again. "Emperor," she continued, "do not let Chairman Baucman cause you pain. I have been able to block these moves, to remind him of the spirit of your father that made these laws. That has always stopped him in the past. I just worry about you if I am not there to stand up to him. If I am retired..."

The Emperor fell back into a wooden chair that groaned under the strain. He looked dejected. Confused. He looked up at her once again. "You have always been loyal to me and to my father. I will say nothing about the change in retirement. I will think on it some more. I just worry of what it will do to all the others," he finished, looking rather lethargic after his recent outburst.

"Of course, Emperor. And, as you think, you could also make it a smaller change. It could be only for citizens necessary for the security of the country. For Councilors and other key individuals. That would eliminate the problem with all the other people," she added, with a consoling tone.

Barahu just nodded to her, not looking up, sunk down in his chair. She walked over and patted him on his shoulder, giving it a squeeze, her small hand making very little impact on his large, muscular shoulder.

"I will come back in a few days and we can discuss it some more. There is no reason to make any decision today. Please, Excellency, go back to your reading. You seemed to be enjoying it so," Tonklin said, moving to the table and retrieving his book. "The Prince. I don't remember ever seeing this book before. Wherever did you find it?" she asked, bringing the book over to him.

"I found it in my father's library. It's old. I thought it would be a story about princes slaying dragons or something. It's not like that at all," he said, not lifting his head but accepting the book from her.

"Well, enjoy it my Emperor, our Most Holy Barahu. I will return early next week." She went to him once again, giving him a slight hug around his shoulders and then moving toward the door. She took one look back at him, watching him sitting, sullen and dejected, slightly rocking back and forth. She closed the door and moved down the long, large hallway towards the exit. There we are, she thought. My future, Jefferson's future, all tied up in an overgrown child. What has this country come to? At least, he was thinking about her proposal. And, as she had suspected, he had no love lost for Baucman. That may be a tool she would need to use in the future. And that may be sooner rather than later.

19

"Gentlemen, I think we're all here," said Andrew Sinclair. While he spoke in barely more than a whisper, this voice echoed off the walls. The four men were sitting in a stone vault, lit only by two portable lights which caused their faces to be largely blackened with shadows. There were only four wooden chairs which sat around a large, flat topped trunk, also wooden, which was used as a table. The vault was old, built into the rock which lay underneath the sacristy of St. John's Cathedral. It was cold but dry, with only one entrance. Few even knew of its existence as it was impossible to see from the surface. A door underneath a carpet on the altar hid its entrance and one needed to descend a ladder to get to this depth. It was the most secure location any of these men knew of.

The four men gathered in the vault all wore serious faces. They had been playing this game for years, decades actually. They had seen millions killed when Barahu took over the government or, more accurately, refused to accept the election that would replace him and declared a state of emergency, implementing martial law in the process. These men had seen friends killed and families torn apart. They detested the government's scientific advancements that had enabled Barahu to do things impossible only a few years before. Cloning and genetic manipulation allowed Barahu and his government to play God, a part that he accepted with relish.

Each of the men had a deep seated, burning hatred of Barahu. And each of them, slowly, day by day, had worked incessantly to disrupt and destroy his government. They longed for the freedom and liberties which they had known as Americans, before the socialists had ascended to power and then refused to leave, even as the American public rejected them. Slowly, this group had held together the Liberty Tree, dreaming of a day when the works of Jefferson and Madison might again be recognized in their country. These were not sunshine patriots, but a determined band of men that would never give up. While they were few, they were linked to hundreds of men and women across the country that remembered or had been taught about the First American Republic. Like a chain link which touched only two others, these people interacted with very small groups, who did likewise in a decentralized system which reduced the risk to the whole while continuing to grow. The group was ready, waiting for the signal to begin an uprising. But, they all realized that a few hundred could do little against the force of Barahu and the Supreme Council. It would take an uprising of thousands. That was the concern as their moment of opportunity seemed to be nearing.

"I've received information that there is a major rift opening within the Supreme Council," began Sinclair, avoiding any niceties. These men were well beyond the "hellos" and "how are yous" of meetings. "Councilor Tonklin is due to retire soon. It seems that she doesn't like that idea and is planning to escape to a stronghold in the West Sector. She's hoping to get protection from Barahu II but, if not, she's prepared to make a last stand. Security Regent Peloreid knows something is happening but doesn't know what. While I don't have proof, I think he's under orders from Chairman Baucman to find out Tonklin's plan and stop her. So, I think our timing is somewhere in the next two months."

The man sitting in the shadows to Andrew's left murmured. "So, Andrew, this is all well and good but we've got to be able to motivate the populace. Where do we stand on the project to alter the sedatives?" asked Justin Pance.

"We're close, but I'm not sure of an exact time. We've told the chemist that we need the new formulation by the end of the month. That would give us about a month to get it into circulation before this happens, if it follows the timing I expect," responded Sinclair.

"If you get me the formulation, I can have it flowing within a week," added Michael O'Connell, who was sitting across from Sinclair. "I've got people standing by to make the change. But, even if we get it in, that's only three weeks to take effect."

"Why do you think we have until the end of next month?" asked Pance. He was leaning forward now, looking sternly at Sinclair. As his face was now lit, Andrew could see both the stress and the determination on his face. Pance was a Director of Security at the Supreme Council. He had a better knowledge of the inner workings there than anyone else in the room.

"It's based on some comments that Tonklin and her team made. Plus, Tonklin is due to be retired soon so I think she'll move within three months. She can't wait much longer."

"I agree," replied Pance. "I'm just not sure that we have that much time. If Peloreid is onto her now, he'll turn up the heat. Word is that Baucman is going to recommend him for Tonklin's seat. He wants someone loyal to him around the table. Tonklin controls a significant block of Councilors. With her gone and Peloreid replacing her, Baucman could do whatever he wants. He'll be unstoppable."

"That is a concern. I'm just not sure we can get it any faster. Speeding up the process could lead to other problems," answered Sinclair.

"Other problems? What type of other problems?" asked O'Connell. He was heavy set, with rosy cheeks and a face that seemed to wear a perpetual smile. That hid an eternal pessimism which led him to lean towards a cautious approach in many critical situations. While viewed as a shortcoming at times, this had also saved the organization on more than one occasion when more high tempered men were pushing for action.

"Without proper testing, the formula could have either a larger or smaller impact than we might like. The thought is that we need to wean people off. A sudden shock could do more harm than good."

"I see," replied O'Connell. "Yes, a shocked population might not do anything. We don't want them in shock. We want them pissed off at their circumstances. We want them to take action."

"Right," added Pance. "Rioting in the streets. I can't wait. I hope they stomp those goddamned purple shirts all into the ground." His blood was definitely up now. Pance had watched the Supreme Council in their deliberations for over 12 years. He had seen the disdain and contempt in which they held the very people that allowed them to live in regal comfort. He had seen them send thousands, tens of thousands to their death by approving various experiments. Or sometimes, simply to save money. He hated them and the Supreme Being and Most Holy Leader Barahu, as well as his offspring. He wanted them dead. Or better yet, to become the subject of experimentation and extermination, just as they had done to others. Barahu had spoken of how all were equal, but he enslaved an entire population and then lived a lavish lifestyle, enjoying the best of everything while others slaved away for him. He was a man of the people, but that man had isolated himself from the people, deeming them unworthy of him. Pance despised the man and the Council which now ruled in his name.

"And, now the big question," continued Sinclair, "the reason I called you together. I feel we must push Tonklin. We must use the leverage to cause a major rift to be played out in public. If not, if the other Councilors and even Barahu II aren't involved, it all happens behind closed doors. She'll steal away in the night. Barahu will either back her or not, and the government goes on as usual. We need to blow this thing apart. If not, Baucman will find out her plan and end it. We must get to her. But, what, how exactly do we push her?"

"We need to push her to allow the people to once again participate in government. We need to be able to elect officials, not just do what the Supreme Council or Barahu want," replied O'Connell.

"Why would she help us in anything?" The question came from the fourth man in the room, the only one that had yet to speak. "Why would she do anything for us at all? Because we threaten her? Threaten to expose her plan to Baucman? If she's got Barahu's backing, it doesn't matter what Baucman says." The man continued to sit back in the darkness, leaning back against the stone wall of the vault. "I believe you are aiming too low, gentlemen."

All faces were looking into the darkness, towards the sound coming from the fourth man. And then, Patrick Ryan leaned forward, bringing his chair crashing down with a bang which echoed around the chamber. The others automatically jumped back at the unexpected movement and sound.

"The way we force the issue is not to threaten Tonklin. It's to threaten Barahu. Barahu won't be afraid of Baucman, but he will be afraid of his successor, Ohnoma."

"So, how do you propose we get to Barahu?" asked O'Connell.

"The way we defend ourselves is to attack. We must attack the government, and that means Barahu. We have to force the Supreme Council to back one or the other. They're already split. That will force the issue. We pit the two Emperors and the two sides of the Supreme Council against each other. That's how we win."

"I'm not following you," said Sinclair. "Are you saying we should or shouldn't use Tonklin?"

"Of course, use Tonklin. Scare her. Ask her for the moon if you want. What we really need is for her to force the issue of her retirement with Barahu. Get her to force him to change his rule. Get him concerned about Ohnoma. But, do the same thing to Baucman. Force his hand. He's not stupid. He knows Tonklin is close to Barahu and will probably go to him for support. We've got to scare him into going to Ohnoma. We've got to get the two emperors fighting. That will split the Council and, thereby, the government. People won't know who to follow, the current Barahu or the future Barahu. That's when we strike. That's when we use our people to disrupt the government. We need to play both sides against each other."

"So we use Tonklin...and Baucman," asked Pance. "I like it. Get them both."

"Yes. Push Tonklin," continued Ryan. "Make her go running back to Barahu. Make her beg him to let her live or go out west or whatever the hell she wants. Then, push Baucman. Let him know what she's doing. Andrew, you have direct access to his lapdog, Peloreid. Feed him the information. He'll love you because he thinks it will get him in good with Baucman. If Baucman thinks Barahu is changing the rules for Tonklin, he'll be afraid that she'll talk him into more than just voiding her retirement. Let's force him to go to Ohnoma. Our goal should be to bring Barahu II and Ohnoma into conflict. To battle for the crown. That's when we make our move. That's when we need to be ready to have the population revolt.

And, I agree with Justin, we don't have three months. This will be settled before then. We need to get this rolled out, even if it's not fully active. We have to move in a month, tops. Otherwise, this will play out. Tonklin will get nervous, whether we push her or not. When she gets nervous, she'll bolt. She'll run before long. We have to act now or we've lost the opportunity."

The men looked at each other. Sinclair and Pance were nodding. O'Connell pinched his lip, deep in thought. "I think we're going to start having some shortages at the plant," he said finally. "We might need to dilute some of the additives that we put in the food. Maybe that will jump start the process until we get the new formulation."

The others smiled and nodded.

"But let's not kid ourselves," O'Connell continued. "That will work for a week, maybe less. They'll be all over my ass about it. We need that formulation."

"Understood," stated Sinclair. "So, are we all agreed then? I'll start the dialogue with Tonklin. I can do that next week I think. Then, I'll begin forwarding information to Peloreid. Make sure he updates Baucman and make him nervous. I'm scheduled to meet the chemist this weekend. We'll have to meet again by the end of next week for an update."

"I'm nervous about meeting too much," interjected O'Connell. "It would be a shame for all this to come crashing down at this late date."

"We have no choice," growled Pance. "We'll meet. We'll push from both sides. Push them right to hell if we need to."

"Very well, gentlemen. We'll leave in the order we arrived. A few minutes between each as usual. Next Friday evening. Seven o'clock. I'll have an update ready on Tonklin and Peloreid," Sinclair paused. "It's really beginning, isn't it?"

The others nodded, all smiling except O'Connell. Sinclair was the last to leave, thinking of the expression that would be on Tonklin's face when he called her.

Tonklin's face was smiling as she arrived in her office the next day. She had reassembled her team to update them on her conversation with Emperor Barahu II. Jefferson Tonklin was the last to arrive and assumed a place to the right of Evelyn Tonklin who was seated at the center of a rectangular, highly polished, mahogany conference table. Johannes was at the end, to her left while Oliver Matthews was seated directly across from her. She waited while the orderly poured coffee and then moved back to sit in the corner, out of the way but available if needed.

"I think I may be getting some good news for all of us," she began, smiling and looking at each of the team members. "I met with the Emperor yesterday and I think it went well. He's very concerned about my retirement and really doesn't seem to trust Chairman Baucman at all. I think I can talk him into changing the law regarding retirement. I will admit, he's reluctant to change a law that Barahu I wrote, but I explained the context of the law, what was happening at the time the law was written, and I think he understood."

"So, he's willing to abolish the retirement law?" asked Johannes, looking very surprised.

"I don't think he'll abolish it. I think he may be willing to amend it to exclude Councilors and other key individuals." With her last words, she looked at Jefferson and, placing her hand on his, gave a small squeeze.

"Other key individuals?" questioned Johannes. He looked at the smiling couple, trying to hide the contempt from his face and voice. Who did they think they were, he wondered. He doesn't deserve her. He certainly doesn't deserve to have access to people like Johannes. I could crack him in half, the old man. He's a leech, living off of her. He doesn't deserve her, or me. Key individual! I wish the man could be retired.

"Vannie? Does that answer your question?"

The Councilor's voice jolted Johannes back. He looked at her abruptly, a little embarrassed that he hadn't caught a word that she had said.

"Yes, Councilor. That's fine," he muttered, looking away and taking a bite of the muffin that he had removed from the tray, seeking to hide his lack of attention.

"So, as of now, our plan is on hold. I am quite hopeful that we will not need it, and we can all maintain our current positions without disruption." Councilor Tonklin was positively beaming, looking around the table and her co-conspirators and holding hands with her beloved Jefferson.

That was not the face Andrew Sinclair was hoping to see as he viewed his video monitor on Sunday morning. The download from Matthews' uniform was flawless. He could make out every line on her face. But today, it was his face that was unhappy. Without the urgency, would Tonklin really disrupt the Supreme Council? Would everything occur with a simple proclamation from Emperor Barahu that he had amended the rule? It was beginning to seem like Ryan's plan was becoming more necessary. He would have to force the issue, with both Tonklin and Baucman, through Peloreid.

Sinclair took a sip from his coffee cup. It would be a long day, working to edit the video tapes into something that he wanted Peloreid to see. This was a good start. Perhaps he would just show him this clip, unedited. That would help to prove his loyalty. Very soon, when more evidence was needed, he would show the previous video which explained the entire plan. Yes, that just might work. He would just have to change the date/time stamp on the earlier video, but he could do that with only a couple of hours work. It was time to begin the engagement. First, a call to Councilor Tonklin. Turn up the heat there. Then, to meet with Security Regent Peloreid. That should really get the pot boiling.

Sinclair made his way down the hall to a little used stairway. The stairs led down to the mechanical areas of the building which held the boilers and some maintenance equipment. As part of his Liberty Tree activities, he had often needed a secure phone line to make calls. While the vast majority of the complex was monitored with video cameras, no one had thought to install them in the boiler room. They also forgot to put a phone there. When one of the maintenance staff complained, they added one. But, this particular phone line was not wired through the normal switchboard because it was an add-on. Sinclair felt this was probably the most secure phone in the entire building because, by adding it to one of the existing lines before it entered the switchboard, it was essentially untraceable.

The only thing that Sinclair ever needed to worry about was the maintenance staff. Years ago, he had needed to bribe them with leftover food from the conferences that were held. The office staff had discovered that the food ordered for these meetings was much better than the normal fare. The staff made sure there was some conference nearly every day, at lunch time, so they could justify ordering in their meals. The staff would then keep the excess and most of them would take it home for dinner. Sinclair would take his to the maintenance staff. This small bit of kindness led to the maintenance staff doing as whatever he wished, regardless of whether it was within the rules or not. The people that felt as if they were the lowest level of the organization were more than willing to help someone that helped them. So, Sinclair would simply go to the boiler room office when he needed to make a confidential call. If someone from maintenance was there, they would leave, no questions asked. But most days, as today, the office was empty.

While he had thought about his words, Sinclair was still nervous as he dialed Councilor Tonklin's private number. Pance had provided a list of all the Councilor's private phone numbers and domicile unit addresses. He suspected they would come in useful in the right circumstances. He was right.

"Councilor Tonklin here," came the voice from the other end. While not cold, it was very official sounding with no hint of warmth. Sinclair had expected this since her caller ID would show no name or number, other than the Sector Security Office.

"Councilor, did you enjoy your meeting with Emperor Barahu?"

"Who is this?"

"Someone that can either be an ally or an enemy. That will be your choice."

"What's your name? What office do you hold?"

"I am someone who knows your plan. I can help you escape retirement…or I can help to ensure that your plan is discovered," said Sinclair, using a deeper voice than normal, his hand shaking as he held the receiver.

On the other end, Councilor Tonklin's face had gone white. While she was still confident that Barahu would not desert her, she had never expected a call like this. "What do you want?" she queried.

"I represent an organization of. . shall we say concerned citizens. The government will not long stand if it doesn't represent the people. We need to work together to make sure that happens."

"Ah, a revolutionary. You must be insane to think that I would work with you. You will not threaten me! I am a member of the Supreme Council and, if you know that I visited Emperor Barahu, you obviously know that I have access to the highest levels of government," she stated, clearly, but with her voice rising.

"Yes, but, will he really allow you to NOT retire? Now, that's the question, isn't it? Because, if he doesn't, your plan to fly west just might be in jeopardy, now wouldn't it." Sinclair spoke quietly and slowly, allowing the words to sink in. He had anticipated her response.

"Who put you up to this? Who are you working for? I demand to know who. . "

"Madame Councilor, your time for making demands is rapidly coming to an end. You are reliant on a man who has never made a decision in his life to allow you to live. He may, or he may not, but either way, there will be consequences to the government. There will be consequences to you. We can help. For a price."

"I don't need your help. And, I'm not afraid of any consequences," she yelled back.

"Of course you are," replied Sinclair steadily. "If you weren't, you wouldn't have designed a plan to escape. We need to revise our form of government. It is beginning. It would be easier with you. But it will come. The question is, where will you fall?"

"I will always fall on the side of Emperor Barahu, never for you disgusting revolutionaries. We have provided every single person in this country with food, shelter, clothing, and medical care. We take care of every need a person has."

"Yes, and how many have died so you could do that? How many have you killed in the name of government welfare? What liberties have you destroyed? You provide security, but you take a person's rights in return. There is no choice in this country. There is no freedom of thought. People do what they are told, told by a small band of corrupt politicians that will do anything, ANY-THING, to protect and expand their own power. This is not government. This is SLAVERY. But soon, very soon Madame Councilor, the people will rise once more. And the slave masters will suffer the fate of all dictators. Again, the QUESTION, Madame Councilor, which side will you be on?"

Andrew Sinclair had risen now, his hands still shaking but more from rage than fear. He had not planned this, had not planned to lecture and sermonize. He had not wanted to lose his temper, but the arrogance of the Councilor had made him lose his self-control.

"I think this conversation is over," stated Tonklin flatly.

"Yes, this conversation is. But there will be another. Situations change. The political animal will adapt since it has no basic conscious to anchor its beliefs. Your situation will soon change. When it does, we will speak again. And then you can make your decision. Good day, Madame Councilor."

The line went dead as Sinclair hung up the phone. His hands were still shaking. He had been more forceful that planned. He had threatened an uprising that would not occur unless others in government played their parts. She could easily ignore his threats, call his bluff and see what happened. But, Sinclair did not think she would. Tonklin was in a tight spot. She had planned on secrecy in case Barahu didn't support her. She still wasn't sure that he would. So, the heat was turned on, he just couldn't tell how high he had turned it.

He made his way to his office, moving now to the next step in the plan.

"Security Regent Peloreid, Andrew Sinclair here," he said into the phone in his office. "There's something I think you should see but I hesitate to copy it to bring to your office. Could you possibly come down here?"

"Is it important?" asked Peloreid, briskly.

"Sir, I think it's what you've been looking for."

"I'll be right there." The phone went dead.

Less than three minutes later, Security Regent Peloreid strode into Sinclair's office. He pulled a chair out, crashing down into it.

"This had better be good, Sinclair. I'm preparing for a meeting with CHAIRMAN Baucman and I can't be late," he stated, slightly out of breath.

"I think it is. Let me close the door and then I'll start the projector."

Sinclair moved quickly to close and, noticeably, lock the door. He returned to his computer, struck a couple of keys and turned to the video screen on his wall. In seconds, he and Peloreid saw a door opening and the interior of an office come into view. Since the viewpoint was from Oliver Matthews, the video was more of what he saw versus a bird's eye view of the room as normal in a surveillance camera.

Sinclair watched Peloreid as the meeting began with the Tonklin's and Johannes around the table. He sat quietly as Peloreid took in the video and listened intently to the words being spoken. It lasted only eight minutes at which time Peloreid instructed him to replay it.

"I believe this is exactly what you were concerned with, is it not?" asked Sinclair.

"Yes. Precisely. So, they mention a plan here. Is there no other mention of it in any of the other videos?" questioned Peloreid.

"No, sir. Only here. It seems like she's asking Emperor Barahu to change the retirement law so she can remain on the Council and, uh, unretired."

"Yes, that's exactly what she's doing. But what does she mean when she says that the 'plan is on hold'? And how dare she insinuate that Emperor Barahu has anything but the utmost respect for Chairman Baucman. It's obvious that she is trying to drive a wedge between the two of them. Oh, this is most important. I need a copy of this to show to…I need a copy of this."

"Of course, sir. I thought of making one but I won't make copies of any of this material without your consent. I wouldn't want something to fall into the wrong hands on my account," offered Sinclair, typing instructions into his keyboard.

"Yes, yes, you're good like that," muttered the Regent, pacing around the office, deep in thought.

A moment later, Sinclair removed a small disc from his computer and handed it to Peloreid.

"There you are, sir. Everything that you've seen is on there."

"And there's no other evidence from any of the files?"

"No, sir," lied Sinclair. "I've filtered through it, reviewing everything that looks of interest."

"Looks of interest? You mean you haven't watched everything?" asked Peloreid, incredulously.

"That would be impossible, sir. There's about 10 hours of video for each day, unless it's his day off and he doesn't wear his uniform. By the time I filter the audio and video, I would need to do nothing else that watch him work. I review every conversation that he's had, every phone call. But, I skip through the parts where he's at his desk alone or in his car alone. I could bring others on the project and they could each review a part of the day," offered Sinclair, defensively.

"NO! No one else. Just you. What you're doing is fine. Keep me informed."

Peloreid moved to the door and attempted to jerk it open. It was locked and he nearly ran into it before he was able to stop himself. He unlocked it, thrust it open, and moved out towards the elevator at a fast walk, nearly a trot.

Sinclair returned to his desk, a sly smile on his face. He sat back in his chair and sipped a cup of tea. He always switched to tea in the afternoon especially since the office coffee was usually lousy. Strong but lousy. He closed his eyes for a moment and thought of the events that he had just commenced. He foresaw arguments and assaults, Tonklin and Baucman at each other's throats, Barahu II and Ohnoma battling it out for superiority. And, while they would be doing that, the Liberty Tree would be in revolt, taking key industrial sites and utilities, fomenting an uprising in the population, many of whom would have no idea what was happening and why they even should care. But they would care. Their eyes would be opened, for some for the first time in their lives. The haze would be lifted. As long as Charles did his part.

20

"Good afternoon, Chairman. Always a pleasure to see you," said the man in his mid-twenties, smiling as he extended his hand in welcome.

"Good afternoon, Excellency," replied the rotund figure of Chairman Baucman.

The two men shook hand as if they were old friends. In actuality, each was studying the other, sizing up the man, having dealt with the other for some time, but never in matters of urgency or importance. For, while the handsome figure of Ohnoma had been groomed to become Emperor, to date he held no authority and, therefore, the Supreme Council had only a limited involvement with him. They met annually to discuss his education and development but, at this point he was not useful to them. As politicians are noted for doing, if you're not useful, you're usually ignored.

From his side, Ohnoma had noticed this. He was aware of politics, having inherited not only the exact genetic traits of his "father" but also his innate political sense, and perhaps even more ruthlessness. While unable to fully utilize these abilities as of yet, they were there, just beneath the surface. He had been inundated by how wonderful his father had been, how much like a god he was, and in all honesty, he had become bored with it. He was going to be his own person, regardless of what dear-ol'-dad might have wanted. He wanted power, all of the power that Barahu I had at his peak. He would rule his kingdom, not just allow others to manage it for him as his "brother", Barahu II had done. And part of his first acts would be to revamp the Supreme Council.

Ohnoma, while ruthless and egocentric, was also very bright and extremely shrewd. He would control the country, but he realized that he would need to use others in his regime. Part of the Supreme Council might be useful but, right now, he was unsure which parts. So, as he stood shaking hands with Chairman Baucman, it was that question that he was pondering, wondering if this man was a keeper or not.

For his part, Baucman was taking a risk. Peloreid had briefed him on Councilor Tonklin's visit with Barahu II. He had seen the video and knew that she was trying to guilt the Emperor into amending one of the standing laws of the nation. Barahu had never done that before and Baucman was concerned that, if he changed one law, he would begin to change others, perhaps even the ruling that Ohnoma should become Emperor soon. He was more concerned that Tonklin would now hold even more sway with the Emperor and that would reduce his control of the Council. He was betting that Ohnoma would not be willing to wait for his turn as Supreme Being and Most Holy Leader. If he provided a service to Ohnoma which forced Barahu II to cede authority, he would be in a prime position to maintain his power and perhaps to ensure Tonklin's demise. He sensed that Ohnoma was aggressive and impatient to assume control. He was hoping to use this to secure his own future.

"It's very nice for you to stop by, but I must admit I'm a little surprised. Typically, we only meet to our annual review," said Ohnoma, moving behind his desk and leaning back in his large chair.

"I thought we should begin to meet for updates as your date of ascendancy is nearing. I thought a weekly briefing of the most serious items of government would help you to be better prepared to rule," answered Baucman, moving to an armchair across the desk from the Emperor in waiting. His large frame had to squeeze between the padded arms of the chair, making him wince.

"Is this similar to what is done with Barahu II?" asked Ohnoma.

"No, the Emperor has had no meetings, at least, not with me," replied Baucman, with emphasis on the last part of the sentence.

"You imply that he meets with someone else. Shouldn't he be able to meet with anyone he likes?"

"Of course, Excellency. I just find it strange that the Emperor has never shown any interest in governing. He had empowered the Supreme Council to handle all facets of government, with the exception of enacting any new laws or amending any existing ones without his approval. However, I have learned that another member of the Council had been meeting with the Emperor, urging him to begin changing the current laws. It appears that he may indeed be considering some changes."

"But, Chairman, is it not reasonable to make changes to laws to reflect current conditions versus those that existed when the laws were enacted? I would certainly review the validity of laws under present circumstances," replied Ohnoma, watching Baucman closely for a response. He was beginning to think that one of Baucman's opponents was trying to get approval for something they wanted and Baucman didn't. A case of sour grapes, he suspected.

"I wholeheartedly agree, Excellency," responded Baucman, now becoming uncomfortable both with his seat and the way the conversation was progressing. "However, it is the change that is requested that most concerns me."

"Oh, what could this Councilor be asking for? A bigger domicile unit? A new limousine? I fail to see what could be so important."

"She's asking for her life," said Baucman bluntly.

"Her life? Explain," instructed Ohnoma, now leaning forward in his chair with an increased interest in the meeting.

"Councilor Tonklin is approaching her 65th birthday. She knows that, after that date which occurs within a few months, she will be facing the mandatory 'retirement', as will her close companion, Jefferson Tonklin. She has asked the Emperor to amend the law to allow them to live."

"I see. And you feel threatened by this?" asked Ohnoma, thinking that he had uncovered the real purpose of the visit.

"No, Excellency, I am fearful for you."

"For me! Why would anyone need to be fearful FOR me. OF me, perhaps," he said smiling, "but not for me."

"I'm sure you are correct. However, it entered my mind that, if Barahu II was willing to change the law to protect a close confidant from 'retirement', would he not also change the law to protect himself from 'retirement'?"

Baucman stared at Ohnoma as he said these words. He saw the reaction he had hoped for. As with many arrogant people, Ohnoma only considered these petty problems to be for others, never himself. It had never entered his mind that his title could be at risk, that anything bad could happen to him.

"I see. You think that Barahu II will change the law so that he doesn't need to give up the throne when I turn 25. Why do you doubt him?"

"Human nature, Excellency. Would you give someone else a gift that you truly valued if you did not have it for your own? Why would he allow Tonklin to avoid retirement and then accept it for himself only a few months later? I think the barrier has always been that the laws were enacted by Barahu I and he could not conceive of changing them. However, that seed has now been planted in his mind by Councilor Tonklin. He could very easily agree with her. And then, how long will it be until she encourages him to delay his own retirement, which will also extend his reign and eliminate yours."

"What basis could he possibly have for that," yelled Ohnoma, rising from his chair and walking around his study. His face had become tense as, for the first time, he felt that something he desired may be refused him.

"Excellency, the law states that the new Emperor will assume the throne when he turns 25 and when the current Emperor turns 50. Barahu II is only 28. Yes, he has held the throne for several years, but that is because of the untimely death of Barahu I. You were born about 3 years later and raised normally, as opposed to Barahu II who had to assume the throne earlier. He could very easily say that he has not reached his 50th birthday and neither has he ruled for 25 years so he does not need to give up the crown. Either of those arguments would delay your ascension indefinitely. That is the danger I see for you."

For a few moments, there was silence. Baucman wiped his sweating forehead as the morning sun filtered through the windows and fell directly in his face. He was uncomfortable in the chair, with its arms pushing into his sides. Ohnoma paced, first with his arms around his back and then with his right hand rubbing his face. Baucman followed him as best he could by turning his head from side to side and shifting in his seat. The meeting had not gone as expected. He thought Ohnoma would immediately want to plan a way of trapping Tonklin, but he had given no indication of that.

Finally, after several minutes, Barahu turned to Baucman.

"I appreciate you telling me this information. I admit that I had never considered such a thing ever happening. But, from everything I know of Barahu II, I cannot imagine that he would go against the will of Emperor Barahu I. I do not see him as having the will or fortitude to do so," said Ohnoma, plainly and calmly.

"Excellency, you must remember that he is doing so at the encouragement of Councilor Tonklin. It is not a battle. He just needs to sign a proclamation and the issue will be done. After, I cannot believe that she wouldn't prepare another proclamation for the Emperor himself. She would never give up her protector and he would be saving his own life. Both would win. Only you would lose."

"And you. Would you not lose?" asked Ohnoma, still seeking for the real reason that Baucman had approached him, feeling that Baucman really didn't have his best interests at heart.

"Possibly, in the future if other Councilors feel that Tonklin has more influence with the Emperor and if he continues to take a hand in government. They could elect her as Chairperson. However, my position on the Supreme Council is for life so the change would be largely insignificant. My greater concern is for your future and the future of the nation," he lied. "How much will this country regress if Barahu II is allowed to alter the laws that Barahu I established?"

Ohnoma stared at Baucman, still not fully believing him but now beginning to feel that, by using Baucman, both could be more secure.

"Do you have any proof of what you claim? Again, I find it hard to believe that the Emperor would begin changing laws when he's never done that before," challenged Ohnoma.

"I do not have anything from Barahu II. In fact, he has not yet altered any law. However, Councilor Tonklin has already discussed the matter with him and we have also learned that she has an alternate plan for escape if Barahu decides against her but she has put that plan on hold. In my opinion, that points to her feeling that Barahu II is close to deciding in her favor." Baucman was guessing at the last part. He had heard the mention of Tonklin's plan being on hold and, while he didn't have proof of what her plan was, he needed something more to use with Ohnoma.

"Again, Citizen Chairman, do you have any proof?"

"Allow me to show you this video which we obtained. I believe it will corroborate everything that I've stated," said Chairman Baucman, a slight smile spreading across his large, sweaty face as the sunlight continued to pour through the windows.

The bright sunlight was also in the face of Charles Johnson as he made his way along the streets. It was still cold, with spring not yet in the air and the snow just beginning to melt. He was anxious, as usual, to meet with Albert and Andrew. He wasn't taking any chances this time. He had removed the medallion which held the security tracking chip and was holding it in his hand. As he walked through the park, he began scanning it for a good hiding place to stow the necklace.

Across the street from the cathedral, Charles saw a dilapidated building which appeared close to collapse. He walked along its side, glancing up frequently to see if any bricks or wood were about to fall down on his head. Near the corner was a window, broken and with its wood casing rotting. He looked inside the building and saw a number of shelves, buried and broken under the weight of the roof which had partially collapsed. He peered in each side of the window, trying to look along the edges for a good hiding place. On the left side, he saw a nail sticking out of a stud which appeared to have, at one point, helped to hold the shelves to the wall. The nail was still connected, although bent downward as it had been pulled when the shelves collapsed. He reached inside, being careful to keep his arm away from the shards of broken glass which still clung to the window frame. He twisted the nail upwards and hung his necklace on it. Turning around quickly, he studied the streets to see if anyone was watching him. From what he could see, the few people out hadn't seemed to notice him. Most were walking alone, their faces towards the ground. He moved away from the window and slowly towards the church, waiting for the people to move further away before crossing the street and entering the alley.

Today, as Charles entered the church, it seemed as though he really saw it for the first time. The windows which had been darkened and discouraging last time, were now bright and vibrant as the sunlight turned the stained glass into stunning colors. Light seemed to burst out of the images of Jesus to fall right upon Charles' upturned face. It was as if a power was being transported from the image to Charles, engulfing him in light. He stopped, looking upward, transfixed by the sight.

"Aren't those beautiful windows?" asked Albert, moving up behind Charles. "I always loved those. Never tired of looking at them on a nice bright day like today. How are you, my boy?" he asked, grasping Charles shoulder with his hand. "How are you holding up?"

"Me? I'm fine. Just trying to complete my mission," replied Charles, turning his head from the windows and looking down into Albert's old green eyes. "And, I left the security chip off this time."

"Ah, good thinking. Nothing seems to have come from the last time but we don't want anything to foul up this plan, now do we? Come along, the others are waiting," he said, moving toward the altar.

"Others? Other than you and Andrew?" questioned Charles, following Albert down the aisle. "I thought I would never meet with more than you two."

"Unusual times call for unusual measures. Not to worry. Just another step in the plan. Now, follow me and watch your head. It's a little dark down here," Albert said as he began descending the ladder behind the altar.

Charles looked after him, a little unsure of the looks of the dark hole and old wooden ladder. But, he followed dutifully, step by step until he hit the bottom. He found himself next to Albert, both squeezed into a small area which led to a short hallway whose end was emitting a faint light.

"Watch your head," instructed Albert as he led the younger man through the opening and into the rock vault.

As Charles entered, he noticed Andrew sitting across what looked like an old sea chest. Albert took a seat on Charles' right. Another man that Charles had never seen was seated to the left, leaving the seat directly in front of him and across from Andrew.

"Charles, so good to see you again," smiled Andrew warmly as he rose, although with his head stooped beneath the low stone ceiling, and shook Charles' hand warmly. "I've thought of you often over the past few weeks. Daily in fact."

"I've missed you, too," admitted Charles, honestly. "I wish we could see each other more often."

Charles was absolutely sincere in these words. His memory continued to improve but only in bits and pieces, memories that seemed to come to him from nowhere and some of which disappeared as quickly. Andrew was still the best direct link he had with his earlier life, his childhood and his parents. He yearned to spend hours with him, learning all there was to know about that life, the part of his memory that the government had taken from him.

"Charles, I want you to meet Michael O'Connell. He's a member of our executive committee and someone that will be very important in bringing this plan to fruition. Michael manages the food preparation facilities. He has direct control over the purchasing and processing of the chemical sedatives added to the food. While closely monitored, he does have influence over many parts of the process. He'll be the one to ensure that your new formulation is in process as quickly as possible."

The two men shook hands and exchanged niceties. Michael had known Charles professionally before the Procedure 23 had been done and the two spoke for a few minutes about the current situation. Eventually, Andrew brought them all back to the topic at hand.

"So, Charles, you see why we need the formulation. If our plan works and we do drive a wedge between factions of government, we must have the population awake, and hopefully confused and angry about the abuses they have suffered by the government's usurpation of their God given rights. We need that new formulation."

"I've got it," said Charles plainly.

The other men beamed at him.

"You've got it? That's wonderful," exclaimed Albert.

"Marvelous!" said Michael with a shout. "When can I get it?"

"As soon as I can get the files out of the computer," replied Charles, lacking the enthusiasm of the others. "But, there are some issues."

The smiles on the men's faces fell instantly. The room was silent. Charles was sitting with his hands clasped together, looking down at his feet.

"For some reason," he continued, "there's been a lock placed on the computer system. No one can retrieve information. I asked about it and they said it was a normal temporary freeze placed by Sector Security. However, based on the feedback from my colleagues, I'm not sure it's at all 'normal'. I'm not sure what they're looking for, but I can't get anything until it's removed."

There was a slight murmur from the men as they allowed Charles to finish. They looked at each other anxiously, knowing that not only was their plan at risk, but their entire organization could be threatened if the Purple Shirts had begun activities against them. So far, the Liberty Tree had only had occasional conflicts with the Purple Shirts. By limiting their activities and biding their time, the Tree had largely been able to avoid detection. The Purple Shirts knew of their existence since dozens of arrests had been made over the years but, since the Tree limited member's knowledge of the true extent of the organization, those arrests had never led to a large disruption of their activities. None of the Purple Shirts and, in reality, none of the Liberty Tree actually knew of the size and extent of their membership. Now, it appeared that one of their most important objectives was in jeopardy.

"There's also another issue," continued Charles after a moment. "At least, I think there might be a problem. The formulation includes an older chemical, Sigma 6, which isn't normally stocked. I don't know how you'll be able to get that into the formulation," he finished, turning to O'Connell as he spoke the last words.

"I don't know how hard it will be to get Sigma 6 into the plant? It depends if they still make it or not. They strictly monitor all of these chemicals. Unless it's still stocked somewhere, it's impossible, at least in our timeframe. It would also need to be approved by the Food Additive Committee if we're not using it currently. I guess that's it. We can't do it!" O'Connell exclaimed.

"Calm down, Michael," admonished Albert. "Let's peel this onion back a little. So, Charles, how do you propose that we solve this? Do you have some idea?"

"I agree with Michael in the fact that this needs to be approved by the Food Additive Committee. So, I need to adjust the results to show them that the new formulation will do what they want."

"Adjust the results?" asked Andrew. "You mean falsify the results, don't you?"

"Yes, I do. From what I see, that's the only way."

"You're insane," replied O'Connell, shaking his head. "Those people aren't a bunch of idiots. They've got some pretty sharp people on that committee. You can't just go in and throw some crap on the screen and expect them to buy it."

"No, I know I can't. When I was running this test in the system, I also ran another one which would be the replacement formulation that they want. It got close to the results they wanted. I need to show those results with my formulation. My only hope is that, since it's a new chemical composition that I'm using, that they won't figure out the switch."

"And, if they do?" asked O'Connell.

"Then, I'm done and so is this plan."

"That's a hell of a risk, don't you think," shot back Michael. "All of us could go down the tubes because of this."

"I wish there was another way. If there is, I'm not smart enough to figure it out. Maybe there's some other mixture of chemicals to do it. Maybe it's part of my memory that got wiped out last year. I don't know. This is all I could come up with."

"We know you've done your best," reassured Andrew Sinclair, softly but supportively. "So, I have a simple question. What if we bypassed the approval committee?"

"You're crazy," answered Michael. "Bypass the committee. I need them to send us the formulation. It can't just come from Charles. It has to be loaded into the system. And these formulations are exceedingly complex. They have to be adjusted for different amounts for different foods so that taste, color, and potency aren't affected. The government doesn't want anyone figuring out that we're drugging them. And, with most new formulations, there's a phase it cycle where amounts are changed weekly, even daily in some cases. There are literally thousands of computations done which adjust the mixture in minute increments. I can't load that manually. I need the file sent by the committee."

"OK, I understand," replied a soothing Andrew. "But, say we were able to load the file from the system, without approval from the committee. Could that be done?"

"Of course, if I had a chip with all the information. Once it's loaded, it flows automatically to purchasing and processing. Once it's in the system, the inspectors only check to see that the actual output matches the computer settings. But, I would need the chip. Usually, the information is just transmitted automatically through the system by the committee once they approve it."

"So, Charles, what we need is the correct formulation on a chip for Michael. Then he can load it."

Charles stared at the men. "I understand. I'm just not sure when and if I'll be able to download anything."

"How did you get the information for your analysis?" asked Albert.

"That's all done by the system so I don't need to download anything."

"How about results so you can prepare your proposal for the committee?" Albert queried.

"Yes, I'll need to be able to download some information for that. I can ask."

"Charles, from what I've picked up, this project is behind schedule, is it not?" asked Andrew.

"Yes, by a couple of months. That's the stall I was able to do."

"So, would you be able to use that to regain access to the system? Use that as leverage?"

"I can try. Once they open up the system, I can download the file on a microchip. That's easy enough."

"Very well then. You work on that. Michael, you prepare how you're going to get the chip loaded into the system. With luck, all of this will occur within the next coule of weeks. If not, we might have real problems."

"Real problems?" exclaimed O'Connell in disbelief. "With all this, we have to wait for the 'real problems'. Wonderful! Good Lord, I can't wait for those."

"Albert, would you lock up after Charles leaves so we can fine tune the planning?" asked Andrew, politely.

"C'mon Charles. That's our cue that we're no longer required here," said Albert, smiling jovially to the group. "I've got something for you anyway."

The men made their way back through the small entrance tunnel to the ladder and up to the altar. Charles looked out over the numerous rows of pews, the huge columns that supported the vaulted ceilings, and, once again, to the stained glass windows. The light had faded some since they had arrived and the windows didn't project the vivid colors that they had earlier. Charles was a little disappointed in this, almost as if the Lord were turning out the lights on the group.

He followed Albert up the aisle towards the doorway on the left side of the church that led to the alley. Albert opened the door and held it for Charles. He moved to his coat which was hanging on the wall near the outside door. Fumbling first in one pocket and then another, he finally removed a small item which he brought to Charles.

"There you go, son," announced Albert. Charles looked at the little capsule which Albert had placed in his hand.

"What is this, a poison pill that I'm supposed to take in case I'm captured?" asked Charles, only half joking.

"Something like that," answered the older man. "Actually, it pulls apart. When you get the micro-chip, place it in there and reconnect the pieces. It's airtight, watertight, and, if you are caught, all you need to do is swallow it. You're body can't break it down so it will just go right through you. Now," chuckled Albert," I won't pretend that getting it back would be a fun job, but it makes it pretty difficult to discover."

Charles looked at the gray hair, green eyes, and ruddy complexion of the shorter, older man. He couldn't help but feel like Albert was what a grandfather must be like, full of life's lessons, with a sense of humor and only out for your best interests. He had developed a real fondness for the man and, standing there alone with him, looking down into those clear, green eyes, felt an affection which seemed new to him. Was this what it was like to love a parent, or in Albert's case, a grandparent? He felt immersed in a feeling of safety and security which the old man brought to him.

Without thinking further, he reached over and gave the man a hug around his shoulders. Albert put an arm around his back and gave a short squeeze back, before quickly pulling away.

"Go on, get out of here now," Albert instructed, turning away and wiping his eyes. Charles could hear the emotion in his voice and the sniffles coming from the man's, now turned, form. He left without saying another word, his own throat a little constricted at the moment.

Albert locked the door after him. He stood there for a moment, one hand on the door handle, the other holding the door closed. What a fine young man, he thought. What a wonderful person, to risk his life to help people that he could not remember, for a cause that had to be foreign to him. Was it because the government had killed his parents, erased most of his memory, or enslaved his generation? Any of these reasons would be sufficient. It was hard to say what motivated some people to fight against the rule of dictators, when most are happy enough to go along. Courage? Conviction? Anger? Who knows, he thought. But he was thankful that there were such people in the world. He remembered the America that he was raised in. How it had changed, gradually and then faster and faster. People got afraid and voted for people offering hope. The people traded responsibility and choice for a promise of security. And, there was security in this country. Yes, if the government allowed you to live, you were fairly well taken care of. You just didn't have much choice in the matter, thought Albert, shaking his head and moving back to the altar.

Outside, the weather had turned cloudy and cooler. Charles made his way towards the broken window where he had left his medallion. Before reaching it, he made a quick perusal of the street to make sure no one was watching him. Having concluded that it was safe, he reached in, pulled out the chain, and quickly made his way towards the exit on the opposite side of the park.

"Area Security Manager Matthews, this is Officer Stukap reporting," said a soft voice into a transmitter. "I have reestablished visual contact with the suspect. He is moving back towards his domicile unit. Orders, please?"

"Continue to monitor his activities. Did you see anyone else at the church?" answered Oliver Matthews' voice.

"No sir. No one entered or left since the suspect. There were no people indicated on the security tracking either, although even the suspect didn't show up on it. I'm not sure if the composition of the building somehow blocked the signal or if there is some other reason. Also, the suspect removed a necklace and hid it outside the building before entering. It had the symbol of a tree. I've never seen it before," said the purple shirted security officer that was now trailing Charles.

"Did you confiscate the object?" asked Matthews.

"No, sir. I thought it best not scare the suspect. I did take a picture of it which I'm now sending to you."

"Good work. Continue to monitor the suspect until he returns to his domicile unit. After you've turned over his surveillance to the agent on premises, return to me at headquarters for a debriefing."

The line clicked dead. The agent continued following Charles, assuming he was headed to his unit, precisely where the officer wanted to head himself. He hated surveillance. He had stood outside that church for over an hour, constantly walking around to make sure there was no other exit that he might have slipped through. The handheld security monitor, which he used to track Charles through the microchip in his neck, hadn't shown any movement. However, he wasn't even sure that the monitor was working right since it had shown the suspect's location as the street, not the church. Usually, the monitor's precision was within a few feet. In this case, it was off by about 100 feet. Stukap made a note to have the monitor serviced when he returned to headquarters. It wouldn't do to lose his suspect next time because the monitor had him located in the wrong building.

❖ ❖ ❖

21

"Dr. Horner, may I have a moment," asked Charles Johnson, knocking on the Chemical Lab Director's open door.

"Yes, Charles. Come in. I was hoping you'd be bringing me an update on your project. It's behind schedule and, if there's one thing Security Regent Peloreid demands, it's a tight schedule," answered the stocky, white haired man.

"I do believe I've got an answer but I can't be sure," began Charles, moving into the office and sitting in a worn, fabric covered armchair.

"Can't be sure? I would think that it would be obvious enough if the new additive worked or not."

"It would, of course it would. But, the testing system is locked down. I can't get the final results and analysis out in order to present them. I ran a test on the new Theta I as well as a formula based on existing Omega materials. I believe the Theta will be superior but, I can't prove it without access to the system," argued Charles, looking pleadingly to Dr. Horner.

"What the hell do you mean, the system is locked down!" roared the older man.

"I couldn't log in on Saturday so I called the technical director. He told me that the Chemical Lab access to the supercomputer had been locked down, by order of Area Security Manager Matthews. I'm sorry sir, I thought you must be aware of it," stated Charles.

Dr. Horner picked up the phone and, after confirming a number on his listing, dialed and waited, impatiently drumming his fingers on the desktop. Charles gazed at him, watching his eyes flicker around the room, his face beginning to redden. Dr. Stoney Horner was an interesting figure. Nearing retirement age, he was renowned for, well for nothing. He had taken over the lab from Ben Jorgenson after Ben had been removed for security reasons. Andrew and Albert had described Ben's arrest for him and Charles knew that it was Ben who had incriminated him while under painful torture. While Charles could not accurately remember the discussions with Ben, he had fleeting recollections of some private talks, discussions that would have been condemning if discovered.

Upon Charles' return, others had talked very little about Jorgenson. By then, Horner had been in place for a few months and everyone was wary of discussing the old regime. But, Horner's appointment had caused many to scratch their heads. First, he was not a chemist, which made one wonder why he was now in charge of a chemical lab. He was a physicist and, based on what people could gather, not a very good one. He was never mentioned in any official literature regarding new developments or research projects. He was not known to have done anything. Even people in the physics department didn't know what he did. He attended all the meetings, making few comments, and never making waves. He kept his head down and did, well, nothing. So of course, he got promoted. Government at its best, Charles thought.

From what Charles could tell, the gossip was right. He had never gotten any advice, comment, or criticism from Dr. Horner. He could have told him that ice cream was made from oil and rock and the only response would have been a nodding of the head and quiet "mhmm, mhmm". While normally a problem, in this instance, Horner's lack of knowledge was a definite asset.

After a few rings, a male's voice answered at the other end, "Area Security Manager Matthews' office."

"This is Dr. Horner. I need to speak to Citizen Matthews," ordered Horner, in a blustery tone.

"Area Security Manager Matthews is out today. I can put you through to his voicemail."

"I don't want his voicemail. I want to speak to him. Give me his direct number."

"That information is restricted. Do you want his voicemail?" asked the disinterested voice.

"No, I don't want his voicemail," bellowed Horner.

"Very well then." The phone clicked dead.

Horner looked at the receiver in amazement. "Damn these bureaucrats. None of them worth a damn," he shouted before dialing another number.

Charles tried his best to hide is smirk. He found Horner complaining about government bureaucracy quiet ironic since most people complained about him being a prime example of worthless government bureaucrats.

"Dr. Horner for Security Regent Peloreid," Charles heard Dr. Horner say into the phone. "Citizen Peloreid, I apologize for bothering you, sir. I have a problem with a security hold put on our computer system by Area Security Manager Matthews. We can't finish the food additive project without the system. The data's all there, waiting for us to extract it but now we can't. If it's not taken off, we won't be able to finish the project on time," explained Horner. "Yes, sir, I understand that it's already late. I was speaking of the revised schedule. I tried Matthews' office but he's out and they won't put me through to him. I was left no choice but to call you. I know how concerned you and Chairman Baucman are about this project, so I thought it best to contact you immediately. Yes, sir, the Chemical Lab access to the Sector supercomputer. Yes, sir, that's right. Yes, sir. Thank you, sir. Yes sir, I'll ensure that you get an update by the end of the week. Thank you, Security Regent Peloreid. Good-bye."

Horner hung up the receiver and looked at Charles with an air of accomplishment. "You should have access again within a half hour, by order of the Security Regent. Now, how long will it take you to complete the download and analysis?"

"I'll have the download done today and the analysis within a couple of days," answered Charles.

"Good. I need an update by the end of the week. Is there anything else you need me to do for you?" asked Horner, a tone of superiority in his voice.

"No, sir. I can take it from here. Thank you, sir. And may I say you handled that wonderfully?" said Charles, standing and making his way to the door.

"You may," replied Horner, staring at his computer monitor and dismissing Charles with a slight wave of his hand.

Charles walked quickly to his office, closing the door as he entered and moving to his desk. He tried logging onto the system but was still denied access. While he waited, he loaded a blank microchip into the computer and fumbled in his pocket for the capsule that Albert had given him. Now, all he needed was for Peloreid to do his job.

Security Regent Peloreid was just dismissing an assistant from his office. "And, after you call systems security, contact Andrew Sinclair. I need to speak to him," he said, turning his back on the assistant and looking out the window.

It was a beautiful, sunny, mid-winter's day. There was a sharp chill in the air which Peloreid usually enjoyed. But, he wasn't smiling today. He needed an update from Sinclair so he could go back to Chairman Baucman. He knew that Baucman had met with

Ohnoma, but had no idea what had happened. He didn't feel comfortable asking Baucman a direct question about it, but he thought if he could give an update on Matthews' movements, he might get Baucman to divulge the details of his meeting.

"Sinclair, do you have any updates on Matthews' yet," Peloreid shouted into the phone as soon as Andrew answered.

"I've received the data download and am processing it now, sir. I will have an update of any suspicious activity or meetings by mid-afternoon," answered Sinclair, calmly. He was lying of course. He had just scanned through the download and was now going back through the most interesting parts.

"I need an update as soon as you can get it," snapped the Security Regent.

"Yes, sir. That is my highest priority," replied Sinclair. The line went dead.

People are certainly in a nasty mood, thought Andrew. Peloreid had never been patient but this job took time, especially since Sinclair had two more uniforms made for Matthews. Peloreid had insisted so the new Area Security Manager had no excuse for not wearing one. Matthews was told that this was standard issue for his new position and seemed to think nothing of it.

Sinclair stopped the tape when he saw Vannie Johannes enter view.

"Oliver, how are you today?" asked Johannes.

"I'm fine. Any word on the, ah, project?" asked an obviously nervous Matthews.

"Not sure. Councilor Tonklin met with Barahu again. Didn't get a firm commitment but he did ask her to draw up an amendment that he could sign if he so choose. Seems like he's leaning in her direction. Just not sure on the timing so we might not need to do it at all," answered the tall, muscular figure of Johannes.

His dark eyes projected vividly in the video and his face was tight as he spoke. "The Councilor is drafting an amendment now and plans on meeting with him again within the next week. I think she should do it right away but she's concerned about making him nervous by seeming pushy. I don't trust Baucman or Peloreid so I'd like to act before they catch wind of something. The Councilor wanted to act faster too but no, Jefferson had to have his way and told her to wait. He didn't want her to seem too needy," said Johannes, sarcastically. "What an idiot he is. He ought to be shot. No one that stupid has a place in society. Politicians, they talk and talk and talk and never do anything. Councilor Tonklin was in operations so she knows how to act not just talk. The others, I'd line them up against the wall and shoot them. Isn't that what governments for, to get rid of the idiots in society? Isn't that our duty? We make the decisions because most people are too ignorant, too stupid, or too lazy to make decisions for themselves. Who wants the average, everyday idiot to be able to make their own decisions? It would be anarchy. Ridiculous! They couldn't do it so the government took over, as it should. Those that didn't like it were exterminated, as they should have been. It is the government's responsibility to manage the population, not the population's responsibility to manage the government."

From Matthews' there was little response. He said almost nothing while Johannes went on for several minutes. Eventually, they parted, with no more information available regarding Tonklin or Barahu II.

But, Sinclair had what he needed. Tonklin had petitioned Barahu II again. She was preparing an amendment at his request. While he would sign, they would be Tonklin's words. It was time now to show Peloreid and, indirectly, Baucman Tonklin's full plan. That would force the issue with Ohnoma. The time was nearing. Charles would come through, he could feel it. The divide was opening and now they would need to exploit it.

Sinclair rose, making his way down the corridor, towards the door to the boiler room. Ensuring that he had privacy, he closed the office door, picked up the phone and dialed.

"Councilor Tonklin here," answered the woman on the other end.

"Good morning, Councilor. How is your amendment coming along?" asked Sinclair quietly.

"Who is this? How do you know about that?" snapped Tonklin, her morning calm shattered by the call.

Sinclair had surprised and startled her, he knew. She was getting nervous, jittery even, based on the sound of her voice. The pressure and stress was starting to get to her. It was precisely what he wanted.

"Councilor, you are in grave jeopardy. Even if you convince Emperor Barahu to sign that document, forces are mobilizing against you. You need a friend, Councilor."

"Oh, is that what you are, a friend? A friend that would destroy the very government that clothes and feeds him. That doesn't sound like a friend to me!" she exclaimed excitedly, her voice rising as was her blood pressure.

"Yes, I will admit that the government provides food and clothing. The food and clothing they choose. The amount they choose. The color they choose. People do not want handouts, Councilor. They want freedom. Freedom of choice."

"Yes, that worked out so well before didn't it? People were failing. The country was failing. Perhaps you are not old enough to remember."

"While not as old as you," countered Sinclair, "I do remember. Yes, people could fail. But with no risk of failure, there is no possibility of success. People cannot achieve greatness unless they are willing to accept risk. Your government eliminated the ability for anyone to achieve greatness, to control their own lives, and make the decisions, good or bad, that they wish. The controls that your government imposed destroyed opportunity, either to succeed or fail based on your own individual abilities and desires. So now, the individual is destroyed but government survives. That cannot long endure. The opposite is better, for the individual to survive and this government to be destroyed."

"You are nothing but a misguided idealist. I will not help you on your mission to destroy the country that I have worked so long to build," Tonklin replied, disgust hanging heavy in her voice.

"Then, will you not help me to save your own life, and perhaps also Jefferson's."

"I do not need you to help me at all. Why can't you understand that! I have the support of Emperor Barahu himself. I certainly don't need your assistance."

"That would be true, were Emperor Barahu not in jeopardy as well. There is a civil war in the making. Your enemies are also enemies of Barahu. They will not allow you to survive. They are preparing. And, unless you have help, you will not be able to fight them, and Barahu will fall with you. Remember, the enemy of my enemy is my friend. I can be a friend to you."

"I do not want your kind of friendship. You are foolish and misguided. Barahu is safe and we will protect each other. And then, we will work to eliminate your kind from the country," warned Tonklin.

"Yes, you do have great experience at eliminating threats. But, you are not ready for your enemies. They are coming, Councilor. If you foolishly refuse my help, then you should act fast.

Your time is running out. You do not have until your 65th birthday. It will happen before that date."

Sinclair hung up. He sat back, smiling to himself. He had expected this conversation to go as it had. In reality, he had no idea of how quickly Tonklin's enemies, namely Baucman and Peloreid, were preparing to move. He just needed to create a sense of urgency, on both sides, but starting with Tonklin. He didn't need concrete plans about her enemies. He just needed to get her concerned about their movements. Like most of the high ranking government officials, he sensed that she had a paranoia of anything that might disrupt her authority. She would sacrifice anything to protect it, and it was that paranoia that he need to leverage. And, as with Tonklin, so too with Baucman since they were essentially cut from the same cloth, although it took a lot more cloth for Baucman, Andrew chuckled.

He was sure that Peloreid had briefed Baucman and that Baucman had in turn gone to Ohnoma to begin building support. A Liberty Tree agent in the Chairman's own office had notified the group of those moves. But, he didn't know if Ohnoma had even taken Baucman seriously regarding the treat. If not, the video showing Johannes giving Matthews the update should move things along.

Sinclair returned to his office and phoned Peloreid.

"Sir, Andrew Sinclair here. I'm not done reviewing all the video but I've come across something that I think could be too urgent to delay. I thought I should bring it up if you have time for me.... Yes, sir. I'll be there momentarily."

Sinclair moved to the elevators and up to Peloreid floor. Waiting in the lobby outside Peloreid's door, he looked out the big windows onto the front entrance to the building. As he watched, Area Security Manager Oliver Matthews strode through the doors, removing his topcoat and straightened his uniform. Ironic, thought Andrew, that the very uniform which brought him such pride would also cause his downfall, and perhaps the downfall of the government. "Pride goeth before a fall" echoed in his mind. Matthews certainly seemed to be rushing towards his fall.

Oliver Matthews was rushing, rushing to meet with Security Officer Stukap. Stukap was waiting outside of the Area Security Managers office when he arrived. He stood at stiff attention and saluted as Matthews walked by, waving for him to follow. Once inside the office, Matthews slammed the door closed and quickly turned to the younger officer.

"Well, what is your report?" he demanded.

"Sir, I followed the suspect, Charles Johnson, as instructed. The only suspicious movement he made during the day was to go to the old church, St. John's Cathedral. He walked very hesitantly, constantly looking over his shoulders to see if he was being followed. I do not believe that I drew his suspicion. He was in the church for just over one hour. During that time, I maintained visibility with the premises and didn't see anyone else entering or leaving," stated Stukap, standing at attention for the entire time of his report as Matthews sat watching him.

"Is that all?" asked Matthews.

"There was only one other thing that was curious. Before entering the church, Johnson removed a necklace and hid it in a dilapidated building across the street. When he exited the building, he retrieved it. I found that very odd."

"Yes, I believe you mentioned that on the phone. However, I didn't recognize the symbol of the tree. I thought it might hold some religious significance, tree of life or some such nonsense that people used to believe in," Matthews replied.

"I was unsure as well, sir, so I took the initiative of researching the symbol. It was used as recently as a few years ago to designate membership in the 'Liberty Tree Organization'."

"The Liberty Tree? That's an illegal organization. I thought they had rounded all of those people up and, well, and eliminated them as a nuisance. The Liberty Tree, active in Regent Peloreid's Sector. Unbelievable!" exclaimed Matthews, partly in disbelief and partly in excitement. "You're sure of this, that it's really the Liberty Tree symbol?"

"Yes, sir. However, the record didn't really say what that was except that it was their symbol and that the organization was illegal. All other information was blocked so I'm not sure what it all means," replied Stukap softly.

"They were a bunch, I guess they ARE a bunch of anti-government radicals. Want to overthrow Barahu and, I don't know, have anarchy or something. Crazy bunch of idiots, all of them. Didn't want Barahu making all the decisions for everyone. But he's the Supreme Being and Most Holy Leader so what do they expect him to do? He's supposed to make all the decisions because he's smarter than everyone else. No, I heard about these lunatics when I was coming up through the ranks. Never met one though. Thought they were all dead. But, here they are in the middle of Peloreid's sector and I'm the one that found them. Isn't that a nice way to begin the day," finished Matthews, smiling and evidently pleased.

Stukap stood there, still at attention, awaiting orders. He was happy to have helped out his superior. He wasn't sure why Matthews seemed to be so happy about something that would certainly embarrass Security Regent Peloreid, but that was none of his concern. His job was to follow orders, not to think. He didn't need to have any moral conviction for the job, since those things just seemed to get in the way of being a good Purple Shirt. No, he just needed to do what his superiors told him and, he was sure, for that he would be amply rewarded.

"So," asked Matthews, "Johnson took off the symbol before entering the church. Must be some religious thing where they can't wear it inside. Lucky for us or we'd probably have never found it. And you said before that no one else was in the building?"

"Not according to the tracking monitor," answered Stukap honestly. He didn't want to mention the fact that his monitor might not have been operating properly since it also didn't register Johnson as having been in the building. The Area Security Manager seemed in such a good mood that he didn't want to bother him with the details.

"Is there anything else to report?" asked Matthews.

"Not at this time, sir. Do you have any further orders for me, sir?"

"Just continue your assignment. Track Johnson anytime he leaves his domicile unit or economic position location. I want to know everyone he sees and talks to. Understood?"

"Yes, sir. Thank you, sir," answered Stukap, saluting Matthews once again.

"Dismissed. And, good work Stukap. Very good work. You have served Barahu well today."

Stukap nodded, a huge smile on his face, and turned to leave the office. Matthews turned to look out the window. There it was. A way to leverage Peloreid. An illegal organization operating right under his very nose. Matthews could now pull Johnson in anytime he chose, as proof of Peloreid's failure. If Peloreid made any move against Councilor Tonklin, Matthews would grab Johnson and use him as leverage to help Tonklin escape. This was perfect. It had fallen right in his lap.

He had been right to have Johnson trailed. When his tracking chip had shown him as being in an illegal location, the church which had now been confirmed a second time by visual surveillance, it had not been that big of a deal. It probably would never have come to his attention at all except for the fact that Johnson had been one of the pilot subjects for Procedure 23. Matthews smiled again. He had forgotten until just now that the reason they began following Johnson was because of Procedure 23, another of Peloreid's projects. A Procedure 23 patient in a restricted area was a red flag that he had decided not to ignore. Now, his intuition was proven correct. Charles Johnson, dangerous enough to require a Procedure 23, was going into restricted areas and had joined an anti-government group. This was a perfect indictment of the Procedure 23 program and of Peloreid's security program for the sector. Two for the price of one. This was turning out to be a very good day.

❖ ❖ ❖

Charles was also smiling, at least inwardly, as he boarded the transport at the end of the day. Dr. Horner's call to Security Regent Peloreid had done the trick. Within 15 minutes, the security lock on the system had been removed and he had been able to download the detailed formula and insertion schedules onto the microchip. The chip was safely ensconced in the capsule which he was holding in his right hand inside his trouser pocket. He didn't notice the additional man joining the group of workers as they all boarded the transport to return to their residence unit. He wasn't noticing how the man kept his eyes on Charles or how he made his way towards the back of the transport where he could continue to monitor Charles' activities. Charles was too pleased with his work that day to notice much of anything. His job was nearly complete. All he needed to do was to get the capsule to Andrew, Albert, or

Michael O'Connell. Then, his role would be done. He could wait until it was time to join in the uprising.

Charles was tired, exhausted actually. All he wanted to do was sleep. The stress of the past few months had steadily built until today. Now, his only desire was sleep. The hard part was over and his adrenaline rush that had fueled him over the last couple of weeks was dissipating. It was time to rest. Tonight, he would rest.

22

"Excellency," said Chairman Baucman, giving a short bow as he entered the study of Ohnoma. Peloreid snapped his boots as he came to attention before also offering a short bow.

"What is it Baucman?" asked Ohnoma, somewhat dismissively as if he disapproved of the interruption. "You said it was urgent."

"I believe it is, sire," answered the overstuffed figure of Baucman, his rotund figure shuffling further into the large, ornate office towards the table where Ohnoma sat. "We have new information for you."

"We?" asked Ohnoma, nodding towards Peloreid.

"I apologize, Excellency. Allow me to introduce you to Citizen Security Regent Peloreid. He's in charge of all security and surveillance activities for the Capitol Sector and is the ranking Security Regent nationwide. He reports directly to me and has been instrumental in uncovering the plot."

With these words, Peloreid once again snapped his boots together in salute and said, bowing, "At your service, Excellency."

"I see. Security and Surveillance? So, you're job is to know all the dirty little secrets of everyone, even Emperor's, eh?" asked Ohnoma.

"I would never issue surveillance for an Emperor, Excellency. However, in this case the person we were observing was involved with the Emperor so, naturally, we became involved in uncovering the plot," explained Peloreid.

"I see. And, how has the status changes since our last meeting?" asked Ohnoma.

"The Emperor has instructed Councilor Tonklin to prepare an amendment to the law allowing her and perhaps selected others to avoid the mandatory retirement. We have just learned that she cancelled her Council meetings for this afternoon and is, at this very moment, presenting her amendment to the Emperor for his approval and signature," answered Baucman, holding onto the back of a chair and beginning to sweat. He took a handkerchief and wiped his forehead and neck as he awaited Barahu's response.

Ohnoma stared contemplatively at Baucman and Peloreid. He was more looking through them than at them. His mind was working through the options. On one hand, he could ignore the situation. An Emperor would have every right to amend laws as he saw fit. Is this an instance that he should even worry about? However, on the other hand, he was amending one of the most sacred ordinances ever written. The authority to forcibly exterminate people because of their age was one of the codicils that empowered the government to manage many aspects of society. This was "cradle to grave" government and, if they had the authority to create replacement human beings from the cradle in their laboratories and nurseries, they must also have the authority to assist their populace into the grave, to make room for more and more efficient replacements. You just couldn't have all these old people cluttering up the place.

But, Barahu II wasn't repudiating the government's right to 'retire' individuals, only their right to exclude certain people from the rule. Shouldn't that be his right? It seemed so. But, if he changed this law, would he change others? Or, stated another way, why wouldn't he change others? And, as Baucman has so clearly laid out in their previous discussion, if he extended the life of others, why would he not do the same for his own?

A tug of war was going on inside Ohnoma's head as the different arguments swung back and forth. His attention came back to the two men standing before him, watching him, wondering what was going on inside his head.

"So, Chairman, what would you propose that we do in the current situation?" asked Ohnoma, not so much from a real desire to hear their ideas but to give himself more time to think before coming to a decision.

"We must stop them," exclaimed Baucman immediately.

"Stop them. How? On what authority?"

"Excellency, I have Purple Shirts positioned around the perimeter of the building and grounds. I would call them in at a moment's notice. We could arrest Councilor Tonklin on the spot," offered Peloreid.

"Arrest her, for what. She hasn't broken a law yet. In fact, she's trying to change the law so she won't be breaking it. How do you arrest someone for that?" questioned Barahu.

Peloreid's face went red and he looked down at his feet, embarrassed by the obviousness of Ohnoma's rebuke.

"Excellency, let us be frank. This is not about lawbreaking. This is about your future. The Emperor will not turn 50 years old for 22 more years. He will not relinquish his throne to you when you turn 25. He will read the language of the law to say that he doesn't need to step down until his 50th birthday. Tonklin will push him to do so in order to protect her protector. If she has enough influence with him to make him change the law to help her, she will certainly have enough to make him interpret the law to help himself. This in not about laws. This is about your right to rule this nation as the Supreme Being and Most Holy Leader

Barahu I, your father, intended. No one should take that right from you. Allowing Barahu II to sign this law, to begin changing and interpreting laws, is a huge risk to your right to reign. That is why they must be stopped. You must assert your authority. If you don't do it now, they will become stronger. What is at stake tonight is nothing more than your future as Emperor."

Baucman paused. The stress was getting to him and he even began regretting the third dessert that he had enjoyed at lunch that day. His stomach was churning. He understood exactly what he was doing. He was recommending a coup in the Imperial Palace, a coup that would remove a legal ruler and replace him with another.

His legal argument would be that this was only a few months earlier than it would naturally occur since, in his interpretation of the law, Ohnoma would assume the throne upon his 25th birthday. The acceleration of this change would be due to Barahu II's incapacity to reign. One look at the malformed figure of their current Emperor would validate this conclusion. No pictures were ever published of II. Few, other than the palace servants and the Supreme Council realized that the images of the tall, thin, handsome figure shown in all the photographs, murals, and statues were of Barahu I, not Barahu II, even if the names said otherwise. The Council had decided upon that move once they saw the disfigurement that the growth hormones had caused. Baucman also realized that this argument would be accepted only if the coup succeeded. If it somehow failed, he would be taken out and shot. Of that, he had no question.

Ohnoma stood and paced around the back of his desk. He had always worried that it would come down to this. He had hoped that Barahu II would prove mentally unstable to the point that he could be quietly pushed aside when the time came. His conversations with the Supreme Council had led him to believe that they would support the move. But, now the Council was fractured. The Chairman would obviously support him, as he was now. But what of the others? His inside information told him that Baucman had a very narrow majority. But, in the next few months, with Barahu II's backing, he was sure that at least one Councilor from that coalition could be motivated, either bribed or coerced, into joining Tonklin.

And then, where would he be? Continually stuck in the background, treated nicely certainly, but not regally. He was Barahu I's son, or at least his clone. He was born and bred to lead, not to follow that monstrosity of a brother, well, a type of brother he guessed. No, the throne was his. Baucman was right. To allow Barahu II to begin interpreting and changing laws was a risk to his sovereignty, a risk he was unwilling to take.

"So, Chairman, how do you see this playing out this evening?" asked Barahu, turning to face the two men.

"As Peloreid said, we have men posted around the building. No one will be able to enter or leave without our permission. This can be done quickly and quietly. We simply escort Barahu II and Councilor Tonklin out. Barahu II can be taken to a quiet location where he can be held under lock and key. We can move to assume authority immediately or we can wait until you reach your 25th birthday. I will take care of Councilor Tonklin. With her authority removed, the Supreme Council will certainly approve of either approach that you wish to take."

Baucman had thought this out well, thought Ohnoma. Yes, perhaps just locking Barahu II up for a few months. Then, under his interpretation of the law, everything would be legal for him to assume the throne.

"I approve. You said that Tonklin is with my brother now?"

"Yes, Excellency," inserted Peloreid. "They are still in his office in the West Wing of the Palace."

"And your Purple Shirts are ready to do my bidding, whatever that might be," questioned Ohnoma.

"They will do as I instruct. There will be no questions asked," replied Peloreid, straightening his back and sticking out his chest, giving Ohnoma a clear look at the many service medals which adorned his purple tunic with its gold braids.

"Then, we should go," concluded Ohnoma. He led the way from his office, into the large, long hallway towards the West Wing of the building. Few people were to be seen. A few heads did turn as he entered West Wing. Once he got there, he was somewhat embarrassed to realize that, while he knew where the West Wing was, he had never been there before and had no idea where the Emperor's office was.

Baucman, seeming to recognize the problem, jumped to the front and led the way, followed by Ohnoma with Peloreid in the rear. As they neared two large white doors, Baucman slowed and stood to the side. Ohnoma paused, looking at the doors.

He turned his head to address Peloreid, who had assumed a position opposite Baucman. "Your men are ready," he asked.

"Yes, Excellency. They are on standby awaiting my instructions," answered Peloreid, somewhat nervously.

Ohnoma nodded in response and reached his hand out for the door handle.

As the office door flew open, the heads of Emperor Barahu II and Councilor Tonklin shot up to look at the intruders. Ohnoma strode forward directly towards the Emperor. Baucman and Peloreid entered quickly and quietly closed the door behind them, locking it. Tonklin's eyes moved from the figure of Ohnoma to his two cohorts. She was immediately aware that this could be nothing good and began to feel grateful that Vannie Johannes, while a terrible elitist, was also a determined pessimist who had foreseen such complications.

"To what can I attribute this unrequested interruption?" asked Emperor Barahu II, attempting to contain the humiliation and embarrassment which he could not stop himself from feeling. He had been uncertain about altering a law established by Barahu I and now, being caught in the act, he felt guilty even as his logic told him that he needn't.

"Brother, I believe you are doing something of which I would not approve," came the reproachful response from Ohnoma.

"Brother?" questioned the Emperor. "Perhaps brother since there is no word to adequately describe our relationship. So, brother perhaps but Emperor certainly. Do not lose sight of that, BROTHER. Now, what is it that you might not approve and, please, for my education, enlighten me on why I should need to care."

Barahu was now glowering at his 'brother'. Overcoming his embarrassment, he was now feeling an anger surge inside of him. He could barely hide his loathing. He rarely saw Ohnoma, mostly just in passing. Now, having him standing only feet away, his contempt was building. Barahu II knew he was not the exact likeness of his father. While not knowing about the growth hormone which he had been subjected to, he could look in mirror. His oversized head looked ridiculous even to himself. His arms and body, while muscular, was also covered with a layer of fat which made him appear pudgy. His brother was an exact replica of his father, tall, thin, muscular, handsome. He was the reflection that Barahu II dreamed of seeing in the mirror, not his own. But he, not Ohnoma, was the Emperor! That was what he had to offset the reality of his appearance. And so now, when his brother's countenance was not only before him but also an arrogant tone was attached to his words, Barahu felt his anger beginning to build.

"Brother," repeated Ohnoma, "you are altering the laws as set down by our father, are you not," he accused. "With your tenure about to come to a close, I would expect that no changes would be made without my knowledge and approval."

"You surprise me, BROTHER," replied Barahu, the volume of his voice rising. "I do not consider 22 years to be nearing a close. You realize, of course, that I am due to rule until I turn 50 and that will not be for many years. At that time, I will happily abide by the law and ALLOW you to reign for about three years until you, yourself, are replaced by Barahu IV. And so, I require neither your insights, opinions, nor approval for what I do. I think I do require an apology for the rudeness of your interruption but I will accept the immediate removal of you and your, uh, your supporters as adequate."

The two men stared at each other, hatred and anger building in both of them.

"You prove yourself ignorant of the law, BROTHER," responded Ohnoma. "It clearly states that the NEW Emperor will be crowned upon his 25th birthday. That will be shortly. You see, you began to become obsolete as soon as I was born, BROTHER."

"You have made your case, which I find to be lacking. And, since I am now the legal ruler of the country, I will decide and it will not be in your favor. Now, leave before I have you removed."

"Your days of making any decisions are over. I will not allow an overgrown failed chemistry experiment to deny me my birthright," shouted Ohnoma, moving quickly towards his brother.

Barahu II, until this point seated behind his desk, rose and moved toward Ohnoma as well. He was taller and larger than his brother and stood inches from him, looking down into his hate filled face.

"You have no authority here," bellowed Barahu. "I control this country and, now that Chairman Baucman has shown his true colors, I will assert my authority over you and the Supreme Council as well. Baucman is hereby removed as Chairman and will be arrested, as will you and whoever this other rat is that you brought along."

"That may be your desire, but you need more than your gigantic body to enable it to occur. And, since the Purple Shirts will follow my orders, your words are less than impressive. Peloreid, order in your officers," instructed Ohnoma.

"I wouldn't move if I were you," shouted the voice of Vannie Johannes as he moved from the shadows of a doorway out into the light. Behind him were two of Councilor Tonklin's security detail and all held weapons targeting Ohnoma, Baucman, and Peloreid.

"Johannes, you condemn yourself tonight," shouted Peloreid. "Do you think we're not aware of your plans? We've known about them for weeks. Your helicopter will not reach the hospital and your planes will never leave the airport. Your plan is destroyed and, unless you wish to destroy the others in your little team, you will lay down your weapons at once," he commanded.

"No, Peloreid. I've seen how you treat your suspects. No, I don't think your torture chamber will see me. Not tonight, not ever. One move by any of you and we will shoot. The only question is whether we shoot to stun or kill," barked back Johannes, never taking his eyes off the three men.

"You're a fool," countered Peloreid. "This building and these grounds are surrounded. You will be arrested the moment you attempt to escape. In fact, additional guards are entering the building as I speak. If I don't give them a command within two minutes, they will be storming inside this very room," he lied.

"Oh, is that why you locked the door when you entered? To make it easier for them to get in? I don't think so. I'm sure you have guards outside but my forces will stun enough of them to allow us to leave. Councilor Tonklin, should I terminate these men now?" asked Johannes. "It would be a pleasure, I assure you," he sneered.

"NO!" shouted Barahu II. "There will be no murders tonight. I am Emperor and I will not allow it, not in this palace!"

"Very well," agreed Johannes. "We'll take them into custody until we can issue new orders to relieve Chairman Baucman and Security Regent Peloreid. Then we can assume control of their forces." He motioned to one of the two security guards to take the men.

Ohnoma burst into a rage. "No, you will NOT take me," he shouted, pushing the guard away from him and leaping towards the Emperor. "I'll see you dead first," he bellowed, attempting to grab the larger man's throat. Barahu II pushed the smaller Ohnoma back, himself falling backwards towards his desk.

In the fracas, Peloreid jumped towards the other guard, grasping at his weapon. The officer turned quickly, more quickly than Peloreid anticipated, and fired a round directly into Peloreid's chest. The bullet, a small piece of electrically charged metal barely entered Peloreid's body but, as soon as it made contact with him, discharged an electric charge that stunned the man, freezing his muscles immediately and causing him to fall sideways onto the floor. The other guard reacted accordingly, firing one shot at Ohnoma and another at Baucman. Those men fell where they stood, their eyes and hand frozen.

"I said NO killing," shouted Barahu II over the echoes of the shots.

"They're not dead, only stunned," Johannes shouted back. "But the shots will most definitely bring their Purple Shirts in. Once they see Peloreid on the floor, they'll open fire so we'd better leave. We should initiate our escape plan immediately."

Tonklin looked at Johannes in silence. She was shocked by the whole scene, which had lasted only minutes. She nodded to Johannes.

"Emperor, I think you should come with us," offered Johannes. "Only until this can be sorted out, of course. We can contact the other Councilors and have them issue arrest warrants for these three. But, we must leave or their forces will capture us all. It's out only option."

"I can't leave this palace," answered Barahu II, quietly. "It is the only home I have ever known." He moved back behind his desk and slumped down into his chair. He couldn't remove his eyes from the three bodies lying in front of him, twitching as the affects of the electric shock continued to coarse through their bodies.

Johannes looked at Tonklin, pleading with his eyes for her to do something. She nodded in reply and moved to the Emperor, putting her soft arm around his large shoulders and leaning down to whisper in his ear.

"Please, Emperor. You will return. I promise you that. We just need to go until we can contact the other Councilors. I'd love to show you the West Sector. It's lovely this time of year. The warmth will help revive you, revive all of us. It's a wonderfully beautiful area of the country. Please, we need to go before something terrible happens," she begged.

Barahu raised his large, brown eyes to look into hers. She smiled at him with a maternal encouragement which seemed to convince him. He nodded his head and slowly rose. Tonklin looked to Johannes.

"Initiate," she said, guiding Barahu II towards the doorway.

Johannes punched a button on his phone.

"Matthews, here."

"Oliver, it's go time. NOW!" yelled Johannes, pushing one guard to the front and the other to the rear of the procession before dropping in step behind Tonklin and Barahu II.

"Now?" asked Matthews incredulously.

"NOW!" repeated Johannes. "Peloreid knows about the plan. He's out of commission for the moment but that won't last long. We need to move. NOW! Meet us at the hospital. Make sure the transportation is waiting."

"Yes, sir," answered Matthews. The phone went dead. It's on he thought. It's on NOW!

Matthews punched a button on his phone. He had prepared for this moment but, based on the conversations of the past week, he didn't expect it to be necessary. A voice answered from the other end.

"Get the bird in the air," Matthews commanded and immediately hung up. He dialed another number. "Get the birds to the nest," he said and once again hung up.

This was it, he thought. And Peloreid knows. Of course he knows. The damned guy seems to know everything. But how? They had been so careful. All the meetings had been in Councilor Tonklin's office. He and Johannes had both checked for microphones or cameras and had never found anything. He had never contacted them from his office. How did Peloreid know?

His heart was racing as he made his way down to the car. Peloreid. Damn him! Well, he had a little trick for Peloreid, didn't he? Would it be enough? He didn't know but it couldn't hurt. He would offer Peloreid to give up Johnson, to let him hide the problem with Procedure 23 and the existence of the Liberty Tree if Peloreid let them go. He hoped he wouldn't need it but, if not, he could release Johnson. What did he care if the Liberty Tree was active in Peloreid's sector? Who knows, maybe they could be useful at some point.

Matthews dialed another number as he got into the back of the car.

"Officer Stukap here," came a muffled voice.

"Stukap, Area Security Manager Matthews here. Are you near the suspect?"

"I'm in the transport with him, sir."

"Excellent. Do you know where Hospital 103 is located?"

"Yes, sir. It's less than 15 minutes from here."

"Excellent. I want you to bring the suspect to me there as soon as you can. How soon can you do that?"

"We're about eight minutes from his domicile unit. I'll take him as soon as we exit the transport. That way no one will see us in case any of his associates are on board. I'll order a car and have him there within 30 minutes."

"Do it," ordered Matthews, hanging up the phone. It would take him about that long to get to the hospital as well. He didn't know where Peloreid was but he'd make sure that he had a surprise for him when he got to the hospital. He was looking forward to seeing the look on Peloreid's face.

Currently, Peloreid's face showed pain. His muscles were beginning to unclench as the electric shock wore off. Without sitting up, he raised his phone to his head and pushed a button.

"Security Regent Peloreid, we were trying to contact you sir," responded the man answering Peloreid's call.

"Do you have Tonklin?" Peloreid forced the words into the mouthpiece.

"No sir. I believe they escaped. We just found several of our officers unconscious. I believe one may be dead," the voice responded.

"Get my car ready and send all available forces to Hospital 103. I need some help in the Emperor's office so get someone up here now. Also, send a message that no helicopters are allowed to Hospital 103. I don't care who is issuing the order. If it doesn't come from me, it isn't followed. Understood?" grunted Peloreid as he forced his body to sit up, trying to loosen his muscles.

"Yes sir. Understood. How should we restrain Councilor Tonklin?"

"Stun only. I want them alive. All of them. Also, someone claiming to be Emperor Barahu is with them. One look will tell you that it's not him. We have the real Emperor here. Make that point clear to everyone."

"Yes, sir. I'm almost at the office now."

As Peloreid struggled, he heard a pounding on the office door. Now, he wished that he hadn't locked it. He rose, now to his knees, still working his arms and legs to loosen them. After a few thuds against the door, it burst open as three officers fell into the room, their combined efforts required to break in the large wooden door.

The men quickly ran toward Peloreid, stopping quickly as they neared the three men, two of which were still lying on the floor.

"Get me up," bellowed Peloreid. "And get me to my car. MOVE!"

Two officers lifted Peloreid, sat him in a chair, and lifted the chair carrying it back toward the broken door. The other officer moved to Ohnoma and Chairman Baucman, helping them to sit up.

"Hospital 103. Get me to Hospital 103 now!" Peloreid demanded.

❖ ❖ ❖

23

Charles exited the transport at his unit and began walking toward the steps. From the corner of his eye, he noticed another man also exiting the transport. While Charles was used to seeing three or four people getting off with him, this man was a stranger. As Charles increased his pace, the man did as well, breaking into a trot. Charles' heart began to race. His hand clenched the capsule more tightly as he rushed up the steps two at a time. Just as he reached the door, he heard a voice call from behind him.

"Citizen Johnson, I need you to stop!"

Charles stopped, his arm extending to open the door. He needed to relax. This may be nothing, just routine, although in his gut he knew this was not routine.

"Citizen Charles Johnson, I am Officer Stukap of the Purple Shirt Security Forces. I need you to raise your hands and come with me," ordered the officer, his voice low, almost a growl.

Charles was frozen. His mind was racing. The capsule, he couldn't let them get the capsule. This was why Albert had given it to him, for just this occasion. Charles began faking a cough as he turned towards the officer. He raised his right hand to his mouth as he continued hacking, hoping the officer would buy his act. As he took a breath, he sucked the capsule into his mouth. He didn't swallow it immediately, but held it in his cheek. He wanted to see how this played out before trying to swallow the oversized capsule, especially considering that his mouth was exceptionally dry at the moment.

"What's wrong, officer?" he asked lowering his hand before faking another round of coughing. "I'm really not feeling too well right now."

"By the order of Area Security Manager Matthews, I'm taking you into custody. You will be told of the charges by Citizen Matthews when you are interrogated. And, don't worry about your illness. Luckily for you, I'll be escorting you to a hospital nearby," Stukap replied, grinning before moving forward and pushing Charles into the wall. He turned him around and handcuffed him before checking his pockets. Satisfied, he made a call ordering a car to his location. He pulled Charles towards the street, waiting by the curb for a few moments until a purple squad car pulled up. Opening the back door, he roughly pushed Charles into the back seat and then got in beside him.

"Hospital 103, quickly," he ordered the driver and the car sped away from the curb.

Charles said nothing. A sense of failure began to permeate his mind and body. The weariness that he felt on the transport seemed to multiply. None of the adrenaline that had helped him through the past few weeks existed any longer. He was tired and now, he had failed. He tried to focus his thoughts on generating enough saliva to allow him to swallow the capsule. It wasn't easy but eventually, he swallowed it. The pill seemed to stop about halfway down his throat but, by that point, Charles had stopped caring.

So, this is life in Barahu's America, being taken on the street, one minute living your life and the next in shackles. Now, he understood better the precautions that Andrew and Albert had required. He thought of Albert, saw his green eyes once again in his memory. HIS memory, he thought. Not the government's memory, HIS memory. This is how the whole thing had started, hadn't it? The government, taking his memory, exerting their influence and control over even the most basic of individual's identity. What they had taken, Andrew and Albert had returned, at least partially. They had helped him remember his parents, parts of his life before the Procedure 23. And he had promised to help them, to help every citizen to recover their freedom from total government control. But, he had failed. He was so close. Perhaps he could somehow get the capsule to someone from the Liberty Tree. If he was sent to prison, perhaps a guard or someone else could take the capsule to them. They seemed to have people everywhere. They must have someone inside the prisons. They had to. Charles convinced himself that he had to hang on, had to keep fighting, had to succeed, even if it cost him everything. He would NOT fail his parents. He would NOT fail Albert. He couldn't let them down. Not again.

"Area Security Manager Matthews, this is Officer Stukap," said the officer into his phone. "I'm just arriving at the hospital with the prisoner. Where should I meet you sir?"

"I'm about five minutes away, Stukap. Find an examination room somewhere, preferably on the floor near the helipad. Once you're in one, call me back and let me know where you are. Understood?" commanded Matthews.

"Yes, sir. Understood," replied Stukap just as the line went dead. "Well Johnson, Citizen Matthews seems very anxious to meet you."

Stukap smiled at Charles. He was enjoying this. He was anticipating a handsome reward for serving his superiors so quickly and efficiently. He was doing his duty. This man meant nothing to him and, if Matthews decided to torture him for information, he didn't really care. He was serving the greater good. If some people had to suffer, it didn't bother him as long as his superiors were happy. And, tonight, they would be very happy, especially Area Security Manager Matthews.

However, Area Security Manager Matthews was not happy at the moment. His ride to Hospital 103 seemed to be taking forever. He hadn't heard any other news from Johannes since the call to initiate the project. It also concerned him that Security Regent Peloreid was aware of the plan. That couldn't be good news. While not impossible to overcome, they had always hoped that they would escape before the full security forces were mobilized against them. That was obviously not the case tonight. At that moment, his phone rang.

"Matthews, where are you?" thundered Johannes voice from the receiver.

"Two blocks away. Where are you?" answered Matthews, mentally willing the car to move faster.

"We just arrived. I'm escorting Emperor Barahu and Councilor Tonklin to the helipad level. We need to get Jefferson as well but I don't know if he's arrived yet. I need you to get inside and set up a defense perimeter around the helipad as soon as you can. I expect Peloreid to have forces there any minute."

"Understood. I can see the hospital now. I'll gather our forces and be prepared to defend the entrances."

"Dammit, Matthews, we don't have time to defend all the entrances. Just the helipad level. We just need to be able to get on the helicopter as soon as it arrives. Just the helipad, do you understand?" shouted Johannes.

"Yes, sir. Understood." Matthews heard the phone click, disconnecting the call. Defend the helipad level? That would be no easier than defending the entrances. The helipad was on the roof of a six story wing of the main hospital which rose 18 stories. Just defending the helipad level would mean that you had to stop troops from coming from that level, below, and above. The entrances were only on one floor. Defending the main ones would delay Peloreid enough to allow the helicopters to arrive and Tonklin's party to escape. And, had Johannes not said that the Emperor was with them, Matthews thought in amazement. If he's here, why do we have to fight anyone at all? Unless, he's a captive. But, even Johannes wouldn't be foolish enough to kidnap the Emperor, would he? Matthews mind was spinning. He was a better at detailed planning than improvisation. This was all happening so quickly. He needed time to think. The one thing he would definitely need to do was to stop Peloreid. He was sure that Peloreid would be leading the forces trying to stop them. He would stop Peloreid.

Matthews' phone rang again. "Matthews here."

"Sir, I have the prisoner strapped down in Examination Room 6A. It's on the same floor as the helipad, just across from the elevators. What would you like me to do now?"

"Stay there and guard him. I'm just entering the hospital. I'll be there in a moment."

Matthews flew out of the car and ran up the steps to the hospital's main entrance. A dozen of his hand picked security detail was waiting for him at the entrance. Originally, this seemed like plenty of firepower to escort them to waiting helicopters but, tonight, knowing that Peloreid was probably on his way, it didn't seem like enough.

"Sixth floor, everyone. We need to find Councilor Tonklin. We'll set up a perimeter there," Matthews ordered, moving to the elevators.

When the elevator doors opened on the sixth floor, Matthews saw Stukap standing outside an examination room. When he saw Matthews, Stukap snapped to attention.

"Wait here. I'll be back shortly," ordered Matthews as he turned left and quickly walked down the long corridor towards the doorway to the helipad. He spotted two members of Tonklin's security detail positioned outside of one doorway. Both men had their weapons trained on Matthews until he neared enough for them to verify his identity. They stood aside as Matthews walked into the conference room that Johannes had chosen for their headquarters.

"Where are the helicopters?" Johannes demanded as soon as he saw Matthews.

Matthews stopped and stared at the group in front of him. Jefferson Tonklin was sitting, huffing and puffing from what Matthews had supposed was his sprint to the room. Tonklin was holding his hand and offering him a cup of water. It was the other man who was commanding Matthews' attention. While eerily similar in features to Emperor Barahu I, this man was overgrown in nearly every dimension. He was obviously taller than normal, but it was his oversized head that caught Matthews by surprise. This, this couldn't be Emperor Barahu II, could it?

"Matthews, where are the damned helicopters?" shouted Johannes, snapping Matthews out of his stare.

Matthews looked down at his watch. It had been nearly 20 minutes since he had called for the helicopters. "They should be here in about ten minutes," he replied.

"Ten minutes. Why aren't they here now?" yelled Johannes.

"We've been through this," stated Matthews, through now clenched teeth. "With no standby instructions, it will take at least 30 minutes for the helicopters to lift off and get here. We were on stand down orders so they weren't ready. If you told me this might be happening TONIGHT, I would have had them on standby."

Johannes glared at Matthews who returned his stare.

"I'm going to see to the perimeter. We should hear the helicopters when they approach, at which time we'll move to the helipad," stated Matthews, turning and moving back down the hallway towards the elevators. As he went, he shouted instructions to the officers to seal off any other service elevators or stairwells.

Near the elevators was a waiting area with windows overlooking the main entrance. He could see the reflections of flashing lights growing brighter. He moved to the windows and saw squad cars and security transports pulling up in front of the hospital. Dozens of Purple Shirts were jumping out and being motioned to their positions by officers. It was beginning. Their only way out would be via the helicopters now.

Stukap again came to attention as Matthews rounded the corner.

"Where is he?" Matthews demanded.

"In here, sir," Stukap replied, opening the examination room door for the senior officer.

"So, Charles Johnson, you had a Procedure 23 just to turn around and join an anti-government group. Good thinking," Matthews said sarcastically, looking at Charles who was strapped to a gurney.

Charles, who had raised his head when Matthews entered, laid it back down again and stared up at the ceiling. He was thinking of his father, of the only conversation with him that he could clearly recall. They had argued and his father had been right about everything. And now, Charles had let him down yet again.

"Should we begin an interrogation now?" asked Stukap, only too eager to please the Area Security Manager.

"Not now. This man has caused a lot of trouble tonight. Stukap, I need you to go down to the entrance. You'll see a lot of Purple Shirts there. An uprising has started and I believe this man is a part of it," Matthews lied. "When Security Regent Peloreid arrives, tell him that I must meet with him here. I need to show him this suspect."

"Yes, sir," shouted Stukap, jumping to attention and saluting. He moved towards the exit.

"Wait, Stukap, where's the Liberty Tree necklace?" asked Matthews, remembering one of the most important points of leverage against Peloreid.

"Oh, yes sir," replied Stukap, moving to Charles, pulling apart his shirt and ripping the Liberty Tree medallion from him. The chain was strong and tore at Charles' neck, snapping his head forward until the force of Stukap's arm overcame the chain and it gave way. Charles' head fell back on the gurney with a thud.

"Here you are sir," said Stukap, beaming and holding the necklace out to Matthews. Matthews took it and examined it before slipping it into his tunic pocket.

"Very good, Stukap. Now, GO. Peloreid," he exclaimed, motioning for Stukap to exit quickly.

Peloreid's body ached as did his head as he sat in the back of the limousine taking him to Hospital 103. He had called all available security forces to the location and shut down the airspace over it, although in reality it was nearly impossible to totally control the airspace. His security forces were prepared for civil unrest, not airborne assaults and did not have anti-aircraft guns or surface to air missiles. He would have to hope that his own security helicopters could ward off the others or that his ground forces could destroy them once they landed. Otherwise, the building was surrounded and he had ordered no forces to advance until he arrived, which would be momentarily.

As his car maneuvered between the squad cars and personnel transports, Peloreid stared out the window, studying the situation. Overall, he was pleased. He could see his Purple Shirts surrounding the buildings exit, with cars blocking the main entrance. Officers crouched behind the cars with their weapons trained on the entrance doors. Peloreid knew this was useless, since the whole reason for choosing the hospital was to use the helipad. Of course, that plan was supposed to entail a surprise escape, not combat. The hospital was not ideally suited for that situation, but, without time to make alterations, Tonklin's group had decided to go with their original plan, Peloreid suspected.

"Security Regent Peloreid, I'm Lieutenant Terrier in command here. The perimeter is secured," announced an officer as she opened Peloreid car door and assisted him in exiting. Peloreid's muscles were still stiff and reacting slowly, although more mobility was being gained as he continued to move.

"Excellent. Do you know where the suspects are?" questioned Peloreid.

"Not exactly, sir. Your orders were to wait for your arrival before entering so we do not have officers inside at this moment," answered the lieutenant, flushed somewhat from the excitement but also from concern that she had not taken the appropriate steps in Peloreid's eyes.

"That's fine. There will be no escape for them. Order the officers to set all weapons for stun only. I want these people alive. Is that understood?"

"Yes, sir. That is the standing order but I will reinforce those instructions."

"Very well. Let's go. Get some troops to clear the front entrance," commanded Peloreid.

Lt. Terrier turned and issued some instructions to some of the Purple Shirts crouching behind the squad cars. Immediately, ten officers ran up the edges of the steps, five on each side. They cautiously peered through the glass doors, weapons at the ready, before storming through them and dispersing throughout the lobby.

In a moment, Terrier returned to where Peloreid was standing. "The lobby is secure, sir. There is one officer inside who insists that he has an important message for you from Area Security Manager Matthews," added Terrier.

"Matthews. There's a message from Matthews?" asked an astonished Peloreid.

"That's what the man said, sir. Should I bring him out?"

"No. Let's go in. Keep the perimeter sealed but we'll move the command to the lobby," instructed Peloreid.

The two Purple Shirts moved into the lobby as Terrier led Peloreid to an office where Stukap was being held. Upon Peloreid's entry, Stukap jumped to his feet and saluted. Peloreid looked at him and returned his saluted.

"Officer, Stukap, is it?" asked Peloreid, straining to read the officers ID tag.

"Yes, Sir, Security Regent Peloreid. Officer Stukap reporting sir."

"And I'm told you have some message for me from Area Security Manager Matthews? What is it?"

"Yes, sir. Citizen Matthews is on the sixth floor and has is holding an important prisoner. He had me capture this dangerous individual and bring him here. Citizen Matthews would like you to join him so he can turn this dangerous person over to you," stated Stukap, beaming with pride at having served his commander so well yet again, and to the Security Regent himself.

"So, Matthews would like me to come to him. Yes, of that I have no doubt. So tell me, Stukap, why is this man so dangerous?"

"He's part of the plot that is causing tonight's uprising. Citizen Matthews is hoping to end the plot and feels that this man has a hand in it. He's part of an anti-government group," added Stukap.

Peloreid paused. He had not expected this. He wondered now, what side was Matthews on. He was not with Tonklin at the palace. And now, he had a prisoner that may be leading the revolt. Could that prisoner be Johannes? Had Matthews never entirely been on board with the Tonklin plan? Perhaps he was following orders and, now that he reported directly to Peloreid, decided that he didn't want to partake in the plot. Was he hoping to secure Peloreid's blessings by stopping the escape single handedly? It was possible. Not many people would risk Peloreid's wrath, particularly when the rumor was being spread the Peloreid would soon join the Supreme Council. This was entirely possible. As Peloreid continued to consider it, it made more and more sense. Yes, Matthews had changed sides, never really supporting Tonklin. Now, as he was a new part of Peloreid's team, he wanted to impress him. Since he was trusted by Johannes, it would be only too easy to capture him in the confusion.

However, thought Peloreid, it could just as easily be a trap. Matthews was seen on tape meeting with Tonklin's team and certainly had a starring role in planning the escape. He decided, he would meet Matthews but would proceed with caution.

"Very well, Stukap. Lead the way. You two, come with us," he said, as he motioned to the officers that had been guarding Stukap to follow.

Stukap moved out of the office to the elevators.

"No," ordered Peloreid. "We'll take the stairs," pointing towards a doorway further down the hall. Stukap nodded and did as instructed, moving up the stairs. He slowed down after the first floor as he noticed Peloreid struggling to keep up with him. The four men continued their march upward until they reached the landing mid-way between floors five and six. Peloreid told them to stop as he caught his breath.

"So, Stukap," started Peloreid, still breathing heavily, "where is Matthew located?"

"He's in Examination Room 6A, directly across from the elevators. I strapped the prisoner to a gurney there," answered Stukap.

"Very good. I'm still a little winded. Be a good man and hold the door for me."

Stukap moved up the remaining steps and reached the doorway. As the other officers began to follow, Peloreid held up his hand, motioning for them to wait. Stukap turned back to look at Peloreid, who nodded to him to continue, acting as if he was following.

As soon as Stukap opened the door, several shots rang out. Electrically charged bullets slammed into Stukap's body, tearing his uniform and unleashing their charge as they made contact with his body. He fell backwards and slid down a few steps towards Peloreid and the others. One officer ran to him and felt his neck.

"He's dead, sir. They must be set to kill," announced the officer, who had turned to face Peloreid, his face going white. He had never before seen someone killed. He had never turned his weapon to the kill setting. Usually, stun was sufficient to disable anyone, but to kill a Purple Shirt. Somehow, it had always seemed that the Purple Shirts were invincible, unable to be scratched much less killed. Wearing the purple shirt entitled you to respect, better treatment, privilege. But not death. No, that he had never even considered.

"They're either set to kill or he had too many hit him at once. The combined charge would be enough to kill him," stated Peloreid blankly. This was what he had been concerned with, a trap. Obviously, Stukap had not known about it. He had been a pawn, useful but not valuable. He probably did the wrong thing for what he thought was the right reason. In reality, it didn't matter. He had served his purpose. He wasn't the first person to be sacrificed for Peloreid and he wouldn't be the last.

"Contact Terrier," Peloreid ordered the other officer. "Tell her to send four more officers here. Then, in three minutes, I want her to be in position to attack Floor Six from the northeast and southeast stairways. They must be coordinated attacks when they hear a concussion grenade discharge. Tell her that we're on the central stairs and not to shoot in this direction. We'll toss in the grenade and then attack from this direction. NOW. Call her!" shouted Peloreid to the stunned officer. He nodded and turned to place the call.

Peloreid waited until the officer returned, assuring him that Lt. Terrier would be in position as ordered. Moments later, four more officers came struggling up the stairs, panting from their climb. Peloreid waited, studying his watch, waiting for the minutes to pass. Finally, he turned to the group.

"You," he pointed to the officer that was standing over Stukap's dead body, "stand on the stairs and pull the door open. You," pointing to the officer that had contacted Terrier, "stand next to him and when he opens the door, throw in a concussion grenade. You four," pointing to the officers struggling to catch their breath, "you rush in and shoot anyone you see. Our objective is Exam Room 6A which is right across from the elevators. The first two there will enter and secure the room. Don't shoot unless you have no choice. I want the men alive and conscious. That's very important. Disarm anyone inside but don't shoot them. Understood?" he asked, peering at the four men standing below him on the stairs.

All four nodded and readied their weapons. Peloreid looked back down at his watch. After a few moments, he nodded to the first officer.

The officer flung the door open. Bullets flew over their heads, bouncing off the walls. Sparks flew as the bullets discharged into the walls. Immediately, the second officer threw a grenade into the hallway. It exploded with a tremendous bang and caused vibrations throughout the stairway. The four officers flung themselves down the corridor, firing their weapons at anything that moved. From other sides of the floor, Peloreid could hear other weapons being fired as the coordinated attack of the Purple Shirts began.

Peloreid followed the other two officers into the hallway, crouching down to expose himself less to the enemy and to improve his visibility in the smoke filled hallway. The three ran down the corridor towards the elevator bank. Through the black smoke, Peloreid could see the first two officers fling themselves through the door leading into Examination Room 6A.

As he approached, one officer came out and announced, "Room secure, sir."

Peloreid nodded as he walked past the man and came face to face with the scene inside. Charles was strapped to the gurney, straining his eyes to see who was entering. Matthews stood, his hands slightly raised, as the other officer kept his gun trained on him. The officer turned to Peloreid and extended his hand which held Matthews pistol.

"Both men have been searched and are unarmed," reported the officer.

"Excellent," replied Peloreid, eying the two with obvious satisfaction. He accepted the handgun and said, "Leave us and see to it that no one else enters unless I call for them."

"Yes, sir," acknowledged the officer, leaving the room and closing the door behind him.

"So, Citizen Matthews, you can lower your hands. I don't plan on shooting you," announced Peloreid. "I'm told that you have a prisoner for me. It appears that I have two prisoners all for myself," he continued, a viscous smile appearing on his face.

"I have an offer for you, Citizen Peloreid. One that I believe you might want to hear," countered Matthews, staring back boldly at the Security Regent.

"I don't believe you have much to offer me. You are part of a conspiracy to overthrow the government. A conspiracy which is failing. What could you possibly have for me?"

"Do you recognize this man?" asked Matthews, motioning to Charles.

Peloreid moved a little closer to the gurney, keeping his eyes and pistol trained on Matthews. He took a quick look at Charles before returning his gaze to Matthews.

"No, I don't. Should I?"

"Not necessarily. But, he could have a very big impact on your life. See, he's what you fear the most. He's proof of your failures. He's proof that you are incompetent. And, unless you allow Councilor Tonklin and I to leave unharmed, he will become very well known."

"Is that so?" questioned Peloreid, continuing his smile. This idiot thought that he could blackmail him, Security Regent Peloreid. Matthews was a moron. I was playing politics and blackmailing people before this cretin was even scheduled for a test tube. How dare he, thought Peloreid? Calling me incompetent!

"Go on," Peloreid instructed. "I am eager to hear this story."

"Procedure 23 was your idea, was it not? You advertised it as a tremendous success, a success that maintained a critical workforce while saving the country enormous amounts of money. Those seem like nearly impossible opposites, but that was your story. This man is one of your subjects from the pilot study. I believe you stated to the Supreme Council that the study was 100% effective. Then, there comes the other part. You've heard of the Liberty Tree organization?" asked Matthews.

Peloreid nodded. His smile was waning somewhat as Matthews continued to speak.

"Yes, I'm sure you have. You've also stated that these vermin were totally eradicated from YOUR sector. Oh, they may pop up in other areas, but not here. Not in the Capitol Sector. Not when you are in control. And yet, this man on whom you administered a Procedure 23 and then sent through reorientation training, this man, within a year, joins the very organization which you say no longer exists. This man, whom you were supposed to treat so he would support the government, is working to destroy the government. Now, I'm sure Chairman Baucman will be willing to overlook these deficiencies. Or will he, since he is backing you for the Supreme Council? Will he really overlook these insignificant details about his favorite? Or, would it be too embarrassing for him? Will he need to find another lapdog to put on the Council?"

Peloreid's smile had faded. The Council! Was this man really threatening his appointment to the Supreme Council? And, what if Matthews' statements were true? How would he overcome these failures? Procedure 23 could probably be explained with simple statistics. In a pilot test, there were bound to be a few failures. He could deal with that. But, the Liberty Tree? He had dealt with them before. Their fanatical views about liberty and freedom had been deemed a significant threat by Barahu I. Anyone involved with them could face immediate execution. The Liberty Tree operating in his sector? That could not only lead to his exclusion from the Supreme Council but to actual criminal negligence charges being brought against him. Matthews was in a tough position and was playing hardball. Peloreid had to outplay him or his entire career, and perhaps even his life, would be in jeopardy.

"I can see that you're contemplating my words," continued Matthews, seeing Peloreid speechless. "So, all you need to do is allow us to leave via the helicopter and the planes that are waiting for us. You can make up some excuse for our escape. Blame it on some of your officers. And, this man's secrets will leave with me. That's the deal. Take it or leave it."

"How do I know any of this is true? You could be bluffing. In reality, a poor ploy like this is your only possibility for escape. I need to see some proof," said Peloreid, half in truth and half to buy more time to consider his options.

Matthews pulled the medallion from his pocket and held it out to Peloreid.

"Here's my proof. A Liberty Tree medallion. We've also trailed him to several restricted areas of the city where I'm sure he had his clandestine meetings." Matthews was stretching the truth and he knew it. He also knew that Peloreid was correct on one point, this was probably their only chance of escape.

Peloreid stared at the necklace in astonishment. It was a Liberty Tree medallion, of that there was no doubt. He had seen them before, worn as signs of solidarity and defiance for Barahu and the government. This man was a Liberty Tree agent and traitor. He was sure of it. But now what? He could not just let them go. Kill them both? A distinct possibility. But, how would he explain that? Matthews was easy. He was shot resisting arrest for the insurrection, although the fact that the legal Emperor was with them could cause a problem if that ever got out. But what about the other man? How would he explain that? There would be reports, paperwork to file, and his body would have to be identified. How big of a lie could he come up with, particularly when his officers had seen them both alive when Peloreid entered the room and had ensured that they were disarmed. No, he couldn't just shoot them both. There would be too many loose ends. And, how did Matthews believe that he would be able to leave the room alive when he had just handed Peloreid his evidence? It was an obvious question.

"You have been generous enough to bring the traitor to me and for that I thank you. You have also given me proof of his involvement. Again, thank you. So, why shouldn't I just kill you both?" asked Peloreid, pointing his weapon directly at Matthews' chest.

"Do you think I'm stupid enough to offer this without having another method of publicizing your failures if you threatened me? I didn't follow this man myself. I had an assistant. He is instructed to turn over all documentation to Emperor Barahu, Chairman Baucman, and Councilor Tonklin should anything happen to me. We have full copies of this man's file, the surveillance records, and photos of this medallion included," Matthews lied again. He was backed into a corner. He had not had time to plan this out fully. He really didn't have a backup plan so he had to bluff. It was his only way out now.

"Really. A clever plan. Or, a bluff," replied Peloreid, trying to sound more confident than he really felt. Chairman Baucman would certainly not be happy to receive that information. Particularly after the events of this evening, he would not want any loose ends and, if these files really existed, Peloreid would be one of those loose ends.

"So, if this cohort is real, he must have a name. Give it to me now and I'll allow you to leave as you wish," demanded Peloreid.

Without thinking, Matthews snapped back, "Officer Stukap of the Purple Shirts."

He knew almost at once that this was a mistake. It was the truth, Stukap had done the leg work behind the prisoner's capture, but he was also there tonight and had brought Peloreid up to meet him. He didn't have time to change his answer.

He really isn't very smart, is he? thought Peloreid, with a vicious smile appearing on his face. "Very nice. Officer Stukap was killed attempting to enter this floor. But, thank you for your honesty," replied Peloreid coldly.

He snapped the lever on the pistol to the kill position and fired. The shot hit Matthews in the chest, entering his body an inch and releasing its electrical charge. Matthews body went rigid, his eyes opened wide and his mouth clenching tightly. With a load groan, he fell forward onto his face, dead before he hit the ground.

Immediately, two officers burst into the room, weapons drawn. The looked around and saw Matthews body lying on the floor.

Peloreid turned to them and ordered, "He tried to attack me so I had to defend myself. Now get me a doctor. I need him at once."

"Are you injured, sir," asked one of the guards.

"Don't question me! Do as I instructed!" shouted Peloreid wildly.

"Yes, sir," answered both men simultaneously as they ran out of the room.

Peloreid turned and closed the door. He could explain Matthews easily enough but had a different plan for his prisoner. He looked at Charles, saying not a word. Peloreid walked to Matthews' body and kicked it over, looking down into the still open eyes.

Charles laid his head back after examining the scene. He knew his fate. It was just a matter of how it came. He was tired, very tired. He had come so close but, in the end, he had failed. The Liberty Tree would continue he knew. As long as there were people like Andrew and Albert, people who craved their freedom, there would be a Liberty Tree. But, he would be gone. He just hoped that he had not endangered them as well. How did they find him? How did they know about his medallion? Was there a traitor amongst the members? Was it all because of his stupid mistake at the church? He didn't know and, at this point, he couldn't do much even if he did know.

A minute later, the door opened and a doctor in medical scrubs was ushered into the room by the two officers. Peloreid nodded to the officers and motioned to them to leave, which they did.

Closing the door, Peloreid turned to the doctor. "Doctor, this man is a traitor to his nation. I am ordering an immediate Procedure 66 to be done."

The doctor stared at Peloreid in amazement. His night had begun normally enough, reporting to work and dealing with a hallway full of patients. But then, Purple Shirts and gunshots had filled the hospital. Patients and medical personnel had fled to the doors only to be crowded back inside by more Purple Shirts. People were scared, crying, unable to understand what was happening. And now, he stood in a room with a senior Purple Shirt, a dead body, and another man strapped to a gurney and was told to perform a deadly procedure. He didn't know what to think.

"I. . I'm afraid I can't do that without proper authorization. I need the appropriate paperwork," he mumbled.

"Doctor, I am Security Regent Peloreid. This man has already had a Procedure 23 performed last year. Unfortunately, it was unsuccessful. Based on the approved regulations and process, he is now to be given a Procedure 66. I am ordering you to do it on my authority," instructed Peloreid sternly.

"But, sir. I don't have the required paperwork," protested the doctor.

"What is your name?" demanded Peloreid, shouting now.

"I am Dr. Bitten, Joseph Bitten," answered the doctor hesitantly.

"Well, Dr. Joseph Bitten, this man has caused an insurrection against the Emperor this evening. And, he chose this hospital as part of the plot. If you don't wish to follow my orders, I have no choice but to assume you are also part of his plot. I will need to arrest you and take you to interrogation," Peloreid threatened.

The doctor's face went white. He, as most, had heard horror stories about the interrogation chambers used by the government. He had no wish to witness an interrogation, much less be its subject. He turned to face Peloreid, his voice unsteady.

"You say that you are authorizing this procedure? You assume all responsibility?"

"I do. Now doctor, there are still other traitors in this hospital, dangerous criminals that are trying to escape as we speak. I need you to do this now."

"Yes, sir. As you wish, sir. I'm not sure if I have the approved drugs in this room," he muttered.

"Do you have anything that will work?" demanded Peloreid.

Dr. Bitten opened one drawer and then another. From a third, he pulled a small bottle.

"This isn't the right one, but it will work. It might be painful," answered the doctor.

"I have no concern over this monster's pain," replied Peloreid.

The doctor moved over to the gurney. Charles looked at him. The doctor had kindly eyes, Charles thought. He didn't resist. He knew there was no point. The doctor was doing what he needed to in order to save his own life. Charles didn't hate him for it. He almost felt sorry for him.

The doctor leaned over and strapped a tourniquet around Charles' arm. He pulled it tight and then waited, tapping Charles' forearm a couple of times to find the proper blood vessel. The doctor took one last look at Peloreid, who simply nodded his approval, before inserting the needle into Charles' arm.

As the chemicals entered, Charles felt a warm surge running up his arm. He could feel the pain, now blinding hot, coursing through his body. His stomach and lungs seemed to be on fire. His body began jerking wildly against the straps that bound him. His brain seemed to boil inside his skull. He was looking up into the light, staring at its brightness.

And then, the brightness began to fade from the outside to the center. His world was growing dark, the light getting smaller and smaller. The pain also began to fade. He looked up again and saw familiar faces above him. It was his father and mother, smiling at him as if in one of his dreams. They were speaking to him. He couldn't hear them at first and then their voices became clearer and clearer. They reached to him, took him by the hands, and pulled him towards them. He went willingly. He wasn't tired anymore.

The doctor turned to Peloreid and said, "It's done."

"Good. Now I want the body disposed of immediately."

"But, sir, I have no authority. There is supposed to be an autopsy performed. There are forms to complete," argued the doctor.

"Doctor, you have just performed an operation with no formal authorization. Now, I can support your claim that it was on my order or, I could refute it. You are in no position to argue. This is a hospital, is it not? You have a crematorium in the basement, do you not? I want this body cremated at once."

The doctor stood there, staring at Peloreid. He was in no position to argue. He made a call on the phone, ordering an immediate cremation. Moments later, an orderly dressed in surgical scrubs, complete with face shield and cap came and removed the body.

Peloreid and the doctor followed the body out of the room. The orderly waited by the elevator, looking around at the destruction which surrounded him. The doctor moved quickly down the corridor, in the opposite direction from where Peloreid was headed. Peloreid, hearing the sounds of helicopters approaching, ran towards the Purple Shirts that had barricaded the hallway near the helipad.

The elevator doors opened and the orderly pushed the gurney forward and then pushed the button to the basement. He looked down into Charles' face, staring at the peaceful visage.

A tear fell from the orderly's old green eyes.